FIC
WINTERS

If you have a home computer with internet access you may:
-request an item be placed on hold
-renew an item that is overdue
-view titles and due dates checked out on your card
-view your own outstanding fines

To view your patron record from your home computer:
Click on the NSPL homepage:
http://nspl.suffolk.lib.ny.us

North Shore Public Library

NEVER
ENOUGH

NEVER ENOUGH

A VIEW PARK NOVEL

ANGELA WINTERS

KENSINGTON PUBLISHING CORP.
http://www.kensingtonbooks.com

DAFINA BOOKS are published by

Kensington Publishing Corp.
850 Third Avenue
New York, NY 10022

ISBN-13: 978-0-7582-1261-0
ISBN-10: 0-7582-1261-5

First Kensington Trade Paperback Printing: July 2007
10 9 8 7 6 5 4 3 2 1

Printed in the United States of America

NEVER
ENOUGH

CHAPTER 1

It is a sad day when a man realizes there aren't any conditions under which he would say no to the woman he loved. This was the state Carter Chase, *the reluctant gentleman*, was in as he watched Avery from the balcony of his family's resort condo in Maui. The woman who, with just a smile made it hard for him to breathe, was sitting with her back to him, reading one of her trashy novels in her usual serene and peaceful way. The sight of her made him weak inside, and he didn't like that at all.

The lesser man inside of him envied her for being so strong, and the better man hated himself for the secrets he kept from her. Despite it all, he felt like he was high every second he was with her. He loved her to death and that wasn't what he had planned.

It had been almost a year since the day he'd walked into her beauty salon with the intention of buying her out for his father's company. He'd been careless about it at first, but his father, a man he had struggled with lifelong, had asked for his help. Well, Steven Chase didn't ask anybody for anything. He'd challenged Carter as he had done all his life to prove he was committed to Chase Beauty, the billion-dollar corporation Steven had built from scratch.

Carter didn't work at Chase Beauty, a major bone of contention between him and his father, but the company was his biggest and most important legal client. The opportunity to get both of Avery's very popular salons was a way for him to do more than shove the contracts across the desk for Steven to sign. Carter hadn't given a damn about Avery or her shops.

That was before he met her. He hated her at first and it seemed ironic to him now that he loved her so much. She was stubborn and obstinate, and for a man like Carter, who was used to getting anything he wanted, especially from women, it was infuriating. Not only had she not given in, but she'd made things worse by taking the struggle to the media—and for the Chase family, that was a big deal.

Everything about the Chase family was a big deal, and if there was one thing Steven didn't tolerate, it was bad publicity for Chase Beauty. Carter chose to take out the grief his father gave him on Avery and destroy everything she had. He wanted to teach her a lesson and he knew exactly how to do it.

Carter knew he was a cream-of-the-crop bachelor in Los Angeles black society. Thirty, good-looking, in great shape, a successful lawyer, deeply connected, Ivy League–educated, and worth millions. He'd sensed a flicker of electricity with Avery from the beginning and intended to use it against her by seducing her and stealing her shops from right underneath her before dropping her like a sack of dirt. There hadn't been a woman yet who could say no to him and certainly this goody-two-shoes neighborhood girl wasn't going to. It hadn't mattered to him that she was already engaged to another man.

Looking back, Carter could see clearly where he had gone wrong. He'd underestimated her strength, her loyalty and her intelligence. He'd also underestimated her partner, Craig Moon, and that mistake had led to disaster, almost getting Avery killed.

By the time Carter realized he had real feelings for her, it was too late. Every attempt to reach out to Avery met with a brick wall, but his determination became a destructive obsession as he ignored his better judgment and pushed his principles aside. When Alex, her fiancé, became the only thing in his way, Carter set him up and made sure Avery wouldn't want anything more to do with him.

The guilt he felt over what he'd done disappeared when Avery, grieving over her now-cheating ex-fiancé, came to his bed. He had won and nothing else mattered. Or so he thought.

Carter was at the height of his player days. He hadn't been a dog, but he hadn't had any intention of commitment anytime soon either. He'd been faithful through most of his relationships, but that didn't count the women he'd dumped in order to pursue someone else. Like most men, he saw most women as territory to explore and then move on. Keep them around too long and they would expect to move in or get a ring. Love would be reserved for later on down the line. This is what he thought with Avery. The fun had been in the getting and once he got her, he would move on.

It didn't work out that way, and as he made his way onto the balcony, Carter accepted that his player days were over. Avery had gotten under his skin, was running through his blood and had staked claim on his sorry ass. It was a bittersweet revelation, but he was man enough not to need to fight it, which had been his first inclination.

He'd spent enough time trying to convince himself it wouldn't work because she didn't come from the world of the upper class like him—didn't have the background that would allow her to slip into that world, which fought very hard to keep others out. He wanted to believe that her simplicity was beneath him and her penchant for being a pushover made her unfit to handle the cutthroat universe of the upper crust. It was all bullshit because every morning when he rolled over and saw her beautiful face, he was floored. She was his home.

"What you reading, baby?" He sat on the down-feathered cushion of the rattan chair next to her, sliding it closer so they were touching. He looked into her large, promising eyes before taking in her full lips and leaning in for a kiss.

Avery Jackson, *the girl next door*, felt her toes twinkle when he kissed her. She missed him every second he was away. He looked incredible, his milk chocolate–brown skin gleaming from the sun, his light brown eyes always intense. "How was golf?"

He shrugged, leaning back. He was starting to feel a little nervous but wiped it away. "It was golf. What you reading?"

"It's a romance, so just shut up." Avery held the book away as he reached for it. She didn't want the lecture.

There was always a lecture with Carter. It was one of the many things she had gotten used to. It was one of the easier things to get used to. Summer homes, charity balls, exotic vacations on every continent and perks people like Avery were never expected to even know existed. This was all foreign to her until she found herself immersed in Carter's world.

In this world, everything was better, glossier, brighter, sleeker, prettier and easier. Private jets, designer clothes, breathtaking jewelry and beautiful places were just the basics. Avery was awed to see how things just seemed to work out for people this rich and was a little disturbed by the ease with which Carter accepted it all.

The privilege, entitlement, pleasure and power had given him many strengths, but it had also given him a level of snobbery that Avery couldn't abide most times. But God help her, she loved him so much.

"Why are you reading that crap?" he asked.

"Why is it crap?" Avery asked. "Just because it didn't win a Pulitzer? Everything you read doesn't have to be culturally enlightening and politically significant."

"There's a lot of room between culturally enlightening and crap."

He reached over and ran his finger up her arm. Her skin was as soft as silk and she turned him on in that tiny pink bikini. Avery had an incredible body, but she didn't flaunt it and Carter loved that. He was turned off by sisters who let it all hang out as if they were putting their body on display for purchase. Avery had class and knew how to look sexy without being sexual. It reassured him that the best was reserved only for him. Just another reason she was perfect to him.

"We're on vacation." Avery giggled in response to his teasing touch. "Trashy novels are required."

Carter looked past the edge of their large balcony at the Pacific Ocean. The scenery couldn't have been more perfect. They were staying in the 2,500-square-foot condo his family had purchased at the newest luxury resort on Maui. Decorated with wood-paneled walls, museum-quality artwork, a grand piano, lavish furnishings, three bedrooms and marble bathrooms, it was perfect and that was what he wanted for their first real vacation. The Ritz, the Fairmont and W were fine for their weekends away, but this was real and Carter wanted seclusion and perfection. Just last night they'd seen a whale through the condo's high-powered telescope from just inside the sliding glass doors.

They were about to start the second of their two weeks away and it was a first for him. He was a workaholic and couldn't fight that little itch making him want to get back to Chase Law, the corporate law firm he'd started only five years ago. He now employed thirteen lawyers and a support staff of more than twenty.

"You enjoy your massage?" he asked, wondering if he should just do it now or wait until after dinner.

"Oh," Avery moaned as she put her book down and turned to him. The smile on her smooth café au lait face, a little red from the sun, was ear to ear. "It was incredible, baby. I had to hold onto the walls just to get back up here."

Carter smiled, pleased whenever Avery acted more at ease with the lifestyle offered her. Sometimes she seemed reluctant to indulge herself just because she could, and Carter couldn't help but feel insulted.

Avery didn't even want to imagine what the two-hour ritual cost. She'd given up wondering about those kinds of things. Carter was used to the best and most expensive of everything, and after a while of feeling self-conscious, she had come to love it. He gave her everything even though she never asked and he never bragged about it. It was nothing for him and she had to admit it was part of why she loved him.

Only part—she loved him for so much more. Once she had been too intimidated by his last name to think she could love him. The attraction had been there from the beginning, but she'd fought it until she couldn't fight anymore. Carter had been there for her when she'd lost her shops and even though he was partly to blame, he'd saved her life. He also had been there when Alex broke her heart and hadn't left her side since.

He was everything any woman could want. He had a presence that sucked up the room and he knew how to make her lose her mind whenever he put his hands on her. It was all too perfect for Avery, so she'd held off. She'd kept her heart away for as long as she could, but there was no fighting this man.

"I was surprised," she continued. "I expected to see some old German woman with hands like a man and a mustache."

Carter laughed. "She wasn't?"

Avery reached over and touched the bottom of his strong chin. Not a hair out of place; this neat freak was clean cut to a sin. She loved him still.

"She was young and beautiful. Very feminine Japanese . . ."

"Japanese?" Carter's eyes widened. "Damn, if I had known that I would've joined you. We could've all worked something out."

She slapped him on his muscular arm, wishing this vacation would never end. Always a private person, Avery wasn't eager to get back to the public life that came with dating Carter. It was all part of the package—she understood that—but it wasn't easy.

"Honey?" She smiled at his rapt attention. "Do you mind if we . . . I really don't want to get ready for a big deal. Can we skip dinner tonight?"

"Sure." Carter swallowed. Okay, so much for his after-dinner plan. It seemed to be now or never. "I'll cancel the reservations. You want to order room service?"

She nodded, glad she didn't get an argument. With Carter there was always somewhere to go for dinner to meet these people or be seen here or there. Living large was more work than Avery had ever imagined.

"How about steak?" he asked, swinging his legs around the chair so he was facing her. He kept his left hand at his side.

Avery sensed something was up. The tense expression on his usually calm face gave him away. "What's going on?"

"Nothing," he lied. Her little button nose made him want to kiss her again. He loved how she could be beautiful, but not to the point where she was too pretty to be cute. She wore hardly any makeup and had a freshness about her that he never got tired of. "I just . . ."

Avery got nervous when he looked away for a moment.

Carter was never at a loss for words unless he was angry. He would shut down and not talk to her, but he wasn't angry now, so what was up?

He looked back at her, noticing the confusion on her face. There was no turning back. "Avery, do I make you happy?"

Avery was taken back by the question. "Of course, baby. Happier than I've ever been."

He bit at his lower lip for a second, forgetting absolutely everything he had planned to say. *To hell with it.* "I want to be all you need, Avery. You've become that for me and I want to be that for you."

She leaned over, placing her hand gently on his cheek. Now she was really worried. "You are, honey."

"You've touched a part of me I didn't know was there," he continued, "and I don't tell you how much I love you very often, but you know I do."

"You could say it a little more," she added with a tender smile, "but I'll take what I can get."

"I'm saying it now." Carter felt his left palm beginning to sweat. "I'm saying it in the way I hope you'll understand I mean it. More than I think I've ever meant anything."

Avery looked down as Carter raised his left hand in between them. He opened his closed fist and her heart leaped into her throat. She didn't know the ring was a brilliant-style high-cut Lucida diamond center rectangular stone of about five carats with two bezel-set side stones. She just knew it was absolutely beautiful.

She looked into his eyes and this powerful man looked like a little boy, waiting anxiously. She wrapped her arms around him and screamed his name. She yelled "yes" at least ten times that she could count. She let him go with tears streaming down her cheeks. Was it real? Was he actually . . . ?

"You and me," he said.

"You and me," she repeated, holding out her hand for him to slip on the ring.

He hesitated. "Baby girl, you know what you're getting into, right?"

She didn't need a moment to get his meaning. They'd had this conversation several times. "I'm marrying the man God made me for. Nothing else matters."

He believed her because he needed to. He believed her because he knew she loved him as much as he loved her and although he didn't believe she knew what she was getting into, there was no way he could be without her. So he slipped the ring onto her finger and raised her hand to his mouth. He kissed the inside of her palm and leaned forward to kiss her cheek. He tasted the salt of her tears and ignored the secret he kept from her. He ignored anything that told him he didn't deserve her because he wanted her too much.

When he kissed her, Avery felt her body heat up like a furnace. She had dreamt of marrying Carter for some time but never gave in to it. He could have any woman he wanted and the women in his world had been born into it. They had family names that meant something and had for several generations. And unlike Avery, they had similar backgrounds and experiences as he had.

Why would he settle down with a plain, simple girl who thought the highlight of the weekend was going to church? She wanted to have him as long as he wanted her, but now she would have him forever and that was all those Sundays in church paying off.

As she jumped onto his lap and kissed him back, Avery wasn't listening to the voice inside that told her she hadn't thought this through. The voice was yelling under the strain of her happiness trying desperately to remind her that although she knew what was in this man's heart, she didn't know everything about him.

Carter put her in position before sliding off her bikini bottom. Avery ignored the voice, hearing only her heart beating out of control as his tongue circled her belly button and went down to her center. He knew just what to do, and soon her moans drowned out the voice completely.

Avery hoped the voice knew it wasn't welcome. She was going to be happy because the man she loved with every inch of her was going to be her husband.

* * *

Michael Chase, *the favorite*, could hear his boys on the other side of his bedroom door and for once he was grateful. He usually wanted a few moments alone with his wife, Kimberly, before the onslaught of the twins began, but not today. He needed the buffer because he knew Kimberly was going to be pissed off.

When he opened the door, both boys stopped playing and screamed his name like they hadn't seen him in weeks instead of since that morning. He put his briefcase down in just enough time to catch them and pick one up in each arm. They were six now and getting too heavy for this, but he wasn't ready to give it up. Daniel and Evan were the lights of his life—them and the angry beauty sitting on the bed among the new bedsheets she'd recently ordered from Europe with a thread count so high Michael doubted it was even the truth.

"You're in twouble," Daniel said, pointing his finger.

Michael kissed them both before putting them down. He smiled at Kimberly, who looked so sexy in a simple peach-colored tank and cotton low-rise shorts, it was sick. He sat down on the chenille sofa to the right of the bed, eerily turned on by her unforgiving glare. She was still the most beautiful woman he had ever seen.

"Says who?" Michael braced himself as Daniel bounced on his lap while Evan chose to jump up and down on the bed; something he'd been told not to do at least a hundred times.

"You're late," Daniel accused, pulling at his father's Charvet tie. "Says Mommy."

Michael winked at Kimberly and she responded by mouthing a silent *fuck you*. He wanted to jump her right then. "Why don't you boys go play in your room?"

"So Mommy can yell at you?" Daniel asked, seeming determined to conquer the tie.

"Exactly, and don't slam the—" Michael gave up as the door slammed behind them. "They're gonna break that damn door again."

Undoing his shirt, he leaped onto the bed, but Kimberly Chase, *the outsider*, held out her hand and pushed him away.

"Not a chance," she said. "You bastard."

She wasn't having it. He had been stringing her along for too long. She glared at him, refusing to return his charming smile as he sat on the bed, caressing her leg. She slapped his hand away as he tried to reach the inside of her thighs.

"I'm not playing with you, Michael." She slid across the king-size bed, determined to resist him. No matter how angry he made her, she always wanted him. After seven years, he still had her lit like a candle.

"I'm sorry." Michael took his shirt off, revealing his trim, muscular physique. He was very dark and handsome, resembling a young Sidney Poitier. He knew he was hot. "I had to work late."

"Bullshit!" She grabbed a pillow and tossed it at him with enough force to knock him back. "I had to cancel."

"It's just a house," he said. "Make another appointment."

"They sold it, Michael. The realtor just called five minutes ago." Kimberly had to get out of this house or she was going to go crazy. "The house is gone."

Michael groaned, feeling guilty even though he hadn't been crazy about that house. "You'll find another house. You have all the money in the world, Kimberly. They'll come back with something better."

"I wanted that house!" Kimberly couldn't get the vision of the five-bedroom, 8,500-square-foot Venetian-style mansion in Pasadena. That house was made for her.

Michael met her anger with resolve. He didn't have time for this.

He went over to his walk-in closet in search of something to put on. He could feel her eyes on him through the wall and it irritated him because he knew she was right. He'd made a promise and he wasn't sticking to it. They should have moved out of the Chase mansion in the mostly black and affluent L.A. suburb of View Park years ago. It wasn't as if they couldn't afford it, but he'd asked for time to be close to his father while he was still proving himself. He wanted a promotion to CFO and a seat on the board of directors and had gotten both in December. Chase Beauty clearly was going to be his, and now it was time for Kimberly to get her wish.

"It's June, Michael. You said we'd have a house by March." She got up and made her way to the window seat, her favorite place in their large bedroom in the west wing of the house. The window looked over the half-circle driveway filled with Mercedes, Range Rovers, BMWs and Jaguars that led to the steel gate built to keep the world at a distance.

Kimberly found it ironic that, coming from the Detroit projects where she'd had to turn tricks after running away from an abusive home, she should think that living in a 15,000-square-foot-palace was a dream, but it wasn't. It was a prison and she had to get out before she killed someone. She knew who that someone would be. Janet Chase, the mother-in-law from hell.

"I want to build a house," he yelled from inside the closet while checking his vibrating BlackBerry. He wanted it to be his brother, Carter, who was supposed to be home soon. "So it's exactly like we want."

"That will take too long." Kimberly didn't want to go over this again. "We can move into a house now and have one built later."

"Call the lady back," he said. "You're a Chase. Use your name. They'll find a way to hold on to the—"

"Michael, stop it!" Kimberly yelled. "It's driving me crazy! Don't you care?"

Michael stood in the archway to the closet, taking in her look. It was a look that told him he wasn't doing his job as a husband, and he wanted to be defensive about it even though she was right.

His father always told him a happy wife meant a happy life, and Michael was paying the price for not heeding that advice.

"It's just not the right time," he said. Another trip to Harry Winston was in order. "I'm very busy with—"

"Please." Kimberly rolled her eyes, making a smacking sound with her lips. "You can't get off your father's nipple because you're scared and you're jealous."

Michael pressed his lips together to avoid saying something he would regret. He took a quick, deep breath before responding. "You don't know what you're talking about, woman, so I suggest you stop while you're ahead."

"Stop what?" Kimberly crawled to the front of the bed and stood up. "Getting to the truth of the matter?"

"What truth do you know?"

"That the reason you don't want to move is because you're afraid you'll lose what little advantage you have over Carter."

Michael's eyes squinted as he felt his breathing pick up. "Shut up, Kimberly."

"Don't tell me to shut up!"

"Don't tell me about my father!"

Carter, older by one year, was Michael's best friend and his biggest rival. Carter's strained relationship with their father had allowed Michael to shine in his father's eyes and it meant the world to him. He worshipped his father, even though the man irritated the hell out of him and scared him a bit. As much as Michael felt for Carter, who wished he was closer to their father, he knew it all meant Chase Beauty would be his, and so would Steven's favor.

"You don't care that I hate it here," Kimberly said. "You don't care that I've lived under this roof for seven years with a woman who thinks I'm ghetto trash, all so you can be close to your daddy."

"You can't place all the blame on my mother," Michael said. "You hate her guts too."

"She never gave me any choice, but that's not the point." Kimberly took an abrupt step toward him. "The point is, Carter and Steven have been getting along and you're scared he's going to take his rightful place as favorite first son."

Michael's stare was threatening, but Kimberly didn't back down. "You've got a complex when it comes to Daddy's approval and—"

"I said, shut up," Michael warned.

Kimberly smiled, pleased to get such a rise out of him. Why should she be the only one with a ruined day? "I'm just telling the truth."

"Do you really want to take it there?" he asked.

Kimberly swallowed, hoping it wasn't as evident as it seemed. She had to stand her ground even though she knew what was coming. His suspicions were getting worse.

"Don't try to turn this on me, Papi."

"Don't turn what on you?" Michael asked sarcastically. "You're keeping secrets from me and you're trying to play me for a fool."

Kimberly blinked, unable to keep her poker face. She was afraid Michael was really beginning to believe what he was saying, and that would ruin everything. "You keep me locked away from the world. You don't like me to have a life, so you act like anything I do on my own is cheating. I'm not falling for it, Michael."

He looked her up and down. Part of him wanted to strangle her; part wanted to make love to her. The woman made him crazy. His hypocrisy made him even crazier. He hadn't been a completely faithful husband, but the idea that she might cheat was more than he could bear. "I know you inside and out. I've tasted every bit of you. Don't you think I can tell when you're lying to me?"

Kimberly huffed, turning to walk away, but Michael grabbed her by the arm and swung her around to him.

"Stop it." She jerked her arm away.

"I'll find out what you're doing," he said, feeling the rage rip through him just at the thought of what he feared. She couldn't possibly be cheating on him. She wouldn't risk everything he was giving her.

"I'm not cheating on you!"

"Then tell me what's going on!"

"You're getting paranoid." Kimberly stepped back as he reached for her again. She slapped his hand away.

She hated lying to him and had promised herself she never would that night before their shotgun wedding when she'd bared her soul. He didn't care that she came from nowhere, had dropped out of high school and had run away from home. He didn't care that she had been a hooker in Detroit for two years until she was seventeen. He had taken in all her lies and gone to great lengths to keep anyone else, especially his own parents, from discovering the truth. For that, he deserved the truth, but she couldn't give it to him because she knew he wouldn't stand for it.

She turned her back to him, returning to the window. He followed her, standing at her side for a while. He stared down at her as she kept her lying eyes focused.

Like Michael, Kimberly had a very wicked side to her, and they connected on a cosmic level. Yes, it was a lot about volcanic sex, but the twins made their marriage, their family, real. He'd once believed he'd given up life as a bachelor at the tender age of twenty-three for her because she was pregnant, but that wasn't it. He had given it up because he knew, as much fun as it might be to keep looking, he would never find another woman with his deviant penchants and beauty that made him lose his stride like this one. He would never get past that twitch he felt from just a glance. Something of him was inside of this woman and had been from the first night he met her. It would always be there.

"Kimberly." Michael spoke in a quiet, controlled tone belying his anger. "Don't make me have to kill somebody over you."

Her head jerked up and she turned to him with wide eyes. She could have asked him if he was kidding, but she knew he wasn't. She knew him too well. So she didn't bother to ask or say anything. Her stomach was clenched tight and she knew she was going to be in trouble if she didn't figure something out soon.

When he finally left, slamming the door behind him, Kimberly felt sick at the thought that he might be going to another woman. There wasn't anything she could do about it, so she threw it from her mind. She had other things to deal with.

To say Janet Chase was a thorn in her side was putting it lightly, and Kimberly made an obsession out of giving the uppity, devilish socialite her due.

It had all begun the day she met her. Kimberly hadn't expected much. She was a model with a recently acquired GED and a dark past who had gotten pregnant after a one-night stand with an MBA student who was just too fine to pass up. After a few drinks and some smooth talk, Kimberly was hooked even before she knew she had stepped on a gold mine.

She hadn't expected Michael to call her again, but he had— and again and again. She had been excited when she found out who he was, but she had no faith anything would last, because nothing good ever had in her life. Men like him only entertained themselves with women like her. She had been poor and alone in the projects, ignored by an alcoholic mother, an absent and mostly in jail father, and an abusive brother on drugs.

Every man in her life had treated her like crap, including the man who'd picked her up at the train station the night she ran away and pimped her out at fifteen. She had lost faith in men and decided that they weren't worth much more than what she could get from them while they were interested. She knew she was beautiful and that was her tool.

Michael wasn't the first man with money who'd offered her anything she wanted, but he was the first who seemed to really mean it. When she'd found out she was pregnant, her first thought had been to get an abortion, but she had done that before and it had killed a part of her. She would never, ever do it again.

She hadn't been expecting a marriage proposal, but she realized that Michael was a Chase and as Janet Chase had made clear to her only seconds after they met, there would be no bastards in this family. The concept of illegitimate children seemed the only thing worse to the ice queen than marrying a piece of trash from nowhere, but that didn't make it okay, and Janet made sure that Kimberly was aware of that from day one.

"You're not good enough for him," she'd told her the second the two of them were alone for the first time. "But my son has a weakness for . . . your kind. I know you're after his money."

Kimberly, not one for pleasantries, had tried to get along for Michael's sake, but it was clear to her that Janet hated her and when she found out that Janet was hoping Michael would divorce her after the children were born, the line was drawn. Janet had spent the past seven years trying to kick Kimberly out of the family, and Kimberly had spent them all just trying to hold on.

She had had enough and six months ago, as she saw the perfect picture of a woman begin to fall apart after a rash of family tragedies, Kimberly saw her window. Janet was weak. Her oldest daughter, Leigh, hated her because she blamed her for the death of her boyfriend. Her youngest, and favorite, Haley, after being embroiled in a political scandal and drug investigation, had to be sent to Europe after losing her damn mind. Carter had been detaching himself even further from the family to pro-tect his new girlfriend. Michael . . . well, Michael had never been Janet's. He had always belonged to Steven, so Janet had nothing except the Valium she popped in her mouth on a much-more-than-regular basis.

All Kimberly needed was that little piece of something to push this woman off the edge and off her throne. She had been doing her research, even hiring a private investigator, to find dirt on Janet. Everyone had secrets, right? Kimberly had plenty of her own and knew if Janet ever found out the truth about her past, her life would be over. Janet had already spent thousands trying, but whatever Michael couldn't use his money to make go away was lost in the world of invisible people in the middle of nowhere. Janet hadn't been able to break through.

Kimberly was suffering the same problem. All of her leads had fallen through and she was getting desperate. Haley was coming back and Kimberly knew that would buoy Janet's spirits. Now, with Michael sure to have her followed to confirm she wasn't cheating, she didn't know how much room she had to get what she wanted. Janet was weak and she had to pounce—but with what?

CHAPTER 2

"**D**addy?"

Janet Chase, *the socialite*, felt her heart warm at the sound of her oldest daughter's voice. At the same time, the pain of what she knew was to come ripped at her insides. "Hello, Leigh. It's Mother."

There was a short silence on the other end. "So you're trying to trick me by calling me from Daddy's office phone?"

"You never pick up when you know it's me."

"Mom, I'm not going through this with you. Goodbye."

"Wait." Janet felt her nerves on edge. She had just taken a Valium, hoping it would prevent her from arguing. If she stayed calm, Leigh usually would talk longer. "This call is not about you and me."

"That's because it's always just about you."

Janet was trying to understand her daughter's anger. She understood now that Leigh had left L.A. to spend a year as a doctor in Africa, in part to get out from under Janet's grip. She had always put too much pressure on Leigh, hoping she would be able to grasp the responsibility that came with being a Chase.

When she came back, Leigh had chosen to open up a free clinic in South Central serving kids with HIV and AIDS instead of going into one of several prestigious private practices waiting in line for her. Janet had hoped her refusal to support Leigh would deter her, but it only made her more determined. Leigh's trust fund was in the millions, but only one hundred thousand was available to her per year until she turned thirty. She emptied out all she could and kept going.

It seemed like nothing could stop her until the clinic was broken into and vandalized. The financial and insurance disaster had given Janet an opportunity—or so she'd thought. Looking back on it, it seemed so ridiculous and cruel but at the time she was desperate when so much in her family was falling apart.

"Haley is coming home today," Janet said. "She'll be here any minute."

"I know." Leigh's response was cold and sharp, so unlike her. "I'm seeing her tomorrow."

"You can come over for dinner. . . ."

"You know I won't, Mother."

"You don't have to talk to me." Janet held back her tears. The Valium was setting in and she was calmer than she usually would be in the face of such rejection. "Just be here with the family. Everyone asked about you again at church this morning."

"I have to go, Mother."

Desperate, Janet gripped the phone tighter. "Leigh, please. You can't keep this up forever. You're the one always talking about Christian forgiveness. It's been six months and you know that I'm sorry."

She was sorry—desperately sorry. What she had done amounted to blackmail. With the other doctors and patients relying on her, Leigh couldn't help but accept the financial support of the Chase Foundation, the family charity Janet ran. Janet had made Leigh agree to play a larger role in the social responsibilities of the family to help counter Carter's and Haley's legal troubles.

She'd also made sure Leigh dated Leo Bridges, the broker son of one of L.A.'s newest black elites transported from Boston. She hadn't known that Leigh was already falling in love with Richard, a doctor at the clinic. When she did find out, Janet ignored Leigh's wishes and pushed her more toward Leo, who'd turned out to be completely insane. Leo's jealousy over Leigh's feelings for Richard resulted in him shooting Richard and then himself. They were both dead and Leigh blamed Janet for everything.

"I have forgiven you, Mother," Leigh said after a short pause. "I just can't have you in my life right now."

"Leigh!" Janet heard the click and felt tears welling in her throat.

With a trembling hand, she put the phone down. She felt alone and desperate inside Steven's darkened office and knew she deserved it. She'd betrayed her child, and the whole family was paying the price.

Being a Chase was never easy, but Janet wasn't new to money. She had been born to two wealthy lawyers with prominent social standing. After Janet had grown up with all the best of New York's high society, meeting Steven while at Spelman College was the defining moment of Janet's life. Although her parents objected to her marrying a man with a background not "up to par," Janet knew she had found a man among men.

Their life together was the stuff of dreams, building wealth and rising to the top of the world. Black society in Los Angeles didn't have the backbone it did on the East coast, but Janet had changed all that. Her presence, her work in the community and her plans over the past twenty-five years helping prominent blacks in positions of power and influence in business, law, politics, medicine and philanthropy had made it something to reckon with.

Chase Beauty now was an international force, Steven was a billionaire and the Chase name was synonymous with influence, wealth and achievement. It also was synonymous with controversy, which seemed unavoidable for people in their position.

Janet had devoted her life to being a wife and mother and making the Chase Foundation mean something in the world. Where in all that had she gone so wrong?

That was the question she was asking the psychiatrist Steven had convinced her she needed to see. Leigh had made it clear she was as good as dead to her; Steven had sent Haley to live at the family's villa in Italy to avoid getting thrown in jail; Carter had distanced himself from the family to protect Avery; and there was always Kimberly.

The piece of ghetto trash Michael had married had Janet more concerned in many ways, than anyone else had. The gold-digging whore was up to something and Janet knew it couldn't be any good. Michael had always had a thing for women who were beneath him, but this one took the cake. He had completely skipped the middle- and working-class and gone directly to the gutter.

There had been no choice but to have him marry her before the twins were born, but Janet did everything she could to help Michael see the light and divorce her while the prenuptial agreement was still intact. He had three more years, and Kimberly's growing challenges to her authority in this house were pushing her to the edge.

She lied to Steven and told him she had stopped taking the Valium, because it was impossible for her not to take it. She had cut down, and that was the best she could do for now.

A cry of relief broke from her lips as she heard voices down the hallway and rushed out of the office.

"Haley!" Janet ran to her baby, her arms open wide. It had been too long.

Haley Chase, *the taker*, smiled from ear to ear. She hadn't realized how much she had missed her mother until she hugged her tight. She didn't want to let go, especially not after the reaming she had just gotten from her father.

"Why didn't you come to the airport?" Haley pouted as she leaned back.

Janet kissed her on both cheeks before running her fingers through her long, wavy auburn hair. She was a caramel-colored fiery beauty with magnetic dark eyes and smoldering features. At twenty-three, Haley had raised more hell than most people could in an entire lifetime.

"Your father wanted time alone with you."

"So you collaborated with him."

Janet shrugged. "He's very worried about you."

"He's not worried." Haley dropped her purse on the table and fell into the soft, plush, grand-scale English roll-arm sofa. It felt so good. Although staying at the villa in Rome and the finest hotels in other parts of Europe had their perks, she missed home. "He hates me and he wanted to hurt my feelings."

"How can you say that after all he did for you last year?"

Haley just rolled her eyes, refusing to show that she cared. Yes, her father had done everything, legal and illegal, to protect her from Rudio, the drug dealer who'd tried to kill her before she could testify against him in court, but it hadn't changed much. She was still the biggest embarrassment Steven had ever known and he never let her forget it.

"That was last year." Haley ducked away from her mother's fussing hands. "He's being such an—"

"Watch it." Steven Chase, *the conqueror*, stood in the archway to the living room and tossed the final two red Burberry suitcases on the floor. Looking distinctly younger than fifty-four, with salt-and-pepper temples, he had a determined face that held an unwavering frown. "You've used up all your patience points with me after cussing me out in the car."

"*You* cussed *me* out!"

"That seems productive." Janet stood up and went to her husband. Leaning up, she smiled at him before kissing him on the cheek. "I thought you wanted to talk to her."

Steven saw every inch of his wife's flawless black hair, luscious nut-brown skin, full, tempting lips and almond-shaped eyes as perfect. Well, almost perfect. He let the glossy look in her eyes pass over him. He didn't want to believe it was anything but emotion over Haley's return. She had promised to stop taking the pills and he had to believe her. Janet never lied to him. Still, he'd scoured the house and thrown away all the stashes she had hidden. He couldn't go further than that. They had trust.

"I tried to." He sent Haley a stern glare. "She still acts like she's the victim in all this. You have no idea what hell she was raising in Switzerland."

"And I don't want to." Janet shook her head. "The last report of you trashing a nightclub in Oslo and running off for two weeks with some royal's husband was enough to make me sick."

"Nobody asked you to be all up in my business," Haley said.

"That's kind of hard to avoid," Steven said, "considering I'm the one who has to pay to cover it up."

"Where will you send me next?" Haley teased, unable to clearly comprehend why she got so much joy out of ticking him off. "Asia? India? Somewhere I can't embarrass you? I don't think that place exists."

"I'm not sending you anywhere." Steven wished he could smack that little smirk off her face. "You're going to behave."

"I'm not a child!" Haley shot up from the sofa in true tantrum form.

Steven took another step toward her. "You would have to be a lot more mature to be considered a child."

"Go to hell!"

"Okay." Janet reached for Steven, who had started for Haley, and pulled him back. "That's enough. Let's all just calm down."

Steven looked back at his wife, noting her relaxed tone. He didn't have time for suspicion. "I have to go. You deal with her."

"Where are you going?" Janet asked. "It's Sunday."

"I have to go to the office. The driver is waiting outside." If he didn't get out of this house, he would strangle Haley.

If it wasn't one thing it was another with that girl. Most of the gray hairs on his head were attributed to his youngest child. She wasn't the only one he had trouble with, but at least Carter wasn't crazy and he was nowhere near as expensive and stressful. His wife made it worse by spoiling her rotten, seeming unable to accept that she was an adult now. She indulged Haley in everything and in return, they only got more grief.

Falling back on the sofa, Haley smiled victoriously as she watched him leave. "He's very worried? Just worried enough to get in a few more hours at the office."

Janet wouldn't make an excuse for Steven and the priority he placed on Chase Beauty. Often Steven would pull away and leave her to clean up the mess. He would step in to be the hero and save them all from a crisis using his influence, power or money, but would quickly retreat to his first love, Chase Beauty.

"I think he's just trying to avoid tossing you across the room." Janet joined her on the sofa.

"No matter what he says, I didn't try to drown any—"

"Haley." Janet held out her hand. "Please, I don't want to know."

"I'm just saying." Haley looked around. "Where's Maya? I'm hungry."

"We sent you to Europe to get you out of trouble and all you do is cause more."

Haley didn't have the patience for another lecture. "You told me to have fun."

"I didn't say any such thing. You're out of control and it's going to get you hurt. It almost got you killed, remember?"

Almost, but didn't. Having fun with Congressman Jack Flay on his boat last summer, Haley had accidentally witnessed a drug deal at sea, and the rest was history. At least to her it was. Everyone else seemed unable to let it go. "Can you make me something to eat?"

"I'm not your maid. I'm your mother."

"Same thing." Haley's smile faded quickly as her mother's face took on a furious expression. Something was wrong. She could see it in her eyes and the leisure with which she responded. "Are you okay?"

"How can I be?" Janet asked.

Haley felt a knot in her stomach and her rage began to build. Anger came so quickly to her. "If this is about Sean, I won't talk about it."

Sean Jackson was the detective assigned to Haley's case, and they had been at war from day one. She hated the judgmental do-gooder and he looked down on her. Despite not wanting anything to do with Sean, Haley expected that he wanted her, like every man did. It irritated her to death that he ignored his attraction because of his so-called principles. She became hell-bent on making him abandon that honorable facade.

Instead, she had fallen in love with him, a first for Haley. Men, for her, were nothing more than amusements in between living her life. Why fall in love? The first man in her life wanted nothing to do with her, so why would she give any other man a chance to turn his back on her?

But Sean was different. He was a genuinely good person and as much as that nauseated her, it endeared him. The sex was good and after she had been secluded in a safe house following a couple of attempts on her life, Sean was all she had. Then he'd become all she wanted.

When he'd dumped her, Haley had become obsessed with revenge. No one had ever dumped her, and some low-grade police detective wasn't going to get away with it. He'd told her he loved her but that they were too different to make it work. Unwilling to live on her trust fund, he wanted them to put together some miserable existence on his detective's salary. How could he have really loved her if he expected her to be poor? He was a fool and he had to pay.

"You'll talk about whatever I want you to," Janet said.

Haley settled in. "You're talking to yourself, then. Sean got what he deserved."

"You tried to destroy his life." Janet had no love for Sean Jackson. She didn't want him anywhere near Haley, but having saved her life more than once gave him a right not to be terrorized.

"He broke my heart," Haley said just above a whisper, as if she didn't want the walls to hear and go tell someone she'd been weak for even a second.

What Janet understood and Haley didn't was that this relationship had been doomed from the beginning. She had been willing to allow Haley her fun with the boy but had assumed that once the danger was gone, the thrill would be too. When she saw that Haley had developed real feelings for him, Janet saw the true danger. Besides the fact that he wasn't good enough for her, he was trying to change her and it was beginning to work.

Haley didn't care; that was her thing. Janet accepted this about her daughter. She was selfish and completely unaware of anyone's feelings but her own. She would never change, and any attempts she made for Sean would be short-lived. Janet wasn't willing to sit by and watch her daughter try to be someone she wasn't for a man who was beneath her. She would be miserable. This was why she had insisted Sean see the light and understand that although he loved Haley, it wouldn't work.

He had done the right thing and paid a high price for it. For two months after it was over, Haley had harassed him at home and work, vandalized his property and paid women to file false complaints of harassment and abuse against him. When it was found out that she was behind it all, the media ate it up. Haley was, after all, their favorite Chase. She had been arrested and responded by filing a lawsuit against the police department. Steven had had enough. He'd pulled strings to get the charges dropped and had shipped her off to Europe.

"It's not going to start again," Janet warned. "I'm very busy planning the Museum Ball and I don't have time to keep an eye on you. You're going to leave him alone."

"I don't give a damn about him anymore," Haley said. "He doesn't exist to me."

"Good." Janet wasn't so sure she could believe that. "You need to focus on graduate school."

Haley moaned, flailing her arms at her sides. "Mom, please."

"Stanford is close and . . ."

"It's June. It's too late."

"It's never too late if you're a Chase."

Haley smiled, never one to run away from the power of her last name. "Let me guess. Daddy will contribute a few hundred grand to the school's new library and somehow I'll be on the top of the list for fall—GRE, transcripts and applications optional."

"Your father is threatening to cut off your trust fund." Janet was pleased now that she had her attention. Money was Haley's first language. "You either go to school or get a job."

Haley pressed her lips together tightly and gritted her teeth. *That damn man.* "What about UCLA?"

Janet cringed briefly. "UCLA isn't the same caliber as Stanford, but it will have to do. And it's closer. I'll start making calls tomorrow. What are you interested in?"

"Whatever's easy." Haley stood up, deciding to figure out how she would get out of that later. Looking down at her mother, she rubbed her belly. "So who exactly is going to make me something to eat?"

The comfort of familiarity was always an interesting concept to Nikki Jackson, *the peacemaker*, and as she watched her husband lounging on the living room sofa of their modest View Park home watching the Dodgers with a can of beer in one hand, she couldn't help but smile. Two years short of fifty, he was an attractive, well-built man with a light complexion from his island heritage.

"I'd rather not yell at you," she said, her hands resting on her pleasingly full hips. She had her long braids pulled back into a ponytail, exposing her smooth, dark skin with specks of oil paint but not a hint of wrinkles.

Charlie Jackson, *the do-right man*, turned his head to look at his wife. "I'm watching the game."

"Should that be your priority today?"

This was his first day off in a few months. As police chief of View Park, he had been putting in extra hours to oversee the installation of a new computer system in police cars. As with all technology, in Charlie's opinion, it was more trouble than it was worth, and after weeks of headaches, he wanted to spend his first day off relaxing.

"Is this about church?" he asked. "Don't worry. I've been praying more this week than I have any Sunday. I'm good with Him."

"It's about your son," Nikki said. "He's here."

"He is?" Charlie was quickly thinking of reasons to avoid Sean.

"I told you he was coming by to work on his car. Are you going to go out and talk to him?"

"Tell him to come in and watch the game with me."

"I'm not telling him anything."

Charlie put his beer down and swung his chair around to face his wife. "Nikki, I know. It's just—"

"It's just nothing," she interrupted. "Go talk to him."

It wasn't as bad as it seemed. Charlie still loved his son and was proud of him. Sean had graduated at the top of his class at the academy and was the youngest officer promoted to detective in county history. Despite receiving flak for being the police chief's son, Sean had proven himself beyond reproach.

That was, until that Chase girl had come into his life and all the rules Sean had broken for her tarnished his reputation.

Charlie had warned him not to get involved with her, but Sean had been blinded by his lust. The fallout had brought embarrassment to the family and the police department. The worst was that Charlie could tell Sean still felt for the girl, after everything she had done. When he'd confronted Sean about it, ugly words were exchanged, and their relationship hadn't recovered yet.

No matter the cause, Charlie knew it was his responsibility to fix things. He was the father. "I'll go . . ."

"They're here!" Nikki rushed to the front door.

Charlie rolled his eyes, slowly making his way to the door. It was only two weeks and his wife acted as if Avery had been gone a year. He was happy to see her too, but she also had that Chase disease.

Avery's face lit up the second she saw her mother and it was because of this that Carter was willing to come here. He didn't care for anyone in her family and preferred to keep his distance. Sean was a weak fool, in his opinion, and Chief Jackson could burn in hell for all he cared. Her mother was some flower child who hadn't caught on that it wasn't the '60s anymore, but she was Avery's best friend and for that, he was fine with making this their first stop once arriving back in Los Angeles.

"I didn't expect you today." Nikki leaned over and gave Carter a polite kiss on the cheek. "I thought you would want to rest, but since you're here, we can have dinner."

"We're just stopping by," Carter offered curtly. He nodded to Charlie, who nodded back. It was the best he could do despite the comments he would get from Avery later.

Avery hugged and kissed her father. "We can't stay. We're too tired, but I had to come by and share the news with you."

"What news?" Nikki felt her stomach tighten, knowing what was coming.

When Avery held out her hand, Nikki smiled in pure joy for her daughter's sake before embracing her. She saw the happiness in Avery's eyes and desperately wanted it to be well placed.

"This is wonderful," Nikki said, figuring very few women would have said no to a ring that size. "It's incredible."

Avery was too excited to notice the cold exchange the two

men shared and too happy to be worried about leaving them alone when Nikki took her hand and led her into the dining room.

"Nice to find out after the fact." Charlie made sure his expression was self-evident.

Carter pasted on his best attempt at a humble grin. "I know I should have asked you first, Chief, but let's face it . . . you wouldn't have given your permission."

"You have a point." If there was anything Charlie liked about Carter, it was that the man didn't mince words. He was a cocky, entitled bastard, but he was honest about it.

"And she is twenty-six," Carter added.

"That's got nothing to do with it," Charlie said, "but I understand. I would have said no and you wouldn't have given a damn. So let's leave it at that."

The men eyed each other, holding a distaste tempered only by a certain amount of respect.

"Hello, Carter." Standing in the doorway to the kitchen, Sean Jackson, *the Boy Scout*, was wiping the grease off his hands and studying with interest the tense exchange before him.

Carter said the man's name and nodded. He couldn't even pull off the grease monkey look convincingly. He was only twenty-five but looked five years younger. He had purity written on his face through and through, only slightly tainted by the damage Haley had inflicted. How he could've been one of the best detectives in the county was beyond Carter, who decided to spend this time entertaining himself.

"Have you heard the news, Sean?" He bit back his smile.

"About what?" Sean sensed he was being set up but had stopped letting anyone in the Chase family get to him.

"Haley's coming back."

Charlie snorted, and Sean sent him an annoyed glance before turning back to Carter. He said nothing.

As he watched his father turn and head back to the living room, Sean knew he wasn't in love with Haley anymore. She'd made certain of that by acting like a crazy fool. Now, three months later, he was getting his life—and his professional reputation—back. Now she was back too.

* * *

"Of course I have time to help." Nikki was writing furiously in the notebook on the dining room table. "The gallery is a little slow and your sister will be helping out when she gets home. You have to agree on a date."

Avery hadn't gotten to that point yet. "I'm just enjoying the moment."

Nikki looked up from the notebook, and the lively, eager smile on Avery's face made her want to melt. "You are happy, aren't you?"

"I love him so much." Avery squeezed her mother's hand in her own.

"I know you do."

Avery caught a flash of her mother's brows furrowing before she returned her attention to the notebook. "Mom, I know what you're thinking."

"Do you?" She never was able to hide much from the girl.

"You think it's too soon after my engagement to Alex."

"That's not what I was thinking at all. I know that Alex closed that door when he cheated on you. But I can't say I was happy to see you jump so quickly into a relationship again."

"What does relationship etiquette matter when you're with the person God meant for you?"

"He's a Chase, baby." Nikki put down her pen and took a breath. "Their money—their status in society—has completely disconnected them from their people."

"What does that have to do . . ." Avery knew Nikki believed that anyone who wasn't a part of the struggle was part of the problem. "They are one of the most charitable families to black causes anywhere. Scholarships, fund-raisers and . . ."

"Yes, they are very generous with their money, but they have no understanding of the real contemporary black experience, and your children will be raised with those values."

"My children will be raised with my values."

"If you're going to marry him," Nikki said, "those values should be the same."

When Avery looked away, Nikki took her hand and rubbed it firmly. "This family has had nothing but trouble with Chases.

Everyone who messes with that clan invites disaster. It almost cost you your life, remember?"

"Carter loves me." Avery didn't want to hear this, especially not from her mother, whom she knew to be almost always right. "I love him. We'll work through whatever comes."

"You've only been his girlfriend. Once it gets out you're getting married . . ." Nikki's shoulders slumped as she shook her head. "He's been protecting you up until now, but he won't be able to do it anymore. Everyone will want a piece of you."

"I'll get through it with Carter." Avery reached up and placed her hand on her mother's cheek. "We love each other so much. We protect each other."

"Love isn't always enough," Nikki said. "You loved Alex."

"Alex betrayed me." Avery still felt a stab of pain at the thought of what he'd done. The pictures of him with that other woman were emblazoned in her memory and made her think of all the nights she'd spent crying herself to sleep. "Carter would never betray me. I know that I can trust him, and I do—completely."

Carter leaned against the wall at the edge of the living room listening to Avery's words. He bit his lower lip as he felt the burden of his transgression press down on him. The past was the past and what had happened was necessary. She could trust him—at least now she could.

CHAPTER 3

"They already ate hamburgers at school today." Kimberly looked at her watch. She was running late.

"Let's go, young man." With her most stern Caribbean accent, Maya, the Chase family maid, ordered Daniel to his seat at the kitchen table.

"What are you feeding them?" Kimberly asked impatiently.

Maya made no attempt at hiding her impatience. "Please, Kimberly, just go to your appointment. It's only snacks."

"Nothing spicy," Kimberly ordered. "You know what that does to their systems."

"That chicken wasn't for them," Maya said. "They're sneaking into the refrigerator."

"Well, I'm off." Kimberly walked around the table and kissed both boys on the cheek. "I'll be home by dinner."

"I'm not making dinner tonight."

"Why not?"

Maya was searching the refrigerator. "Mrs. Chase told me not to."

"Did she give you a reason?"

"She just said don't bother." Closing the fridge, she brought two juice boxes and graham crackers to the table. "Ask her why. She's in her room, but don't bother her now."

"Why not?"

Maya shrugged. "She's making an important phone call. She just said not to bother with dinner and kicked me out."

An important phone call, one she didn't want Maya to hear. Maya, the woman who probably knew more secrets about Janet than Steven did. Kimberly's intuition kicked in and she rushed through the house, up the grand staircase and down the east wing toward the Castle Room, what the Chase children called the master bedroom. The door was closed, but she could hear a voice and she quietly, carefully pressed her ear to the door. Janet, who probably was sitting on the bed, sounded muffled, but it was clear to Kimberly that she was emotional.

"I can't . . ." Janet sighed. "I can't do it again. Someone from the museum board almost saw me. With everything that happened last year, I was barely able to get enough votes to stay chair of the board. Planning the ball could easily be taken away if it gets out that I'm seeing you."

Kimberly pressed harder, hoping the door would hold up.

"Dr. Gai— Yes, I know, but you know who I am. The museum ball is the social event of the summer and my place on it is crucial to my family's image."

Kimberly deduced that Janet was talking to the psychiatrist, to the old-money rich Eleanor Gaines, one of the worst-kept secrets in the family but one of the best-kept as far as the rest of the world was concerned. Kimberly wasn't supposed to know. She'd forced it out of Michael after overhearing him talk to Steven about it. She'd had to promise Michael she would never let on that she knew, because Janet would lose it. Kimberly was holding it in her lockbox of possible attacks, but she had to be smart. Releasing it to the press now would only bite her in the butt.

"I do need to talk to you." Janet's voice broke through her tears. "It's just . . . I need you to come here. I know it's not . . . My stress levels are back up and I'm feeling on edge."

Kimberly's lips formed a wicked smile. These were the little delights that held her together until the big payday.

"If you could just come tomorrow, I promise . . ." Janet let out a loud sigh. "Thank you, Dr. Gaines. I . . . really . . . these lies are just tearing me up inside."

Kimberly felt her heart begin to beat faster.

"My home office will do. Yes, we'll meet then. . . . I'll see you tomorrow."

On tiptoe, Kimberly rushed down the hallway, the stairs and out of the house. Speeding off in her hunter-green Infiniti for her spa appointment, she couldn't stop laughing. She didn't care that she would be late. What could a hot stone massage do for her that dirty secrets about Janet couldn't do better? This was going to be something; she would make sure of it.

Listening to Bessie Smith sing the blues wasn't really working for Leigh Chase, *the angel*, right now. She felt safe, considering she was having a good day. The clinic's philanthropic funding for the year had come through. Another doctor, a leading pediatrician from the prestigious Cedars-Sinai hospital, had agreed to volunteer at the clinic a few hours a week. Lab results for two girls she'd been treating, both teenage prostitutes, had come back that day showing negative for HIV past the six-month mark of unprotected sex. Having recently lost a friend to AIDS, both girls seemed determined to use condoms, and Leigh had a good feeling she could believe them.

Besides, Haley was back, and as much as her little sister got on her last nerve, she loved her and missed her. They would go to dinner, drink too much and have a good time.

Then she saw the letter bunched in with the rest of her mail and her mood quickly did an 180° turn. She looked at it for a second, feeling angry and guilty at the same time. Was she being petty? Was she being spiteful? She thought she was a giver, having tried to give her entire life. She wanted to do the right thing and make others proud. Somewhere everything had gotten warped and she'd lost her priorities, and the man she loved was dead because of it. It wasn't just about her mother, but it had a lot to do with her.

And that was why Leigh tossed the letter's expensive, perfectly stitched stationery into the bin on the console table with the twenty others her mother had written in the past six months. She hadn't yet worked up the courage to toss them out.

When she heard Haley ring the doorbell, Leigh rushed down the hallway of her downtown L.A. condo, just six floors under her brother's penthouse. Haley wasn't into hugging and kissing anyone except their mother. Despite that, Leigh reached in for a kiss, happy to see her baby sister looking as beautiful as ever.

Haley leaned away from the hug and sauntered down the hallway. "So have you made any changes to my condo since I was last here?"

"Are you still on that?" Leigh shut the door behind her. Haley hadn't let her forget that this condo was supposed to be hers. "That was a lifetime ago—your own words."

"Daddy bought it for me."

"For you and Sean despite the fact that Sean told you he wouldn't live in a home paid for by his girlfriend's father."

In the kitchen of granite countertops, cherry wood cabinets and Sub-Zero appliances, Haley helped herself to the refrigerator. "Details. The point is, this place is supposed to be mine. The only reason you have it is because you're too poor to buy your own place 'cause you burn all your money in the clinic. And of course you refuse to live at home."

"At least I didn't lose my damn mind and have to be shipped off to Europe."

Haley looked up, surprised by the edge from her usually sweet-lipped sister, older by three years. "Daddy didn't think you deserved it either. He just felt sorry for you because of your dead boyfriend."

"His name was Richard," Leigh said harshly.

Haley stuffed half a slice of cheesecake in her mouth as she looked Leigh up and down. Her straight, light brown hair was a little longer, just past her shoulders, but besides that, nothing had changed. She still looked like an angel with barely a speck of makeup and still wore clothes she bought off the rack at department stores.

"Don't look at me like that," Haley ordered. "You're not the one with a right to be pissed. I am."

Leigh was simply too easy a target to take her anger out on. Every time she came here, Haley was reminded not only of the disaster with Sean but also that their father loved Leigh more than he loved her. He would move the earth for his precious doctor daughter. He'd found the private funding to keep the clinic going after Leigh had refused any money from the Chase Foundation and he had rectified her trust fund so she could pull more than the annual limit to live from. All the while, he was completely happy with the little brat rotting in Europe. It had been this way forever.

"I'm not pissed," Leigh said, "but don't talk about Richard if you're going to be nasty."

"When are you going to get over that?" Haley asked. "I mean, it's not like he was the love of your life. You hit it for three months."

Leigh didn't bother to explain her feelings for Richard Powell, the doctor from Chicago who'd swept her off her feet last year. "At least I keep my grief to myself."

"I wasn't grieving over that asshole. I was getting my much-deserved revenge."

"At everyone's expense."

"You're one to talk," Haley said. "You're killing Mom. Dad is the one who sent Leo over the edge when he had him kidnapped and beaten, but you blame her for everything."

Leigh fought the emotion. "Let's not talk about Mom."

"Let's not," Haley said, mocking Leigh's annoyingly proper tone. "Let's not say anything that might make you feel bad about sending her to a psychiatrist."

"Mom needs a psychiatrist," Leigh said. "She is way too controlling. Besides, I'm seeing a psych too, and she says that I need this time to—"

"That's all very interesting, Leigh. Can we go out to dinner now? I'm getting sick of being around this place."

"I'm not the only one sending Mother to a psych."

"You don't have to worry about me." Haley helped herself to a wineglass from the see-through cupboard. She had the feeling she would need to be drunk to get through another introspective evening with Ms. Let's-talk-about-our-problems. "Sean

Jackson isn't even on my mind. I'm looking for something new to sink my teeth into."

Leigh's lips thinned with concern. Why was that not at all reassuring?

Despite being outside, Avery could feel the thick tension among the family as they sat around the pool at the Chase mansion for after-dinner drinks. With the silence and empty small talk during dinner, she was surprised that Janet had even suggested they do this, but Avery was still trying to get her head around the family's weird rituals. When she questioned them, Janet's only answer would be that things were done because they were done that way among fine families. It made no sense, but Avery was learning that a lot about high-society expectations made no sense and that was the way they liked it.

Sitting by herself on a fluffy lawn chair with an untouched glass of South African cabernet, she felt alone. Among the three acres the Chase family had acquired from buying out their neighbors, the vanishing-edge, piercing-blue pool with tumbled marble and rainbow stone deck was one of the most impressive pieces. It was like a work of art in itself, helped along by the shimmering lights from below that made it seem almost magical.

The fifteen-foot outdoor kitchen with a roof was made from red stone and was equipped with everything from a refrigerator to a gas grill, rotisserie and barbecue-pit smoker. It had been featured recently in *Homes in Color* magazine along with the basketball court, which was equipped with some kind of electrical baskets that Avery didn't understand.

Behind her, the Caribbean-style, two-thousand-square-foot guest house was still covered with a few of the decorations from the last party the family had given to raise money for a new youth center in Long Beach a few days before she and Carter had left for Hawaii. It was unlike Janet to let a detail like that go unattended for so long.

Avery remembered the party, and the air had been tense then as well. There was always a tightness around the Chase family, but Avery sensed only those who weren't members actually felt it. The Chases themselves seemed completely at ease. Thinking of her own family, Avery always felt a sense of warmth and protection around them even when they were having problems. Here, she just felt exposed.

She also felt invisible at times—like now. Steven and Janet were together on a sofa in deep discussion, probably arguing over Haley, who was supposed to show up for dinner but hadn't. Carter and Michael were standing at the bar at the end of the pool trading punches in the arm, both in that world where only the two of them were allowed.

In her heart, Avery wanted to be excited about the news she and Carter would share as soon as Kimberly returned from putting the boys to bed, but she wasn't. Her stomach tensed just at the thought of it being known, because she felt something escaping her grasp.

Kimberly felt the draft from Michael's cold eyes as she returned to the family. She wished she could have stayed with the boys, but Avery had made her promise to come back. Despite the jealousy she felt over Avery's easy entrance into the family compared to her own, Avery had quickly become Kimberly's only real friend.

Carter knew it wasn't a good sign that Kimberly sat down on her own. "You gonna tell me what's going on?"

Michael just shook his head. "I don't want to talk about it."

"If it's about that house . . ."

"I don't want to talk about it." Michael swallowed the rest of his scotch just as Avery approached. He knew Carter loved her, but she should have been gone by now.

Avery tugged at Carter's arm and he leaned in. "Maybe not tonight."

Carter frowned. "We have to, baby."

"We don't *have* to."

"We can't hold off any longer. Trust me, we need to just get it over with. It'll be okay."

He wrapped his arm around her, squeezing tight, and Avery felt a lot better. With Carter at her side, she was up for anything.

"Avery and I have an announcement to make," Carter said.

Janet was off the sofa and headed for Avery before any more could be said. With a wide smile on her face, she opened her arms, waiting . . .

"Well?" Steven asked, although it wasn't necessary. This was expected—maybe not so soon, but expected. He was just happy to see Janet so pleased.

"We're getting married." Avery took the ring out of her pocket and placed it back on her finger. She suddenly realized where most of her anxiety had been coming from, because it went away the second the sparkling jewel was back where it belonged.

"Wonderful!" Janet wrapped her arms around Avery, grateful that she hadn't taken a pill that night, even though she had been tempted. She wouldn't have been able to enjoy this moment, the one bright spot in her day.

She had taken to Avery from the beginning. There was something about the girl. Generally she wouldn't have considered her "Chase" quality. Besides her father's authority, her family had no standing, no name, no heritage of note. Avery herself didn't have the credentials, but she was impressive. She had a grace, modesty and sense of quality about her. Janet would work with the rest.

Kimberly stood up, feeling her blood run green with envy at the sight. Her own engagement announcement had gone somewhat differently.

Michael held out his hand to Carter, who shook it vigorously with a nervous smile on his face. "So you're joining the club."

"I told you I was."

"You told me you were thinking about it."

"Well, I thought about it and . . ." Carter turned to his father who had taken his time in approaching.

"Congratulations." Steven fought the urge to hold out his hand for a shake. Things were changing between him and Carter, and the methods of communication they had shared for the past twenty years no longer applied.

Carter was taken off guard when his father hugged him, not by the action but by his own reaction. He felt the emotion well in his throat, unable to remember the last time this had happened.

Michael took one step back, feeling out of place as the two men embraced. He glanced back at Kimberly, who was facing him with a haughty smirk. He had to fight an anger that had no right to be there.

Janet held her hand to her heart, her mind racing a million miles a second. "We can have the wedding at St. Claire's and . . ."

"I'm Baptist," Avery said. She looked to Carter, who squeezed her hand tight.

"But Carter is Episcopalian," Janet countered, "and it's our family church."

"Mom," Carter pleaded, "we haven't decided where we're getting married yet."

"Then St. Claire's should be at the top of the list." Janet looked around. "I wish I had a pen and paper. It's okay; I'll remember. The rehearsal dinner can be at the Regent and the reception should be at . . ."

"Mom." Carter's tone was stern. "Let's not talk about those things tonight."

"Let the girl plan her own wedding," Kimberly said.

Janet ignored her. "I'm sorry, Avery. It's just that I'm so excited. It's been so long since . . ."

"Since the last Chase wedding," Kimberly said, her hand tugging at her chin. "I remember how excited you were to help me plan that one."

Janet gritted her teeth, staying focused on Avery. "With you going back to work tomorrow, you'll be swamped with too many things to do. You'll need some help. I know the best wedding planner in Los Angeles."

"That won't be necessary." Avery swallowed, feeling a lump in her throat. "My mother is helping me plan the wedding."

Janet pasted on the best smile she could to try to make up for the quick twitch of her eye. That hippie den mother was not going to be in charge of a Chase wedding. "She might be busy as well. She has that art gallery and—"

"We've already discussed it," Avery said.

Janet pressed her lips together to keep from saying something she would regret.

"Shame on you." Kimberly was unable to hold back her grin. "You told the Jacksons first."

"It doesn't matter," Carter said. "Everyone knows now."

Kimberly was having too much fun. "Yes, but—"

"That's enough," Janet spat at her. Despite her best efforts to keep Kimberly away from Avery, the two had formed a friendship, and Janet could see that becoming a problem.

"This isn't going to go well," Steven whispered to Michael as they both watched from a slight distance. "Fix me a drink."

Michael did as told, pouring his father a glass of London dry gin. "Kimberly has a right to be angry."

"You have to say that," Steven said. "You're—"

"Husband or not," Michael argued, "the double standard is pretty nauseating."

"Don't take it out on me," Steven said. "I've been good to her."

Michael found that statement somewhat comical. "Your idea of being good to someone is not treating them like crap most of the time."

"Good enough. Just be happy for Carter."

"You're the one who has a problem with her."

"Not in the same way you do." Steven liked Avery as a person, but having her work at Chase Beauty was a mistake. He didn't like the soft style of business she practiced. "Now that she's getting married, she'll quit her job."

Michael laughed. "Don't hold your breath, old man. This is the twenty-first century, and she's as hardheaded as they come."

"I'm sorry, Michael," Maya said over the phone. "She didn't say where she was going. Try her cell phone."

"I've tried it!" Michael gripped the phone tighter. Where was his wife? "She isn't answering."

"Maybe she left it here," Maya said. "She does that sometimes."

"Tell her to call me when she gets home." Michael slammed down the phone, not bothering with a goodbye.

When Carter entered, the look on Michael's face told him it had to be Kimberly. She was the only person who could make him this angry. "What she do now?"

"Don't you knock?" Michael asked.

"Since when do I have to?" Carter sat down.

Michael sighed, leaning back in his oversized Italian leather chair. "What's up?"

"That was Kimberly, wasn't it?"

"Why you asking?"

Carter frowned. "Since when did you start keeping things from me?"

"You're one to talk."

Carter let out a frustrated groan. "I told you I was gonna propose."

"You said you were thinking about it."

"I showed you the damn ring two days before we left."

"I didn't think you'd have the nerve."

Carter eyed his brother sternly as Michael's lips broke into a quick smile. He knew what Michael meant and he didn't like it. "You amusing yourself?"

Michael shrugged. "I'm just saying . . ."

"I'm not worried. I can handle this."

"Things weren't supposed to go this far," Michael said. "You've kept too many secrets from her."

"One secret."

Michael laughed. "A pretty big one, don't you think?"

"It was your idea." Carter regretted listening to Michael even though he knew he couldn't blame him.

"Whatever lets you sleep at night," Michael said. "But we both know you paid Lisette to sleep with Alex because you had no intention of keeping Avery around. Lisette travels in our social circles."

"Not anymore," Carter said. "That was part of the deal. Part of the $250K."

"Have you been—"

"Yeah," Carter said. "Of course I have. She spent a few weeks in Amsterdam and goes to Paris pretty often, but no . . . Lisette hasn't come back to the States."

"What if she comes back?" Michael asked. "You know what she's capable of?"

Carter had dated the British model of Jamaican heritage for less than four months. They had great sex, but nothing more. She had been after his money and he had been after her ass. They had never been exclusive, and after the fascination had worn off, he'd ended it. She was incredibly beautiful and devious, and she would do anything for money. She had already been married a few times by the age of thirty-two, and after recent legal problems with the children of her last husband, twenty-eight years her senior, she was hard up for money. She had a lifestyle to maintain.

Carter had never done anything so debased and would take the guilt to his grave. "I'm not letting anything mess this up."

Michael nodded to his left. "So are you here for lunch with your new fiancée?"

"No," Carter said. "I'm having lunch with Dad."

Michael blinked. "For what? Why?"

"Business." Carter glanced at his watch. "I'm gonna be late. Look, I wanted to ask you something."

"What business?" Michael asked. "Anything I should know about?"

"No, just contract stuff." Carter stood up with a wide smile on his face. "I need to ask you—"

"Yes," Michael said with a satisfied grin.

"Can't I at least ask?"

Michael threw his arms in the air. "If it amuses you, fine."

"Will you be my best man?"

Jealous thoughts of Carter and their father bonding over steak at the local business club went away. Carter was his boy forever. "Yes."

She was finally gone.

Kimberly thought she was going to explode waiting for Janet to leave the house. It had been almost two hours since Janet's private session had ended and Dr. Gaines had left. Kimberly had bitten at half her lower lip, aching to get into Janet's private office and retrieve the looping recorder she'd taped to the back of the sofa.

The door to Janet's office was locked as usual, but Kimberly had learned to pick locks when she was six and had picked this one several times before in her search for dirt on the "monster-in-law."

Once inside, she rushed to the sofa and with one hard grunt pushed it away from the wall, grabbing the tape recorder. Not willing to take any chances, since Maya was around somewhere, Kimberly quickly made her way back to her bedroom as she re-wound the tape. She giggled like a little girl as she clicked the Play button. The good stuff came just a few minutes into the session.

Janet: I just feel (sigh) . . . I just feel this growing depression sweeping over me. It's like a cloud. I could barely get up this morning. I . . . (sniffles) . . . I . . ."
Dr. Gaines: Take your time, Janet.

There was a short silence, and Kimberly pressed Forward.

Janet: (inaudible) that wedding. I can't believe she's shutting me out.
Dr. Gaines: Did she say she was shutting you out?
Janet: She didn't have to. I thought, for just one second, that finally there would be something good in my life, and it was snatched right away from me. After everything I have done to make that girl feel welcome. I just . . .

Janet was full-out crying now.

Dr. Gaines: Janet, do you believe Avery's choosing her mother over you to help her plan her wedding is the cause of your depression?
Janet: Everything is. The wedding, Leigh, Haley, the lying.
Dr. Gaines: The lying? Are you still taking the Valium even though you promised Steven you would stop?

There was a short pause and Kimberly started to feel let down. Everyone knew Janet was still taking the Valium.

Dr. Gaines: Your husband believes you stopped in October.
Janet: I tried, but that sneaky little bitch. . .

Kimberly smiled, flattered by the inclusion.

Dr. Gaines: Let's stay on the Valium. I would consider prescribing you something for the depression, but I can't until you stop taking the Valium. The mix could be deadly. You can't even be sure you need them until your system is clear of the Valium.
Janet: I will stop. I . . . I can stop. No, seriously, Doctor, I can. I don't want to take them. I hate lying to Steven. I've never lied to him be—
Dr. Gaines: Is there something else you're keeping from him?

Kimberly felt her stomach tightening.

Janet: It's not about this. It's from years ago. Decades ago.
Dr. Gaines: But from your expression just now, it obviously has stayed with you.
Janet: Of course it has.
Dr. Gaines: Maybe you can invite him to a session and get it out.
Janet: I could never tell him this.
Dr. Gaines: Can you tell me?
Janet: No, I want to forget it ever happened.
Dr. Gaines: If it's related to your situation . . .
Janet: It isn't. This was the summer after I graduated from college. I was in Paris and I had an affair.
Dr. Gaines: You never told Steven?
Janet: We were engaged, but I won a chance to study at a prestigious design school in Paris. I couldn't pass it up, and Steven was busy working in New York.

There was a long silence and Kimberly was frozen in place. Something told her this was going to get better. Even someone as anal-retentive as Janet couldn't be this upset over a brief pre-marital fling.

Janet: Steven believes he's the only man I've ever been with.
Dr. Gaines: You've had more than thirty years of marriage. You believe the truth would turn him against you after all this time?
Janet: It's not just the affair with Paul. It's . . . I did something awful. I . . .

As she listened to Janet break into loud sobs, Kimberly waited patiently for more. She was disappointed when Dr. Gaines agreed to let the topic go and talk more about Haley's return and Janet's anger over being left out of the wedding. Still, she had gotten enough to feel a second wind.

I did something awful was what she had said, and Kimberly took that to heart. Janet was never critical of herself, so this had to mean something. Kimberly contemplated all she had—having an affair before the wedding, lying about the Valium and doing something awful. It wasn't enough. Kimberly knew she had to get her PI to find out who this Paul was and what Janet had done.

It suddenly occurred to Kimberly that she had a chance to do something she'd never thought possible. All this time, she had been waiting to get out of the Chase mansion. Never once had it occurred to her that she could get *Janet* kicked out. Just the idea made her toes curl in delight.

Mrs. Perfect was going down.

CHAPTER 4

Avery set the pint of ice cream on the table and picked up the remote. Looking at it, as usual, it was like reading Japanese. She'd been living in Carter's condo for two months and was still getting used to his state-of-the-art lifestyle. She'd thought it would be nice to be able to afford the newest and best of everything, but it was just too much work. She would have to take a class before she could work that stereo.

Setting down the remote, she planted herself on the sofa and opened the first of the seven bridal magazines she'd purchased earlier that day. Carter was running the streets with Michael and she would have the evening all to herself.

Then the doorbell rang.

Of course it was too good to be true. Avery was thinking of excuses to give to whomever it was to get rid of them as soon as possible. When she peeked through the keyhole, she jumped in excitement. The door flew open and the sisters rushed into each other's arms.

"Taylor!" Avery dragged her baby sister inside. "What are you doing here?"

"I'm home for the summer, girl."

Taylor Jackson, *the schemer*, hurried down the hallway of the luxury penthouse in one of the most sought-after buildings in downtown L.A. She took everything in at lightning speed.

"I'm just a few days early. I had to let that fool loose."

"What fool?" Avery followed as the beautiful nineteen-year-old surveyed the condo with wide eyes. "You've been here before."

"I know." Taylor sat down on the sofa and grabbed the pint of ice cream and spoon, helping herself. "I just love this place. It's so . . . classy."

Taylor was tall and dark with a natural, unruly curly cut that went wild on the ends. She had big doe eyes and tiny features. She was also one of the rare genetic freaks who were thin with perfect, natural curves.

"It's nice," Avery said, "but we're selling it."

"Why?"

Avery pushed the magazines out of the way and sat down. "It's too sharp and modern for me and we're right in the middle of all these lights and nightlife."

"This is the best place to be." Taylor just didn't get her sister. "Everyone who's anyone lives around here, and you live on top. You're close to the best clubs. Do you know how many celebrities are in this building?"

"I didn't know any celebrities lived here," Avery said. "But if they do, all the more reason for us to move out. I want to move into the suburbs after we're married. You know, a nice home where—"

Taylor laughed, showing her pearly white, perfect teeth. "Girl, you are a trip. You're young and rich. You're supposed to live in the city and be where life is happening. I would give anything to live out here."

Taylor was still trying to think of a way to maneuver herself into that second bedroom next to the office. She dreaded the idea of another summer spent in the boring 'burbs and her mother's art gallery. After hearing the good news about the engagement, Taylor had known this summer could be different.

"I'm not rich," Avery said.

"You will be when you get married—which is when?"

Avery shrugged her shoulders. "We haven't picked a date yet. By 'that fool,' you meant Tyrell?"

Taylor nodded. "I was just tired of his ambitionless ass."

"He's in college, Taylor. You have to give him time to figure out what he wants to be."

"I know what I want to be," Taylor said.

Avery respected Taylor's desire to be a model, but, like their parents, she hoped Spelman would encourage her to do something less glamorous. She was afraid of that lifestyle. "You have to finish college."

"Who said I wasn't finishing college?"

"I thought you loved Tyrell."

"I did for a while." Taylor offered Avery the ice cream and reached for the remote. "He just ain't about nothing. He wants to work with young black boys—you know, the absent black father thing."

"It's not really a 'thing'," Avery said. "Absent fathers are taking a devastating toll on black children. What he's doing is admirable."

"I could see it as admirable if he wanted to be a politician one day, but he just wants to . . ." Taylor waved a dismissing hand. "I'm looking for someone who wants to be somebody, to be about something."

Avery was disturbed by Taylor's notions of worth in society, especially considering they both had been brought up with the same values. "What would Mom think if she heard you?"

"I'm down for our people," Taylor said. "I just want to do something on a higher level, like you are."

"You want to run a salon chain?" Avery asked. There were days when she wished she was still sitting in the back office of Essentials. At least then she'd felt connected to the community.

"No, I mean how you've latched on to the Chase family. You can't lose."

"I haven't latched on to any family. I fell in love with Carter. It's not about his money."

Taylor made a smacking sound with her lips. "You want to play holier-than-thou, try someone else. Even you can't pretend you didn't see those dollars."

"I didn't see them first." Avery wasn't comfortable with the direction of this conversation. "And as for being with a Chase, remember Sean."

Thinking of Sean, Taylor only wanted to rip Haley Chase's head off. The only problem was that Haley, as insane as she was, was still one of the "it" girls in L.A., and Taylor didn't have a chance of getting in without her.

"Tyrell wasn't throwing down in the bedroom anyway."

Avery was a little shocked, but held her tongue. She wasn't in a position to say anything; living with Carter and not married yet.

"Please tell me you were using—"

"Mom and I already had this talk." Taylor couldn't hold back her laughter. Avery seemed more uncomfortable than their mother had been when she'd found out. "She lectured me about the statistics on HIV and black women."

"Twenty a day are diagnosed positive, Taylor." Avery had recently read the report herself, and it had frightened her to death after Leigh explained the epidemic.

"I want to talk about this wedding." Taylor's eyes jumped as she shifted upward. "Can I go to the mansion?"

Avery wasn't encouraged by Taylor's enthusiasm. It didn't say much that her first instinct was to keep Taylor as far away from the Chase clan as possible, if for nothing other than their mother's sanity. "Baby girl, it's not all it seems to be."

"I can judge that for myself."

Taylor had already judged that this marriage was going to work for her. As happy as she was for Avery, this wasn't just about her sister's joy. She was going to be officially connected to one of the richest black families in America.

Black society was just like any other exclusive group; they did everything they could to keep out those who weren't born in. Every now and then one could slip in but rarely would reach the inner circle. The Chase family was in the center, and Taylor saw her future taking her there.

"That should be enough, shouldn't it?" Kimberly asked into her cell phone.

She enjoyed walking through her spacious closet while gently running her fingers along her clothes. There were so many choices, all hot designs and the latest styles—exactly what she'd dreamed of as a child.

She stopped at the lingerie. She wanted to wear something wicked for Michael when he came up after his regular Sunday basketball game with Carter.

"If it's all you have," Neil answered, "it'll have to be, won't it?"

Kimberly had hired Neil Owen after hitting a brick wall over and over again. She hadn't wanted to bring anyone in because of the damage it could cause if it got out. Fortunately, a model friend, now safely tucked away in Sweden, referred him as uniquely discreet for the right amount of money. Neil was former CIA—the kind who couldn't even tell his own wife what he did for a living.

"I know I can count on you," Kimberly said. "Call me as soon as you have something."

"Who is that?"

The phone fell out of her hand as Kimberly turned to see Michael standing in the doorway to the closet, pulling his sweaty T-shirt over his head.

"Who are you talking to?" Michael asked, trying to ignore how exceptionally tasty her dark skin looked against the canary yellow silk bra and panties.

"You scared me." Trying to slow her heartbeat, Kimberly picked up the phone, placing it on the closet island that housed her hats and belts. "You're home early. You must have been losing."

She made her way to him.

"Carter had to go meet Avery for some wedding thing." Michael let her wrap her arms around him, feeling himself come under that familiar spell. He thought of the old Prince song "Joy in Repitition." "Who were you talking to?"

"Ms. Cregan," she lied. "From the boys' school."

"Why is she calling you on a Sunday?" He didn't believe her for one second.

Their marriage worked because neither of them was particularly sensitive. They said what they meant and let the chips fall anywhere—usually into bed. Their passion for each other and love for the boys was strong enough to get past anything. It was because of this honesty that it was very easy for Michael to tell when Kimberly was lying.

Kimberly kissed him on the lips, the favorite weapon of the distracting wife. "She's calling all the parents to remind them that next week is the last week of school."

"That's ridiculous," Michael said.

"We pay them twenty-five thousand bucks per kid in tuition every year," Kimberly said. "It's not too much to ask for a Sunday call, even for the obvious. I was thinking of something nice I could—"

"I have to take a shower." He pulled away from her and walked over to the desk.

"Mind if I join you?" Kimberly wasn't used to putting too much effort into arousing her husband. They were like magnets, drawn to each other without cause or need for much seduction.

She tugged at his shorts, trying to pull them down, but he guided her hand away. She didn't let it deter her. Neil would find something soon. Until then, she would have to keep things together.

"I just want to shower." Michael checked his BlackBerry for messages.

"I'll get it started," she answered. All she had to do was get his hands on her and it was all instinct from there.

"Fine," Michael answered flatly. "I'll check my messages and be there in a second."

He watched as she winked at him and switched her hips into the bathroom. She was too fine for her own good.

Michael put down his BlackBerry and darted for Kimberly's closet. Grabbing her cell phone, he checked the last incoming call. He didn't recognize the number and knew it wasn't the school, because Kimberly had all of those numbers on speed dial. Checking her call history, he noticed that several incoming and outgoing calls were devoted to this number. He selected the last one and pressed Send.

The older male voice on the message didn't bother with a hello. "You've reached 310-555-CAPI. Leave a message."

Michael hung up and quickly memorized the number, writing it down as soon as he got to his desk. He would have Matt Tustin, one of the family's many private investigators, get right on it.

But first . . . time for a shower.

CHAPTER 5

The trends in L.A. nightlife changed at the drop of a hat, but not much had changed since Haley had been gone. The only difference was Pearl, the newest nightclub on the scene, which had opened one month ago. With the requisite number of celebrities and athletes showing up on Friday and Saturday nights and subsequently getting kicked out, Pearl had temporarily stolen the spotlight. Wannabes and hopefuls stood in line for hours when even the hottest women were turned away.

Not Haley Chase. She was a queen on the night scene, a celebrity for being a spoiled rich girl who knew how to set a party off. Despite the trouble she often caused, club owners knew that if Haley paid them a visit, they would be in the gossip blogs on Monday.

She hadn't been in the club for ten minutes before a minor baller for the Lakers sent over one of his posse to invite them to his little roped-off corner of the club.

Haley grabbed Tia, who was always too eager for her own good. Haley smiled at the boy because she pitied him more than anything. It was sad that he was wearing the jersey of his master.

"No thanks," she said.

"Why not?" Tia asked.

The young man, a light shade of caramel with a dark, wavy

Afro jutting out in every direction, scratched his chin. "Do you know who my boy is?"

Haley placed a hand on her hip. "He's someone who sends his minions to get girls for him. That's all I need to know."

He looked her up and down with a sneer. "Who do you think you are?"

Tia laughed as if she knew something was about to happen.

Haley rolled her eyes. "Someone who doesn't come when called."

She turned her back to him and could hear him make a smacking sound with his lips before he walked away.

Tia leaned in. "You went too easy on him. You're losing your touch."

"Baby player was the sensitive type," Haley answered. "Besides, this isn't where we want to be."

"Meaning?"

Haley was disappointed. Despite being the daughter of one of Hollywood's hottest black male actors from the '80s and a famous German model, Tia still acted as if she was grateful for getting the extras. She was a beautiful girl, golden-colored with long, unruly hair and legs half a mile long. But then again, that was every other girl in L.A.

"Up there." Haley nodded in the direction of the elevator, guarded by two Clydesdale-looking types. The elevator went to a second level where private parties were taking place and a theater balcony looked down on the rest of the club. "Let's go."

Tia reluctantly followed. "I tried that last weekend and we couldn't get in."

"Who were you with?"

Tia listed names that included a few current budding socialites, an actress and her semi-famous publicist.

"Of course you didn't get in with that skank," Haley said. "Just shut up and let me talk."

The two Clydesdales didn't flinch as Haley approached, but one of them looked her up and down. She would start on him.

"Private party." His voice was low and intimidating enough. "Sorry."

"Don't apologize," Haley said without breaking a smile. "We want to go up."

"Are you on the list?" he asked, annoyed.

Haley placed both hands on her hips and leaned back. "Do I look like I wouldn't be?"

He smiled, pursing his lips briefly, but he seemed prepared to stand his ground until the other guard leaned in and whispered something. He gave Haley another look and smiled in recognition before nodding and stepping aside.

When the elevator opened up on the VIP floor, all eyes turned to them. Haley knew she was looking fierce in a Sue Wong silk, blush-pink, lace-trimmed dress. The V neckline went down to her belly button.

Some of the women waved her over, but most just rolled their eyes because they knew her arrival put an end to any chance they had to be the center of attention. Haley did a quick survey of the men, recognizing most of them and having no interest in any.

But one man in particular caught her eye. He was standing at the edge of the bar, at least six feet tall with a shaved head and cinnamon-brown skin. Although the textbook Armani was a little disappointing, he set it off with a mulberry silk shirt. But it wasn't his style that made her look a second more than she should have. There was something about the way he was looking at her, with a sense of intrigue and sinfulness she connected with. Besides her brief insanity with Sean, Haley had a preference for men who would cause her nothing but trouble.

Everyone's eyes followed both women as they made their way across the floor to the corner, but Haley could feel his above anyone else's. When a group of women quickly surrounded her, she pretended to be interested in their compliments and questions about her European vacation, but she kept him in the corner of her eye.

He didn't take his eyes off of her, not even when two barely dressed women latched onto him. So he was a player. Haley didn't really care; she'd broken the best of them, and with the way this one had targeted her, she was beginning to find him too easy a task to bother with.

Then the tray came to the table. Everyone except Haley immediately began devouring the Russian beluga caviar on toasted brioche, terrine of fois gras, truffles and lobster medallions.

"Who is this from?" Tia asked with a mouthful of food.

Haley rolled her eyes. Didn't this girl know anything? "Stop acting like you're off the street. It doesn't matter who it's from."

"It's from Mr. Reman," the waiter said, nodding toward the mystery man, who now was leaning against the ledge that overlooked the downstairs dance floor, with two new pieces of slutty jewelry on each side. Still, he had eyes only for Haley. "He's the manager of the club."

Haley didn't return his smile. She felt that Tia's frantic waving was more than enough to feed his ego. Men were just so damn disappointing, assuming women were impressed with anything that might sparkle.

She wasn't looking for a husband, so she felt no need to make a man something more than he was. Being men, they were worth only so much in the first place. The most he could be was a diversion until she came up with a better plan for getting back at Sean.

Haley looked at the plate of expensive goodies the sows around her were finishing off. With a disappointed sigh, she stood up and headed for the bathroom. As she'd suspected he would, he quickly inserted himself within her line of sight so she couldn't avoid him. He thought he was charming.

Haley stopped and looked at him with an annoyed expression, saying nothing.

"I'm Chris Reman." He spoke in a deep, confident tone as he offered his hand.

Haley tilted her head, not moving an inch.

He didn't seem too fazed by her rejection. "Can I ask for a name at least, sister?"

"Sure, I'm the woman who is gonna piss on your floor if you don't stop blocking my way to the bathroom."

"I'm willing to risk it," he said after a quick blink, "because I don't think you'll do it. Public urination doesn't seem your style."

"You have no idea what my style is."

"That's obvious," he answered. "You didn't like my spread."

"Did you really expect me to?" She held up her hand to halt his response. "And please don't embarrass yourself by telling me how much it cost."

Chris leaned back, looking like he was trying to figure her out. "It was just a gesture. Beautiful women are always welcomed in my . . ."

"You were trying to impress," Haley interrupted. "But a word of advice. If you think some fish eggs on bread will get you some, you might want to set your sights a little farther down the food chain than me."

"Whoa." Chris laughed, giving Haley another once-over. "Well, maybe I can invite you to dinner at a place that better meets your standards."

Haley mocked him by looking him up and down in the same way. "It seems too hard a task for you, but thanks for the offer."

She circled around him and continued to the bathroom, hiding the little smile that formed at the edges of her lips. There were worse diversions one could find.

"The door was open," Michael offered in his defense as his parents, engaged in a kiss, looked to him with ill-tempered expressions. "And it is a place of business."

"It's my office." Steven reluctantly let go of his wife. "You walk in like you think it's yours."

Michael's lips curved into a smile just at the thought of the day this office would be his. "We have a budget meeting with Avery's team in fifteen."

Janet collected her purse from Steven's desk. "I was going to stop by her office and see how the wedding plans were going."

"I thought she asked you to stay out of it," Michael said.

"Michael." Steven's tone made saying any more unnecessary.

"As a matter of fact," Janet countered, "she's allowed me to plan the engagement party."

"Finally," Michael said, "an engagement you can be proud of."

Janet pressed her lips together as she held eyes with her son. They had been through this before and Janet knew where

Michael's heart was. Patience was her only choice with him. She knew something was going on between him and Kimberly and was only hopeful it would work in her favor.

"You two enjoy your meeting." Janet reached up and kissed Michael on his cheek.

"You need to watch yourself," Steven warned after she was gone.

Michael didn't respond as he made his way to the back wall of floor-to-ceiling windows. He wasn't in the mood to be scolded.

"Whatever is going on between Kimberly and Janet is between them." Steven returned to his chair. "You stay out of it."

"How exactly do you stay out of something involving your wife?" Michael asked with a sarcastic tone. "Unlike you, I can spend only so many hours away from home."

Steven swung around in his chair, showing an unmoved expression. "I'm not impressed with your crack. Your mother is happy and I'm not going to let anyone get in the way of that, including you."

"God forbid," he said, just above a whisper.

"Hey, I—"

"Back off." Michael surprised himself when he heard the words escape his mouth. It was a capital offense to piss off King Chase and as he felt his father's eyes penetrating him like daggers, he knew it was too late to care.

Steven held his temper. He knew he would have enough to deal with in fifteen minutes; he didn't need to add on.

"We're moving out," Michael said, turning to him.

Steven was uncharacteristically caught off guard. "When?"

"I don't know, but soon." Michael sighed. "We have to."

"You've been saying that for three years now." Steven met his son's glare head-on. "Don't be angry with me; it's the truth. What makes this—"

"Don't act like you don't know something is going on."

Steven nodded, feeling torn. It was right for Michael to move and be the king of his own castle, but he didn't want him to. He loved having his boy—not to mention the twins— around in a house full of women.

"It's the right choice," Steven said. "It will make Kimberly happy and—"

"What is this?"

Both men turned as Avery stormed into the office, waving a sheet of paper in her hand. She slapped the memo on Steven's desk, only becoming more infuriated as he looked up at her without expression.

Michael stepped forward, determined to enjoy the entertainment. "Our meeting isn't for another ten minutes."

Avery ignored him, staying her focus on Steven. "Those prices are unacceptable."

For six months, Avery had been in a war with Steven over the prices at Chase Expressions, Chase Beauty's chain of twenty L.A.-area salons she managed. Both of her old salons were among them, and she took great pride in creating the premier salon style and service with neighborhood prices.

"Avery," Steven said calmly, "if you have an opposition to my suggestions, you can bring it up at the meeting."

"I don't think you want to hear what I have to say at the meeting," Avery shouted. "And let's not pretend that these are suggestions. This memo clearly states that this is a decision you've already made and—"

"After careful consideration, I—"

"Cut the crap." Avery was too full of angry adrenaline to realize how close to the edge she was treading.

Michael's eyes widened as he saw his father react. "Avery, take it easy."

"You want to shut out the very people you said Chase Beauty was targeting." She pointed to the memo. "These are the same prices the most expensive salons in L.A. are charging. We agreed not to do this."

"I understand," Steven said. "That's the problem."

"It was the solution," she argued.

"We are getting the reputation of being the cheap salon," Michael offered. "We can't have 'cheap' and 'Chase' spoken of in the same breath."

"We aren't cheap," Avery argued. "We are less expensive and we've been successful so far because people want to support their own. Yes, View Park and Ladera Heights can afford this, but most of our customers can't. We'll lose business once these increases are announced. It's dishonest."

"That's how business is sometimes," Steven said. "If they'll pay these prices at other salons in L.A., they'll pay them here."

Avery couldn't get why this man didn't understand. "The whole idea was to give them the same quality and service but at better prices so every woman, whether she is from L.A. or Compton, could—"

"The decision has been made," Steven said.

"You waited until I was on vacation and went behind my back!"

Steven shot up from his desk and Avery jumped with a gasp. Michael stepped aside; he had warned her. Now it was too late.

"How dare you?" Steven's eyes turned to slits as he stared her down. "The name on that door and on your paychecks is mine. I don't need to go behind anyone's back. I've appeased you because it pleases my son, but don't you think for one second I won't fire your ass if you ever talk to me like that again."

Avery swallowed, her inherent fear of this man's force hitting her like a brick. "It . . . it won't work. It's going to . . . to backfire."

Avery wasn't so sure she wanted to turn her back on a man with such a fierce look on his face, but she braved it and walked as fast as she could out of the office, trying desperately to catch her breath.

Steven sat back in his seat, waiting for his boiling temper to calm down. He looked up at Michael. "What are you smiling for?"

Michael straightened the smile on his face. "Nothing."

The little battles between Steven and Avery had come to an end. The war was beginning and it signaled an end to the truce between Carter and their father. That's what Michael was smiling for.

Kimberly couldn't remember feeling this happy since . . . since she'd found out Janet had a big, fat skeleton somewhere in Paris. Sitting at the vanity in her bedroom, she gazed at herself in the mirror, reveling in her pride and beauty.

"Of course it's good news." Neil's voice could barely be heard over the airport traffic swirling around him.

Kimberly spoke into the Bluetooth, leaving her hands free to brush her hair. "It has to be. Not only did she have the affair, but it was with her professor?"

"I can't be sure if that's the Paul we're looking for," Neil said, "but he's the only one at the school at the same time she was."

"But he was her teacher?"

"The equivalent of a . . . yeah, you can call him a teacher."

Kimberly felt her toes tingle. "When will you be in Paris?"

"My flight to London is leaving in one hour. Then I'll buy a train ticket to Paris. I have to go."

"I'm running out of time."

"I'll do what I can."

When Michael entered the bedroom, he heard Kimberly say goodbye. She was on that damn phone again and the smile on her face made him only guess who it might be. Caught up in whatever she was talking about, she didn't notice him until he slammed the door behind him.

Kimberly shot up from her vanity and rushed over to him. "Hey, Daddy."

He turned his head as she brought her lips to his, but she didn't hesitate to kiss his cheek instead.

"Who was on the phone?" he asked.

"Can we not do that again?"

He turned to her, loosening his tie. "Who was it?"

Kimberly rolled her eyes, letting the lie roll off her lips with the ease that only a woman could do. "It was Avery."

Michael froze, his eyes bearing into her like daggers. He wanted to strangle her. "Avery?"

"Yes." Kimberly ran her fingers across his chest and began undoing his shirt. "I love it when you wear this shirt; salmon pink looks so good against your skin. It makes me want to—"

Kimberly gasped as he grabbed her wrists and pushed her hands away. He was looking into her eyes with a fire that frightened and excited her.

"Shut up." He grabbed her hair, pulling her head back before his mouth came down on hers, hard and angry. His kiss was intended to punish her, to hurt her for how easily she could now lie to him.

Kimberly turned her head away, trying to pull her arms free of his painful grip. "Michael, don't . . ."

Ignoring her, Michael was fueled by a fury tainted with passion. He grabbed her by her hair and pulled her head back again. Leaning down, he brought his tongue to her neck and blazed a trail up to her chin. He lifted his head just in time to catch a slap across the face.

"Don't try to brand me." She backed away as he started for her again. There was an insanity to the way they were pulled to each other. Everything she knew was telling her that he wanted to hurt her, but she still wanted it.

"My brand has been on your ass for seven years, baby. Maybe you've forgotten."

With the pounding in his head drowning out everything else, Michael grabbed her again, picked her up and threw her on the bed. The look of fear in her eyes turned him on more than he'd expected. He ripped off her blouse.

Kimberly let the tornado in her belly rush through her. She reached up for him, but he slapped her arms away. It hurt her that he wouldn't look at her, but it hurt more not having him touch her, so she just closed her eyes and pretended she couldn't tell.

Kimberly let out a tortured groan as his mouth took her left breast. When he bit hard on her nipple, she winced and pressed against his shoulders. He only bit harder and she let out a scream.

"Michael, please!"

He ignored her, hating himself more then he hated her because he wanted her so bad. He leaned down, putting the full weight of his body on top of hers. Taking her hands in his, he pinned her arms to her sides and stared down into her beautiful, lying eyes. She believed this hold she had on him could protect her, but she was wrong. There would be hell to pay and it would start now.

"I'm going to hurt you," he whispered through heavy breaths.

Kimberly nodded even though she knew this was different than all the other times he'd *hurt* her. Michael liked it rough, especially when he'd had a hard day at work. She found something frighteningly sexy about being used by him in a selfish way. All she asked was that he give her a warning so she could brace herself. Only his eyes told her something else this time. They were clouded by an anger that scared her and she knew all the bracing in the world wouldn't protect her from what he was going to do.

When the knock came at the door, Michael felt a sense of reality return to him and the wicked pleasure of seeing the look on Kimberly's face in a few seconds satisfied him more than it should have.

He lifted up, yelling, "Come in!"

"Michael!" Kimberly pushed against him. She turned to the door. "Just a second!"

Michael grinned as he stared down at her, taking his sweet time getting up. He sat on the edge of the bed as she scrambled to her closet. "Come in!"

Kimberly fumbled with the first shirt she could find. She couldn't see who had just entered the bedroom, but the second she heard the voice, her knees went so weak, she had to reach for the wall just to keep standing.

"Where is she?" Avery asked, feeling slightly uncomfortable by the mischievous grin on Michael's face as he sat on the edge of his bed.

Michael slowly turned to Kimberly and a smile spread across his lips in response to her blank stare. She was several shades lighter. "She's right over here."

Kimberly swallowed hard, unable to tear her eyes away from Michael, whose expression quickly darkened. She felt her stomach trembling as he stood up and began buttoning his shirt.

"Hey." Avery made her way to the other end of the room, where she saw Kimberly standing at the edge of the closet, halfway dressed.

Kimberly blinked and tried to smile as Avery came into sight. She prayed for the legs to support her as she finished putting on her shirt. She opened her mouth, but nothing came out.

"You okay?" Avery wasn't sure what was going on, but she knew it wasn't good. She looked back at Michael, not liking the dangerous glare in his eyes.

"I forgot to tell you, baby." Michael licked his lips, taking in every bit of fear on his wife's face. "Avery's car isn't working. She drove here with me. She needs to talk to Mom about the party and she asked me to get you for her. Her cell battery wore out."

For some unknown reason, Kimberly felt the urge to laugh although there was nothing funny about this. As Avery nervously asked her if she wanted to help plan the engagement party, she watched Michael give her one last hateful glance before turning and walking out of the bedroom, slamming the door behind him.

When she turned back to Kimberly, the look on her face made Avery rush to her. "What's wrong?"

Kimberly stumbled to the bed, with Avery following closely behind. "He knew."

Avery just shook her head, her confusion beginning to turn to fear. "You're scaring me. What is going on?"

Kimberly looked at her and despite the affection she felt for her future sister-in-law, she couldn't trust her with this. She was too close to Janet and too fond of doing what was right. No, the only person she could trust was Michael and she would have to find a way to tell him the truth or she would lose him, and that was not an option.

As she stood alone in the foyer of the Chase mansion, Taylor couldn't keep her mouth closed. She had seen pictures of the house in magazines but none of them compared to the real thing. The foyer was soft and warm with marble flooring and sleek, modern furniture, but it was the double staircase that made her want to get out her cell phone and snap a picture.

Everything around her was steeped in luxury, and Taylor felt a sensation close to sex as she imagined herself living this way. Looking around, she was itching to ignore Avery's orders to stay where she was until she came back downstairs. From where she stood, she could see the great room on her left and a formal sitting room on her right. She was aching to run her fingers over everything.

Taylor tensed as she heard footsteps, not sure why she felt like she had been doing something wrong. When a middle-aged woman in black uniform pants and a sensible white oxford shirt came from around the corner, she felt like she'd been caught.

"Can I help you?" Maya asked.

"I'm Avery's sister." Taylor nervously stuffed her hands in her pockets. "She told me to wait here. She wanted to drop something off for Mrs. Chase before—"

Taylor jumped when the doorbell rang. It was louder than she had ever heard, but she guessed it needed to be for such a large house.

"Excuse me." Maya made her way to the door.

Why was she so anxious? She was just as good as any Chase. She was going to be a member of the family. So why did she feel like she didn't belong here? What was she afraid of? *Who* was she afraid of?

"Haley!" Maya placed the lavish bouquet the delivery man had just given her on the brass-mounted mahogany wall table. She looked it over approvingly. "Someone is trying to impress."

Taylor smiled nervously, knowing she was missing something. Although the tall flowers were beautiful in the brightest combination of white, purple and pink, it was just a bouquet. "What are they?"

"Hyacinths," Maya answered. "Someone went for the money. Even Mrs. Chase only gets these for special occasions. Whoever he is, he's in for a surprise. It was all for nothing."

She turned to Taylor and offered a quick "It was nice meeting you," before rushing off.

She most likely was very busy, but the woman's abrupt exit made Taylor feel invisible. As she walked slowly over to the bouquet, the sound of her hard heels hitting the marble floor echoed around her. She felt stupid for having less knowledge than a maid about the flowers. How was she ever going to fit in?

She wondered how much the vase had cost. It looked expensive—tall, sea-blue glass with melting waves at the side. She took hold and lifted it up to see if a label was on the bottom. It was heavy—another sign it was expensive.

"What are you doing?"

Taylor jumped, tipping the vase and spilling water on herself and the floor.

"Dammit!" As she put the vase back on the table, Taylor cringed at the smile on Haley's face as she made her way down the stairs. "I'm . . . I'm sorry."

"Who let you in?"

Taylor gritted her teeth, forcing a smile. How she hated this trick. "Avery. She's my sis—"

"I know who she is." Haley was going to have to find a way to put a stop to this. "And I know why you're here."

"I was just looking at the—"

"It's not going to happen." Haley lips pressed together and she leaned forward with a menacing smile.

Was she trying to read her mind? Taylor didn't know what to think. "W-what?"

"This wedding." Haley felt sick just thinking about it. "My mother told me about it and it's not going to happen."

"I don't think you have much say in it."

Haley smiled. "I don't care what you think, and you're wrong. There is no way in hell I'm letting the Jacksons into this family."

Taylor couldn't believe the gall of this chick. She was completely serious. "Why can't you just be happy for your brother?"

"I don't give a damn about my brother," Haley said. "And it's none of your business."

"I'm not the one who brought it up."

"You brought it up the second you walked in this door." Haley leaned to the side, looking behind the tall girl. "Where's your ladder?"

Taylor rolled her eyes, thinking she was going to have to work harder to get past this psycho. "I'm having lunch with my sister. I'm not trying to be a social climber."

Haley laughed. "I appreciate you understanding you have no chance, because it would really press my time to have to get rid of you, as well as your sister."

"You're not going to do it," Taylor warned. "Carter and Avery's love for each other is stronger than your elitist hatred. You won't get rid of her. None of your plans work. Like when you thought you could ruin my brother's life."

"What makes you think I'm through with him?"

Taylor's hands formed fists at her sides, and Haley noticed with pleasure. "Your sister is a lot weaker than Sean. She'll be easier to break."

"Avery may be soft," Taylor said, stepping forward, "but I'm not."

"Is that a threat?" Haley leaned back with a smirk on her face.

"It's just my way of saying I've got my sister's back."

Haley wanted to smack that confidence off her face. "But who's got yours?"

Taylor wouldn't back down even though she knew this woman's elevator didn't reach the top floor. What she did know is that she had a better chance of getting Haley's respect if she stood up to her than if she cowered.

"You can stare me down all you want," Taylor said. "I'm not leaving until my sister comes back downstairs."

"I wouldn't waste my time," Haley answered. "I'm just keeping an eye on you. You look like the klepto type. I already caught you trying to steal my flowers."

"I wasn't stealing anything," Taylor said. "And how do you even know they're for you?"

Haley reached for the card attached to the bouquet. "They're always for me, little girl."

"My name is Taylor."

"And your brand is Wal-Mart," Haley said, looking her up and down, "so it really doesn't matter what your name is."

"No wonder my brother dumped your ass." Taylor felt victorious in knowing she had hit a nerve, as Haley shot her a dangerous look.

Haley took a moment before responding. "Your brother is insignificant."

She opened the letter, quickly reading the message from Chris Reman. His choice of flowers was trying too hard to show his means, and he'd taken too long to track her down. There was no way she was going to call him. He'd have to come up with something else.

"Is that why you've been busting your ass to get back at him?" Taylor felt on steadier ground now. Sean was an asset in her battle with Haley.

"Nobody crosses me and gets away with it." Haley tossed the envelope on the table next to the bouquet.

"Something we have in common," Taylor said.

"You wish." Haley exaggerated her yawn. "Instead of trying to climb into an upper class, why don't you do something more suited for your level and clean up this mess you made?"

Taylor could feel her nails digging into her palms. "It was nice meeting you."

Haley sauntered past her and out of the house, happy for the unexpected entertainment.

Taylor groaned out loud, trying to get her temperature back under a thousand degrees. Noticing the card, she reached for it and opened it up.

Ms. Haley Chase,
   Now that we know each other's names, is it too much to ask for more? Maybe just another chance to prove my culinary taste is much better than you think.

The bottom of the stationery read "Chris Reman, Manager, Pearl Nightclub."

Okay, so the girl most likely was the spawn of Satan, but she could get into Pearl, a place where Taylor didn't have a chance no matter how good she looked. Visions of herself hanging out on the VIP floor, mixed with visions of country club dinners, Rodeo Drive shopping sprees and front-row seats during Fashion Week in New York, twirled in Taylor's head and assured her that she could suck it up a bit longer.

The L.A. Athletic Club may have been considered third or fourth on the list of prestigious business clubs in L.A., but it was

Michael's first choice. His father favored the old money clubs like the California Club and the Jonathan Club, but they were too old and stuffy for Michael's taste. All three clubs were more than a hundred years old and had taken almost that long to admit blacks as members, but his father had been one of the first to receive an invitation and made a point of regularly doing business at the stuffier clubs. They were traditional, which made them Carter's type as well, but the Athletic Club, like the City Club in Bunker Hill, had more color and more life. They were more like Michael.

"Can I get you another drink, Mr. Chase?" the waiter asked as he approached Michael's booth in Duke's Sports Bar on the second floor.

"Not yet." Michael had already downed two drinks waiting for Matt Tustin. He knew he might need the cushion to take whatever news Matt had for him, but he wanted to take it easy.

Matt Tustin was one of those invisible types, which made for a great PI. He was such an ordinary man that he could just blend in anywhere. He wasn't too tall or too short. He was white, but not pale and not dark. He was forty-five but looked anywhere between thirty-five and fifty. His hair and eyes were brown, not light or dark, just brown, and his clothes were bland. Everything about him was so incredibly average that he could shoot someone in a room full of people and no one would be able to identify him.

That was why Michael didn't notice him until he was standing at the booth.

"How you doing, man?" Matt asked with a generous smile on his face.

"Sit down."

Matt shrugged and took his seat. The waiter was there in a second, as they always were, but before he could open his mouth, Michael interfered.

"He won't be here long enough for that."

Matt appeared offended for only a second before he slapped a manila folder on the table. "Your brother always offers me a drink."

"I'm not my brother."

"That's the truth." Matt looked around. "I've never met him here. This is nice. How much does membership cost here?"

"More than you can afford." Michael leaned forward. "What do you have?"

"You'd be surprised what I make," Matt said. "There are a lot of neurotic, obsessive, paranoid rich people out there."

"Just get to it."

This already had taken too long for Michael's taste. He'd expected Matt to use the phone number and get something right away. It was usually all he needed, but after several days, he had been able to produce only a name: Neil Owen from Pasadena. It was driving Michael nuts.

Everything had been downhill since the day Kimberly lied to him about talking to Avery. He'd left and hadn't been home since, spending the night at Carter's place. Kimberly had called him, piling lie on top of lie to try to cover up, and he was grateful he wasn't near her, because he would have done something he would regret forever.

He missed her, he missed his boys and he knew he didn't have the guts to stay away much longer. After the anger subsided, there was the pain of knowing that no matter what she did, he couldn't live without Kimberly. He hadn't been the perfect husband and he was living by a double standard, but he wasn't going to let this happen. If she was cheating, it would have fatal consequences for somebody, but he would keep her.

"I've got good news and bad news," Matt offered.

"Stop messing around."

"Hold on a second. Our Mr. Owen is good, but so am I." Matt opened up his folder and slid his report across the table. "He's one of my own."

Michael's curiosity was piqued. "He's a PI?"

Matt nodded with a proud smile. "A damn good one too. He's barely traceable, but I put everything I had into it like you said—spared no expense. He's former CIA."

Michael flipped through the thin report, wondering what in God's name Kimberly was doing with this man. "He's fifty years old?"

"Yup. White male, fifty years old and"—he reached into the folder and slid copies of two glossy photographs across the table—"rather ugly if you ask me."

Michael studied both pictures, one of a hard-looking man with no expression in a crisp black business suit and the other with the same man forcing his lips to form a weak smile as he stood next to a woman and two teenage boys.

"Where did you get these?" he asked.

"You don't want to know," Matt answered. "The guy's office is like Fort Knox, but his home surprisingly isn't."

"You could have been caught."

"He's in London," Matt said. "At least that's where he went three days ago. No return flight and his trail goes cold after Heathrow."

"You think he's working for Kimberly?" Michael asked.

"I'm telling you, the man is smooth, but I was able to see some of her account withdrawals around the dates of his deposits, and four of them are dated just one day after Kimberly's credit card receipts show she was either eating or shopping in the area of his office."

"I need to see him and Kimberly together." Michael tossed the report on the table. He gestured for the waiter to bring him that next drink.

"Not gonna happen until he comes back," Matt said. "I do this for a living, sir. I don't think your wife is hitting it with this guy."

Michael glared at him, wanting to sock him for even saying the words. "I don't care what you think. I want more proof."

Matt shifted his eyes nervously. "Sorry, I . . . That's fine, Mr. Chase. Would you like me to wait until he's back or just stay on your wife?"

"Stay on Kimberly for now." Michael nodded a thank-you as he took the drink. He finished it in one gulp, letting the fire run down his throat and clear his mind for just one second. He slammed the glass on the table, garnering a few looks from the power lunch crowd in their crisp three-thousand–dollar suits, knowing they hated him because his suit cost six thousand. He turned to Matt, who was staring at him with a dumbfounded look on his face.

"What are you still doing here?" he asked.

Once alone, Michael looked at the photo of Neil Owen and convinced himself that Kimberly wouldn't let this man touch her. She could never be attracted to him, and he had no money.

Michael had been successful in spending the past seven years forgetting that his wife spent a small part of her youth having sex with men who probably looked like Neil Owen. It wasn't her fault. She had been a teenager trying to survive, and the second she could get out, she did. She hadn't had much choice; poor beautiful girls all alone in the projects rarely did. In the silence of late night while in their bed, she had cried in his arms, remembering the nights she'd wanted to kill herself. It was crazy to Michael, but it all only made him love her more. He had saved her, and for that, she would never leave. And she wouldn't risk losing him by cheating on him.

So, whatever else in the world she was lying about, it wasn't an affair. Michael knew who Kimberly was—all her good and bad—and he loved all of it because he knew she was his. She knew she was his. She knew that he had made her and she wouldn't betray that by letting any man put his hands on her. It just wasn't going to happen.

That settled, what in God's name was she up to?

CHAPTER 6

Kimberly thanked the country club waiter as he placed the plate of oysters on her table. He offered only a half smile in return before walking off, but she didn't care. When she'd asked for the food to be delivered poolside, she had been told no food was served poolside. She would have to sit in the poolside café if she wanted to eat. She would be able to see her boys at their swimming lesson just fine from there.

Unfortunately, the waiter was new and didn't know who she was. This fact was made very clear to him by the manager of the café who scolded him harshly and promised Kimberly she would have the oysters anywhere she pleased in five minutes. She acted as if she hadn't noticed how pissed off the waiter was even though she suspected he didn't like being put in his place by a black woman.

It was all funny, really. In the world Kimberly came from, the idea of anyone white serving a black person was a joke. Almost as funny as the sight she was watching right now: her boys swimming in the Olympic-sized pool with the club's swim coach. Black folks don't swim; at least that's what she was told as a child and believed. She grew up with so many limitations, lines she couldn't cross and doors she couldn't open.

It was ironic that her first taste of black money had come

when she started tricking. Her pimp, David, had found her wandering the streets at the age of fifteen after she'd had had enough and run away for the last time. Although most of his girls worked the street or the clubs, Kimberly's beauty placed her on the menu for his higher-end clients. She would meet men in posh hotels and restaurants because she could clean up well enough to look as if she belonged and could pass for older.

It was in this role that she first met black men with college degrees who owned their own businesses, were actually married to the mother of their children and made six-, sometimes seven-figure salaries. They lived in McMansions in the Detroit suburbs and had never touched a football, a basketball or a baseball bat or cut a rap record. As much disdain she felt for them for not even bothering to ask what her name was, she admired them for not buying into all the things she had—like that black folks don't swim.

As she watched her boys flap around the pool, looking as if they were a second from drowning, she knew they were going to swim, go to college, own their own businesses, make seven or eight figures and be married to their children's mother. And she would do everything in her power to make sure they would never pay for sex with a child whose name they didn't bother to ask.

They would have everything she never had and it was because of Michael. It was because of the doors he had opened for her, the love he had shown her and the ambition he had taught her. Every man in her life had treated her like crap until Michael, and it had taken her more than a year to realize that he wasn't up to something. He was going to be good to her. He was going to stay.

She loved him with all of her heart, but it wasn't just her heart she was thinking about when she knew she had to keep Michael. She would never give up this life, being a Chase. Not even destroying Janet was worth that.

She needed Michael home. The relief she'd felt when Avery called to tell her he was staying with them and not with some other woman had been short-lived. No matter how hard they had fought before—and they'd had knock-down, drag-out fights—Michael always came home.

So last night, Kimberly had made the choice to tell Michael the truth. If she had to give it up she would. Michael always sided with her when he was forced to pick sides, but there was no way he would accept her trying to break up his parents' marriage and send his mother over the brink. There was nothing she could do, and she couldn't wait another day for Neil to save her life.

But spotting Neil's familiar phone number on her cell, Kimberly grasped that last sliver of hope that was seconds from escaping her forever.

"Please give me good news," she said.

"I have better than that," he answered. "I think I've got what you've been dreaming of."

Kimberly had to hold on to the arm of her chair as she took in everything Neil told her. She didn't want to believe it could be this good.

The summer before their wedding, Janet had matriculated at the Ecoles de la Chambre Syndicale, a prestigious fashion school in Paris. Her teacher had been a young man by the name of Paul Devereaux. By methods that Neil would not disclose to Kimberly, he had accessed school files from that year and found exactly what he'd suspected. Paul had been subject to disciplinary action for inappropriate behavior with an unnamed American student.

After contacting two of Janet's former classmates, one a small-time fashion designer in London and the other a modeling agent in Milan, Neil was able to hammer the nail into the coffin. Not only had Janet and Paul engaged in a sexually intimate affair, but there was a rumor Janet had gotten pregnant and had been taken to the doctor used by all the rich girls in Paris who needed confidentiality to protect their family's good name. A medical procedure had been performed.

Two weeks before the summer session ended, a depressed, despondent Janet returned to America and Paul was fired, supposedly at the request of her powerful lawyer father from New York.

"If you're lying to me," Kimberly said, her voice shaky, "I'm going to have you shot."

Neil laughed. "Baby, it was easy. This is what I do."

"She had an abortion?"

"Now *that* I couldn't get," Neil said, "but let's face it. What else could it be?"

"I need your proof and some way to track him down."

"I'm not finished, beauty queen."

"You've found him?"

"He's right here in Paris," he answered. "He's a hotshot fashion designer."

"Paul Devereaux?" Kimberly racked her brain, reaching back into her New York modeling days. "I keep up on the fashion industry and I've never heard of him."

"He's one of those sub-designers, works under the Gaultier label. That famous enough for you?"

Kimberly's hand went to her chest as she felt it tightening. "Jean-Paul Gaultier? Shit, Neil, do you know what you've done?"

"I've earned a bonus," he answered. "I know exactly what I've done, runway girl."

After she hung up, Kimberly couldn't stop laughing. She didn't care how crazy she looked to anyone who might notice. As she gulped down the oysters, the first food she'd eaten in a couple of days, she felt her whole soul being energized.

"Mommy, look!" Evan screamed out as he made it one foot before going under and needing to be retrieved by his coach.

"I see you, baby!" Kimberly waved to him as she let out a long sigh. Falling back against the chair, she already had her plan in place.

She had just begun to believe that her own past wasn't going to come back and destroy her life. She had been living in the middle of nowhere, her family part of the invisible in America; which is why Janet had come up with much of nothing from her childhood when she'd done her background investigation. She had some information on where Kimberly had grown up, but her family was gone or dead and no one had ever paid much attention to her before she'd run away. Michael had made sure that his mother would run into brick walls, and Kimberly knew Janet was utterly frustrated with the black hole that existed until

Kimberly showed up in New York at the age of seventeen on the arm of a man she had met in Atlantic City, who promised to make her a model.

She had been lucky as hell that she was a non-person to those men she'd slept with. Most of them wanted her on all fours, so they never bothered to look at her face for more than the second they met her. They would never recognize her or remember her, especially now that she looked and dressed as if she had been around class all her life.

Still, she knew it wasn't all luck. Michael had made sure she stayed out of the spotlight, limiting her exposure. He wouldn't tell her what he'd done, only that he'd erased what could hurt them, and she didn't protest or question more.

As for the rest of those street people she'd met along the way in that dark, distant place, what happened in the world of Chase meant nothing to them. So she was safe.

Janet wasn't, not anymore. Kimberly was certain this was a sign from God. Paul was a fashion designer under a leading label, she was a former model and her husband was CFO of Chase Beauty.

It was all too perfect.

"What's the point?" Haley tossed the UCLA application papers back to her mother. "I'm already in, aren't I? Can I have a drink, Dad?"

Standing behind the bar just outside the family's game room, Steven said, "It's Sunday and it's only one in the afternoon."

The game room, in the basement of the mansion, had been recently redecorated by Janet, who regularly expressed her flair for design by changing rooms in the house or certain offices at Chase Beauty. Gone was the red and black modern minimalist. Now everything was dark cherry wood and hunter green with splashes of pomegranate. The pool table was still in the center of the room, but the fifty-inch plasma flat screen was usually the center of attention. The new Vegas corner had poker, blackjack and roulette tables, all ordered online from a real play table distributor.

"You're drinking," Haley argued.

Steven wondered why he continued to indulge his wife in these after-church family get-togethers. "That's because I have to put up with you."

"Steven." Janet wished he wouldn't provoke Haley.

Steven rolled his eyes. "Fine. What do you want?"

Haley smiled, leaning back on the stool. "Mojito!"

"Appease me." Janet pulled out the only incomplete section on the application. "Just pick a topic, Haley. I'll write the essay."

"You pick a topic," Haley whined. "Besides, Daddy's money is getting me in. Why do I have to write a stupid essay?"

"How hard can it be to write one essay?" Steven asked. "It isn't like you don't have the time."

"Because I'm sitting on my ass all day, right?" Haley's stubborn grin was erased by that look on her father's face that said *not today*.

No matter how much she fronted, Haley had a healthy fear of her father. It wasn't a physical fear; she knew he would never lay a hand on her. It was just a fear of his power and his status as head of this family.

It was his distance and cold stares that made her feel small and the disregard with which he responded to her sarcasm made her think he didn't really care.

Haley pushed away from the bar and hopped off the stool. "Never mind the drink. I've gotta go."

"Haley." Janet's tone was stern. "What about an experience with Junior Achievement?"

"She was kicked out," Steven said.

Haley groaned. "I'm outta here."

"Thank you," Janet said to her husband. "You made that much easier."

Steven took a sip of Absolut. "These bonding moments are your idea, not mine."

"Which is the problem." Janet helped herself to Haley's drink. "You're the head of this family. Why am I the only one trying to keep this family close?"

"You're asking too much. She came to church. That's enough for one week."

Janet gave up, knowing it was the truth. She would have to

write the entrance essay herself. It was a small price to pay to get the girl into school.

Steven watched as Janet took another sip of her drink. She was tired, and her mood had been erratic over the past weeks. He'd been watching her as closely as he could, but it was hard and Maya wouldn't help him. She was on Janet's side.

"Are you all right?"

Janet nodded and laughed because it was the truth. She hadn't taken a Valium since meeting with Dr. Gaines. After testing tomorrow, she would be able to take the medication Dr. Gaines had prescribed, and Janet was hopeful things would begin to clear up.

Janet smiled, reaching out to squeeze his hand in hers. The idea of confessing to Steven about taking the Valium frightened her, but she wanted to do it. He would forgive her, she didn't doubt that, but at what cost? He would wonder what else she had been lying to him about.

"Is there something you want to say?" Steven asked.

Janet wasn't ready and was grateful that Steven's attention was taken by Carter and Avery, who were intensely focused on each other on the sofa a few feet away. Janet remembered being in love the way they were, caught up in each other so much that the rest of the world disappeared. Planning their engagement party was one of the few bright spots in Janet's life right now.

"You have to get along with her," Janet said.

"That's easy for you to say," Steven answered. She was actively lobbying against the new price increase and pestering him every day with other ideas to improve the image of Chase Expressions salons without raising prices. "I've had enough of her."

"She's going to be family." It was Janet's pleading that had convinced him to offer the job to Avery in order to make peace with Carter. "I promise you, if you put forth the effort, it will all work out."

Steven smiled, leaning into his wife. "Well, that does it. If you promise, I have no choice but to believe you. I haven't regretted it once."

Janet's eyes weakened and she felt her stomach tickle with the fear that only secrets and lies can bring.

*   *   *

Avery craved that sweet, heated flirtation that came with every kiss from Carter. Just the taste of his lips and she wanted to be all over him.

"Let's go upstairs to one of the guest rooms," Carter whispered into her ear before gently biting her lobe.

As he pulled her closer to him, he remembered wanting to crack the code to the power she had over him, but he had given up. *It's okay to be completely in love*, he reminded himself despite some instinct that told him to run from it. It was okay to love the way she smelled, get drunk on the way the ends of her curls would go in unplanned directions like they had a mind of their own. Avery wasn't like most women. She would completely love him back. She could be trusted. It was okay to give her everything, tell her everything.

"I will go with you." She wrapped her arms around his neck and leaned into him. "If you tell me what the heck is going on with Michael and Kimberly."

Carter looked behind them. With their boys playing at the miniature football table just feet away, Michael and Kimberly were making out like a couple of horny kids, just like old times.

"What do you care?" Carter asked. "He's out of the condo. That's what you wanted."

Avery quickly glanced in Janet's direction. "I just want to know what caused it. They fight all the time and I know it has something to do with Janet, but he's never left before. Kimberly was hysterical on the phone."

"It was a misunderstanding and she cleared it up." Carter had to get used to Avery wanting to penetrate his confidence with Michael. She was going to be his wife and they couldn't have any secrets from each other—at least, not anymore.

"Misunderstanding," Avery huffed. "Please."

"You know how dramatic they are," Carter said. "They aren't happy if the world isn't coming to an end, but it's all over now."

"Janet must have thought she was in heaven."

"For a few days at least. Dad said he couldn't remember seeing her so happy."

Avery sighed at the mention of her future father-in-law's name. "Your father. He's driving me crazy."

Carter was shaken by the degree to which even the semblance of pain in her expression reached so deep inside of him. He ran his fingers through her hair and cupped her chin with his hand. "Don't worry, baby. This will all pass."

Avery checked her temper. This seemed to be Carter's only response to her complaints about how difficult Steven was making things for her at Chase Beauty. It was beginning to really bother her.

"We've already begun to lose customers," she said. "Now he wants to slash half the radio ads planned for the fall."

"You have to trust him, Avery. For all his faults, Dad is a marketing genius. He just doesn't make mistakes."

"He's making one now." Avery leaned away from Carter, looking him squarely in the eye. "And I can't believe you of all people are trying to suggest he's infallible."

"Not when it comes to business," Carter answered. "Chase Beauty is his kingdom; he's king. End of story."

"He's undermining me at every meeting," Avery insisted. "It's personal, Carter. I know it."

"You're making it personal." Carter caught her fed-up look and tried to recover with an understanding smile. "You're too emotional about this, baby. Chase Beauty is a billion-dollar international corporation. Personal feelings can't get in the way of profits."

"You sound like him," Avery said, unsure of how to feel about that. She was the one who'd urged him to reach out to his father after they'd begun officially dating. "Are you sure you're not the one who's being emotional?"

Carter was enjoying the truce between him and his father. They were actually getting along and it was more than he imagined they could ever do after being at odds as long as Carter could remember. Now he actually believed they could be close.

"I'm not sacrificing you for the sake of my relationship with him," Carter assured Avery. "I wouldn't hang you out to dry, baby. He's my father, but you're going to be my wife. I'll always choose your side."

Avery's heart melted because she knew he meant it. To look at him and know he would always be there and on her side made her want to give him the world. What had she done to be so lucky?

Haley ignored her mother's request that she lower her voice. She didn't care that this was L'Orangerie, and she didn't give a damn about the snobs who were glancing in their direction. They could all kiss her ass. Nobody was going to take her money.

"It's mine," she insisted with a biting tone. "He can't keep it from me."

Janet remained calm, dabbing at the edges of her lips with her napkin. "Until you're twenty-five, he can keep every cent from you."

They were arguing over Steven's freezing the funds from Haley's trust. Janet hadn't been in favor of it, but Steven felt it was the only way to make her cooperate with their plans for her to attend graduate school.

"With everything I'm doing," Janet said, "I don't have the time to chase after you. The Dean just wants to interview you. With all the strings the school is pulling, it's the least we can do."

"What about my credit cards?" Haley asked.

"They aren't your credit cards. They are our credit cards with your name on them, and we can cut them off anytime we want."

"Two more years and that fund is mine." Haley pushed away her barely eaten plate of roasted turbot with olive paste. "Then I can drop out if I want."

"We've been through this before," Janet said. "When you're twenty-five you can take money out without asking permission, but we still have the option of placing limits until you're thirty."

Haley wanted to spit. "He loves this, doesn't he? Controlling me the only way he can—with his money. And you don't do anything about it. You always pick his side over mine."

"Cry me a river." Janet took a delicate bite of her food as if she were demonstrating etiquette on camera. She knew people were looking at her, waiting for her to slip, but things were changing. She was getting better, clearer, back on her game. "Let's schedule this for Friday morning."

"Can't," Haley said. "Tia and I are going to Mexico for the weekend."

"Oh, for Pete's sake. You can go to Mexico next weekend."

"We're going *this* weekend. There's a big festival thingy going on at a resort on Playa del Carmen."

"Sounds like fun," Janet said sarcastically, "but unless Tia is floating you the cash . . ." Janet cocked her head to the side, feeling her point was made.

"If you get him to unfreeze my account, I'll tell you what Leigh has been up to."

Janet felt the familiar stab in her heart at the mention of her angel's name. Thinking of Leigh was the only time she'd felt tempted to take a Valium. "Is there something to tell?"

"I think so," Haley said. "She's got a date this weekend and she's got some big plans for the clinic."

"Ms. Chase?"

Getting a quick glance at the young man who had just approached their table, Janet knew this wasn't going to go well. He looked low class even though he was dressed in a cream-colored, flashy Italian suit. He was entirely too eager for Haley's approval.

"It's nice to see you here." Chris Reman held his arms behind his back.

"You're not stalking me, are you?" Haley asked, suddenly reminded of how fine he was.

Chris smiled, turning to Janet. "You must be Mrs. Chase."

Janet nodded, not saying a word.

"It's nice to meet you," Chris said, glancing from mother to daughter.

"I can't introduce you," Haley said. "I don't remember your name."

If he was offended, no one could tell. "My name is Chris Reman, Mrs. Chase. It's very nice to—"

"My daughter and I were having a private conversation," Janet said. "I hope you don't mind."

Chris's smile faded, but only for a moment. He rebounded quickly and Haley took notice. He wasn't giving up despite both of them giving him the cold shoulder. She wasn't sure whether to be impressed or to pity him.

"I won't take up much of your time," he said. "I was just hoping for permission to call Haley."

"For what?" Haley asked.

"I wanted to invite you to the Prince concert at Staples this Friday. The owner's private box offers the perfect view."

Haley was prepared to tell the all-too-eager-to-please man no until she saw the look of disgust on her mother's face. Janet was a queen at hiding her distaste for someone in public. She could smile the sweetest saccharine for someone she hated. If she wasn't able to hold back, it was because she found someone particularly distasteful.

"Well," Haley answered slowly, "since my Friday plans were recently canceled, I'll think about it. You can call me if you have the number, because I'm not giving it to you."

"I wouldn't expect you to." Chris showed no hint of impatience before bidding a polite goodbye to both women.

"You can't be serious," Janet said. "Who is he? No, don't tell me, because it doesn't matter."

"He owns a nightclub." Haley smiled victoriously. "Cute, isn't he?"

"Here we go," Janet said, tossing her napkin on the table. She had suddenly lost her appetite.

CHAPTER 7

From the kitchen, Avery hadn't heard Carter come home until he turned down the stereo in the living room. She smiled instinctively, like she always did when he came home. His footsteps coming down the hallway excited her and the sight of him coming around the corner, undoing his silk tie, made her feel like her world was perfect, if only for that second. The traditional girl in her loved this time of day. Her man was home.

"Smells good, baby." Carter leaned against the entrance to the luxury kitchen, a wicked smile on his face as he took in her trim, curvy figure. She knew that he loved those little thin cotton sweatpants that hung low on her hips, revealing her soft, flat stomach and cupping that round ass he couldn't keep his hands off.

Avery smiled with her eyes seductively low. She couldn't resist the flirtation because he looked so damn fine in those expensive suits. She felt her toes tingle as he made his way to her, tossing his jacket on an island stool.

From behind, he wrapped his arms around her waist, pulling her body against his. She tilted her head back, looking up with those big, innocent eyes promising all the love he needed and more than he deserved. He kissed her with a moan to express how good her lips tasted after a hard day at the office.

"Why don't you put that on simmer for a second?" He rested his head on her shoulder.

"Nothing we do gets done in a second."

"Okay, let's try something else to make you happy."

"Give it to me." She reached for the bowl of shrimp, adding them to the boiling-hot pot. "I need something nice today."

"Monday, I'm talking to Dad about you."

Avery turned around, more interested in Carter's emotions than her own. She searched his face for a hint of discomfort, but he only smiled. "You don't have to."

"I know, but I will. It shouldn't have taken this long, but . . . whatever the case, I'll deal with him."

"Are you really okay with this?" she asked.

"You're my baby girl. Nobody messes with my woman."

"We should go over what you're going to say. I don't want to make it seem like I'm a child who needs—"

"Hold on." Carter backed away, leaning against the island. "I know how to talk to my father. Don't give me instructions."

"Sorry." Avery sighed. "I'm just eager. I got it from 'both ends' today. Put that salad in the bowl, honey."

Carter did as he was told. "What do you mean 'both ends'?"

"Your father knocked down every suggestion I had for community sponsorship this fall. Everything I wanted was too— what word did he use?—oh yeah, working class."

"I've told you about this," Carter said. "Chase Beauty is a high-end product. It can't sponsor little 'hood events."

That comment rubbed Avery the wrong way. "Okay, some of them were small community gatherings in Compton, Long Beach, and places like that, but the Black Family Reunion is not a 'hood event. It's a twenty-year tradition on the Mall in Washington, D.C."

Carter stopped, looking at her to see if she was really serious, and it bothered him that she was. "Baby, you have twenty salons in L.A. I'm sure Dad plans on expanding one day, but people in D.C. aren't going to catch a flight to get a touch-up."

"People come from all over the world to that event, including Los Angeles. Besides, sponsoring events is about branding, not getting more customers."

"Everything is about getting more customers."

"If this is how you plan to argue on my behalf," Avery said, "don't bother."

Carter smacked her on the butt. "Watch it, woman. You know I got your back even when you're wrong."

She turned around and kissed him, her stomach fluttering. "I'm not wrong."

"Then don't give up," he advised. "You can be stubborn as hell when you really want something."

"I don't intend to give up," Avery said. "I would just prefer not to have to declare war on my future father-in-law."

Carter helped himself to a glass of Bordeaux. "You've got a lot to learn about being a Chase, Avery. You see, King Chase loves war. It's a natural state of being for him."

"You sound like your mother." Avery's tone held a hint of disgust.

"What now? I thought you loved Mom."

"I do, but . . ." Avery took a deep breath to keep from getting worked up again. "She invited six members of the press to our engagement party. I don't want *any* press at my engagement party; I sure don't want six."

"Avery, you're going to be—"

"Don't!" She surprised herself just as much as Carter with her tone. "Don't say that I'm going to be a Chase. I can't stand it when you say that."

Carter put down his glass. "I'll stop saying it when you get it. Don't look at me like that. I'm not the bad guy here. I've been protecting you, but I can't anymore."

"What does that mean?" Avery felt her teeth grit at his condescending tone.

"I've been doing everything I can to keep you away from all the crap that comes with being a part of my family, but you said you understood that it's going to be different. We talked about it in Maui."

He grabbed the bowl of salad and headed for the dining room.

Avery followed closely behind. "What exactly have you been protecting me from? The gossip-column lies? The pictures people take of me when I'm filling my tank with gas? The random women who call me or come up to me at parties to spit their jealousy in my face? Or maybe it's those endless parties with people who don't have anything better to do than talk about the burden of being upper class."

"That's enough," Carter warned.

"It's enough when I say it's enough." Avery paused, seeing the dark turn Carter's expression was taking. "I know what I'm dealing with, but that doesn't mean I have to give in to it. Keep fighting, you said."

"Some things you can't fight." Carter slammed the bowl on the table. "And all those parties, gossip columns and jealous women aren't the worst of it."

"You don't have to tell me," Avery said. "I'm the one who was almost blown up last year because of you."

Avery immediately regretted her words the second she saw Carter's hurt reaction. They'd made a promise to let go of the damage each had inflicted on the other when they'd first met.

"I remember," Carter answered. "I also remember I was the one who saved your life."

The phone ringing broke the thick silence between them as they eyed each other. Avery rushed to get it if only to avoid the embarrassment she felt from acting so childishly.

"Hello?"

"Is this Avery . . . Jackson?" The woman's voice held a harsh edge.

"Yes, it is." Avery glanced down at the caller ID. "Laura Chapman?"

"Yes," she said. "Maybe you remember me. I was the woman who was dating Carter before you came along and stole him away."

Avery's mouth opened, but no words came out.

"You're a man-stealing little ho, and now you think you're going to marry him?"

"How dare you call here?" All of Avery's patience had been used up. It was bad enough these tramps would try to confront her at parties, but now they were invading the peace of her home. She wasn't having this.

"Is it true?" Laura asked. "Are you engaged?"

"That's none of your business. Don't call here again!"

"That is not your house, bitch!" She had a cold laugh. "I slept in that bed before you, and I can tell you now, you don't have what it takes to hold on to him."

Avery gasped as Carter ripped the phone from her hand. She stumbled back, looking at the expression on his face.

"Laura." Seeing the confused look on Avery's face only made Carter more furious. "What the fuck do you think you're doing?"

Avery watched as his breathing picked up pace and his grip on the phone tightened. She had never been afraid of him, but she had never seen him like this before. He looked on the verge of an explosion.

"I don't give a shit. Don't you ever call here again. You understand me?" He turned away from Avery and put some distance between them. "That's a lie and you know it. You call here again and I will make you regret it for the rest of your life. Do you understand me?"

Avery wasn't sure what she was hearing. Was he threatening a woman?

"Just tell me you understand!"

When he hung up, he turned back to face her and with a calm tone said, "It's okay."

"It's not okay," Avery answered. "Did you just threaten her?"

"I didn't mean anything physical," Carter said. "You know I'd never hurt a woman."

"But—"

"The dinner is burning." Carter pointed toward the kitchen.

Avery rushed to remove the pot but quickly returned. "Who is Laura Chapman?"

"No one." Carter sat down. Before Avery, picking women hadn't been his strong point. "I'm hungry, Avery."

"Who do you think you're talking to? I'm not some girl, you know. I'm your fiancée. Do you think I'm just going to pretend like that never happened, like some Stepford wife?"

Carter sighed. "She does this all the time. The second she reads about me in the paper or sees me with someone else, she calls and tries to threaten the woman to mess it up for me."

"She's never called me before."

"Yes, she has," Carter said. "You just didn't pick up. The news has gotten around that we're engaged."

"Is this woman crazy?" Avery asked. "Should I be concerned?"

"No." Carter's tone was definitive. "She's just a jealous, gold-digging ex who thought her last name could buy her a Chase husband. She moved to Philly two years ago. She won't come back to L.A."

"How do you know that?"

Carter knew he had already said too much. "I just do. Now, can we eat?"

Avery knew she wasn't going to get any more out of him, and deep down inside, she didn't want to. Something told her she wouldn't like what she heard. There was an undertone in his voice and she knew this was like those other times when he wouldn't tell her something she wanted to know, probably something only Michael knew.

"I'll make you a plate," she said, turning back to the kitchen. "But you can eat alone. I've lost my appetite."

"No." Michael reached for Kimberly's hand to prevent her from covering her mouth. "I want to hear you."

Unable to fight him, Kimberly let out a primal scream as the orgasm rushed over her. Her back arched, her head went back and her eyes rolled up as the sweet, torturous sensation swept through her entire body. When it was over, she collapsed on top of him and slammed her fist into the pillow.

"Fuck you, Michael," she said in between breaths.

Michael was laughing as he brought her face to his and kissed her long and hard. "Don't be mad, little mama."

She pushed against him. "You know they heard me."

Michael sat up, too exhausted from hours of sex to care that he was sweating like a pig. He reached up, slapping his hand against the wall behind the bed—the wall separating their bedroom from the boys. "See, nothing. It's two hours past their bedtime. Besides, psychologists say it's good for kids to know their parents have a healthy sex life."

"Not at six years old!" She socked him in the chest.

"Hey," Michael said. "I work hard all day. If I want to hear somebody screaming my name at the end of the night, I'm gonna hear it."

Kimberly leaned over the night table and grabbed her glass of wine. She was too happy to care about anything now. Her husband was back home and her plan was in action.

"Are you going to talk to Steven tomorrow?" she asked.

"I've told you that we have to at least put some kind of business plan together first. I can't just go up to him and say I need $75 million to start a fashion line."

Michael wasn't too excited about Kimberly's plan for Chase Beauty to start a fashion line. She had brought up the idea before and Steven had decided it wasn't the right direction for the company. It was too far away from cosmetics. Michael wasn't too sure it was a good idea either, but when Kimberly had shown up at his office promising to tell him everything she'd been up to, he was so relieved that it seemed like the best idea he'd ever heard.

"You own the purse strings at that company," Kimberly said.

"Dad owns everything at Chase Beauty, remember that."

"I've put so much into this, Michael." Kimberly had gone straight to work after the boys' swim practice. She'd made her calls, done her research and laid the groundwork to make it seem as if this had been her idea all along. She'd had Neil rewrite all of his reports to fit right in with what she was doing. Two days later, she'd run to Michael's office to explain that she'd been spending the past three months doing the legwork on a plan to start a Chase Beauty fashion line.

"You didn't have to do it alone." He was still bitter about her secrecy. "I would have hired someone to help you. My staff will—"

"You laughed at me the last time I suggested it," Kimberly said, "you and Steven."

"I didn't laugh at you. I never laugh at you."

"Steven did."

"Because you were just floating out an idea." Michael waved his arms mockingly in the air. "'Let's start a fashion line. Let's start—'"

"I had to keep it secret." She laughed, grabbing at his hands and pushing them down. "You would've done anything to discourage me. You don't want me working."

"You don't need to work."

"You don't want me working," she repeated. "You want me to stay away from the world. Stay home and be pretty, waiting for you."

"There are two children to raise." This was how Michael wanted it. He had to control her exposure.

"See, there you go." Nothing was going to keep Kimberly from getting Paul Devereaux to Los Angeles. "You owe me this."

"I owe you $75 million?" Michael turned to his side, wrapping his arm around her. He nestled his head in between her breasts. Her moist skin turned him on. "You had me going crazy, Kimberly. For no reason."

"There was a reason and you know it." She felt bad for making him think the secrecy was his fault, but she had no choice. Nothing else could excuse her keeping this from him after all the secrets they'd shared over the past seven years.

"I remembered everything you said, Michael. The industry was too different. Fashion from the West Coast won't fly. Who would the designers be? Who is the target audience? Blah, blah, blah."

"All that blah, blah, blah is called a business plan for investment, and it's crucial to get as much as a buck from Dad."

Michael wasn't so sure he was eager to believe Kimberly because it made him feel better or because all of her excuses and answers seemed to make sense. She had all the documents to prove what she had been up to, but that was what bothered him. It was all too careful for Kimberly. That just wasn't her style. She was someone who winged it, thought things up just in time. She wasn't a planner.

But he believed her when she said this was different. He believed her when she said she had been so careful about her contribution to the Chase legacy and didn't want to be distracted or discouraged. Most of all, he believed that she wanted to keep it from Janet because they both knew Janet would do everything she could to dissuade Steven from helping her.

"Well," Kimberly said, "you're going to get 75 million of those bucks from him."

"When I get the business plan together, I'll push it to him."

Kimberly stroked his head gently. She was working him, but she had done it a million times before when she was determined to get what she wanted. "You have to do more than push. I know you hate battling the old man, but it will be worth it."

It wouldn't be. Michael knew that, regardless of a business plan, his father would say no just as he had three years ago. But Michael wasn't going to say no to his wife. He was going to do all he could for her because she deserved that.

Deep down inside he was glad Steven would say no. He wanted her to have another child and stay home. He wanted her to be there for him and the boys, focusing on their needs. He wanted to protect her from the world because a part of him felt like she would miss it too much if she got a better taste. He wanted to feel less vulnerable to her past by limiting whom she came in contact with. But more than all of that, he wanted her to be happy and would push Steven as far as he could no matter how doomed the idea was.

Haley wasn't sure if it was all the liquor she'd been drinking or the weed she'd been smoking, but Chris was starting to piss her off. That or he was piquing her curiosity enough to make her mad at herself. She'd thought she had his number, but he wasn't so simple.

The evening had started off well enough as he picked her up in a private car—better than a limousine. They'd had a little to smoke before arriving at Staples, and Haley had to slap him only once for trying to kiss her. He seemed to like it, his eyes dancing a bit.

Haley was no stranger to the VIP section of the Staples Center. It was first-class as far as sports arenas were concerned, with plush furniture, high-end decorations, serious security and all the other perks. It wasn't anything to write home about, but there wasn't a second that one wouldn't be reminded that they were better than any of those other slugs sitting out in the arena. That's what VIP was all about.

The Prince tour was the concert event of the year, and everyone who was anyone on the West Coast was there. Unlike during a basketball game, when concerts performed at the arena, it was all about the luxury suites.

Their box had a who's who of Hollywood, music and sports. *US Weekly* and Page Six both would have sacrificed a virgin to be there. Haley enjoyed watching the illicit hookups and got her fair share of attention. It was curious to her that Chris hadn't seemed to mind all the men, and a couple of the women, who were hitting on her. He watched it all and seemed more amused than anything. Haley assumed he was trying to play it cool, not wanting to appear intimidated by men with means and fame far above his own.

He made no claim on her attention, spending time working the room for his club. He seemed more interested in the latest rapper topping the charts than in Haley, and that rubbed her the wrong way. She was impressed that the man thought about business at every opportunity, but there was a line to playing aloof that he was close to crossing.

When the concert was over, the party moved to Pearl, and Chris's behavior changed drastically. He was all over Haley, and she was beginning to think she preferred the aloof game.

"You having a good time?" he asked as he tried to position his hand in between her thighs while they sat at his private table.

Haley pushed his hand away. "Take it easy, brother."

"Can't nobody see." He pressed his lips against her neck. "It's under the table."

As much as he annoyed her, Haley's body reacted to him and gave him a little room to move. Maybe it was listening to Prince singing about sex all night long.

Chris had a forcefulness about him that she appreciated. She didn't have to think when she turned her head to him, and he took her mouth with a command without any drunken clumsiness.

"You gonna tell me more about you?" he asked as they separated.

"What else do you want to know?"

"You're a wild one," he said with a mischievous smile. "You leave a trail of fire behind you. Is that true?"

"You're about to find out," she warned. "If I want you to know something about me, I'll tell you."

He leaned back in the booth, laughing with amusement. "I like your bite, girl."

"Are you sure it's mine you like?" She slapped his hand away as it worked its way up her right breast. "You've spoken to so many girls tonight."

"I own a club, baby." He gestured to someone on the other end of the room. "You know how it is. Hate the game, not the pl—"

"Spare me the tired clichés. I'll hate whoever I want, and I don't need to know how it is."

Chris simply shook his head with a smile.

"What?"

"Every single syllable you speak, your tone, your . . ." He looked at her. "Everything you see is clouded by your security blanket."

"Whatever." She rolled her eyes.

"You don't fear or care," he said, "because you are protected in ways most people never understand."

"I've heard the moneyed-privilege speech before."

"But what you have is more than that." He gestured to the crowd. "These guys—the rappers, actors, athletes—they are rich, and that money brings power, but . . ."

"But what?" Haley was interested and surprised this guy actually had something to say.

"You can only have so much power and respect if you got it from dancing a jig."

Haley laughed. "I think they would argue. He's got a fashion line. He has an export business. She owns five restaurants. That brother . . ." She pointed to each person.

"But it all came from dancing a jig," Chris insisted. "No matter what they make of it, that's the origin. They shuffled their feet and entertained white folks, who put a quarter in the cup."

"Millions of quarters," Haley said. "Money is money. At least it's legal."

"But they don't have real power because ultimately, they are entertainers; they made their millions entertaining white—"

"Dancing a jig," she said impatiently. "I get it."

"They'll never have the same power and respect that a man like your father has. They'll never be him." Chris leaned back as if he'd made a point. "I'm just saying they know power, but not real power. Not the kind you can't question. That's what your world is all about and that's why you are the way you are."

"Because I can be," Haley said.

Chris smiled. "Exactly."

Haley figured he didn't know what he was talking about, but at least he had something to say.

Not so for the young brother who, dressed like a street thug, approached the table and sent Haley a nervous glance before sliding into the booth next to Chris. She watched as they touched hands and the man quickly retreated without one word.

Haley watched as Chris prepared the cocaine on the table. "Aren't you about three decades late for coke in the club?"

"It's making a comeback, baby." He grabbed the straw from Haley's glass and offered it to her. "Ladies first."

"Weed is as far as I go." Haley would never forget the bad trip she'd had the first time she ventured beyond marijuana. It wasn't going to happen again.

Chris took a snort like a pro, lifting up and letting his head fall back. His eyes bulged and shook a little. With renewed energy, he turned to Haley. "Coke is safe. All the shit that's come since is killing brothers. Going back to the old school is the way to do it."

"How impressive." Haley reached for her purse and started out of the booth. So much for a brother with something to say.

He grabbed her by the arm and pulled her back to him. Haley was taken aback by the menacing look on his face, but only for a second. Her hand came up and his head flew back as he let her arm go. He might have been expecting a slap, but not a fist.

"You must want to die young," Haley said.

Chris looked at her, eyes flinching a bit from the pain before a wide smile formed on his lips. "Beats getting old."

He reached for her again, this time by the neck, and pulled her head to his. Haley pushed against him, but he was too strong. His mouth came down roughly on hers, trying to part her lips, until the heel of her Jimmy Choo made contact with the top of his foot.

"Dammit." Leaning back, Chris inhaled with pain.

Haley was curious at the sight of his growing excitement. "You're letting the coke get to you."

"You're getting to me," Chris said. "Everyone has had your attention tonight. It's my turn."

"And you use it to school me on my privilege and offer me drugs? I think you've lost your turn."

"There is no impressing you, Ms. Haley." He leaned back, gently touching the spot on his cheek where she'd decked him. "You don't like my food, my flowers or my . . . amenities."

"Nothing is flooring me yet."

"Well." He offered a lazy, confident "There is more."

Usually that would have been enough for Haley to hit the road and never look back, but there was something about him. It wasn't anything she could put her finger on, probably because her mind wasn't clear enough to do so, but it was there. It was hard to explain what made her decide to stay and later go back to his place and have sex until five in the morning.

Or maybe it was all because she didn't have anything else to do.

"Good job, son." Steven slid the contract across the desk to Carter as they sat in his office at the Chase mansion.

Basking in the momentary but immeasurable pleasure of his father's approval, Carter thanked him and folded the contract for a new ad agency for Chase Beauty into his briefcase. He wondered if there ever would be a day that it didn't matter so much that his father approved, but Carter didn't think so. He had heard more good words from his father in the past six months than he had in the previous ten years.

Which made what he was about to do so hard.

"Dad, I need you to lay off Avery." Carter knew his father preferred it laid on the table, no sugar coating. "I know you've been having some disagreements."

"Disagreements?" Steven asked. "Don't make it sound like we're coworkers, Carter."

"I'm not making it sound like anything other than what it is. You've been giving her a hard time since she came on board."

"Because she's been making mistakes since she's come on board."

"Avery is smart and she understands business. That's why we wanted her salons, remember? Because—"

"Don't remind me of what I told you," Steven replied, tired of arguing with his sons over the women in their lives. "I didn't say she wasn't smart. She just isn't Chase Beauty material."

Carter pressed his lips together, the familiar state of being coming back quickly to him. "Don't insult her."

"Get your head out of your pants, boy," Steven said. "I'm talking business."

"This isn't just about business," Carter said. "You didn't want to hire her in the first place."

"But I did, didn't I?" Steven leaned forward. "I did it for you because you were in love with that girl."

"She has a name," Carter said. "And she's going to be my wife, so you're not going to treat her like you'd treat anyone else at that company."

"That company?" Steven stood, shaking his head. "You got some nerve, boy. You mean the same company that made it so you can have everything you have now?"

Carter sighed, throwing his hands up. "This was a waste of time."

Steven came around the desk as Carter stood up. "That same company that you refused to come work for but now want to tell me how to run?"

Carter turned to him. "I want you to back off."

"I know you love her, but I also know you understand business. She's too soft and she won't even try to get what I'm doing." Steven studied his son, the crease in his brow telling him there was more to this than Carter would share. "I'm not going to put my company at risk because you feel guilty."

"I don't feel guilty," Carter argued. "This isn't about me."

"I'm glad you see that," Steven said. "It isn't about her either. It's about Chase Beauty and for me, nothing else matters. She's not working out, Carter. If you love her like you say you do, then—"

"Don't question my love for her." Carter gripped the handle of his briefcase tightly.

"Don't interrupt me," Steven said slowly and deliberately. "If you really want her to be happy, convince her to quit. It will save everyone a very uncomfortable situation. She loves you and she'll listen to you."

"She's stubborn," Carter said. "She doesn't obey me like Mom obeys you."

Steven laughed. "What house did you grow up in?"

"You need to give her another chance," Carter said. "She has a vision for the chain."

"Visions don't mean anything when it comes to the bottom line. She approaches everything with too much emotion."

"Marketing," Carter said. "It's a popular concept."

"Don't be smart," Steven warned. "Precision, not emotion, leads to profits. If she wants to do what's right, she can work in community relations."

Carter wouldn't bother to explain to Steven how much taking Avery's salons away from her crushed her spirit. Steven didn't get that level of emotion, and he hadn't been there to see Avery doubt everything about herself. His father was right; it was about Carter's guilt as well as his love for Avery. He had been the impetus to the demise of her dream and wouldn't let anyone get in the way of his attempt to make it up to her.

"She deserves this job," Carter said.

"She had her chance," Steven answered. "The fact that she sent you here just confirms she can't handle this herself."

"She didn't send me," he said. "I'm here because someone is messing with the woman I love and I'm not gonna stand for it."

Steven looked Carter over, conscious of his distaste for things to return to what they were. "It's just a job, son. Are you willing to risk the progress we've made over a job you know deep down inside she isn't right for?"

"For my woman," Carter said, "I'll risk anything."

Feeling like a concrete stone was in the middle of his stomach, Carter turned and headed out before stopping at the sound of Steven calling his name. As much as he wanted to keep walking, he couldn't do it. His father's firm and final tone initiated an instinctual deference.

"I'll give you time to convince her." Steven was speaking to his son's back. "You can make this less painful, but she's going, one way or the other. No one decides how to run Chase Beauty but me."

As Carter walked down the lavish hallway of the place he could never really call home, his frustration grew. There was no way to win this. He was going to ruin what he had built with his father, and Avery would lose Chase Expressions anyway.

CHAPTER 8

Haley's full lips formed a spoiled pout as she leaned against the back entrance of Pearl. Chris had kept her waiting there for almost fifteen minutes while he talked to the latest rap group, which would be performing a private concert Friday night.

"This is some bullshit," she said to herself as her arms folded across her chest. She was sure it was a game, but he wasn't playing it right.

No one made her wait, and Chris knew that, but his behavior since the night they'd slept together was confusing. The sex had been good; Haley knew her stuff like no one else, but Chris hadn't seemed too impressed. She appreciated that; a strong brother just wasn't supposed to give it up so early. Since that night, he'd made it clear he was still interested, but he hadn't been falling over himself like Haley was used to. He continued to flirt with other women in her presence and seemed almost amused by the attention men showed her.

So he was different. Haley was cool with that because she'd had enough of the same, but if he didn't get in line soon, she was going to move on. There were too many other opportunities out there for her. Chris's window was closing fast.

When he turned to her, flashing what he seemed certain was

a winning smile, Haley kept a stone face. There was something about him that told her he knew he had to please her, but he was determined to do it his own way.

"Sorry about that, babe," he said as he approached, reaching out for her arm.

Haley backed away from his reach. "Don't call me babe."

"Business," he said. "You know Daddy Chase didn't make his millions by wining and dining beauties alone."

"First of all, it's *billions*, not millions. And second, now you want to play like you know my daddy?"

Chris nodded, seeming to get that she was going to have an attitude. "I know what you need. Come with me."

"I beg your pardon?" Haley didn't take one step behind his lead.

"Get your mind out of the gutter," he said, not halting in his stride.

When they arrived at his office, the first thing Haley saw was a pair of bimbos lounging on the sofa, smoking cigarettes.

"What is it," she asked, "break time for whores?"

Chris laughed, gesturing for the women to leave. "You know I work with models."

Haley leaned against his desk as he fussed with the lock on the top drawer. "You shouldn't waste your time lying. I don't care enough for you to bother."

He paused, looking at her as if trying to read her mind. "I hire women to be beautiful and sexy. There's nothing dirty about it. No sex with me or anyone else."

"Like I said—"

"You don't care either way." He offered up a gray velvet box. "I heard you the first time."

Haley didn't lift a finger. "Open it."

Chris sighed, shaking his head. "You're a spoiled brat."

"And you're a perceptive genius."

Haley was prepared to be impressed the second she saw the Harry Winston label on the box, but she had to pause at the sight of this one. If there was anything Haley knew, it was jewelry, and the platinum, sapphire and diamond flower bracelet before her was absolutely stunning.

As he closed the clasp around her wrist, Chris's mouth went to Haley's neck and he surprised her with a bite instead of a kiss.

She winced, leaning away. "Don't think you can get away with everything just because you bought me a trinket."

"I don't need to get away with everything." His eyes darkened as he grabbed her by the waist and pulled her to him. "But I really need to get away with something right here, right now."

Haley didn't bother to tell him she was more turned on by the sight of bling than anything else he had to offer, because he knew that. She took his hand in hers and began leading him backward toward the Italian leather sofa, but he refused to budge.

"You didn't hear me," he said. "I said right here, right now."

He pulled her to him again and took her mouth with his. She let him lower her to the floor as she tasted his fresh, cool breath. As he positioned himself between her legs, she let the feel of him kissing her, touching her, turn her on.

"Fight me," he whispered into her ear.

Haley leaned back. "What?"

Chris grabbed her by the shoulders and slammed her against the floor. "I want you to fight me."

Haley blinked from the jolt of contact with the floor. "Wait, what do you—"

He was pulling at her Jill Stuart blouse now and Haley was not cool with that. "Stop, Chris. Stop."

"That's it." He ripped the sleeve off her shoulder.

By instinct, Haley lifted her knee and kicked him in the groin. He let out a moan, doubling over and grabbing himself.

"What is wrong with you?" Haley asked, feeling the pain of a ripped $700 blouse. "Do you know how much this—"

"I'll buy you ten more." Chris's voice was dark and husky as he knelt over her. "You've got the idea, but not there again."

"Are you turning into a freak on me?" Haley asked.

Chris looked at her as if he was certain she was joking. "I'm disappointed, Haley. I thought you had a bit of adventure in you. I guess that bland detective domesticated your sex life."

Haley was fuming. "How dare you?"

"What?" he asked. "Act as if I know? Everyone knows. I

thought it was just a blip on the screen, a momentary weakness on your part, but apparently you have more vanilla in you than I thought."

Haley grabbed him by the back of his head and brought his lips to hers. She kissed him hard before saying, "You want a fight? You got one."

His eyes lit up in a way Haley hadn't seen in a man before. She didn't have a problem with rough sex, but there was something about the intensity in Chris's smile that unnerved her.

As she struggled against him, it was clear he was giving her push because she genuinely couldn't compete with this strength. Haley felt an erotic panic sweep over her as she pushed harder and he grabbed her by her hair.

Pulling her head back, he grunted the word "bitch" as his mouth headed for hers.

Haley halted him with a right hook and he fell over to the side. When he turned back to her, Haley saw his lip was bleeding, and fear swept all of her passion away.

"No," she said as he started for her again. "You're bleeding. We can't."

Chris licked at the blood trailing his lips and wiped at it with his shirt sleeve. "It's okay. It's just a little cut. It'll stop bleeding in a second."

Haley winced as he grabbed her by the wrist and dragged her to him. "Just don't . . . don't kiss me."

He looked into her eyes with a greedy smile and said, "I promise I won't."

He didn't. While he battled her, subdued her and made rough love to her, Chris never kissed her. He barely even looked at her.

"What?" Janet asked, feeling her anxiety grow at the look on Maya's face the second she opened the door. "What's wrong?"

"I didn't say anything," Maya answered, accepting the Hermès and La Perla bags from her. "Where do you want these?"

"In my bedroom, of course," Janet said. "But not until you tell me what's wrong. Has Haley done something?"

"Of course she has," Maya said, "but not that I know of. It's just . . ."

"Just what?"

"You said you wouldn't be back until four."

"Maya, don't mess with me."

Maya leaned in. "Leigh is here."

Janet gasped, her hand coming to her chest. "She is? She's back?"

"No." Maya hurried after Janet, who headed for the staircase. "Mrs. Chase, no."

Janet turned back to her, overwhelmed with emotion. She was already near tears at the thought of seeing her baby back home. God was blessing her for being so good. She had stopped taking the Valium completely, and the Welbutrin pills Dr. Gaines had prescribed were working. She was alert and aware and doing everything she could to be a good wife to make up for lying to Steven. God had brought her angel back home.

"She's not back," Maya said. "She's just . . . here. She came to see Haley. She only came on the condition that you wouldn't be here."

"How would she know? You're not feeding her my schedule so she can avoid me, are you?"

"Just go on to your office," Maya said. "I'll put your bags away and bring you a drink."

"So now I'm being marginalized in my own house?" Janet asked.

"You don't want to cause any trouble. You know how you get about her."

Janet sighed. "It's different now. I'm different. Just spare me your lectures. Where is she?"

"I'm right here."

Seeing Leigh standing at the top of the staircase almost made Janet lose her step. She was speechless, not having set eyes on her for four months. It had been an ugly scene in which Janet, high on Valium, had been thrown out of Leigh's condo following a screaming match. She was as beautiful as ever in a white T-shirt and jeans, her skin glowing with natural youth and vitality.

Leigh started down the staircase with Haley's violet Versace gown draped over her arm. Her stomach tightened and she felt her palms begin to sweat. Her mother's tortured-bird look always had that effect on her.

"I'll take these to your room." Avoiding eye contact with anyone, Maya sprinted up the staircase.

"You look lovely," Janet said as Leigh made it to the bottom of the steps. She was pained by the look of discomfort in her daughter's eyes and resentful at being made to feel a burden to someone she had given birth to.

"Thank you." Leigh's tone was flat and barely audible as she tried to conceal any sense of emotion. "I just came by to—"

"It doesn't matter." Janet had to squeeze her hands into fists just to keep from reaching out and touching her. "You're always welcome. It's your home."

Leigh walked a circle around Janet, afraid if she came too close she would get sucked into her mother's emotional hole.

"Leigh, wait." Janet felt like her heart had been grabbed out of her chest and was being dragged along the floor with Leigh's every step.

Leigh turned back, unable to look her mother clearly in the eye. She kept telling herself that the guilt trip wasn't legit, but she knew her mother loved her and it made even the necessary brutally painful.

"Mom, I don't want to talk."

"It's about the engagement party," Janet said, grateful to have a real excuse to keep her there, if even for just one second longer. "It's next month."

"I can't come."

"You have to. Please, dear, this isn't about us."

"You make everything about us."

"It's Carter's engagement. You two are so close, and you're close to Avery now, aren't you?"

Leigh only shrugged and watched as her mother's expression hardened.

"Do you enjoy this?" Janet asked. "By withholding every aspect of your relationships with everyone else in this family, you can really stick it to me."

"Again," Leigh said, "it's all about you."

"I can make a promise," Janet offered. "I'll stay away from you if you come. It's a family occasion, Leigh. Too many of them have suffered because of this thing between you and me."

"This thing?" Feeling her anger rise, Leigh put up her hand to stop herself. "No, I'm not . . . I have to go."

"Leigh." Janet started after her.

Leigh's escape was halted by Kimberly and Avery, who entered the house with wide smiles that quickly evaporated at the scene in front of them.

"Surprise, surprise," Kimberly said as she glanced from Leigh to Janet, whose stricken expression made her smile. "Haven't seen you in a while, Leigh."

"What are you talking about?" Avery asked. "We all had lunch last week."

Kimberly flipped her head back and laughed in Janet's direction. "That's right. I see Leigh all the time. Sorry 'bout that."

Avery rolled her eyes, seeing how she had fallen into Kimberly's trap.

Janet ignored the dig, expecting nothing less from trash. "Avery, I was just inviting Leigh to the engagement party."

Avery turned to Leigh, who was such an open book. She wore her emotions on her sleeve, and Avery had empathy for her. "No pressure, Leigh."

Leigh smiled nervously, feeling the heat of her mother's eyes bearing into her back. "I'll talk to you later. I have to—"

"I'll walk you out," Avery said, dropping her bags.

"That was fun," Kimberly said once she and Janet were alone. "Mother and daughter back together again."

"Shut up you little tramp." Janet couldn't stop the tears, although she knew they would only feed Kimberly's fire.

It was surprising to her that, in the past seven years, the two women had gotten into *only* two physical fights. They had come an eyelash's length from about a dozen more, but most of their arguments were very civilized; accusations, insults and threats. Right now, Janet was ready to tear her hair out and kick her in the gut.

"Ouch." Kimberly stood with her hands on her hips, feeling

refreshed from a trip to Rodeo Drive. "And I thought I was being nice."

"Don't waste your attention on me," Janet said. "You have your failing marriage to worry about."

Kimberly laughed bitterly. "I know you must have thought it was Christmas in June around here, but it was just a fight, Queen."

Janet shook her head, wiping away her tears. "You've taken to underestimating me lately. You and I both know that this time was different. I heard the fights and I heard you crying yourself to sleep at night. The ice is thinner and I'm going to make sure it cracks."

"I never underestimated you, you over-the-hill, drug-addicted debutante."

Janet lunged at Kimberly, but Kimberly stepped out of the way just in time. Her laugh grated every nerve Janet had, and she wanted to kill her. "This is *my* house. You don't—"

"For now it is," Kimberly said. "But things change and I feel a change coming on. I think you feel it too. You might see it in the spring in my step. It's a good thing you've kicked your habit, because you're gonna need all of your senses when your birds come home to nest."

The women separated just as Avery returned. Janet felt her balance giving way and she abruptly retreated down the hallway toward her office. The second she was out of sight, she stopped and put her hand to the wall to keep herself steady. She craved a Valium now more than she ever had since giving them up.

It was true. Ever since Michael had returned, Kimberly had been acting different. She seemed more confident and much more secretive. Janet wasn't sure if it was just her Valium-free clarity, but now she knew better. Kimberly was planning something, and this was more than her usual failed attempts to embarrass or humiliate Janet.

Janet had to be prepared.

"You cannot be serious," Steven said as he eyed his son across his desk. These boys and their women were going to be the death of him.

"I am." Michael had never won a staring contest with his father and he probably never would, but he could last long enough to make Steven choose to give in. "We had record profits last year as well as the first quarter of this year. The second quarter is looking like a record because of the South Africa market and—"

"What does increased revenue in South Africa have to do with emaciated models in L.A.? Nothing."

"We can afford it," Michael said.

"We can't." Steven glanced down at the hastily put-together business plan Michael had presented to him. "We're going to focus on stabilizing the salon chain this year. Next year, we'll look at expanding it into New York, Chicago and D.C."

"I'm looking for exploratory funds," Michael said, "starting with looking at ideas from some top designers."

"Starting with . . ." Steven pulled out the profile on Michael's first choice, attached to several pages of his designs. "This guy is going to be expensive."

"You sound like Avery." Michael's smile faded when his father sent him a lightning-bolt glare.

Steven tossed the folder back on his desk. "If all you wanted was exploratory funds, you wouldn't be here. As CFO you have discretion to allocate that amount without even telling me. You want millions."

Michael nodded, having already spent several thousand on the plan in the past week. "And I want them now."

Steven ignored that. "Look, son, I know you're having some marital problems, but—"

"This is about more than that," Michael said, suddenly feeling ashamed.

"It isn't," Steven countered. "You need to understand that all that has to be left outside that door."

"You haven't even looked at the plan. Chase Beauty is a major player in Paris. We're the second-largest ethnic cosmetic brand. Paul Devereaux is famous in the elite fashion community."

"Most Americans don't care about France," Steven said, "and those who do only care enough not to like it."

Michael waved his hand dismissively. "That stuff is over and it never applied to fashion. Besides, look at all the black fashion brands that have been blowing up for the last five years. They're showing no signs of stopping. We're offering an even higher-end line with the highest-end last name. We can steal a huge piece of that pie."

"I admire your affection for your wife," Steven said calmly. "But money is money and I've learned my lesson with Avery."

"And yet she's still here." Michael didn't care that he was working his father's last nerve. "So you make exceptions for Carter, but not me."

"Careful," Steven warned. "This is a cost decision. Investors get antsy when a company appears expansion-greedy. I'm not willing to put Chase Beauty at financial risk to keep your wife happy."

"Well, I am," Michael said.

Steven wasn't sure what he was getting at, but he assumed it was more than just words spitting back. "Well, Chase Beauty is not your company."

"I don't need it to be." Michael stood up. "I know how to run my own company. I know how to get investors better than anyone."

Steven's lips thinned with irritation. "Do not threaten me, boy."

Michael blinked, uncertain of where to go. He hadn't planned to suggest he would leave. It had just come out, and it was too late to take it back. Besides, he knew he would lose Steven's respect if he tried to.

"I just want a chance to explore," Michael said. "Five million should get me started. We've spent a lot more for a lot less."

It seemed to Michael like an hour passed as Steven just stared at him. He knew his father was working in his head how he would make him pay for bringing it to this, but he also knew he was going to get what he wanted. No matter what Steven's newfound relationship with Carter was, Michael knew he was the favorite.

After a moment, Steven set his anger aside. There was no

way Michael would ever leave Chase Beauty. He salivated over running this empire too much. But Michael had made a good bluff and Steven would give his son a small reward for having the balls. A small reward and a big punishment for the threat.

"You need to understand what you've done today."

"Dad, I—"

"Shut up," Steven said. "Do you see this chair I'm sitting in?"

Michael nodded.

"It's much farther from you today than it was yesterday." Steven paused to make sure Michael understood what he meant. "And if you go too far with this, it will be out of your reach. Eventually, Carter will come around, and I will give this company to him. Do you understand?"

Michael swallowed hard, feeling his stomach about to cave in. Kimberly would have to do a lot more than back off on moving out of the mansion to make up for this.

"Yes, sir."

Steven looked down at the papers in front of him. "Now get the hell out of my office."

"Give me that." Carter reached again for the remote, but this time Avery stuck it behind her back, in between her and the sofa. "Don't think I won't go after it."

Avery laughed, speaking with a mouth full of popcorn. "I'm picking the movie this time."

It was Thursday, which was movie night. It was the one night of the week that Avery could be assured that Carter would be home by 7. With the hours he worked at his firm, it was a precious time for her, especially now that they were planning a wedding.

"You pick it every time." Carter leaned back on the sofa, laughing not at anything Avery had said or done but at the situation.

It was funny how completely domesticated he was. He used to be on the streets with his boys or out wining and dining someone beautiful. Now Thursday meant movie night, at home eating popcorn, selecting On Demand off of digital cable like a married man. Where was a good bullet to the head when you needed one?

Then he looked at her, sitting next to him with her brows slanted in a stubborn frown while surveying the on-screen choices and chewing way too loud to be classy. There really wasn't anywhere else he would rather be. That was love.

"You don't even know how to use it." He reached for the remote again, this time victorious. "Let me do it."

"It has fifteen million buttons." Avery slid over to him, wrapping herself around his strong arm. The way he smelled, the way he looked, with his eggplant Ralph Lauren polo shirt sticking out of his jeans, made her want to jump on and ride. "I want to watch a family movie."

"Baby, you're killing me. I can't sit through that crap, you know that."

She rubbed the inside of his thigh, knowing what it did to him. "I want to see a beautiful black family like we're going to be."

"Why don't we just work on our family instead?"

Avery leaned back as he made header for her lips. "Oh, you want to work on the baby making, but you don't want to see what life will be like with a baby."

Carter was a smart man. He was never too distracted to miss his window. "Let me ask you a question."

"Is this a nasty question? 'Cause I told you I wouldn't do that except on your birthday and—"

"When we have kids, you're going to quit work and stay home, right?"

Avery nodded enthusiastically. "We talked about that, baby."

"I know," he said. "It's just important to me. We're going to start our family real soon, right?"

Avery frowned, unsure of where this was going. "I thought we might be married for a couple years. You know, just get used to each other. We haven't been together long, and—"

"I only said it because I know you don't enjoy working for my father. If you need an out—"

"I don't need an out," she protested. "I'm not like that. No, I don't enjoy working for your father, but the salon chain is my responsibility and it's going through so many changes. I need to fight for the idea I was originally brought on to make it into."

"Dad doesn't want that anymore," Carter said. "And you know he'll push—"

"That's just it." She smiled from cheek to cheek. "He hasn't been pushing lately. Since you talked to him, he's backed off. Thanks to you, I feel like I can manage it there, and I want to stay and do that."

Carter smiled, tugging at his collar. Dammit! He hated it when his father was right even though he should be used to it by now. This was going to be a lot harder than he'd thought.

"At first I felt bad for letting you intervene." Avery leaned in and kissed him, feeling her stomach tingle. "But you came through. Whatever you said, I feel the heat off of me, and I owe you."

He closed his eyes, forgetting everything that happened up until the moment her hand slid down his chest and rubbed against his groin. He let out a frustrated moan before grabbing her and pulling her to him. Kissing her, he could think only of the passion he felt for her and tried to ignore how he had to trick her into quitting.

"What about that movie?" Avery positioned herself on his lap.

"Idea of the century," Carter said suggestively. "I'll get the video camera."

"Unh-uh." Avery was already pushing off when Carter took hold of her arms to keep her in place. "Not a chance, fool!"

He was getting excited just thinking about it. "We can put the tape in the safe in the bedroom. No one can get to it."

Avery was stone-faced.

"Okay, we can tape it." He nodded as if taking her step by step, like a child. "Then we can watch it real quick and then destroy the tape."

They both heard footsteps coming down the hallway, and for once Avery was grateful for one of Michael's uninvited intrusions.

"Saved by the brother." She hopped off Carter's lap. "Did

you talk to him about ringing the doorbell, knocking, maybe even calling ahead? It's not just you here anymore."

Carter stood up just as his brother entered the living room. He wasn't too crazy about Michael's pop-ins anymore, but he wouldn't do that to his boy. "What's up, man?"

Michael nodded to Avery, who looked annoyed to see him. He wasn't here to see her anyway. "What you doing tonight?"

Carter made a head gesture in Avery's direction. "I'm generally otherwise occupied from now on. Remember?"

"So it's going to be like that, huh?" Michael had gotten used to being able to hang with his brother whenever he wanted to. There had never been a woman Carter picked over him.

"Yeah, it's like that," Avery chimed in. "Speaking of, where is your 'otherwise occupied'?"

"She's having drinks with some modeling friends of hers at Koi." Michael went straight for the bar against the wall and poured himself a glass of a sixty-year old scotch. "I'm meeting her later. Thought I'd come and drag Carter with me for some male support."

"Sounds interesting," Carter said.

"Drinks with a bunch of models?" Avery asked, standing up. "I don't think so."

"Can he at least go out on his own terrace and have a drink with his brother?" Michael's question was laced with sarcasm.

Avery just rolled her eyes and walked off.

"Where you going?" Carter asked.

"Bedroom," she answered, not thinking to look back. "So much for movie night."

"Damn," Michael said. "She running things already?"

"Hell, no." Carter made himself a drink.

"Then you can come?" Michael struggled to open the balcony door.

When they were outside, they sat at the table facing an unobstructed view of the hills. "No, I can't."

"So she *is* running things."

"No, but Avery isn't Kimberly." Carter knew more than he needed to about Michael and Kimberly's sex life. "She's not the 'get the appetite wherever you want, but only eat at home' type."

"You haven't told her—"

"Stop asking me that!" Carter was offended. He was the only one who knew about Kimberly's past and had promised Michael he would take it to his grave.

There was a silence between them as Michael settled into the trust. He didn't want to doubt Carter. He hadn't thought twice about telling Carter about Kimberly, even after Carter had tried to talk him out of marrying her. Never before, even when Carter had claimed to be in love, had he worried the secret might be shared—that was, until now. Michael was afraid of how powerful Carter's feelings for Avery were.

"Have you done it yet?" Michael asked.

Carter lowered his head. "I tried, but . . ."

"Dad will fire her."

Carter took a sip of his scotch and let the burn light him up inside. "He wouldn't. The publicity alone will keep him . . . Mom wouldn't let him."

"He gives Mom everything she wants except when it comes to that company." Michael was shaking his head. "He'll make it look like she quit, but he'll fire her."

Avery returned to the living room in search of the popcorn bowl. Her intention was to grab it and return to the bedroom, but curiosity got the best of her. There was something so intriguing to her about Michael and Carter's relationship. Sometimes it seemed as if they were not just brothers, but twins.

She tiptoed to the wall next to the terrace doors, getting close enough to hear what they were saying.

Carter cleared his throat. "Plan A backfired."

"What's Plan B?"

"I might just tell her the truth." Carter shook his head as Michael laughed. "I'm serious. We're getting married. Why can't I be honest with her about it?"

Avery bit her lower lip to keep from saying something. She knew she shouldn't be listening, but she couldn't step away. What was he keeping from her?

"You won't do it," Michael said. "It would hurt her too much."

Avery felt her stomach tightening.

"Forget it," Carter said. "I have enough drama to deal with now. I'll come up with a Plan B."

"What drama could you have?" Michael asked. "Ruining movie night?"

Carter couldn't hold back his laugh even though he was deadly serious. "I'm talking about Laura."

"Oh, that crazy bitch." Michael sat his empty glass on the table between them.

Avery still had a bad taste in her mouth following that phone call, but more from Carter's anger than the woman's hopefully empty threats.

"You take care of her?" Michael asked.

Carter nodded. "I wasn't playing, man. I sent Marco to Philadelphia. He took care of it."

A quick and disturbing thought flashed before Avery's eyes.

"You think it's over?" Michael asked.

"For her sake, it better be." Carter couldn't risk Laura messing things up between him and Avery. He had tolerated her crazy antics before, but not anymore.

Finding it difficult to breathe, Avery knew she had to get away from there. She didn't want to hear any more. What she was thinking couldn't possibly be . . . couldn't mean . . .

She jumped when the phone rang, popcorn flying all over the place. She was frozen, unsure of what to do. She wanted to run, but the second she could move, she bent down and began picking up pieces of popcorn that had jumped out of the bowl.

When Carter stepped into the living room, he at first was surprised to see Avery where she was. Then only one thought was in his mind. What had she heard?

"Avery."

Avery stood up straight, looking him in the eye. She opened her mouth, but nothing came out. His jaw was clenched, his eyes slightly narrowed, and it scared her a little bit. What was even weirder was that she was excited. He suddenly was very dangerous and she couldn't ignore that it turned her on. It was all too confusing for Avery to fully comprehend.

"Did you want something?" he asked, his words methodical as his eyes bore into hers. So it wasn't right that he keep secrets from her, but he wasn't going to have her spying on him.

"I . . ." Avery held up the popcorn bowl. "I came . . . I wanted the popcorn."

Carter looked down at the bowl, then back at Avery, and in a calm, cool manner asked, "Do you want to ask me something?"

Avery swallowed hard, feeling her body begin to tingle all over. It scared her more that she was so aroused.

"Because if you want to ask me something," he added, "then ask me."

Avery felt a shiver run down her spine just as Michael stepped out from the balcony and broke her trance.

"You spying on us?" Michael asked, intending it completely as a joke before feeling the tension in the room.

Ignoring him, Avery gripped the popcorn bowl to her chest as if it meant her life. She took one last look at Carter, who hadn't blinked once, before returning to the bedroom.

It wasn't news that she didn't know much about the mystique of the Chase name. Her world had never met his and there was no need to. Of course she knew who the Chase family was, but the rumors that the last name meant power and influence in ways good and bad hadn't meant anything until she had come up against it. Now, having heard what she'd heard and felt what she felt, it really hit her. What had Carter done?

"What did she hear?" Michael asked, returning to the bar to make himself another drink.

Carter waited until he heard the bedroom door close, wondering if he could let this go. "I don't know."

"Know what you gotta do?"

"Close the balcony doors?" Carter joined him at the bar, his mind focused only on what Avery might have heard.

"If you hit that real good tonight"—Michael made a fist with his right hand—"she'll forgive everything."

Carter smiled but couldn't bring himself to laugh. Based on

the charge he'd gotten from her just a few seconds ago, he didn't see any problem with that. As a matter of fact, it was time for Michael to leave.

Haley didn't care for the look Leigh was giving her as she sat down on the sofa in her living room. It had become general practice for Haley to sleep over at Leigh's after a night clubbing downtown instead of driving all the way back to View Park. Had the rules changed while she was gone?

"What?" she asked.

"You look . . ." Leigh glanced her up and down with a shrug. "You look like you had a hard night."

"Don't get me started." Haley kicked off her Pradas and fell back on the sofa.

She was tired. After kicking it at LAX with Chris, they'd gone back to his place in Century City and had rough sex. Haley had found herself excited at first; Chris was relentless and she liked the pairing of intensity and carelessness. It felt wrong, illicit and deliberate.

That was, until he'd put his hands around her neck and began to squeeze while he was pounding inside of her. She pulled at his arm, saying no as he pleaded for anal sex. She had to dig her nails into his wrist before he let her go and pulled out. She wanted to slap him but knew that would only excite him more.

So she left. He only asked her once to stay, promising to keep his hands off, but Haley's mind was already made up.

"I thought you had a date," Haley said.

"I did." Leigh pointed to the clock on the wall. "It's three in the morning. My date was over at midnight."

"How virginal of you."

"It wasn't really a date anyway," Leigh said. "We just wanted to talk about some new—"

"Do you have any ice cream?"

Leigh sighed. "What's wrong with you?"

"I want some ice cream."

"You eat ice cream when you're up—" Leigh gasped at what she saw when Haley raised her hands to rest her head in as she leaned back. "Oh my God!"

Haley was jolted as Leigh grabbed her arm and pulled it to her. "What are you—"

"Where did you get these?" There were bruises, some fresh and some old, all over her arm.

Haley jerked her hand away. "It's nothing."

"Who did this to you?"

"Leigh, give it up."

Leigh reached for the phone. "I'm calling Daddy."

"No!" Haley grabbed the phone from her. That was the last thing she needed. "He doesn't care anyway."

"Stop that and give me the—"

"You go ahead and call him," Haley said. "Remember what happened when he heard Leo had threatened you over the phone? Two people died. What do you think he'll do to Chris?"

Leigh lowered her outstretched hand. She'd learned all too well that there was a good and bad side to having a father who could and would do anything to protect you. "Chris did this to you?"

Haley nodded. "But it's not what you think."

Leigh had seen these types of bruises on some of the prostitutes who came into her clinic after a john had gotten too rough. Seeing them on her little sister made her sick to her stomach.

"What are you doing?"

"None of your business." Haley was unfamiliar with the sense of shame she was feeling. Leigh was so holier-than-thou. "He likes it rough."

"You obviously don't."

"Do you have some ice cream or not?" Haley got up from the sofa, looking down at her sister impatiently.

"I don't like him, Haley. He's sleazy and—"

"You don't like him? Surprisingly, I like him even more now." She turned to walk away, but Leigh reached up to grab her. She pressed against a bruise and Haley winced.

"Watch it," she warned.

"I am a doctor," Leigh said. "You can talk to me if—"

"I'm not one of your street hos or drug addicts." She jerked her arm away. She was only a few feet away before turning around.

Leigh was hopeful. "I won't tell Mom or Dad."

"You won't tell anyone," Haley ordered.

Leigh nodded and waited patiently. She knew how difficult it was for Haley to feel vulnerable, but the fact that she was willing to do it meant something serious was going on.

Haley took a deep breath. "Do you . . . Have you ever had anal sex?"

Leigh kept her physician's face, looking completely unfazed despite the alarm. "No, I haven't. It isn't my thing. I don't think it's your thing either."

"How would you know?"

"You've known me all your life, but you can't make eye contact with me and you're wringing your hands together. You're obviously uncomfortable."

"Maybe I don't like talking about experimental sex with someone who's only done the missionary position on Saturday nights."

"You done joking?" Leigh asked. "Because this isn't a joke. Anal sex is . . . God, Haley, please tell me you're using condoms with him."

"Of course," she answered. "I'm not crazy."

"You are," Leigh said, "which is why I asked. It's dangerous. The pressure can break your blood vessels, and that makes it much easier to transfer disease."

"Okay!" Haley held her hands up. "Enough of the very disturbing after-school special. People do it, Leigh. They're not all freaks."

"I didn't say they were, but I see your bruises and now—"

"Don't judge me," Haley said before turning and walking away. She didn't like this sudden sense of losing her grip. She was just too tired to think about anything now.

"And stop smoking that weed!" Leigh yelled after her. "That's how you get into these situations in the first place. Impaired judgment—"

The guest bedroom door slammed shut, but Leigh knew this wasn't going to be the last of it.

CHAPTER 9

"Am I missing something?" Duncan James's ocean-blue eyes were begging for an explanation as he sat on the other side of Carter's desk.

Carter smiled, appreciating his confusion. His successful but small Wilshire Boulevard law firm had recently added Duncan, a bright young Stanford Law grad who never complained about ninety-hour workweeks.

"Yes," Carter answered, leaning back in his chair. "You are missing something very important."

"This is a simple bogus discrimination case." Duncan reviewed the file. "She's claiming she was fired because of race despite having several documentations of performance problems. She was a horrible worker."

"It's never that clean-cut," Carter said.

"What about the fact that she's Japanese and the woman they hired to replace her was Filipino?" He waved a revealing sheet of paper in his hand. "And the woman who fired her was Mexican. Why is this even going to court?"

"It seems simple," Carter said, "but you never assume that, Duncan. You know better. The woman doesn't have a case, but what you're missing here is not her case."

"It's our client," Duncan offered with a nod. "They're scared of something. Otherwise they wouldn't be listening to talks of a settlement."

"It might not have anything to do with this case," Carter said, "but you have to find out what it is. Use every resource we have. If we don't use it—"

"Her lawyers will."

"I'm trusting you on this," Carter said. "It's yours."

"You've had this client for three years. I need your help."

"I'm not going to be around as much as usual." Carter cringed just hearing himself say the words.

Chase Law was his first love, and he'd never imagined a world where he would want less of it. But he wanted more of Avery. Ever since that night he suspected she'd overheard him and Michael talking on the terrace, things had been different. He sensed a part of her that trusted him less, but for some odd reason the sex had risen to another level. What had been great before was now mind-bending. There was a dangerous edge to every interaction they'd had since, and it turned them both on. He couldn't stand to be away from her, always waiting for the next chance to get his hands on her.

"I trust you, Duncan." He leaned forward with a reassuring grin. "You don't need me."

The speaker buzzed before Patricia, Carter's executive assistant, spoke. "Carter . . . you . . . you have a visitor."

"Who is it?"

"It's Ms. McDaniel."

Carter blinked but didn't move. He remained calm despite the sudden pounding in his head. He must have heard wrong. He had paid someone a great deal of money to be told immediately if Lisette left London.

"Who?"

"Lisette McDaniel."

Carter's expression went blank as he looked at a clueless Duncan. Of course he was clueless, Carter thought. He had no idea that his boss' world had just come crashing down on him.

"Send her in." Carter's tone showed no sign of his panic. "Duncan, we'll talk tomorrow."

Lisette always took her time when entering a room. She

wanted to give everyone an eyeful of her distinct beauty and style. At thirty-five, she looked better than ever—tall and elegant with long black hair and eyes like coal, her dark skin glowing with health and expensive care.

Carter wanted to strangle her, but the expression he offered as she reached his desk was just cold enough to tell her he didn't want to see her, but not so cold to make her think he was scared. But he was scared.

"Is this the best you can do?" she asked with her decidedly upper-class British accent. "Didn't those expensive prep schools teach you to stand up when a lady enters?"

"Yes," he answered, remaining in his seat, "they did, and I always do."

Lisette's smile quickly faded. "I was lady enough for you once."

"If you were lady enough, it wouldn't have been just once."

Her expression went flat. "I didn't expect you to welcome my return, but I don't think you want to piss me off."

"What do you want?" He gestured for her to sit down. "And quickly."

Lisette slowly slid into the chair, placing her chunky, expensive purse on Carter's desk. "Do you want the whole story or should we cut to the chase?"

Carter grumbled.

"I lost my appeal for my husband's estate to his two bitch daughters."

"Which husband would that be?"

Lisette snickered. "I lost count. What matters is that I need money and I think you're in a giving mood."

"What makes you think that?"

Lisette reached her finely manicured fingers into her purse and pulled out a folded bright white envelope embossed with two rich red roses and black stems. She laid it on the table before Carter, who didn't bother to look at it.

"One of my former friends sent it to me," Lisette said with a wry smile. "I have to hand it to Janet. This design is exquisite. She is about the classiest woman I've ever met."

"Classy enough to see your game a mile away."

Lisette laughed. "Janet liked me enough. She knew I wasn't going to bow to her and that was that. I imagine Avery bows easily. She looks like the sheepish type."

"She isn't," Carter said. "Trust me."

"Oh, I trust you. She had enough backbone to dump her fiancé the second she found out I slept with him." Lisette grabbed the invitation back. "A lot of women would pick a wedding ring over self-respect any day."

Carter's impatience replaced his fear. "You're not getting any money."

"Your plan was to get old Alex out of the way so you could steal his girl. But of course she could let him go. She was trading up."

"You need money," Carter said, "get a new husband."

"I'm working on it. But until then, you can be my husband. In cash only, of course."

"I'm done with you," he said. "I left your cash on the dresser. It's all you get."

Rage transformed Lisette's beautiful face. That must have been one insult too many. "You're not a stupid man, Carter. I don't need to explain your situation to you."

"Then why are you wasting my time?"

She stood up, reaching for her purse. "I'm at the Westin. You remember the scene of the crime. Call me soon. Real soon."

"Don't hold your breath," he offered as she turned to leave.

Carter stared into space for a minute or two to get his wits back. He wasn't thinking of anything, just letting the reality set in. When his mind cleared, he went back to the day he and Michael had decided to include Lisette in their plan.

He played the possible scenarios in his mind, and nothing looked good. He could deny everything; he was a good enough liar, but Avery had a way of seeing right through him. He knew she loved him, but she would never forgive him for this. He could imagine himself explaining that he was drunk with love, but she wouldn't buy it because it wasn't true. He hadn't loved her, he'd just wanted her and he was willing to break her heart to get her.

He couldn't lose her. He needed her, and the thought of being without her made him feel desperate in a way he never had before.

"What you want, man?" Michael asked as he picked up the phone.

"I'm fucked," Carter answered.

Michael laughed. "What did you do now?"

Carter stood up and went to the window, staring blankly at the skyline. "Lisette was just here."

Michael let off a line of swear words. "I knew it! I knew she'd come back. She wants more money, doesn't she?"

"What do you think?"

"What did she say exactly?"

As he repeated the conversation, Carter had to deny the panic that swelled in his throat like nausea. It was going to be okay. No matter how hard, there wasn't anything he couldn't handle.

"She thinks she has you by the balls."

"You think she doesn't?" Carter asked. "Avery can't find out."

"You can always deny it."

"Of course I'll deny it," Carter said, "but that might not be enough. I can make her out to be a liar, but pictures don't lie. It will be too much of a coincidence."

"Does Avery still have those pictures?"

"She thinks she does, but I threw them away when I found them a couple months ago. It doesn't matter. Avery won't forget her face. It's only been seven months and she was devastated."

"You can't pay her, Carter."

"Don't tell me what I already know!"

"Calm down," Michael urged. "We'll figure something out."

Carter wondered what security his mother had hired for the engagement party. The press would be there, television cameras. It could get ugly. "There isn't a lot of time."

"I'll talk to her."

"No," Carter protested. "I can—"

"You can't be seen with her," Michael said. "It's bad enough she came to your office. The engagement party is next week. It would make things worse."

"They really can't get much worse."

"Oh, yes, they can. Look, Lisette has something to lose here too."

"She doesn't care about American society crap," Carter said. "So threatening to ostracize her wouldn't frighten her."

"She's in the business of getting married," Michael said. "She needs rich men who give a damn about the reputation of the women they date. If I convince her that we can make it so no man with a bank account worth squat will want her, she'll start to listen."

Carter felt his breathing began to slow down.

"Let me do my thing," Michael said.

"Okay," Carter said just above a whisper. "Hey, thanks, bro."

"No problem," Michael answered. "I love this stuff."

Sean could feel the eyes on him as he made his way to his desk at the View Park Police Department, but he had no idea why. Maybe it was jealousy. After a long night, he and his partner, Marino Chavez, had shut down a major prostitution ring with a pimp who had girls as young as eleven working for him. It was a big deal for most, but not Sean. He was a relentless detective and dreamed of making it to Homicide. Besides, he had a lot to make up for after the past year.

"Can't believe you came in late," Marino said as Sean sat across from him. "You're always fifteen minutes early."

Marino was one of those cops made for the vice squad. In a matter of seconds, he could look like an eighteen-year-old gang banger or a thirty-year-old drug dealer from several different countries. Or he could look like a Harvard grad who'd made it big-time after growing up on the streets. The thirty-year-old native of El Segundo was a master of disguise.

"I think we earned it after last night." Still more looks, and this time Sean could distinctly hear someone laughing. Was he getting paranoid after only four hours of sleep? "Don't you?"

"I always do," Marino answered. "I only came in on time because I've got to keep up with you. I wish you'd told me."

"I'm only twenty min—" Sean looked up at Ted Bryan, who was sitting a desk away with a smirk on his face. "What? What's wrong with you?"

Ted shrugged and turned back to his partner, not bothering to answer.

"Take it easy," Marino said. "I think they're happy for you."

"Why?" The perception that Sean was given special treatment because he was the chief of police's son made him no one's personal favorite in the squad, but his work had earned him enough respect not to get sneered at. "'Cause of the case?"

"Not the case." Marino reached for a folded tabloid at the other end of his desk. "Not this one, at least."

Sean snatched the paper, feeling a sense of dread creep up on him. When he saw the picture on the front page, he didn't need to read on, but couldn't stop himself.

RUCKUS AT HARBOR INVOLVES CHASE DEBUTANTE; ARRESTS MADE

Members of the usually quiet, private Los Angeles Yacht Club were treated to a night of wild and ultimately illegal entertainment as local debutante Haley Chase hosted a party on *Beauty*, the well-appointed Chase family yacht. After several visits from club security, police were called in. To their surprise, it wasn't the beautiful young Chase who gave them a hard time, as is her usual way. It was her new boyfriend, club Pearl owner Chris Reman, who got into it with law enforcement and had to be taken away in handcuffs.

Sean wanted to put the paper down, but he couldn't. He focused on the picture of Haley, her legs entwined with the current man whose life she would destroy. Sean tossed the paper back to him. "I'm relieved."

"That's what we were saying before you got here. At least she's on to some other fool. She'll leave you alone."

Sean nodded, knowing he should be happy, but there was no getting a woman like Haley Chase out of your system completely. After turning on his computer, Sean went directly to the database. He told himself it was curiosity, not jealousy, that made him enter Chris Reman's name. He wanted to find out everything he could about the man Haley had moved on to.

It all suddenly made sense to Janet, and she was fuming. Did Steven think he could drop that bomb on her and just walk out of their bedroom?

"Steven!" She grabbed her bathrobe off the edge of the bed and rushed out after him.

"What?" Steven didn't slow down as he made his way down the hallway toward the stairs. He knew there was no escaping, but he wasn't about to stand around and get a lecture.

"You must have lost your mind," she said, barely finding the words. "You can't possibly be allowing Kimberly to—"

"This isn't about Kimberly." He was understandably reluctant to tell her about his funding of Kimberly's idea, but he couldn't hide it after she'd overheard him discussing it with one of his employees over the phone just before leaving for work.

"I forbid it!" She slammed her foot to the ground, but Steven didn't stop, so she rushed to catch up to him. "You can't be doing this!"

"It's about Michael." Steven turned to her before starting down the staircase. He appreciated that these days his wife was more alert, like her old self, but he'd forgotten how stubborn she could be. "I don't think Michael will leave, but I don't want him to feel like he has no choice. I know what I'm doing. Don't meddle in my business."

"This explains so much," Janet said. "The way she's been walking around with her chin stuck in the air. The things she's been saying to me."

"What has she been saying?" Steven asked.

Janet wasn't going there. "This is simply out of the question."

"It's already underway." Steven accepted his briefcase from Maya. "Thank you, Maya."

"You can stop it," Janet urged.

"But I won't." He stopped at the front door. "The driver is waiting, Janet."

"He'll wait some more. You can't give Kimberly the idea that she's—"

"What?" he asked. "A member of this family? She is, honey. She has been for almost seven years, and considering how far Michael is willing to go to make her happy, it's obvious she will be for a very long time. You have to accept it."

"I . . ." Janet pressed her lips together, trying to calm herself and keep her head straight. Her fingers went to her temples to ease the threat of a headache.

Placing his briefcase on the floor, Steven went to Janet and wrapped his arms around her. "Dear, you're under a lot of stress. With planning the museum ball and Carter's engagement party, worrying about Kimberly is more than you need."

"I can't afford not to." Janet pushed away.

"It's just exploratory." He reached down for his briefcase as Janet opened one of the massive mahogany front doors. "There is no commitment."

"It's the thought that counts," she said. "It's going to bring trouble, Steven. I promise you."

Steven frowned. "Promise me you'll just focus on staying healthy and behaving at the party when Leigh shows up."

Janet frowned, unwilling to let him think this was over.

"Promise me," he repeated. "I know if you promise, you'll do it. You've never lied to me."

That was just the icing on the cake. Janet hid her anguish as she smiled. "I promise."

After a quick kiss, he left and Janet felt every source of stress building up at once. The lying, Leigh, planning the museum ball, Haley, the engagement party; it was all closing in on her.

Then there was Kimberly, whose plotting had reached another level. She was now going after Steven's support and Janet could never, ever have that. Now she had to figure out how to stop this fashion nonsense. All the while, there was a voice in the back of her head begging her to take just one Valium. She couldn't give in no matter how hard it got.

She was at war.

* * *

"That was a first." Avery took her seat at the table the waiter led her and Kimberly to at Melisse in Santa Monica.

They'd made a commitment to meet at a new restaurant on a biweekly basis and promised to talk about everything but the Chase family, but always ended up discussing family anyway. With the party less than a week away, Avery needed the break.

"A first? You've had dress fittings before." Kimberly accepted her menu.

Avery shook her head. "Don't get me wrong, I love dress-up as much as anyone, but it just seems like so much."

"It's not just any engagement party," Kimberly admonished, "it's a Chase engagement party. Haven't you figured that out yet?"

Avery glanced down at her menu. "It doesn't feel like *my* engagement party."

"You're the one who let the Queen Mother take over."

"I had to."

"I'll have a Blue Sky martini," Kimberly said to the waiter.

"I'll have the same." Avery waited until he was gone before continuing. "You saw how upset she was when she thought I was shutting her out."

"It was the highlight of year."

Avery didn't like being in the middle of this archaic feud between the women, but neither spared Avery her contempt for the other. "Let's not go there. I want to forget it all for an hour."

Kimberly shook her head. "Let me—"

Just then, a young, fair-skinned woman with a cheap Beyoncé-blond weave approached the table. "Kimberly? How are you?"

Kimberly looked up at the woman without a word.

"Katrina Phillips." She appeared offended that Kimberly didn't recognize her.

"Oh, yeah." Kimberly still didn't recognize her. "This is Avery—"

"I know who you are." She held out her hand to Avery and shook it vigorously. "Congratulations. You struck gold."

Avery didn't respond, sensing the bitterness in her tone to match the insulting comments. These women were a trip.

"We're actually having a private lunch," Kimberly said.

"I know. I'm on my way out." Katrina looked around suspiciously before leaning over. "I just hope everything is okay with you and Michael."

"Why wouldn't it be?" Kimberly asked.

Katrina shrugged as if she was completely innocent and genuine. "Well, I saw them yesterday and . . . they just looked so . . . cozy."

Kimberly wanted to smack that smile off her face. "We're really busy here."

"I know." She nodded, flipping her hair back. "Just tell Michael I said hello. I didn't want to disturb his lunch with whoever she was. They just looked so intense."

Kimberly didn't blink.

"If you don't mind," Avery said firmly, "we'd like to get back to our private conversation."

The woman pasted an "eat-me" smile on her face. "Of course. And congratulations again to you. Hope you can hold on to him."

Avery waited until Katrina was out of earshot before spitting out, "What a bitch!"

Kimberly took a deep breath, trying not to let the jealousy cloud her mind. "Ignore her. They're all bitter and jealous. There's a shortage of good black men out there. Especially here, where they're either chasing white women, are gay or they're such hos can't no woman call them her own. Then they see us, who have not only good black men, but the cream of the crop. It makes them sick to their stomachs."

Avery took a sip of her drink the second it arrived. She thought maybe she should have ordered something stronger. "It's just so catty. Even when I got engaged to Alex, the only women who were happy for me were the ones already married. It was like my single friends didn't want to be with me anymore."

"You reminded them of something they can't seem to get no matter what they do."

"So they try to make up for it by being hurtful," Avery said. "Why not just be happy for a sister?"

Avery noticed that Kimberly's attention was gone—gone inside. "You aren't letting her get to you, are you?"

"No." Kimberly snapped out of it. "It's just that they're always there. You can't trust anyone. At that party next week, all those women are going to be smiling in your face and saying how happy they are for you. But in reality, they're going to be hating you and thinking of how they can get in your place."

"They'll have a fight to match Armageddon on their hands." No one was taking Carter from her. "They can try all they want."

"Good," Kimberly said, "because, trust me, they will. Hey, let's talk about something else."

Avery looked around as if she expected to see someone eavesdropping. Maybe she was just paranoid, but the curiosity was eating at her. "Remember when I asked you about Laura, Carter's ex?"

"Crazy heifer." Kimberly laughed. "Once accused me of coming on to Carter because I gave him a hug."

"I overheard him talking to Michael about sending someone named Marco to Philadelphia to see her."

"Who's Marco?"

"That's what I was going to ask you. You've never heard of him?"

Kimberly shook her head. "Did you ask Carter?"

"I couldn't." Avery shifted nervously in her seat. "I wasn't supposed to hear it."

"Sneaky." Kimberly raised her glass before taking a sip. "I like that."

"It wasn't on purpose. It just . . . It didn't sound good."

"That's what you want," Kimberly said. "Trust me. That trick is nuts."

Avery nodded uncertainly. "Would he have her hurt?"

"Carter?" Kimberly contemplated for a moment. "I don't think so. A man maybe, but not a woman."

Both women took a second to place their orders with the waiter although neither of them was really very hungry anymore.

"I'm worried," Avery said. "It bothers me that he seems so determined to keep these things from me."

"He should. It's his baggage, not yours."

"But what if—"

"Don't question him," Kimberly urged. "You might not be happy with the answer."

"Maybe he didn't hurt her," Avery said, "but he could. Couldn't he?"

Kimberly studied her for a moment, wondering if Avery was really ready for what she was getting into. The past seven months had gone by quickly, and she was probably blinded by the man that Carter was.

"Of course he *could*," Kimberly answered. "I know you're scared because even though you don't like it, it kind of turns you on, too. The power is pretty intoxicating."

"It feels so wrong." Avery felt her toes tingle as the thought of how intense the sex had been with Carter over the past week. "It feels . . ."

"Dangerous." Kimberly was getting her appetite back. "This powerful man who can have anyone he wants, anything he wants and can manipulate other people's lives while staying wrapped around your little finger. You don't know what he could do any second, but you know he'd do anything for you, and it's such a rush."

"I do genuinely love him," Avery said as if she had to. "And I don't want secrecy."

"You have to make compromises if you want to be a part of this family."

"I just want my own family."

Kimberly leaned forward, looking intently into Avery's frustrated eyes. "Get out of your fantasy world. You're going to be something that was acquired along the way, an accessory to a family that already exists. This is a family that decides what is right and what is wrong based on what they want. Do you get it? You're going to belong to the Chase family. Your children will belong to the—"

"Stop it." Avery didn't want to hear any more.

"You'll belong to them," Kimberly warned. "Understand that there are payoffs and, trust me, you'll love them. But even though your last name will be Chase, if it's not in your blood, you'll always just be an accessory."

A gentle smile lightened Maya's face as she entered the game room and saw Carter playing pool with Michael.

"Nice to see you here." She gestured to Daniel and Evan, who were chasing each other around the sofa. "A rare treat these days."

Carter moved out of the way to avoid the boys as they ran to her. He felt bad, but he was glad they were leaving. He usually wanted to spend time with them when he visited the house, because he loved being the fun uncle, but he wasn't in the mood of late.

"Can I get you something?" Maya asked. "Are you staying for dinner? We're having veal scaloppine."

"No, thanks. Avery and I are having dinner with friends tonight."

"Thanks, Maya," Michael said as she left the room. He turned to Carter. "Your turn."

Carter leaned forward, trying to focus on the shot. "3-ball, corner pocket."

Michael smiled, leaning back. "This is going to be the easiest thousand bucks I ever made."

Carter made the shot. "Even easier than the millions you make filing your nails at Chase Beauty?"

Michael laughed at the jab as Carter made the shot. After the ball fell, he walked over to the stereo and turned up the music.

"No one can hear us," Michael said as he approached.

Carter leaned his stick against the wall. "You said the news wasn't good."

"I did what you asked," Michael said, "against my better judgment. There's nothing we can do to help her get her husband's assets. It's gone to the highest court and the kids won."

"So?"

"You know what the problem is?" Michael asked. "There

isn't any more shame in this world. It used to be you could threaten a woman's reputation with lurid rumors about three-somes and lesbian excursions, but now . . . they don't give a damn."

"That's what you did?" Carter asked. "Threatened to spread rumors?"

"Photoshop, baby. It makes a rumor the truth."

Carter was angry. "You think this is a joke?"

"I was as serious as a heart attack." Michael shrugged. "She just didn't care. Everyone is doing that stuff now—everyone except you and Avery."

"Was there a Plan C?"

"I broke into her hotel room."

"Are you serious?" Carter threw his hands in the air and they fell at his sides. "I guess it's too much to ask to keep this legal. When will I ever learn?"

"We moved past that when we decided to do this in the first place," Michael said. "But no, I didn't break into her room. I paid someone to do it while I was meeting with her in the hotel restaurant. I wanted to see if she had the photos there."

"She's not stupid," Carter said. "And we don't need to involve any more people."

"We need to take it up a notch."

Carter knew what always happened when Michael said that. "No. We have to think of something smarter. Now what we have is an angry, vengeful woman with no morals."

"Pretty much, yeah." Michael surveyed the table. "The good news is Mom has strong security for the party."

"We need more." Carter wondered how he could ramp up security without his mother asking questions. "I can tell Mom about Laura calling again."

Michael's smirked. "That's weak. The best defense is an of-fense."

"Sometimes the best defense is having a shitload of money."

Michael slammed his stick against the edge of the pool table. "Hell, no! She's already got her hands on your balls. Don't let her get a tighter grip."

Carter was shaking his head. "There's just too much to lose."

"You won't lose her." Michael went to the bar and took a sip of his drink. "Avery gets the promised land if she marries you."

Carter's ego was big enough to have thought that often. He was the full package, the kind of man women sold their souls to the devil to marry. He'd thought all of that and assumed Avery thought the same, but he wasn't a fool.

"You don't know her," he said, "not like I do. All the reasons that I love her are the same reasons I know she'd walk away from me if she finds out about this."

"She'd be angry," Michael said. "She'd dump you, but you'd win her back. Women will always pick a rich, powerful man over—"

"Self-respect?" Carter asked. "Trust? Not Avery."

And he wasn't going to let that happen, no matter how much it cost him.

CHAPTER 10

Haley stayed calm as her arm was grabbed and she was swung around. She knew it was Chris and she expected the angry look on his face. He was getting off easy, so he had no right to be mad.

He'd told her to be at Pearl by ten and she'd responded by telling him she would be there when she felt like it. He was calling her names when she hung up, and usually that would be enough to not see him again, but not with Chris. He rarely showed emotion and acted as if he didn't give a damn about much of anything, including her. So she found joy in ruining his day whenever she could.

She showed up at one o'clock with a group of girls in tow. Making sure he could see her from his perch, she flirted with a celebrity or two before he made his way to her. If he expected her to come to him, he'd have to be trained better.

He growled about her coming late, but she ignored him. When he had to attend to some paperwork, he told her to stay where she was until he came back. Of course she left her spot, joining her group of girls at the upstairs bar. She imagined he would be angry after having to find her again, and she was right.

"What in the hell is wrong with you?" he asked, speaking just loud enough to be heard above the club chatter around them.

"Take it easy." She pulled her hand away. "We're not in your bedroom. No rough stuff in public."

"You think you're funny?" he asked. "I told you not to move from—"

"Which was about the third mistake you've made today." She pointed her finger in his face. "I'm here. Be grateful for that."

Chris looked as if he wanted to say something but thought better of it. He looked over her shoulder at the group of girls sipping martinis. "I take it all these drinks are on the house?"

"Did you expect my friends to pay?" This boy was *so* close to his last days. "If you want to dominate in the bedroom, that's one thing. But in public, you're going to come correct or be ass out."

Chris laughed as if he'd decided to be amused by it all before wrapping his arm around her waist and sliding her toward him. He took her hand in his. Lifting it to his mouth, he kissed it tenderly and smiled apologetically. "I'm tense when I'm on the job. You know how it is."

"No," she answered. "I've never had a job."

His laugh held a bitter, jealous tone to it. "That's because you're a little spoiled princess and I'm just trying to keep my little princess happy. Now, if you'll come with me, I would like to show you something I think you'll like."

"If you only think, then don't waste your time."

"It's about money."

Haley's eyes sparkled a little. "Then what are you waiting for?"

They walked down a hallway past his office. Haley didn't even know there was a corner to turn that far, but there was and it led to a steel door labeled SUPPLIES.

Chris typed in a code, and as the door made a whirring sound, he turned to her and winked after slapping her on the butt. When he opened the door, Haley wasn't sure what to expect, but she had to admit she was surprised. That was, after the two bodyguards, each as big as a house, stepped aside.

The room was small, but it was designed just like a private high-roller section in a top-line Vegas casino. The room had about six tables of different games with no discernable difference from those you would see in the Bellagio, Venetian or Mirage. The dealers had on all-black uniforms and there were girls, lots of beautiful, sexy, barely dressed girls keeping the players company.

After nodding a hello to a couple of famous hoops players, Chris turned back to Haley. "Didn't know about this, did you?"

Haley shrugged. "So you have an illegal card game in the back of your shop. Not much worth knowing about."

"Okay, smart-ass." He led her around the room. "This card game is quickly becoming the biggest game in L.A. Every single person sitting at these tables has a net worth of at least five million."

"I spend more than that in two weeks at St. Tropez."

"No, you don't." Chris leaned into her, grabbing her ass. "Don't tell me you aren't a little excited."

"Not as excited as I'll be when I read in the paper about you getting busted."

"Not gonna happen," he said. "I have several cops on my payroll."

"So you think you're Tony Soprano here?"

He laughed, shaking his head. "It's the rush, baby, not even the money. I'm getting away with it. I've taken all the top players from other clubs. I'm doing appointments now. I got this game going every night."

Getting away with it did light Haley's fire a little bit. She leaned in to kiss him and was enjoying it until she felt his teeth bite her lower lip. She leaned away and slapped him across the face.

"What the—"

"I told you about biting me." Haley checked her lip for blood and was grateful he hadn't penetrated skin.

"Stop treating me like I have a disease." Chris looked too embarrassed to check if anyone was looking.

Haley pushed everyone in her path out of the way as she stomped out of the room. She could play his stupid games if that was what he wanted to do, but he had to play safe. That was not negotiable.

The second she was out on the main floor, she intended to get her girls and head to Club LAX, but the man she came face-to-face with made her take a step back. She didn't like being taken off guard. At least she didn't like letting it show, but she was shaken.

"Hello, Haley." Sean stood out in the crowd. His dress was so conservative compared to everyone else that it almost looked like a costume.

He'd been preparing for this moment, grateful it was at least somewhat on his own terms. Still, he couldn't deny he felt a little tug at the sight of her, which he figured would be his punishment for getting involved with her in the first place.

"What are you doing here?" Haley asked, not sure why she suddenly felt so angry.

"I came looking for you." Actually, he'd come to get a glimpse of Chris in his element but was hoping he would run into Haley. He only hoped they could get through this without the usual apocalypse.

Haley smiled coldly. "Isn't it way past your bedtime?"

"I just got off my shift."

She fanned herself. "I never get tired of hearing that. 'I just got off my shift.' It's so blue-collar. Very sexy."

Sean smiled when he realized her insults didn't really hurt anymore. "Where's your boyfriend?"

"Is that what you came here for?" she asked. "To check out the next victim? It's a bit too obvious for my taste."

"Do you know who you're dealing with?"

Now she was really impressed. "Detective, are you telling me that you've done some research? Well, I guess you've missed me."

"I didn't miss you at all," he said. "Believe it or not, I prefer a life without a psychotic stalker."

"You think that was bad? I picked up a few tricks in—"

"He's got a record," Sean said. "Drugs. Does that sound familiar? You eager to get into that again?"

"It's none of your business."

"He's from Chicago. His brother was a high-ranking Disciple."

"What, like a priest?"

"It's a street gang. You may lack principles, but you don't have a death wish."

Haley blinked innocently. "I don't know what you expect me to say."

"You don't have to say anything." Sean knew this was going too easily to be true.

"It's just . . ." She took a step closer to him and tilted her head to the left, the way he liked—"the sex is so damn good. It's not 'pleasant' like with you, Sean. It's exciting and dangerous."

Okay, Sean thought, *that one hurt.*

"Who's this?" Chris asked as he joined them. He wrapped a possessive hand around Haley's waist, looking Sean up and down. "You an accountant or something?"

"He's a nobody," Haley said.

Sean kept his attention on Chris. "I'm Detective Sean Jackson with the View Park police, and I know who you are."

Chris laughed, but it was clear that he wasn't comfortable.

Haley's disappointment was shown clearly after Sean had walked away. "What was that?"

"What?" Chris asked. "He's a cop. I got L.A. on my payroll, not View Park. I don't need any problems with him."

"So you laugh like a nervous little girl?"

"That's your drama, Princess," he said. "That's for you to handle."

Haley slapped his hand away from her waist. "Then what in the hell do I need you for?"

She took two steps before he grabbed her by her wrist and jerked her back to him. "Don't walk away from me twice."

"What are you going to do about it?" Haley let her anger at Sean walking away from her ride up.

Chris's expression switched from anger to pleasure in a quick second. Haley knew she was talking his language, and for the first time, she felt no apprehension about it. She was ready for whatever was coming.

Michael tossed his jacket onto the bed and headed for the bathroom and the sound of Lauryn Hill. Seeing Kimberly in the tub, rubbing the white bubbles against her perfect chocolate skin, made him forget all of his problems.

"Hey, Daddy." Kimberly smiled as he sat on the marble molding and tugged at his tie. "You're home early."

"I had to get out of there." Tossing his tie away, he moved on to his twelve-hundred-dollar cuff links. He could smell the lavender in the water. "Where the boys at?"

"You see me naked in the tub and that's your first question?" Kimberly shook her head. "I must be losing my touch."

"Not at all." He leaned in and kissed her, smiling at the hunger. "I'm just . . . I'm used to them being in the way, if you know what I mean."

He slowly reached his hand into the water

"Well, no one is in the—"

"Damn!" Michael's hand shot out of the tub. "That water is five hundred degrees, woman."

"You know I like it hot." She reached out and pulled at his shirt. "Join me."

"Hell, no." He leaned back. "I already got third-degree burns on my hand."

"Not willing to suffer a little pain for pleasure?"

"I'll hit you up when you get out." He jumped to evade the small tide of water she slapped his way. "Don't mess up my thousand-dollar shirt with your cheap little oils."

"You wish they were cheap." She knew he was just playing, but it only made what had been on her mind all day beg her even more for an explanation. "Did you enjoy lunch yesterday?"

Michael was slick. It didn't take even a second for him to get that she was asking about his lunch at the Westin with Lisette. How in God's name had she found out?

"You spying on me?" he asked without a hint of unrest.

"No, that's what you do, baby." Kimberly was agreeing to be civil until he gave her a reason not to.

She knew she had married a man women would do anything for a piece of, a man who had relaxed morals when it came to certain things. She didn't want to believe he would cheat on her, but she knew he probably had. Unless she had proof, she wasn't going to let herself believe any of it.

"I had a business lunch with a beautiful woman," he answered after deducing that she didn't know it was Lisette. "Perfectly innocent."

"That's not what I hear."

"Oh, really?" he asked. "Who did you hear it from? One of those jealous chicken heads, always swarming around our marriage like a buzzard?"

"Who was it?"

"Just a woman from the accounting firm." He shrugged, trying to give the impression that it really wasn't a big deal. "You satisfied?"

"Never," she answered.

"Your boy is coming in for an interview next week." Michael knew his best play was to remind Kimberly of all he was doing for her.

"You don't have to tell me." Kimberly was excited just thinking about Paul Devereaux's visit. "He knows who we are, right?"

"What do you mean?"

"He knows about your parents," she said, "that we are *the* Chase family."

"Everyone knows who we are. I'm sure he did his research. He wasn't so easy to get over here. I don't think he'll want the job. He's got it too good in Paris."

"But we're planning an incredible week for him," Kimberly said.

"Which I'd say is about three days too long, but yes . . . it's a good week." Michael repeated the list Kimberly had painstakingly planned for Paul's visit.

"Did he mention your parents at all?" Kimberly knew that once Paul realized the Janet Chase being referred to was his Janet Allen, it would be enough to make him decide against coming, but she was hoping whatever the secret was would be enough to compel him. Deep down inside, everyone is a curious animal.

He had to remember her. Despite the fact that Kimberly hated Janet, the woman *was* unforgettable. If he'd done his research, he must have seen pictures of her, looking ten years younger than she really was without a single nip or tuck.

"We don't need to go all out." Michael was admiring himself in the mirror. "Besides, the second he sees you, if that doesn't sell him, nothing will."

Kimberly smiled in anticipation as she leaned her head against the spa pillow. This was going to be sweet.

Through the mirror, Michael looked down at his satisfied wife. He didn't have the heart to tell her that this plan wasn't going to work. He didn't have the guts to tell her what her picture in magazines nationwide could do to his family if the wrong person recognized her.

No, there was no way this was going to work.

Haley's eyes closed as she let out a guttural moan. Riding on top of Chris, she picked up the pace, succumbing to the pleasure rippling in waves through her. His hands reached up and gripped her grinding, curvy hips, pushing her down on him harder. It sent a rush of fire from her groin through the rest of her body, making her head fall back.

But her eyes flew open and her head shot right back up from the pain of Chris grabbing both her breasts and squeezing hard. She took hold of his wrist, trying to push his hands away, but he pulled her forward. Looking into his eyes, she had come to recognize that look. Things were about to get serious.

He had already gotten too rough in the limo on the way back to his condo, pulling her hair and squeezing her nipple. Haley was so angry after Sean had walked away from her that she didn't think to stop Chris. The pain made her feel good; it made her anger feel justified.

"Don't make me walk out on you again," she warned.

"You'll like this." He let go of her breast, pulling out of her as he positioned her on the bed next to him. "Give me a kiss."

She did as she was told, feeling her stomach flutter with a mixture of fear and excitement. It was amazing to her that she would ever enjoy feeling vulnerable, but she was beginning to. She didn't know what this crazy bastard was going to do next and a part of her got off on it.

She laughed as he positioned her on her side, sliding up behind her. Lifting her leg over his, he entered her again, slowly.

She bit her lower lip, drinking in the feeling. He was by far the most well-endowed man she had ever been with.

He grabbed her chin, turning her head to the side to face him. His eyes danced with an illicit excitement as he said, "I'm going to strangle you."

The flutters stopped as Haley's eyes opened wide. "Come again?"

He smiled, not missing a beat. "It's okay. I know what I'm doing."

His hand slowly lowered to her neck, but Haley stopped him. "Hold up."

He stopped moving. "I'm gonna go limp if—"

"Strangle me?" She didn't give a damn about his erection.

"It's exciting, baby." He leaned forward and kissed her cheek. "It's liberating. The intensity takes the pleasure to a level you would not believe."

"Or it could kill me."

"Would you rather we just keep up this suburban married couple shit you used to do with the cop?"

Oh, hell, no. Haley slapped his hand away and moved away from him so fast he let out a whimper of pain. To make it worse, she reached down and grabbed his quickly softening penis, squeezing it hard.

"You like it rough?" she asked. "Is this rough enough for you?"

She ducked his swinging hand and let go. Backing up to the edge of the bed, Haley met the fury in his eyes with her own. "You don't know who you're messing with, fool. Don't you ever try that reverse psychology shit with me."

Chris looked ready to pounce. "You are by far the most difficult piece of kitty cat I've ever had."

"And the best," she said. "So if you want to keep getting it, you better check yourself."

Chris lifted his hands in the air. "I give, Haley. You rule the coop. You're the player here. I'm just trying to bring a little extra flavor to the game."

Haley's arms folded across her chest as a satisfied smile formed at her lips. "What's the safe word?"

"Ahhhh." Chris crawled over to her. "You're learning the lingo."

She slapped his reaching hand away. "Answer the damn question."

"No."

"No?"

"It's tried and true," he said. "I like keeping some things simple."

"I say 'no,' you stop."

He nodded, a grin from cheek to cheek. "You can trust me, baby."

"Never," she said, despite letting him take her by the arms, lift her body up and throw her on the bed.

CHAPTER 11

The Regent Beverly Wilshire was an elegant European-style hotel well known for having one of the most expensive suites in Los Angeles. It was old elegance with new technology, the exact way Janet liked to entertain. Nothing flashy or modern, but everything money. Le Grand Trianon was the perfect room for Chase and Avery's engagement party.

Everything was going as planned. The caterers were providing impeccable service, and the band played on cue. The media stayed in their designated corner and the room was full of the best of Los Angeles, celebrating Janet's masterpiece of party planning.

Despite it all, Janet could think of only one thing: Leigh's calculated plan to stay as far away from her as possible. It was more painful than Janet expected, being the first time she'd been in the same room as Leigh without Valium to ease her mind and control her behavior. She thought herself a fool to think that if she kept her part of the bargain Leigh would give an inch. As time wore on, it was becoming clear to Janet that Leigh had no intention of acknowledging her existence. All she had left was to once again send her spy.

Watching Leigh and Haley stand together, looking like women with their own lives, made Janet feel old. These girls she believed couldn't live without her were not little girls any-more. They didn't need her. Carter and Michael hadn't needed her for some time, but her girls . . . she didn't want to let them go. No one but Steven needed her now.

She could see a life where Leigh would keep her at a distance even after she gave up this nonsense of not speaking to her, their relationship damaged forever because of past mistakes. Polite nods would replace hugs and kisses. Was it possible things could deteriorate to that level? Janet couldn't bear it.

"She's looking at us right now," Haley said.

"Stop it." Leigh refused to take Haley's bait and create a con-flict with her mother. "Things are peaceful. Leave it alone."

"You could at least look at her." Haley grabbed a glass of Pinot Grigio from a passing waiter. "It's not fair what you're doing."

"What would you know about fair?" Leigh asked. "And you're drinking too much. You pick up alcoholism from your gangster boyfriend too?"

"I can hold my liquor."

"You are on edge, aren't . . ." Leigh squinted, leaning for-ward. She reached out to touch the silk Hermès scarf around Haley's neck.

Hurrying to make sure the scarf was positioned correctly, Haley took a step away from Leigh. "Stop touching me."

"Did Chris—"

Haley regretted ever telling her about Chris's fixation with rough sex. "It's nothing."

"How do you get a bruise"—Leigh gasped, quickly getting angry—"Did he try to strangle you?"

"Keep your voice down." Haley looked around nervously, thinking she should have applied another layer of makeup. The bruises just weren't fading fast enough.

Leigh snatched the glass out of Haley's hand just as she was about to take another sip. "Answer me now or I'm calling Daddy over here."

"Daddy doesn't care about my sex life," Haley said. "I'm not you."

"He'll care if he sees these bruises," Leigh warned. "You've taken this too far."

"I'm fine." Actually Haley enjoyed it more than she'd expected to. It took a few times of saying no before Chris would stop, but eventually he did. "It was safe."

"Of course it was," Leigh said sarcastically. "What wouldn't be safe about autoerotic asphyxiation?"

"Don't use medical terms on me."

"It's not a medic—" Leigh sighed. "This kind of stuff kills people, usually women who think they can trust a guy to loosen his grip even though he's in the throes of passion."

Haley laughed. " 'Throes of passion'? A little dramatic, Leigh."

"When are you going to get sick of this one?" Leigh asked. "I hope it's soon, because I'm afraid you're going to get really hurt."

"Don't worry," she answered. "His time will be up when I want it to be. I know who I'm dealing with."

"Do you?"

"I didn't invite him here, did I?" Haley looked around. "Don't tell me you've never slummed before."

"What do you think he's going to do when you decide you don't want him anymore? He already likes to hurt you for fun. What will he do when he really gets mad?"

"You think he's a psycho like your boyfriend Leo?" Haley smiled as her sister's face contracted before she stormed off, but her smile quickly faded.

She'd never thought of what a man would do when she dumped him. Usually he would beg and plead, send her gifts and promise to be a better man than he was before. With the exception of a few complete losers, it didn't last too long because when Haley made up her mind, it was made up. There were one or two stalkers, but most knew better than to go against someone as high-profile as her.

Haley wasn't going to let Leigh make her worry. Chris wasn't a particularly violent guy. He was actually calmer out of the bedroom than she preferred. Besides, there was that I-don't-give-a-damn-about-much-of-anything way he had about him that told her kicking him to the curb when his time came would go smoothly enough.

"What are you doing?" Avery giggled, looking to see if any-one was spying on them as Carter led her away from the guests. "Where are we going?"

"To be alone." Carter looked both ways before guiding her into an empty dressing room.

Once he closed the door, he lifted her into his arms and took her lips with his. Clumsily, they made their way to the closest wall and he pressed her against it. He slid his tongue inside of her mouth, giving her that familiar ache.

As his mouth made its way down her neck, Avery felt a tingling sensation come over her. She must be dreaming. The day she'd feared because of Janet's excessiveness was turning out to be like a fairy tale. It was really happening. She was going to marry a prince.

Yes, Carter seemed distracted, but everything was working perfectly. Her parents were having a great time, not too bothered by the display of wealth. The decorations were beautiful, the service beyond reproach, the food exquisite. She looked incredible in her new dress and Carter looked like a billion dollars. The press was under control and everyone was getting along.

"Let's do this right here," Carter whispered into her ear.

Maybe it was panic or fear, but ever since Lisette had come back on the scene, he was constantly anxious and only sex with Avery took the edge off. Touching her kept him sane.

"Carter." Avery's mind knew it wasn't a good idea, but her body was too heated up to make it easy. It was amazing, as if they had found a new level of passion. "The door."

"Forget the door." He pressed his body against hers, feeling the blood surge to his groin.

"Not all the way," she whispered.

"What is this, high school?" He didn't want any limits with Avery. "I need you."

"Please." Avery didn't know how much longer she could stick with reason. "The media. Someone will come . . ."

"We should leave," Carter said and he wasn't kidding. To have gotten this far without any problems was a blessing he didn't want to ignore.

"This party is for us."

"A party is a party," he said. "They don't need us. Besides, all the speeches and crap are over. As a matter of fact, let's go on vacation, baby. Let's buy two tickets to Fiji and—"

"We just got back from vacation. You hated leaving Chase Law for that long. Now you want to go again?"

"Things are different now," he said. "You've brought balance to my life."

"That's what I'm here for, Daddy, but I've got a job too."

"You're the boss's soon-to-be daughter-in-law. You can leave as often and whenever you want."

"That would look awful."

"You sound like my mother."

Avery gasped, socking Carter in the stomach hard enough to make him bend to the side. "Don't ever say that. I love Janet, but I am not like her."

"I should be offended, right? You just dissed my ma."

"You want to get away?" she asked. "How about a weekend in—"

"Monte Carlo!"

"No." Avery rolled her eyes.

"Vegas?"

"Try somewhere you can't sneak off and spend the night at a strip club."

"Well, forget it, then." He turned to walk away, but Avery grabbed him by the arm.

"Hey." She wrapped her arms around him, reaching up to kiss him on the chin just as his phone rang. Avery didn't hesitate to let him go. From the ring tone, she knew it was Michael.

Carter grabbed the phone, feeling doom set in. It was the signal. Lisette was here!

When he looked at her, Avery could see something odd in his eyes. Fear? "What is it?"

Carter pulled himself together quickly. "Nothing, but I have to find my boy."

"Your boy can wait, can't he?" Avery was surprised that he was already at the door. "Hey!"

"It's business," he said. "We were waiting for a call. It must have come."

"Why are you doing business today?" She thought they had already discussed that.

"Will you wait here for me?" he asked.

"For how long?" Avery didn't know why she'd bothered to ask, because she wasn't going to wait.

"I'll be back in a second." He rushed back to her and kissed her on the forehead. Looking into her trusting eyes, in that second he hated himself. "Stay here. I love you."

"I—" He was gone before she could finish.

"Where are you?" Carter asked into his cell.

"Out front." Michael clearly sounded angry. "Get out here now!"

When Carter stepped outside, he looked around trying to keep his anger in check. Fortunately, none of the press was out there. If they had been, they would have gotten a clear view of Lisette dressed in very flattering cream-colored silk pantsuit, waving her arms and yelling at Michael, who held a threatening finger in her face.

When he showed up, Carter grabbed Lisette by the arm and dragged her from the entrance and off to the side, where more people were hustling between the shops. Michael was following close behind.

"Let me go!" Lisette struggled to break free. When Carter let her go, she stumbled back a few steps.

"You are out of your mind," Carter's voice grated harshly.

"She doesn't know who she's messing with," Michael said.

Lisette stood up straight, but her eyes gave her away. She was intimidated by their united front. "I just came by to give you my congratulations."

"You don't want to mess with me," Carter said menacingly. "Not like this. Not in front of my family."

She folded her arms across her chest and managed a weak smile. "I'm not afraid of you. You're the one who should be afraid of me."

"You're nobody," Michael shouted. "Do you understand that? You think because you know important people that you're important, but you're not. You don't know what it means, but you will if you try to go against someone who is."

Lisette made a smacking sound with her lips and turned to Carter. "I've been learning a lot about your little common fiancée this past week. She's very—what's the word?—yeah, pious. It's a lost quality in today's world. Thank God."

"Just go," Carter grumbled, his hands forming into fists at his sides.

"Those types don't take well to deceit, manipulation, lying and secrecy, and I think you've covered all that." She inhaled quickly as Carter took another step toward her.

"I haven't covered everything," he warned, wishing he could strangle that beautiful neck of hers. "There's more I could do."

"And you will," she said. "I want five million."

Michael growled, "You are one insane—"

"Or what?" Carter asked.

"Let's not waste each other's time," Lisette answered.

"I'll make you a liar," Michael said. "I'll make it so no one will believe you even when you say the sky is blue."

Lisette ignored Michael, keeping her concentration on Carter. "We were only together for a few months, but I know you. You're only good despite your best intentions, and I figure she knows this now too. She may love you, but she knows what you're capable of. And unlike me—who would just want your money and all the things that come with your last name—I think she'll care."

"That's enough." Michael reached out to grab Lisette's arm and began dragging her toward the curb. "I'm calling you a cab and getting you out of here before you do something to destroy what pitiful life you have."

"Wait!"

They both turned as Carter approached, and Lisette broke free of Michael's grip.

Carter held up his hand to stop Michael's protest. "What makes you think you'll get away with this?"

"Because you really love her," she answered. "Basically,

you're a snob, Carter. You're the type of man who thinks about the social advantage in everything, including marriage. You were supposed to marry someone like yourself, well-heeled, from a family with an important name, connections, stellar education and lots of money. So the fact that you're marrying a nobody tells me that you must really love her. That's why I'll get away with it."

After a moment, Carter turned to Michael. "Give us a second."

"Hell, no!" Michael yelled. "She's not getting a cent. I swear if you even think about giving in to her, I'll tell Avery myself."

"One second," Carter ordered. "Get her cab."

Michael wanted to knock some sense into Carter, but he held back and did what his big brother told him to. He understood that Carter was in love, and that made a man vulnerable and stupid. Michael knew it would be up to him to deal with Lisette.

"You know I'm right," Lisette said when Michael was gone.

"You are," Carter said. "I love Avery more than anything. That means I'm willing to do whatever it takes to keep her, including get rid of anyone who tries to take her from me."

Lisette swallowed, trying bravely to hold her chin up. "You know how to get rid of me, Carter. The ball is in your court now."

"It's always been in my court," he said. "You're going to find that out soon."

As the cab pulled up, Carter followed Lisette to the curb. Stepping out of the way, Michael glanced around to make sure they hadn't gotten any unwanted attention. Just then, he saw Avery in the revolving door of the hotel, one second from stepping out in front. She was already looking around.

It was too late. In a few seconds, she would see them. She would see Carter's hand on Lisette's back as he gently pushed her toward the cab.

"Get in," Carter ordered, speeding her along.

Lisette resisted slightly as the door opened. "I'm not going to wait around forever."

Michael pushed Carter away from Lisette and grabbed her himself. Carter was taken off guard by the action but quickly realized what Michael was doing. When he turned around, Avery was already walking toward them.

Carter blocked her line of sight as Michael shoved Lisette into the car. Despite his panic, he kept relatively cool, quickly studying her demeanor. She was curious, confused and a little angry.

"Who was that?" Avery asked, trying to get a glance into the back of the cab as it drove off onto Rodeo Drive. She wasn't sure what she'd seen, but Avery knew something was wrong. "Who was that woman?"

"I told you to wait for me," was Carter's only response.

"That was no one," Michael said.

Avery looked from Carter to Michael and back to Carter. Her perfect day was over. "Carter, who was that woman?"

"No one for you to be—"

"Don't fuck with me," Avery stated with authority.

Both men blinked, neither expecting that response from the well-mannered cop's daughter. They looked at each other and, without a word, Michael left.

Carter took a second to calm down. "Don't talk to me like that in front of—"

"Don't dismiss my questions," she said, "and I won't talk to you like that. Who was she?"

"Does everything have to be your business?" he asked.

Avery wanted to slap him for that, but she wouldn't give in to her anger so he could blame this on her. "I'm not going to ask again."

"Who do you think you're talking to?" Knowing he had no right to be angry only made him angrier.

"This party is over. I'm getting my parents and leaving." Avery turned to head inside, but Carter reached out and pulled her back. "Get your hands off me."

"People are looking, Avery. Don't make a scene."

With every second, Avery felt closer to exploding. "You're not going to treat me like this. I see you with a woman who—"

"She's an ex." Carter let go of her, trying his best to appear apologetic. "She's just jealous. Michael spotted her and we just got rid of her before she could make a scene. I'm not trying to shut you out. I just don't want you to have to deal with my baggage."

"Who was she?" Avery had suspected that at least one of the many jealous women who wished they were going to be Mrs. Carter Chase would find a way to make some noise. "Do I know . . . Is it Laura?"

"No." Carter placed his hand on the small of her back and turned her toward the hotel. "You don't have to worry about Laura at all."

"Why not?" Avery asked, even though she knew she wouldn't get the truth.

"Because I said so." When she turned to him, he sighed impatiently. "Laura isn't coming to L.A."

"Because she can't?" Avery asked.

Carter stopped, curious about what Avery had been up to. He should have known she wouldn't let what she'd overheard go. "What do you mean by that?"

"I don't know," Avery said. "You won't tell me anything."

Carter surveyed the woman he was going to spend the rest of his life with and reminded himself that her stubborn attitude was one of the reasons he loved her. "Let's go inside."

"It can't stay this way," Avery said. "You have to tell me. How did you handle Laura? Who was that woman in the cab? I need to know who has it in for me."

Carter took her by the shoulders and faced her squarely. "Listen to me, baby. No matter what happens, I will never, ever let anyone hurt you. I will protect you at any cost."

She believed every word he was saying, and that was what scared her. "I love that you're my knight on a white horse, but I can't be in the dark. I'm not that kind of woman and you know that. I need to know what's going on."

"I'm ashamed of a lot of the choices I made before I met you," he said softly. "So you can understand that I'm not too quick to reveal them."

"I won't judge you for anything you did before we were together." Avery reached out and tenderly touched his cheek. "You made mistakes. So did I. Look at Alex. He was the biggest mistake of my life. But it's all in the past. It's just you and me now. We have to trust each other."

"I know, baby." Carter leaned down and kissed her on the forehead. "Let's go inside."

He needed this woman in ways he learned anew every day. Being without her wasn't an option. Neither was losing her trust and respect. When he thought about cost in those terms, five million didn't really seem like that much. He had more than twice that in his trust fund, which he rarely touched. Avery was worth so much more.

But damn, he hated losing.

As soon as she saw them return to the ballroom, Leigh rushed to Carter and Avery. She didn't want to leave without thanking them, but she had a plane to catch.

"I thought you'd left," she said, noticing that they both seemed somewhere else and angry.

"We just needed some air," Carter answered. "What's up, kid?"

"I have to go."

"It's still early," Avery protested. "What is it? Did Janet upset you?"

"It's not Mom. I have a flight at eight. I'm going to Nepal."

"What are you going there for?" Carter asked.

"There's been some conflict and it's left a lot of impoverished civilians with injuries. They need doctors." Leigh didn't expect Carter to understand. He was like her parents in believing that charity was dressing up for a party and writing a check.

"You're such a sweetheart." Avery hugged her but was unable to hide her concern. "But it's still dangerous there. I've been listening to the news."

"What kind of security do you have?" Carter asked.

"What are you talking about?"

Leigh sighed at the sound of her mother's voice. Slowly, she turned around to face her.

"Where are you going?" Janet felt anxiety tighten her chest as she approached. She was careful to keep her distance, but overhearing what she had, she couldn't keep it up.

"She's going to Nepal," Carter offered when he saw Leigh's reluctance. He didn't really want her to go, but he had his own problems to deal with.

"It's work," Leigh said. "I'll be fine."

"When were you going to tell your family?" Janet asked.

"I left a message for Daddy and I—"

"A message?" Janet laughed. "Why not just e-mail us? Sounds more appropriate. You're going off into the third world and—"

"Janet." Avery turned to her. "Please, it's not—"

"Stay out of it," Carter said, taking her by the arm. "Let's go."

"No, Carter." Avery stood her ground. "I'm sure she'll be fine, Janet. There is a security detail with those groups, right?"

"You need your own security," Janet said. "I'll get my purse and call the Attaché. We'll send a couple of their men with—"

"You can't, Mom," Leigh insisted. "I won't let you."

"This is your safety," Janet said. "I'm not concerned with what you think of me."

"Carter." Leigh urged her brother for help, but Janet had already headed for Steven, who was talking on his cell phone several feet away. "Please stop her."

"You stop her," Carter said. "She won't listen to me. Besides, it *is* dangerous. You live on the edge enough with that clinic."

Leigh groaned with a fist in the air. "I shouldn't have told anyone."

"That's not fair," Avery said. "Your family has a right to know when you're going into harm's way."

"Dad's gonna be angry you left him a message," Carter said, "so there's no chance he'll take your side over hers. Just accept it."

"Think of it this way," Avery said, "it's not wrong to be worried about your safety. It's her job. Besides, she didn't once try to talk you out of going. She is changing."

Leigh shook her head, knowing there was nothing she could do right in this situation but leave. "I'm sorry to leave so early. Thank you so much for helping the center out. We really appreciate it."

Gifts were not expected at an engagement party, but one

could not pass up an opportunity that brought the upper crust together. Guests were encouraged to donate money to the Hope Clinic, Leigh's center.

"It wasn't my idea," Avery said. "It was Janet's."

Leigh wasn't impressed. "Probably to force me to show up."

"Or to show you that she loves you," Avery said, even though she knew that Leigh's assumption more likely was the truth.

"I don't want to be treated differently than the other doctors."

"That's your problem," Carter interjected, "you *are* different and you can't face it."

"You're not helping," Avery warned.

"You're a Chase," he continued, ignoring Avery. "You're a target for all types of people just because of it. You have to protect yourself!"

"What was that for?" Leigh asked as Carter stormed off. "He knows no one in Nepal knows who I am."

Avery sighed, feeling guilty for not wanting to go after him. "Ignore him. He's angry. Ex-girlfriends."

"Well, I have to go." She started to walk away.

"Leigh, wait."

"No." Leigh stopped mid-stride and turned. "I understand what you're saying, but I have to go."

Even though she would much rather leave, Avery stayed put knowing that Janet would be back. This time she was with Steven, who looked even angrier than his wife.

"She's gone," Avery said.

"Steven." Janet felt her anxiety begin to scream at her. She needed a pill. "I have to know she's safe."

"I'll stop her," Steven assured Janet.

"You can't do that," Avery said. "She's not a child. You have to—"

"Stay out of it," Steven said. "This is family business."

As they both rushed past her, Avery was left alone in amazement. She wanted to believe he was just angry and scared for his daughter, but Kimberly's warning crept into her thoughts. No matter who she was now, or who she would be, she wasn't a Chase by blood. She was an outsider.

CHAPTER 12

"This is what Carter wants." Avery pulled out the brochure from Bastide. "It's absolutely beautiful."

Her mother, Nikki, put her crab panini sandwich down and took the brochure. She looked it over with a frown.

"We went there a few nights ago." Avery stole a bite from Nikki's plate. "The Chases are big on French restaurants."

After a morning of shopping, Avery and her mother were sitting in the back room of Hue, the thriving art gallery Nikki had started a decade ago for local minority artists. The pair intended to discuss a place for the rehearsal dinner over takeout.

"Always going somewhere fancy." Nikki put the brochure down. "Little Avery, a woman of the world."

Avery smiled. "It's exhausting, Mom. These people go nonstop. They don't understand the meaning of a quiet night at home."

"You're talking about yourself, you know." Nikki felt bad the second Avery looked at her. "I'm sorry. I didn't mean to upset you."

"You didn't." Avery shrugged. "It's true. It's what I've become. There are just so many expectations."

"Like this." Nikki slid the brochure toward her daughter. "The rehearsal dinner is one thing, but a reception at the Four Seasons? Your father has pride, you know."

"I know. I want him to help pay for the wedding."

"He doesn't want to add pennies to millions."

Avery sighed impatiently. "What do you want me to do, Mom?"

"Don't get upset."

"I'm marrying Carter Chase." Avery pushed the file of brochures across the table. "Dignitaries, politicians, royalty, billionaires and multimillionaires will be there. I can't have a reception at the local community center."

"You're the bride," Nikki said. "You can get married anywhere you want to."

"No." Avery felt herself getting emotional, something that seemed to happen so easily these days. "I can't, Mom. That's what I'm trying to tell you. I know this is hurting Dad, but it's out of my hands."

Nikki wrapped her arms around her baby, wishing she could make her feel better. She wanted to say so much but knew it would only upset Avery more.

"I'm sorry." There was no stopping Avery's tears now. "I just feel . . . I just want to get married and have a beautiful wedding."

"I know. I know."

"I love him so much, Mom." Avery sat up, wiping her face with a napkin. "I want to be his wife. I don't doubt that at all. It's just everything else."

"You can't separate any of it," Nikki said.

With a nod, Avery tried to smile. "It's really not bad. I mean, I'm lucky to have found someone like him. That he would want me. I could be alone."

"That's not the only alternative." Nikki rubbed Avery's back. "You have to talk to Carter about this. I know you haven't."

"He'll just lecture me on understanding what it means to be a Chase. He doesn't get where I'm coming from."

"You have to make him understand."

"Mom, you know what I'm dealing with right now." Avery hadn't told her mother the whole truth about Laura, but she did know about the phone call. She also knew about the mystery ex Carter had shoved into the cab. "I can't become the jealous fiancée."

"You will," Nikki said. "As long as he's being secretive and you're too scared to get to the truth, it's inevitable that you'll become that person."

"I don't care about his past," Avery said.

"That's good for his past," Nikki said. "But these women are making it very much his present. Avery, I'm really worried."

"Don't be." Avery took her mother's hand in hers and squeezed. "I'm stressed, but I am happy. I love him, and he loves me so much."

"Love isn't enough," Nikki said. "You have to have trust and the truth. How can you accept what you have to deal with if you're kept in the dark as to what it really is?"

As the waiter set the plate of zucchini-blossom beignets with summer truffle vinaigrette in front of her, Kimberly nodded a polite "thank you." She was too nervous to be charming. There was so much to lose, but as she waited in the famous restaurant at the Hotel Bel-Air for the guest staying in the $1,300-a-night Grand Suite, the anticipation of all she could gain made her just as worried.

Known as the most romantic hotel restaurant in L.A., it was one of Kimberly's favorites. Michael had taken her there during her first week in L.A. Although most people wanted the hottest, newest thing in Beverly Hills, Kimberly kept returning to the outdoor dining of the bougainvillea-draped terrace, which reminded her of when she had fallen in love with her husband.

"Mrs. Chase?"

Kimberly lowered her glass of wine as she looked up at the guest accompanying the maître d'. Paul Devereaux was everything she hoped he would be. Thoroughly European, he could get away with his keen sense of style and not be assumed gay. He was tall, looked about ten years younger than sixty, naturally tanned with the traditional Romanesque features of a strong nose and hard jawline. He wasn't as attractive as Steven but could hold his own.

"Your guest has arrived."

Paul nodded a "thank you" as he took his seat. "I knew you

would be even more striking than your pictures, which by the way are too difficult to find for a woman as beautiful as you."

Kimberly smiled, enjoying his French accent. "Why did you think that?"

"Your voice over the phone." He nodded to the waiter who came to pour him a glass of wine. "I know how beautiful women sound. More important, I know how beautiful women of leisure sound—not at all hurried, but aware of their importance."

Kimberly wasn't so sure that was a compliment. "I hope you're enjoying your stay."

Paul accepted the menu and ordered quickly.

"My suite is impressive. You have done well." He leaned back in his chair, looking as if he'd known Kimberly for years. "I have not done much since I arrived. I look forward to meeting with your husband tomorrow. I have to tell you, I was surprised to hear from you this morning."

"I was eager to meet you alone first." Kimberly's confidence grew as his smile widened.

"Is it too early to ask what you are up to?" he asked.

"That depends. How much of a sport are you?"

"Not a good one I am afraid. That is, unless there is something in it for me." His voice was smooth like a man used to little resistance. "I was surprised to get a call from your husband. It is such an unlikely pairing. It is not something I would be interested in at all."

"Then why did you come?" she asked. "A free trip to L.A.?"

"You know why I came," he said softly.

"You want to see her, don't you?" Kimberly was so excited, she gripped the arms of her chair. He understood everything.

"Of course I do." Paul smiled as if remembering fondly. "I've always thought of it."

"Why haven't you?" she asked. "I mean, before now."

Paul's confident smile faded and there was distinct emotion on his face. "It didn't end well."

"Would you like a chance to rectify that?" Kimberly sensed there might be true affection there, and she wasn't sure that was a good thing.

Paul looked down at the glass of wine in his hand. "I don't . . . I don't think that's possible. It's been more than thirty years and her marriage appears strong, from what I've read."

Kimberly leaned forward. "I need you to understand that this is between you and me. My husband isn't a part of it."

"Do you think that is wise?"

"It's necessary." She sat back.

"You know my next question."

"Patience." She waited until the waiter had placed Paul's plate in front of him and left. "I need to know I can count on you."

"Why do you want me to seduce Janet?"

"I need her distracted," Kimberly said. "It's complicated."

"Not really." He looked her up and down. "I think it's easy to imagine what the problem is, but I don't care to hurt her."

"I don't need you to," Kimberly said. "As a matter of fact, I'd prefer you make her very happy. What I really need is for you to stick around."

"What about her husband? Steven Chase is a formidable man, and I doubt he will appreciate his wife's ex-lover coming around."

Kimberly laughed. "Now, Paul, I wouldn't put you out there like that. He knows nothing about you, the affair, the . . . abortion."

Paul's smiled faded as he set down his glass of wine. "How could you possibly . . ."

"It's not important how I know. It's only important you understand that Steven knows nothing. You have to keep your past hidden from him."

"It is not a wise choice to surprise a powerful man."

"Steven is powerful, but you'll be going back to Paris when this is over, and he doesn't have any power in that world. Besides, you won't be the problem. She will."

"I think you underestimate her."

"I think you underestimate me."

"That may be true." Paul no longer seemed to be enjoying himself as he circled the top of his glass with his finger. "Still, I must be protected."

Kimberly reached into her purse and pulled out a check. She slid it across the table. "This is a start. Now let's talk about what I need you to do."

Avery felt the warm tingling sensation tickle her body from head to toe as she heard Carter coming up behind her.

This weekend had been a godsend. Although she knew the family had sold its home in the Vineyard years ago, she wasn't aware they had a place in Sag Harbor in the Hamptons. When Carter suggested they spend a four-day weekend there, it was just what she needed. And beside a few calls to his office, she'd had him all to herself.

It seemed trivial that she was feeling so sorry for herself. Here she was sitting on a cushioned chair in the backyard of a beautiful eighty-year-old home looking out over Long Island Sound with her rich, gorgeous fiancé, who had made love to her for two hours the night before.

"I have something for you." Carter sat on the chair next to hers with both hands behind his back.

Avery sat up eagerly, wondering what was going on. Carter was a generous man, but yesterday it had been an eighteen-karat gold mesh bracelet with round brilliant diamonds set in platinum. Two days before they'd left L.A. it was a pair of Tiffany rose pearl earrings.

"Are you trying to apologize for something?"

Carter smiled, not showing a hint of the anxiety he'd been feeling since the close call at the engagement party. "Aren't I always?"

"Lay it on me, Daddy." She held her hand out.

He slapped two small sheets of paper in her hand. "You decide."

Avery frowned when she realized what she was holding. "Carter, please."

"An art gallery exhibit in Hampton Bays or a benefit for ovarian cancer at the Sag Harbor Yacht Club."

"What happened to 'yeah, baby, it'll just be me and you'?"

"Do you know how many events I've turned down? There are about four parties a day out here this time of year."

"I thought no one was supposed to know we were even here."

"They intended to invite the Stathams but found us."

The Stathams had been renting the house for the past three seasons but had a family emergency in Pennsylvania keeping them away this summer.

"So they don't really want *us*," Avery said.

"They would actually prefer us." Carter stuck out his lower lip in a pout. "Trust me, it will get back to Mother that someone was out here and didn't show up for anything."

"I know." She waved the cancer-benefit invitation. "But I don't have a formal."

"Not necessary." He pointed to the "Hamptons casual" written in bright red at the bottom of the card. "You're set, baby girl."

She took a deep breath, looking out at the bay. "I just love it right here. It's so peaceful."

"We can buy a place," he offered. Anything to make her happy. Anything to make her not want to leave her life with him. "Our own place."

"I would like that." She warmed at the thought of inviting her parents here for a summer vacation, walking along the bay with her mother.

Carter said, "I think I know a place. An old friend has a place in East Hampton. She's trying to sell it."

"She?" Avery asked suspiciously. "Another ex?"

"Are you serious?"

Avery laughed, pretending like she wasn't. "I . . . I'm sorry."

"Come here." Carter opened his arms as Avery moved in to him. He held her tightly, knowing what it took to make her happy. Avery liked feeling safe. "You don't have anything to worry about, you know that."

"I trust you, baby. I just . . ." She felt ashamed of her suspicious thoughts. "I just feel like there is this whole part of you that I don't know about, and I don't see how we can really be married and have these voids."

"She is a friend of the family," Carter said. "Well on the wrong side of sixty."

Avery laughed, slapping him in the chest. "I'm being very serious."

"So am I." He leaned down, kissing her on the forehead. "The mistakes I've made in my past, I don't need you to know about. I don't need you to know that part of me."

Avery leaned away, looking up at him. Sometimes she wished he wasn't so disturbingly handsome. "I want every part of you. Your past doesn't make a difference to me. I'll still want to love you, take care of you, make you happy forever."

Carter knew she meant every word. There was no way he could lose this woman. "What do you want to know?"

"Laura." She observed him rolling his eyes. "You asked the question."

Despite his better judgment, Carter sucked it up and told her the truth about Laura, a woman who had pretended to be something she wasn't. When he'd found out she was just on the prowl for a rich husband, he'd dumped her and that was when the crazy came out. She stalked him, harassed the other women he dated and generally tried to make his life miserable.

"I just had to take care of it."

Avery wasn't satisfied. "What does that mean? I heard—"

"You shouldn't have been eavesdropping on us, Avery."

"I know. It's just that I . . . Who is Marco, and how did he take care of her?"

"He works security for my family in certain situations. He's like a . . . messenger. My family paid Laura to go away. She signed papers with severe financial penalties if she sets foot in L.A. ever again. Marco went to . . . remind her."

"You can't legally keep someone out of a city." Avery expected Carter to agree, but he just stared. "But he didn't hurt her?"

"I would never do that," Carter said. "I won't lie to you, Avery. I've used money and influence to my advantage in ways that weren't fair, but I'm not a violent person."

"I believe you," Avery said in a clear voice. Unsteadily, she said, "But that day . . . you . . . you and Michael were talking about something else."

Carter wasn't a romantic. Lying to a woman was part of life.

There was so much they didn't understand, so much they didn't want to understand no matter how much they said they did. Telling them the truth all the time only meant disaster.

Avery looked down, poking at the button on his linen shirt. "I thought you were talking about . . . about me."

Carter ran his fingers through her hair. "I was figuring out how to tell you I wanted to go to Koi with Michael. But I'm glad I didn't. What you and I did later that night was much, much better. Against the dresser, on the floor . . ."

Just the memory got her going, and when his lips were on hers, everything else disappeared.

"No matter what," Carter said as their lips separated, "you can trust me, baby. I love you more than I love myself."

As they made love in the breeze of a warm Sag Harbor afternoon, Carter knew he was going to give Lisette whatever she wanted.

"Get me out of these," Haley moaned as she tried to get her concentration back. She wasn't sure what was wrong with her. She had smoked a little weed, but nothing more. Why was she so out of it? "Dammit, Chris."

"I can't find the key." Chris was laughing as he wandered the bedroom of their suite at the Beverly Hills Hotel, his glass of Courvoisier spilling all over the place.

He was looking for the key to the pair of handcuffs holding Haley to the bed, but she figured he was too coked up to think straight. And when he fell down, face flat on the floor, she was beginning to think she might be in trouble.

"Quit messing around, you cokehead." She squeezed her eyes shut to stop the blurring.

She wasn't going to put up with this anymore. He'd been pounding away at her for an hour but was too high to get anything done. It was all a complete waste of time.

"Get these off me now!"

"I see it." He crawled across the floor toward a pile of clothes.

Haley was ready to lose it. This fool was so past his expiration date. Even making Sean jealous wasn't worth this. "If you don't hurry, I'm going to—"

The doorbell to the suite rang and Haley's stomach tightened in panic.

"I'll get that." Chris grabbed the edge of the bed, trying to right himself.

"Don't you dare!" Haley yelled. "Don't you let anyone in while I'm—"

"Hold on." He waved his hand at her before stumbling out of the room. "I know who it is. It's cool."

She didn't have the energy to yell anymore. What she felt, she couldn't describe, but it was as if she had run a marathon in the pouring rain. She wondered exactly what had been in that weed she'd smoked. Or maybe it was the wine. Either way, she was going to kill him.

She heard voices and laughter and was beginning to feel scared. She was naked, handcuffed to the bed and completely helpless. Who was he talking to? What would they do to her?

"Sean," she said his name in almost a whimper. She needed him to help her.

The door slammed and Chris showed up in the archway with a plastic-draped red dress hanging on a wire hanger.

"Are they gone?" Haley asked.

Chris nodded, stumbling toward the bed. "This is for you."

"Boy, I swear if you don't—"

"Oh yeah." Tossing the dress on the bed, he went back to his pants and pulled out a key. "You want this?"

Haley felt homicidal as he waved the key in front of her. "You want to live?"

As he slid next to her, the inebriated expression on his face disappeared. His eyes were dark, his mouth turned down in a threatening frown. "You wear that dress to the club tonight."

"To hell with you." She wasn't wearing any ho-bag slut dress he'd picked out.

Haley's reflexes were slow, so she had no chance to elude his hand as it grabbed at the back of her neck and pulled her toward him.

"You wear the dress," he repeated. "Do what your daddy tells you, little princess."

"You're not my daddy." All she could do was jab him in his side with her knee, but he had no reaction. "Get these off."

"But I am." He let her go and began fumbling with the cuffs. "You said yourself Daddy Chase doesn't care about you. That only leaves me."

"When did I tell you that?" Haley asked.

"Just a few hours ago," he answered with a laugh. "Don't you remember?"

"No, I don't. You put something in my . . ." Finally free, Haley concentrated on rubbing her sore wrists. "My daddy is none of your business."

"And he chooses for you to be none of his," Chris said, "so I'm your daddy."

Mustering all the strength she had, Haley's fist connected hard enough with Chris's jaw to send him flying off the bed and onto the floor.

Standing up, she grabbed the dress and tossed it at him. "You wear it. You make a better bitch than I do."

She could hear him calling her all sorts of names as she slammed the bathroom door behind her. When she turned on the lights, the vision in the mirror, a woman bruised and drugged out, was so foreign it frightened her. Who was this? What happened to the devastatingly beautiful temptress she was?

Haley knew right now she was in one of those moments where you decide to go one way with your life or another. She was familiar with these moments.

"Oh, hell no," she said. And that was that.

Vivian, Steven's executive assistant, was laughing and gossiping with her assistant, Tess, but both women quickly came to attention when Janet entered.

"Mrs. Chase." Vivian sat up straight and painted the most welcoming smile on her face.

"Good morning, Vivian."

"You look absolutely gorgeous," Tess said. "Who are you wearing?"

"Tess." Vivian tried to laugh off her assistant's lack of taste. "With all this fashion line talk, Tess is getting a little too into it."

"Of course." Janet resisted the urge to roll her eyes. "It's Chanel, but I don't care to discuss the fashion line."

"Of course." Vivian was looking at her computer with a frown. "Dropping by for a hello? He's just finished a meeting and he'll be off to lunch."

"I'm here for lunch," Janet said. "I'm not too early, am I?"

"You're joining them?" Vivian reached for the phone. "I only made reservations for three at Gardens. I'll have to change it."

"Maya told me the office had called and asked me to come here for lunch with Steven," Janet said, certain she wasn't forgetting. She had a lot on her plate, but Maya's message seemed clear.

"Did you?" Vivian looked at Tess, who promptly shook her head and shrugged her shoulders. "I'm so sorry. I don't know what happened. I didn't call you at all."

"Well, what is going on?" Janet asked impatiently. "Where is he now?"

"He's in there, but he has a meeting and—"

They all heard a round of laughter on the other side of the door.

"Sounds like the meeting is over," Janet said as she made her way to the door. "I'll handle this."

When Janet entered the office without knocking, everyone in the room turned to her. Steven was sitting at his desk with Michael sitting across from him and Kimberly on the sofa against the wall. Although both men looked pleasantly confused, Kimberly was smiling ear to ear.

"What are you doing here, honey?" Steven quickly got up from his chair and made his way to his wife.

She tilted her head so he could kiss her cheek. Kimberly's smile told her immediately something was up. "Did you ask me to lunch?"

"No," Steven said. "But you're welcome to join us."

Michael stood up, not certain this was a good idea. What was his father thinking? "Well, we're talking business and I know you don't care to hear that, Mom."

"What business?" she asked.

"Fashion business," Kimberly offered. "But of course you can join."

"I know I can," Janet said. "I'm just wondering who left that message for me."

"What message?" Steven asked.

Before Janet could answer, she heard the toilet flush in Steven's private bathroom.

"We're interviewing a designer," Michael said in response to his mother's curiosity.

"You have to meet him." Kimberly stood up as the door opened. If only she had a camera. "He's great."

When Paul exited the bathroom, he had eyes only for Kimberly, but when he turned to the others, the image of Janet clearly stole his attention.

He played it perfectly and Kimberly was very proud. He didn't even blink. Janet, on the other hand, played it better than Kimberly would have wished. Her eyes widened and her mouth opened slightly as if she would have gasped if she was a woman less used to surprises of a scandalous nature.

Steven offered introductions. "Dear, this is Paul Devereaux. He works under the Gaultier label in Paris. Mr. Devereaux, this is my wife, Janet Chase."

Janet could barely stand as every emotion known to man assailed her at once. How could this be? How could . . . She immediately composed herself as Paul offered his hand to her. She was afraid to touch him.

"How lovely," Paul said. "Mr. Chase is rich in many more ways than money."

"Thank you." Janet's voice was like a wilting flower, void of the usual social mastery. He appeared intent to pretend as if they didn't know each other, but she knew he remembered her. "It's very nice to meet you, Mr. Devereaux."

Their handshake was quick and brief, obviously cold to

everyone around them. Kimberly saw her chance and stepped up to the group.

"You don't remember him, Janet?" Kimberly's eyes pierced into Janet's unsteady glance. "Paul told me that he knew you in Paris years ago."

"It was so long ago," Paul said. "You probably don't remember."

"You went to design school," Kimberly offered. "Paul was a teacher there."

It suddenly hit Janet what Kimberly was doing and for the first time in seven years, Janet was afraid of her. "Well . . . I . . . I think I . . . Yes. Paul, how nice to see you again."

Kimberly's eyes darted to Steven and she saw him blink with a confused frown. It was only a split second, but she got what she wanted. Steven had noticed Janet's slip of memory and how she didn't play it well at all. He wiped it away just as quickly, but it was planted and Kimberly would water it when the time was right.

"When was this?" Steven asked.

"More than thirty years ago," Paul said. "I don't think we really knew each other. Of course your last name was different. I just would never forget such a beautiful woman."

"Please stop." Janet smiled. "You're embarrassing me."

Kimberly had to laugh at that. She had no idea just how much.

"You can't be old enough," Steven said.

"I was only a student teacher. Not the real teacher."

"Small world." Michael glanced at his watch. "We should make our way to Gardens. The drive will be hell."

"My wife will be joining us." Steven wasn't appreciating the way Paul was looking at Janet, but he was used to men admiring her beauty and unattainability.

"Even better," Paul said as he grabbed his jacket from the back of the chair.

Janet took hold of her husband's arm, hoping her knees wouldn't give out on her as he led her out of the office. She prayed to God for coincidences, but even as she said "amen," she knew better.

Kimberly was stone-faced as Janet looked back at her quickly before turning the corner out of the office. Reaching back, Kimberly grabbed her purse and when she turned around, she was face to face with her husband. He had that look.

"I'd ask you what you were up to," Michael said, "but you'd lie, wouldn't you?"

Kimberly wrapped her arm around his waist as her body rubbed against his. "What's wrong, Daddy?"

"Why are you being nice to Mom?"

"I don't want Paul to know about the family strife," she explained. "He's already very on the fence. I want this to work."

"How do you know about him and Mom?"

"He told me. We had lunch yesterday." She circled around him. "Now let's go. They're waiting."

Michael reached out and pulled her back to him. "Lunch? Yesterday?"

"We'll talk about it later." She took his hand in hers and squeezed.

Michael let it go because he wasn't in the mood for an argument. Kimberly's ecstatic mood meant great sex, less stress and no fighting. He just wanted her to be happy about this as long as possible.

CHAPTER 13

Avery reached for her briefcase in the back of the driven town car, expecting to get out in only a second, but was surprised as the driver kept going.

"Will, where are you going?" she asked.

"I have to drop you off around the front," he answered. "There's construction starting this week. It's too dirty back there."

"I don't mind." Avery did mind getting dirty, but she preferred not to be seen when she was dropped off at Chase Beauty's offices.

It was Carter's idea she use a personal driver so she could avoid the stress of driving in L.A. traffic and get work done in the process. It was a convenient luxury that she admitted she enjoyed. Having just driven from a meeting with the new manager of the newest Chase Expressions salons in Long Beach, she felt it was the perfect time to catch up on her messages.

This didn't mean she wanted anyone to know about it. For that reason, she asked her driver to drop her off at the back entrance of the building, near the garage.

"I was talking about me." Will laughed. "It's too dirty for this pretty car."

"Okay." Avery gripped her briefcase, feeling ridiculous for

being ashamed. Anyone in their right mind would make this choice if they had it.

Her life was going to change. It was already changing and she had to stop feeling guilty about it. So what if a few people saw her step out of a driven car? She had to stop caring what other people thought or whispered about her.

"Now what do we have here?" Will asked as he slowed to the curb.

Avery's stomach tightened as she saw the group of people in front of the building. She couldn't read all the signs, but she could see one that said BETRAYING YOUR OWN.

"What's going on?" She reached for her cell phone. "Are they protesting?"

"It looks like it." Will came to a full stop.

Avery watched as her arrival got the attention of several people. She was grateful that Vivian quickly answered. "Vivian, I need to talk to Steven. There are protestors outside."

Vivian informed her Steven was at lunch with Michael and had been told. She encouraged Avery to go around the back but put her on hold before Avery could explain why she couldn't.

"Do you want to drive around?" Will asked.

"I . . ."

"The cop is waving me on, Ms. Jackson. I can't stay here. If you're afraid, I can—"

"No." Avery reached for the door handle. "I can handle it."

When she stepped out of the car with tinted windows, a few curious looks turned into excitement. She saw the local media enough now that she was with Carter, but these people noticed her because many of them worked for her as managers at Chase Expressions or were regular customers.

Seeing Janice Wells, an old friend and now the manager of what used to be one of Avery's own salons, Avery headed for her. Within a few feet of Janice, she was caught off guard by the angry voices directed at her.

"Stop the price hikes!"

"Keep your promises!"

"Janice." Avery approached. "What's going on?"

"What does it look like?" Janice was a young, cinnamon brown–colored, full-figured woman with large black eyes and a brunette weave that went down to her breasts. "We're protesting the price hikes. You guys have gone too far this time."

Avery had to raise her voice to be heard above the yelling. "Janice, you know I'm on your side."

"So you say." Janice took a step back as if she didn't want to be seen too close to Avery. "You said this was going to be a high-class salon chain at neighborhood prices, but this latest hike forces us to raise prices to the same or higher than most L.A. salons. Actions speak louder than words, Avery."

"Ms. Jackson!" A young woman with reddish-blond hair and dressed in a short power suit approached with a miniature microphone. "What do you have to say to the protestors? They accuse Chase Beauty of lying to the black community to get their service and hiking up the prices."

Avery tried desperately to remember everything Carter had told her about dealing with the press but could recall only his warning not to talk to them, no matter what.

"I don't have anything to say," Avery said.

"So now even the words are gone," Janice said accusingly.

Avery looked at her, unable to hide the hurt she felt at Janice's betrayed tone of voice. "Janice, this isn't the answer to our problems."

"Can you speak up?" the reporter asked as she scooted closer.

"I'm not talking to you." Avery caught her own tone before it took too harsh a turn.

"You've changed, Avery." Janice was shaking her head, disappointed. "I guess you're one of them now."

"Janice, I—"

"Is that true?" the reporter asked, her voice carrying above the crowd. "Have you lost touch with the community now that you're in the Chase fold? Are you on the side of the rich now?"

"Don't say a word, Avery." Vivian barreled through the crowd with authority, grabbing Avery by the arm. "Come inside."

As she was being led into the building, Avery turned to look back at the crowd and it stuck in her gut that the once familiar, friendly faces all were directing anger and betrayal at her. It made her want to cry.

"He's not getting away with it," Avery said as soon as they were safely in the building.

"Don't threaten Steven," Vivian warned. "He's made up his mind about this, and that is that. Ultimately, they'll come around."

"At what cost?" Avery asked. "I thought this family was so concerned with PR and image. They don't care now?"

"Who is this *they* you're referring to?" Vivian asked.

"The Chase family."

Vivian smiled. "That's you, honey."

Avery opened her mouth to protest but found nothing to say.

"You coming?" Vivian asked as she stood in the elevator door.

"I'll be up in a second." Avery flipped open her phone. "I have to make a call."

Carter's sympathetic ear had Avery crying within seconds of relaying her experience to him.

"Just quit, Avery. It's not worth it."

Avery leaned against the glass wall in a private hallway, wiping her eyes. "Just give up? That can't be what you think I should do."

"What's your alternative?" he asked. "Going up against Dad again and again? I love you, baby, but you'll lose. So would I. No one beats him."

"So I just let him get away with this?"

"He'll get away with it whether you let him or not," Carter said. "Just leave there now and come to my office. We'll talk about it."

"It's wrong," Avery said. "What will it look like if I back out on all of them after I promised to fight for what we agreed to?"

"It won't look any different if you stay." Carter sighed. "You don't understand. You're in a different world than them. They've figured it out; you haven't."

This made Avery profoundly sad because she knew it was true.

"You have to stop thinking like they do, Avery. You're smarter than that."

Avery's anger overtook her sadness. "You're insulting me, Carter."

"I'm not," he said. "It's just a fact that—"

"No one can win against the Chases," she finished sarcastically. "Well, maybe it's time that long-held truth changed."

As she leaned into the mirror of the elegant bathroom at Gardens, Kimberly took her time applying her makeup. She didn't expect to wait long after she excused herself from the table. And she didn't have to.

Janet recognized the smirk on Kimberly's face the second she entered. It was the same one she'd had all during lunch. Janet was going to smack it off and then some.

"What do you . . ." Janet took a second to glance toward the stalls.

"Don't worry," Kimberly said. "It's just you and me—for now, at least, so make it quick."

"What do you think you're doing?" Janet slammed her purse onto the counter.

"I'm reapplying my lipstick," she answered. "I know you're old, but you're not blind yet."

"How did you know about me and Paul?"

"Is there a you and Paul?" Kimberly asked. "I got the impression that you barely knew each other. That's why you didn't recognize him at first, isn't it?"

"Cut the bull." Janet stepped to within inches of Kimberly, but she didn't flinch. "I know you're up to something, so give it up."

"Give what up?" Kimberly only smiled, making sure to keep a calm voice. "Is there something you're hiding from me?"

Janet leaned back. "Do you think I've been hard on you all these years? It's nothing compared to what I'll do if you—"

"If I what?" Kimberly asked. "Does this have something to do with your past with Paul? Would that explain why he was so eager to come here?"

"I assume he told you about us."

"That he knew you," she said. "That he remembered you and he'd followed you over the years."

Janet softened at the thought. Not everything about her memory of that summer made her sick with regret.

Kimberly tilted her head to the side. "Aww, you seem touched."

Janet's expression turned stone cold. "Whatever you planned, not only will it not work, but I'm going to bury you in the dirt for even trying."

"But there's more," Kimberly said. "Isn't there? I mean, the way he was looking at you. The way you're acting now. I only hope that if it's scandalous, Steven doesn't find out."

Janet waited for Kimberly to leave the bathroom before breathing again. She turned to the mirror, seeing the beautiful, composed woman she always projected to the world. No matter what, she held her chin high. She was Janet Chase, and everything would eventually work out in her favor. Eventually everything did.

All Janet had to do was make sure that Paul was on her side. The pain that centered on their breakup was more than she was able to deal with right now, but she would come up with something. And after she did, she would obliterate that ghetto trash off the face of this earth.

But first she needed help. She needed help to keep her mind about her, help to stay calm and not let her emotions take over. Help not to remember the awful decision she'd made in Paris more than thirty years ago that she regretted deeply to this day. Help not to panic when she thought of Steven knowing about her lies.

"Hello, Dr. Knots."

"Janet Chase?" Dr. Knots's German accent always sounded short on the phone. "It's been a while."

"Yes, Doctor." Janet kept her eye on the bathroom door. "I need your help."

"Is something wrong?" he asked.

"My Valium," she said. "I need another prescription."

"Well . . . if you come in, I can take a look at you and—"

"I don't have time for that," Janet said. "I've always been able to count on you, Doctor. I need to be able to count on you now."

After a short silence he said, "Of course you can count on me, Mrs. Chase. Please come by tomorrow."

It was just one pill she needed, Janet assured herself as she returned from the ladies' room of the family's country club to rejoin Avery and Nikki. No one would even notice. Besides, she was still taking the Welbutrin, so she wouldn't look too relaxed. She needed them both with everything that was going on. In addition to her own very real problems, which were substantial enough, there was the museum ball and trying to keep some sense of class in these wedding plans.

She couldn't sleep at night thinking of Leigh still in Nepal facing God only knew what. When she did get some sleep, she had nightmares of that afternoon more than thirty years ago in the doctor's office and Steven finding out about her past with Paul. She was on edge, trying to anticipate Kimberly's next move, even though she felt somewhat confident she could handle Paul.

Then there were little scenes like this. Watching Nikki and Avery laugh and rub shoulders on the sofa in the country club's lounge area made her downright jealous. That closeness and tenderness was out of the question with Haley, but she'd shared it with Leigh once. Would she ever be able to again? Nikki and Avery's friendship was so real, tangible and pure. There was complete trust and unconditional love—the way a mother-daughter relationship should be. They would never be able to do without each other.

"What did I miss?" Janet asked as she sat down.

"Just an inside joke," Avery said, "about a ghetto wedding some cousins of ours had in Detroit."

Janet painted a smile. "How charming."

"It was one of the funnest events I've ever been to," Nikki said honestly and proudly.

Avery was still laughing. "It was fun, wasn't it? Just gettin' down without any pretentions. I had a ball."

"Don't worry, Janet." Nikki could see the woman's eyes widening. "We won't have any of that fun stuff at this wedding."

Janet cleared her throat. "I get the joke, Nikki. Of course I don't want the wedding to be pretentious and I do want everyone to have fun. That's what weddings are for. I would just beg you to reconsider the church. Every good family gets married at—"

"We've already decided on View Park Baptist Church," Avery interjected. "It's a compromise since the reception will be at the Four Seasons, where you wanted."

"It's bigger than our family church," Nikki said, "but it's still Baptist. It won't fit four hundred, but not that many will come to the wedding anyway."

"But they will," Janet argued. "I know how these society weddings are. They want to see the church, the decorations, the bridal party—all of it."

"We'll fit who we can," Avery said. "Be happy, Janet. You won on the reception."

"You're aware," Janet said, "that the only reason we could get the Four Seasons on this date is because of—"

"Your name," Nikki finished for her. "We know and we appreciate it. Can we move on?"

Janet took a deep breath, beginning to feel relaxed. "Go right ahead."

Avery collected the wedding planner book from the table. "Next let's talk about—"

"What did I miss?" Kimberly asked as she rushed over to them.

She had been gone for only a short time to check on the twins, who were attending the birthday party of a major studio executive's daughter near the kids' pool.

Janet felt nauseous at the sight of her, so happy and self-confident. This wouldn't last; it couldn't. "Where are the men?"

"I saw them driving the cart out to the grounds." Kimberly noticed the dip in Janet's eyes. "Are you all right, Janet? You look . . . tired."

Realizing she had been slouching a bit, Janet sat up straight. "I'm fine. Thank you so much for your concern."

Avery felt the chill all around them. "Kimberly, we're going to decide on the table favors."

"This is so much fun," Kimberly said, waving the waiter over. "I never got to do this for my wedding."

"You'll get the chance," Janet said, "for your second wedding."

"Janet." Avery warned, but Janet was already reaching for her ringing cell phone.

"Saved by the bell," Nikki whispered. "Is it always like this?"

"Not always," Avery answered. "Sometimes they just pretend like the other isn't there."

Kimberly laughed.

"Please excuse me," Janet said as she stood. "It's about Leigh. I have to take it."

"Is she all right?" Avery asked, worried.

"We've sent someone to make sure she is." Janet quickly made her way to a private corner.

"What does that mean?" Nikki asked.

"Margarita!" Kimberly barked at the waiter, before turning to Nikki. "It means what you think it means. Its par for the course for this family to have people followed or investigated. No matter where you go, they'll find you and find out what you're doing."

Nikki turned to Avery with a confused frown, but Avery just looked down at the planning book. She didn't want to get into it.

Nikki was angry now. "It's like what Carter did with you when he found out about your partner, Craig, and his money problems."

"She's worried about her daughter," Avery said. "Put yourself in her position."

"No, thank you," Nikki offered with a frown that was quickly replaced with a smile. "Well, look who's here."

Taylor, dressed in white jeans and a barely there satin peach tank, slowly made her way to their section in the lounge. From her expression, anyone could see she was having the time of her life. Country club living was definitely for her.

"Where have you been?" Nikki asked. "That was the longest bathroom trip I've ever heard of."

"I was just looking around." Taylor fell into a plush chair next to Nikki. "This place is incredible. More black folks than I expected. Avery, do you have a membership? 'Cause I need to be up in here on the regular."

"No, you don't," Nikki said. "These are not our values, Taylor."

"What values would that be?" Taylor asked. "Having fun? Relaxing?"

"It's not all bad," Kimberly said. "As a matter of fact, I'm going to hold a press conference here when I announce my fashion line."

"So they're true!" Taylor slid her chair closer to Kimberly, having tried her best not to blurt out that she thought she was about the most beautiful woman she'd ever seen. "The rumors about a Chase fashion line?"

"You'd better believe it." Kimberly wished Janet could be here to witness her gloat. "It's going to change everything."

"Can I model?"

"Wait a second." Nikki held up her hand. "We've been through this. You are going to—"

"Mom." Taylor spoke through gritted teeth. "Don't embarrass me, okay? I'm just asking."

"We won't have a line until next summer," Kimberly said, looking her over. "So I wouldn't have anything for you now, but you do have a look."

"Will it be in New York?" Taylor asked.

"New York?" Nikki clearly was getting upset. "No one is moving to—"

"Don't worry, Mrs. Jackson." Kimberly reached for the mommy beeper given to her by the club day-care center. "Everything Chase is based in L.A., but we'll have to spend a lot of time in New York. That's just the reality."

"Sounds exciting," Taylor said. "Besides, it's the summer, so it won't interfere with school . . ."

"That's the party." Kimberly stood. "I have to go see what they want. One of the boys has probably broken something expensive."

"Can I come with you?" Taylor jumped up with beaming eagerness on her face. "I want to hear more."

"What about us?" Nikki asked. "We're here to plan the wedding."

Taylor waved goodbye as she was already trailing Kimberly to the elevators.

"She isn't serious, is she?" Nikki asked.

"You know how much she wants to be a model," Avery answered, flipping to the next page in the planner. "Carter thinks we should have something like a—"

Nikki reached over and closed the book. "I won't have this, Avery."

"What are you telling me for?" Avery asked. "I don't have anything to do with that."

"I'm already losing one daughter to this family. I won't lose another one."

Avery blinked, showing the pain her mother's words caused her. "Mom, you'll never, ever lose me."

"You know what I mean."

"I know exactly what you mean and I'm telling you, you haven't lost me."

"What about Taylor? It's bad enough she wants to model, but for her to get caught up with the Chase family . . . Can't any of you just keep away from them?"

"Stop, Mom." Avery rubbed her arm reassuringly. "You know how flighty Taylor is. Who even knows what she'll want next summer. I'll keep an eye on her. I'll protect her."

Nikki's brows centered as she somberly asked, "But who will protect you?"

"Dad," Michael pleaded, "can we just play golf and not do this?"

Steven stopped discussing a supplier contract with Carter and turned to Michael. "It's too difficult to get in touch with this boy these days. You're avoiding me, right?"

Carter didn't want to start anything. He had enough on his plate. "I've been busy."

"Busy, my ass," Steven said. "I know you've gotten my messages. The way that girl showed me up in front of my—"

Carter slammed his nine-iron into the ground. "Her name is Avery!"

Michael quickly stood between them. "Take it easy. We're at the good country club today. And Dad, everyone was hot about the protestors."

"But only"—Steven leaned in for effect—"*Aaaveeerrry* took it upon herself to yell at me in front of three of my EVPs. No one gets away with talking to me like that."

"You went behind her back," Carter said. "Those salons are her responsibility and you hiked every possible fee more than 10 percent despite telling her you wouldn't."

"I could hit you with this club for even suggesting that I went behind her back," Steven said. "You sound like her. Are you under the impression there is any decision at Chase Beauty that isn't solely mine to make? Besides, I never told her I wouldn't. I told her I would hold off. I was giving you time to do your job and get her to quit."

"I never agreed to that." Carter practiced his swing.

"I didn't ask you to agree to it," Steven said. "I told you to make it happen."

"In other words, you ordered me, right?" Carter pitched long with a full swing but turned to his father instead of watching his own ball. "How's that method working out for you?"

Seeing the tension between the two men as Steven looked ready to knock his nine-iron against Carter's head, Michael felt silly for ever feeling he might lose his place in the pecking order. So Avery was good for something after all.

"Carter, you and I agreed about Avery," Michael said. "Dad is right."

"I never agreed to make her quit." Carter stepped aside as his father came to the tee. "There are other things I'm dealing with right now."

"That's too bad." Steven swung and leaned back as he watched his ball land on the green closer to the hole than Carter's. "Because I'm going to fire her."

"No, you're not." Carter stuffed his club into the bag and went to his father. "Dad, I swear to you if you fire Avery, I'll—"

"What?" Steven laughed. "Remember who you're talking to, boy."

"She's going to be my wife!"

"I'm happy for you." Steven nodded Michael over for his turn. "But that's got nothing to do with how I run my business. No one gets away with cursing me out in front of other employees. If it had been in private, it might be another thing. But she's going to go, and that's all there is to it."

Michael purposefully walked between them on his way to the tee. "If you guys throw down, people will see you."

"There's no need for violence," Steven said. "What's done is done. It isn't as if Carter can change my mind."

"You think she's a mouse, don't you?" Carter asked. "You think she'll put her tail between her legs and run off."

"Trust me," Steven answered, "after the things she said to me last Wednesday, I don't think that at all. I have cause and you and I both know she won't take legal action. She is going to be your wife, and you won't let her."

"I don't control what she does," Carter said.

"That's your problem," Steven said back. "You don't control a damn thing about her."

After the men stared each other down for a few seconds, Carter blinked and said, "Well, it was fun while it lasted."

Steven knew exactly what he was referring to, and it genuinely hurt him. "This doesn't have to be about you and me."

"Anything about my future wife is about me." Carter slid into the front seat of the golf cart.

"Well, that's too bad." Steven took a seat behind him. "Let's move on. People are waiting."

Michael looked from Carter to his father. "Is that it?"

"Apparently," Steven said. "Let's go."

"Dammit, Dad!" Carter turned to face his completely unaffected father. "You can't do this!"

"I can do anything I want." Steven leaned forward, pointing his finger. "I got into this for you, remember? I've put up with this for you. You got what you wanted. Now it's over."

Michael sat in the driver's seat.

"Two weeks," was all Carter said as he gritted his teeth.

After a short silence, Steven sighed before nodding his head. "Two weeks."

Carter turned to Michael. "Just go."

As he drove, Michael waited until their father was talking on his cell phone to say anything, keeping his voice low. "You just have to take the balls you use to stand up to him and use them with her."

"I'm not going to bully my wife," Carter said. "I'll figure out something. I still might just tell her the truth."

Michael laughed. "I wouldn't recommend it."

"No offense, bro, but I don't want your marriage."

Michael turned to him. "What the hell does that mean?"

"I don't want to control my wife. I don't want to handle her so that she's dependent on me, kept away from anything that might make her want more than I want her to have."

"Ouch." Michael brushed it off. "You just make sure you can make her your wife before you start preaching about how you're going to treat her. You still have Lisette to worry about."

"Not anymore," Carter said. "I called her. I'm going to pay her."

Michael shook his head. "Five?"

"I negotiated it down to three."

"She'll come back for the other two at the wedding reception."

"She's not coming back," Carter said. "I'm making sure of that."

"You can't make sure of anything with crazy bitches. They just don't care."

"Just shut up and drive," Carter ordered.

"Did one of you say crazy bitch?" Steven asked as he got off the phone.

"No," both men answered in unison.

Haley was just beginning to enjoy herself in the VIP section at the Bali-inspired nightclub Mood when Tia nudged her, almost making her martini spill all over her Rocawear tube tunic.

"What's your problem?"

Tia nodded her head in the direction of another VIP section. "Isn't that your brother?"

Haley made a face noting her displeasure. "I can't escape them, I guess."

"His wife is so incredible-looking."

"'Incredible-looking'?" Haley asked. "I don't think that's proper English."

Tia snapped her fingers. "Sounds like you're jealous."

"Please," Haley said. "I could never be jealous of anyone unfortunate enough to be dragged into my family. Let me go say hello before they come over here and embarrass me."

When she approached, Haley stood above Michael and Kimberly as they made out like horny teenagers. Realizing she was basically invisible to them both, she grabbed an ottoman footrest and slid it up to them.

"You do have to breathe at some point," she said, finally getting their attention.

"Hey, girl!" Michael leaned forward and slapped Haley on the thigh. "What are you doing here? I thought your joint was at Pearl."

"Old news," Haley said.

"That was fast," Kimberly said, "even for you."

"It was out of my hands." Haley shrugged with a smile.

"You want to hang with us?" Michael asked.

"You're joking, right?" Haley asked. "I'm with friends. I just came over here to make a request."

"Anything for the little princess," Michael said.

"Since we're related and people recognize us, can you please not have intercourse in public?"

Both Kimberly and Michael laughed as they turned to each other and resumed making out. Rolling her eyes, Haley stood up to leave but came face-to-face with Taylor.

"Hi," Taylor said, not bothering to hide her lack of enthusiasm at the sight of the crazy one.

"How did you get in?" Haley asked.

"She's with us," Kimberly said. "I invited her. She's going to be one of my models."

Haley felt ill. Why was everyone so eager to pull the Jacksons under the Chase family umbrella? "You mean for the fashion line Mom says is going to happen over her dead body?"

"Hopefully." Kimberly shielded herself from Michael's threatening fist as they both laughed.

"Don't start anything, Haley," Michael warned.

"You lucked out," Haley told Taylor. "That social ladder is turning into more of an express elevator for you."

"At least I'm trying to work," Taylor said, "not sitting on my ass being a psychotic pain in the neck to everyone I cross paths with."

"Only because you don't have that option," Haley admonished.

Taylor contemplated the consequences of slapping her right at that moment. There were too many cons, but she knew it would have felt so good.

"Haley," Michael called out, "here comes your old news."

Haley looked past Taylor and felt a brick in her stomach at the sight of Chris walking toward her. She had to give it to him; the man was picture-perfect on the outside. Who would know he was a drug addict freak?

"Surprised to see you here," Chris said. "You're looking good for someone too sick to answer the phone."

"I never said I was sick," Haley said. "I just told my maid I wasn't taking your calls. She makes up whatever lie she wants. If you were smart you would have caught on by now."

"You don't have to worry about me, sweetheart." He turned to Taylor, looking her up and down rudely. "You are about the finest thing up in here. Your legs are, what, six feet long?"

Taylor smiled, placing her hands on her hips. "You must have just walked in."

"Don't sell yourself short," he said. "You have something."

"Be careful or you'll catch it," Haley said.

Taylor held her hand out to Chris. "I'm Taylor Jackson."

"Nice to meet you, Taylor." Chris took her hand gently in his and with his other, he reached up and gripped her upper arm. "Chris Reman. I know you're a model."

"Please." Haley didn't need to hear any more of this. Did he think he could actually make her jealous? "What are you even doing here?"

"Have to check out the competition," Chris said, keeping his attention on a flattered Taylor. "I have an agency. I just signed a contract with Katalyst. You know who they are?"

"Of course I do."

"I've seen enough," Haley said. "I don't want to go blind, so I'll leave you and your new best friend alone."

Haley expected Chris to call her back, but he didn't, and she was annoyed with herself for giving a damn. No, she didn't want him anymore, but she was damned if she was going to let him hook up with that socialite wannabe.

She fought the urge to turn back and look, knowing how much of a giveaway that was, but she couldn't help it. When she did look back, Taylor and Chris had both sat down and were deep in conversation, with Michael and Kimberly making out behind them.

"I know that is not you-know-who over there," Tia said as soon as Haley returned.

"Just look away," Haley said.

"Who is that girl?"

"Trash," Haley answered. "Nothing more, but much less."

Tia seemed unconvinced as she placed a hand on her hip. "If she's trash, then how did she get into the VIP section? How did she even get into this club?"

"The same way you did." Haley gestured for the waiter to come her way. She needed something much stronger than what she had now.

CHAPTER 14

Janet didn't know whether to scream or faint when Maya entered the kitchen and told her Paul Devereaux was waiting for her in the great room. Her first thought was of Steven, who no doubt was in his office. After taking a Valium, she composed herself and headed out to meet him, all the while wondering whose side he would be on.

As much as it broke her heart to remember the abortion, Janet knew that she and Paul had shared something special that summer. She wasn't young and beautiful like Kimberly, but she had their history to use in her favor.

"Janet." Paul shot up from his seat as she entered, smiling from ear to ear.

She wanted to be happy to see him, wished that she could be. "Paul. How nice of you to come by. Did you have an appointment with my husband?"

Paul's smile faded somewhat. "No, dear, I came to see you."

Janet didn't have time to school him on the etiquette of conducting a single male–married female relationship in high society. She could always say he was gay.

She smiled politely and gestured for him to sit down. When he did, she made certain to sit on the sofa opposite him. "I hope you aren't angry I didn't recognize you immediately at my husband's office."

Paul smiled knowingly. "Actually, I was under the distinct impression that you recognized me immediately."

Janet offered her poker face as she quickly deciphered his expression and tone. "So to what do I owe the pleasure of this visit?"

"I was upset you did not return my call. I even left a message at the Chase Foundation."

"I haven't been there much." Janet at least could be honest about that. "I'm planning the museum ball. I'm heading the committee and we're in the last stages. It's an incredibly important social event. I've been overwhelmed."

"I can see," Paul said. "You look tired. Don't take that the wrong way. You look incredible. As a matter of fact, Janet, it is unbelievable to me how well you have held up."

Janet offered a pleasant laugh. "Well, Paul, I'm rich."

Paul leaned back, nodding with a smile. "That you are."

"If you've come here hoping I'll convince you to sign on to Chase Beauty, you're going to be disappointed."

"I sensed no love lost between you and Kimberly." Paul stood up and hastily made his way to the sofa. "But that is not why I'm here."

Janet's smile faded at the gesture of closeness. "Paul, it really isn't appropriate—"

"How do you live with regret?" he asked.

Janet swallowed hard, trying to hold her feelings at bay. "I can't do this."

"Can't do what?" he asked. "It was more than thirty years ago. Surely you can discuss it now."

Janet looked around, praying that Steven would stay in his office and that Maya was not around. She knew if it came down to it, she could count on Maya's silence, but she didn't want to be in that position.

"The choice I . . ." She took a deep breath and faced him squarely. "The choice *we* made was the only choice possible at the time. I was engaged to Steven and—"

"I was a poor teaching assistant."

"Your finances never played into it. At that time, Steven was just as broke. I had more money than both of you."

"But you loved him." Paul's tone was resigned. "I know you did; you told me."

"I wanted it to be clear," Janet said. "I cared about you, and what I had with you was about feeling free for the last time. I knew Steven would be the only man I would ever love—make love to for the rest of my life."

"I was your summer-long bachelorette party." Paul laughed, halting any protest from Janet. "I just wish it could have been different, don't you?"

"Of course." Janet dug her nails into her palms to keep from letting the tears come. "When I look at my four children, all I can think of is what our baby would have looked like, what it would have become."

"I have no children, Janet." Paul's head dropped and he sighed heavily.

"None?" Janet felt awful for him. Had she been his only chance? "I . . . I'm sorry, Paul."

"I regret that," he said, "but not as much as I regret not try-ing harder with you. I still care for you, Janet. I still—"

"No." Janet slid away from him. "Paul, it's impossible for you to say these things."

"I have to," he said. "That is why I'm here. That is why I have stayed here, because I have to see you, alone. I have to . . ."

Janet leapt from the sofa as she heard Steven's commanding footsteps coming from the marble-floored foyer. She struggled to pull herself together, knowing that he could read her emotions from a mile away.

Paul turned to Steven when he entered, and Steven first no-ticed the expression of emotion on Paul's face.

"Mr. Devereaux, what are you doing here?" Forgoing polite-ness, Steven wasn't interested in playing games in his own home. He hadn't forgotten how this man had admired his wife all during the lunch they'd had together. "We have no busi-ness."

Paul stood up slowly, appearing annoyed at Steven's presence. "No, Mr. Chase. I came to say goodbye to you and, of course, Janet. I am on my way back to Paris."

Janet felt her body release when she realized that Paul wasn't going to make this harder. "Isn't that nice of him, Steven?"

"Wasn't necessary."

"Of course it was," Paul said. "You were so hospitable with the hotel suite and—"

"That was all my son and his wife." Steven made his way to Janet, wrapping his arm possessively around her. "I guess Maya forgot to tell me you were here."

Paul continued to keep a kind face, although he must have gotten the meaning of Steven's gesture. "Well, I don't want to keep you from your evening."

"It was nice of you to come by." Janet was proud of herself. Despite the turmoil raging inside of her, her voice came across as smooth as ever. "Have a safe flight."

"Yes, I can show myself out." Paul nodded a goodbye to Steven before turning to leave the room.

Steven felt Janet's tense body relax in his arms. "Why was he here?"

"He told you." Janet broke free of him and made her way to the bar. "Would you like me to fix you a drink?"

"Cognac." Steven studied her every move. "But why was he *really* here?"

Janet avoided eye contact, pretending to concentrate on the drink she was pouring. "Steven, are you tired?"

"He was upsetting you," Steven said. "Your expression, your posture and your breathing—Janet, I know you."

Janet sighed, placing the glass down. "What do you expect, Steven? Do you want me to ignore that you're allowing Kimberly to invade Chase Beauty? I'm not happy about any of this. I was only being kind because I knew him once."

Steven understood her frustration, but he couldn't tell her he'd already decided against the fashion line. She wouldn't be able to keep her happiness to herself, and it would cause too many problems with Michael.

"He's more than fond of you," he said, accepting the drink. "He had no intention of speaking to me today. You know that."

"Of course I do." Janet rubbed his arm. Even after thirty years, she could distract him with her beauty, and it made her love him more. "You should be proud, not jealous."

"I'm not either," Steven said. "I don't like him and I don't appreciate the fact he would assume so much with you."

"When he knew me I wasn't Janet Chase. I was just another spoiled rich girl."

"But you're not anymore. He should know that and act accordingly."

Janet shrugged. "The French—they have their own way."

"Why do I feel like there's something you're not telling me?"

"What do I know?" Janet asked. "With the ball, the wedding and this terror over Leigh, I haven't had time for anything else, including Frenchmen."

"Leigh is fine. I've taken care of her."

"I won't be happy until she's back in L.A."

Steven walked over to his wife, wrapping his arms around her. "She's very difficult to reach, but I'll try to call her."

"She'll know you're doing it for me and stay just because."

"She's not that spiteful," Steven said, "not anymore, at least. That's more Haley's game."

"Don't mention her name." Janet made a smacking sound with her lips. "She didn't show up for her interview at UCLA."

"Dammit!" Steven let go of Janet. "I've had it with her!"

"Call the provost," Janet urged. "Promise more money. I'm sure you can smooth it out."

Steven was shaking his head angrily. Why bother? She would drop out by the holidays. He was ready to say the hell with it all, but then he looked into Janet's eyes. They were tired and stressed, and he realized how he had neglected her over the past weeks. She was dealing with so much; he knew he had to do whatever it took to make things easier for her.

"I'll call him now." Steven kissed Janet on the forehead. "Then I'll try Leigh again."

As he headed for his office, Janet walked over to the Picasso chaise near the front window. She wanted to forget the past twenty minutes.

Steven would fix this mess with Haley, and Leigh would promise to come home. Now that Paul was returning to Paris, it could be over soon. She thought of regrets, decisions made in Paris that would pain her until her death. There was nothing she could do about that choice; it hadn't really seemed like she'd had choices then. Not telling Steven about that summer was the right thing to do. It would have ruined everything, and enough had been ruined.

It was times like this, when she had to sneak around her own home, that Haley thought seriously about getting her own place. Her parents had it in for her over this school mess. She knew her father was at work, but there was no telling what corner Janet was lying in wait.

It was okay so far. She'd made it downstairs into the back of the house. There was always an occasional hired help for the day lurking around, scaring her half to death, but Haley hadn't even run into any of those.

She saw her way clear to the pool, planning to bask in the sun as long as she could. As she placed her towel on the chair, she looked over at the bar, wishing she could get Maya to make her a drink without her telling Janet she was out there. She would have to do it herself. After tossing the most recent copies of *People*, *Us Weekly* and *In Touch* magazines on the circular glass table next to her, she headed for the bar.

Pouring herself a drink, she sensed movement to her right, and fear quickly squeezed her stomach. Someone had been in the guest house and was coming out. Haley couldn't help but think of the day Rudio had died. She and Sean had been at the pool of the hotel where she supposedly was under heavy security. Rudio's revenge was more about killing her to get back at Steven for trying to ruin him than to prevent her from testifying.

That day, Sean had put a bullet right between Rudio's eyes, and Haley remembered feeling full of rage and satisfaction at the same time.

Haley grabbed the ice pick, ready to use it or whatever else was there until she saw who came out.

"What are you doing here?" Haley yelled.

Taylor closed the door to the guest house behind her, hating Haley for breaking the good mood she was in. "Just looking around. I was invited."

"I doubt that," Haley said.

Why did good things happen to bad people, Taylor asked herself. That guest house was as large as an average house and looked like paradise.

"No one lives there?" Taylor asked.

"It's a guest house," Haley said, "not an apartment."

"I thought maybe Maya—"

"Maya has a wing off the kitchen. You want to invade her personal space as well?"

"It just seems like a waste," Taylor said, "not to have anyone living there. Two bedrooms, huge bathroom, fully furnished with a large-screen TV, DVD player, fully stocked bar, a kitchen and—"

"I know what's in there," Haley said. "What, did you write it down or something?"

Taylor gave up. There was no dealing with this heifer. "It's just nice."

"Of course it's nice," Haley said. "What did you expect? I used to live there, but . . . It didn't work out."

"You mean you messed it up."

"None of your business." Too many hard parties, one silly drunken near-drowning and her father had made her move back into the main house. "You just love seeing how the better half lives, don't you?"

"*Better* is a subjective word," Taylor said. "I'm here with Avery."

"I don't see her anywhere."

"I don't need to be supervised. I'm not the one whose profile in *Angeleno* magazine including getting caught stealing from La Perla. That was you, right?"

Haley was unfazed. "Are you tracking me, Taylor? How stalky of you."

"Me stalking you?" Taylor laughed out loud. "You wrote the book, sister. It was pretty pitiful how you acted last year."

Haley slammed the glass in her hand on the bar and smiled

as Taylor's eyes widened. She was a little scared, and she should be.

"You thought last year was something? I was just practicing with your brother."

"Because he dropped your ass like a hot sack of dirt?" Taylor asked.

Haley contemplated jumping over the bar and tossing her ass into the pool but thought better of it. Her parents were pissed enough at her. "You must have lost your *Social Climbing for Dummies* book."

"I have to admit," Taylor said, "I was pretty envious of you until last year. You came off pretty pitiful after that. And with what Chris tells me—"

Taylor jumped back as Haley came around the bar and started for her. She was within inches of Taylor in a second.

"What did he tell you?" Haley snarled. "That little hood is a liar and a coke fiend. Maybe that's the kind of man you like— leftovers with habits."

Taylor didn't budge, didn't step back. "What does that say about you, Haley? He was a hood and he still didn't want your ass."

"Do you really think he dumped me?" Haley asked. "I mean, I know what guys have to say to keep face, but think about it. You know last Friday night was all about me."

"In your mind I'm sure it was." Taylor's hands came to her hips as she felt her adrenaline pick up. "So why did he keep talking to me for two hours after you left? He's invited me to Pearl next Friday to meet Katalyst."

"You might as well work in the Sears catalog," Haley huffed. "Purely local shit."

"It will do until the Chase fashion line is up and running."

Haley took in Taylor's smug impression. "So you think your little plan is working out real well for you, don't you?"

Taylor only smiled. *Bitch, this is just the beginning.*

"Don't get too excited, darling." Haley leaned in. "'Cause there are some mountains even the best-laid plans can't get you on top of. Especially if someone already on the top doesn't want you up there."

"Taylor!" Avery called from the sliding doors of the Florida room. "We have to go. Come on."

"Go ahead to your plain-Jane sister." Haley waved her away as Taylor turned to leave. "Enjoy all this while you both can."

Avery wasn't going to cry, no matter what. She was done feeling sorry for herself. After all, she'd made her bed when she'd yelled at Steven last week in front of the entire marketing team. It had been the wrong time and place, but he had pushed her too far with what he'd done to the salon chain.

It was all part of a plan, she decided as she came home. They had been neck-and-neck until Carter intervened. What Avery had thought was a truce was really just an attempt to lull her into a sense of security. Then came the right hook. He'd pushed her to the edge and she'd pushed back. Today was just another nail in the coffin.

When she'd come back from a late afternoon meeting with a wedding caterer, Avery knew she wasn't supposed to see Alan Marcell, vice president of product development, leaving Steven's office, from the guilty look on Alan's face. After she'd grilled him for an hour, he confessed that he and Steven were meeting to discuss a line of children's hair conditioning treatments to be sold exclusively at Chase Expressions. He was told specifically not to tell Avery or her staff about it yet.

Steven was starting to exclude her from all important decisions regarding her own business line! Avery's first thought was to explode, but she realized this was what Steven wanted. He wanted to get rid of her and he was going to make her do it for him. No, she had to think. She had to figure out what her next move was going to be. But first, she had to get out of that building before she did something she'd regret.

It was only four in the afternoon, so she expected to be alone for at least another four hours. Despite his promises to spend less time at work, Carter was still coming home past seven on a regular basis. It was okay tonight, she thought.

Avery wasn't looking forward to telling Carter about this. She could see the pain in his eyes when she told him about the strife between her and Steven. She was confident he would pick her side; he'd proven that, but it was still hard on him.

Carter would be home in a few hours and she would feel better when in his strong arms. He would comfort her in that way only he could. Until then, a hot bath and a glass of merlot would have to hold her.

But as she went to the master bedroom, Avery heard a voice, a deep voice coming from somewhere. She thought maybe she had left the bedroom television on, but realized the sound was coming from the opposite direction. There was a television in Carter's office as well, but it was rarely on.

Cautiously, she tiptoed toward the sound, and as she got closer, she realized it wasn't a television. It was Carter. What was he doing home at four in the afternoon? And why did he sound so angry?

"Don't you dare!" Carter yelled into the phone. "You're pushing me farther than you want to take me, woman. We agreed on three. That's it."

Avery stopped outside the office door. She couldn't hear anyone else's voice, so she assumed he was alone and on the phone.

"Don't flatter yourself." His voice was seething with contempt. "I've dealt with women like you all my life. I've always won."

The tone of his voice reminded her of when he'd threatened Laura on the phone. It frightened her.

"No more discussion," Carter dictated. "I'll meet you at the Westin tomorrow at three. I won't wait one second past for you." After a few seconds, he sighed impatiently. "Don't be so sure of yourself, sweetheart. I've got more cards than you think. You know me intimately enough to know better."

Avery didn't want to hear any more. She couldn't think of anything to do but get out of there. As if it would allow her to ignore all of her doubts, she rushed away from the door, grabbed her purse and quietly left the condo.

Outside the building, she was quickly lost in the crowds on the busy sidewalk. She wasn't going to cry; there had been enough crying. There had been enough of everything, including secrets and lies. Avery was tired of being the one left out, the one always guessing. No more staying in the dark. She wasn't going to ask any more questions. She wasn't going to be dependent on explanations that didn't make sense. She was going to find out for herself what was going on, starting with whoever Carter was threatening on the phone.

"Mrs. Chase."

Janet reached into her purse to check her cell phone. It was working. The reception inside the museum was just fine. So why wasn't she getting a call?

"Mrs. Chase."

As she placed her phone back in the purse, she heard the jingling of her pill bottle and was tempted to take some. She was trying to stay clearheaded in the final stages of planning the museum ball, but every second that phone wasn't ringing made her worry.

"Mrs. Chase, please."

Janet snapped out of her trance and turned to Jeannie Hall, the Chase Foundation's newest assistant. "Yes, Jeannie?"

"The chef will be here in ten minutes with the new dessert selection." Jeannie, a petite Irish girl with flaming red hair, bright green eyes and a face full of freckles, glanced nervously down at her clipboard. "You only have fifteen minutes with him before the acoustics man is here."

"It will be fine, Jeannie," Janet assured the girl.

"I . . . Okay." Jeannie frowned, seeming uncertain before walking away.

Janet couldn't stand the wait. According to Steven's sources, Leigh's volunteer stint for Doctors Without Borders had come to an end and she should have been back in the U.S. by eleven last night, but it was already noon and Steven had yet to confirm she was back in the States.

When her phone rang, Janet jumped into action. "Steven?"

"Sorry to disappoint you," was the French-accented response.

"How did you get this number?" Janet asked.

"I know how to get what I want as well as anyone. Janet, I must see you."

"You're in Paris . . ."

"I never left L.A."

Even though there wasn't anyone within earshot, she resorted to whispers. "Why did you stay, Paul?"

"You know why. I want to see you."

"That is out of the question." Her voice took the tone of a scolding mother. "I'm a married woman, a very high-profile married woman who is in love with her husband. I will not see you."

"I do not want to have an affair with you, Janet. Although I find you incredibly beautiful, please understand what I am asking."

"Whatever it is," she answered, "it's too much."

"The pain is still there, Janet. I can hear it in your voice."

"What you're hearing is frustration, Paul. I'm sure Kimberly hoped you and I would rekindle something and put my marriage in jeopardy, but it won't happen."

"What about our child?" he asked.

Janet closed her eyes, feeling the pain at the edges of her temples. "We have no child. If you really cared, you wouldn't have waited more than thirty years to ask."

"Unlike you?"

"I have repented," Janet insisted. "I have prayed and found forgiveness in—"

"There is no such thing as true repentance when you still keep secrets and lies."

"How dare you?" Janet asked. "Don't call me again."

"I will leave if you come see me," he said quickly.

Janet laughed even though she found none of this humorous. "How much has Kimberly paid you? Is she sleeping with you?"

"That is rather crass for a lady of your distinction."

"So now you care about etiquette? You didn't seem to mind when you came to my home while my husband was there."

"This is why I am suggesting you come to me at the Bel-Air instead of us meeting in public." Paul sighed. "I am considering your situation, but I feel this is . . . Janet, I do not intend to leave L.A. until we talk about this uninterrupted."

"There is nothing to . . ." Janet took a moment to calm herself. She needed a pill and she needed it bad. "You regret it. I regret it. That's all that can be said, because it's over and we can't—"

"I will not leave, Janet."

"I'll find out how she's paying you," Janet warned. "When I put a stop to it, I'll bet you'll leave. Whatever you planned simply is not going to work."

"Do you want me to tell you what that plan was?"

Janet wasn't sure how to respond. Was he confessing?

"Come to see me," he insisted, "and I will tell you what it was all about and then I will tell you why I decided not to go along with it once I saw you."

There were some things Janet couldn't resist. She could expose Kimberly and get rid of her for good. "I'll be there at three this afternoon."

"I am—"

"Then," she said forcefully, "you'll leave L.A. for good."

She hung up without waiting for his response. She popped the pill in her mouth after making sure no one was looking, forgoing the glass of water. She could handle this.

"Mrs. Chase!" Over by the caterer's entrance, Jeannie was waving her hands wildly in the air. "The chef is here. Please."

With a deep breath, Janet grabbed her purse and started for the kitchen. She could definitely handle this.

"You're letting her get the best of you," Tia said as she and Haley bypassed the line into Pearl. "You've never done that before."

"I'm just curious," Haley spat back. "This isn't about Taylor."

Neither was it about Chris. Haley knew this was about her own insatiable desire to screw things up for people she didn't like. She found a certain sick satisfaction in knowing she could ruin everything for someone if even for a few moments and get away with it.

"I just think it looks petty." Tia followed Haley diligently, as she always did. "Will you even get in . . ."

There was no need to finish the question as the two men guarding the elevator stepped aside the second they saw Haley approaching. She knew Chris wasn't stupid enough to have her banned.

"Just shut up and do what I told you." Haley checked herself in the mirrored walls of the elevator. She looked incredible, as usual.

Everyone's attention turned her way when she stepped out onto the floor.

"Check it out." Just as Tia lifted her arm to point in Chris's direction, Haley knocked it down.

"Stop acting ignorant." Haley pasted on a fake smile as several girls approached to show the usual fake adoration. "I see them."

Looking without looking like you're looking was an art, and Haley had it down. She could carry on conversations with several different women around her and drink her appletini, while watching Chris present Taylor to Katalyst's representatives as if she was a prize he'd won.

She looked great; Haley would give her that. Actually, she would give the credit to Chris, because she was certain Taylor didn't have the sense of style or money to afford to put together the getup she had on.

Haley was distracting every man in the place, but Chris in particular. She knew he hadn't expected her to come back, and his ego was blowing up. Their eyes met once and Haley didn't blink, but looked away, not too fast or too slow. She wasn't here for him.

It wasn't until one of the many whores who hung on him every night at the club called him away that Haley saw her opportunity.

"Let's go," Haley ordered.

Taylor's stomach tensed at the sight of Haley approaching. She knew something was up once the girl walked into the VIP room. She could only brace herself.

"Taylor." Haley stopped, blew a few air kisses. "You look great. I didn't know Wal-Mart had such a snappy collection."

Before anyone could reply, Haley turned to the man Taylor was talking to. "You must be with Katalyst. I'm Haley Chase. You know my father, Steven Chase."

His small eyes lit up as his once-annoyed expression turned to excitement. He jolted from his seat and thrust his hand forward. "Of course, Ms. Chase. It's nice to meet you."

Taylor felt a little queasy.

"You have a big contract with us," Haley said, finding unforgivable joy at Taylor's stricken expression. "Your models do several of our local beauty salon ads."

"All of them, actually." He gestured for Haley to sit down. "You'll join us, won't—"

Haley shook her head in refusal, tapping at her chin with her index finger. "But your contract is up for renewal in two months, isn't it?"

"We're confident—"

"I wouldn't be if I were you." Haley looked Taylor up and down. "If this is what you're offering . . ."

"Hey!" Taylor wasn't going to stand for this.

Haley stepped back, holding her hands in the air. "I'm just saying. I know what my daddy is looking for."

"Your daddy isn't looking for anything," Taylor said. "It's Avery Jackson you deal with, and she's my sister."

Taylor smiled, looking at Haley as if to say, *your move, bitch*.

Haley's petite nose wrinkled, excited by the challenge. "My father makes the decisions."

"He'll listen to my sister before he'll listen to you," Taylor said. "From what Chris tells me, Daddy doesn't value your opinion for shit."

The man, who had become invisible, jumped out of the way just in time to avoid Haley as she lunged for Taylor. She grabbed her hair first, then part of her shirt, ripping at the sleeve. The crowd quickly made space as the two women screamed and grabbed at each other.

As she pressed her palm against Haley's face, Taylor was hit by a hard left hook. She fell back a few steps, but she wasn't down for the count. Angrier than ever, she lunged for the girl but this time was pulled back.

"Let me go!" Taylor struggled to get out of the grip of whatever giant had grabbed her. Looking up, she could see it was one of the bouncers. "Let me go!"

Haley didn't bother to make any requests to the bouncer who'd taken hold of her. Pulling on her self-defense lessons, she elbowed him in the rib with one arm and kicked him in the groin with her left heel. He moaned and stepped back but never let go.

"Stop." Chris stood between the women, gesturing for both of the men to let go. He zeroed in on Haley. "What do you think you're doing?"

Haley smiled, bruised but victorious. "I'm doing what I do."

Chris, seeming only mildly annoyed, grabbed her by the arm and pulled her aside.

Haley jerked her arm free. "You're not hitting this anymore. Save the rough play for someone else."

"You have a serious hook," he said as he cornered her against the wall. "And I know that personally. You're going to bruise her pretty face."

Haley shrugged carelessly. "I was just making conversation. She's the one who went crazy."

"Please," Chris said. "You and I both know which one of you is crazy, so stop it."

"Your attempts at making me jealous won't work," Haley offered.

"I know this will shock you," he said, "but everything isn't about you."

"So you're telling me you're really interested in that piece of trash?"

"I'm not interested in her for myself," Chris said. "I'm interested in her for . . . Well, she's not for me, but I can use her. I'll keep it at that."

Haley didn't like the smug look on his face. "For modeling? She's got 'amateur' written all over her."

He rolled his eyes. "For a college graduate, you're not too smart. Remember the room I took you to downstairs? My other business?"

"You want her to work in that dump?"

"She can make me a lot of money," Chris said. "The white boys in particular like the dark-skinned girls."

Haley's expression turned to disgust. "You're sick."

"I thought you figured that out a couple months ago." Chris leaned in for a kiss, but Haley put her hand up and pushed his face away.

"Not on your life," she said.

Chris leaned back, winking at her as if he thought this was all part of a game. "Another time, then."

Just as he turned and walked away, Tia approached, looking oblivious.

"That was not the plan."

"Let's go," Haley said.

"I didn't even get to do the part where I congratulate her for entering rehab for her crack—"

"Shut up!" Haley grabbed her by the arm. "Let's go."

Haley didn't ever want to set foot in Pearl again.

Carter returned Lisette's smile with a hard, stone-cold expression as he reached her. Sitting off the hotel lobby in a small area leading to offices behind the front desk, surrounded by dark blue walls, she was waiting for him at the only table there, a circular glass table with two white chairs and a bright lamp.

He looked around before stopping to sit down across from her. With his back to the lobby, he didn't like this at all, but he just wanted to get it over with.

"Let's go somewhere else," he said. "This is too dark. It's too . . . suspicious."

"You're a very publicly engaged man, Carter. How will it look if you're seen in the bright lights of the lobby with me?"

"It won't look as bad as being seen in a dark corner off the lobby with you."

"Always thinking." Lisette nodded approvingly. "You're like your mother in that sense. Always aware of the public."

"Let's just get this over with."

Lisette pulled an envelope out of her purse. "Here are the negatives."

"You mean the ones you were supposed to give me with the pictures you took?"

"A woman on her own has to be more careful than that," she said. "I'm giving them to you now. There are no more."

"There better not be."

"Don't threaten me, Carter. This doesn't have to be—"

"Shut up." Carter reached across the table, grabbing her by the wrist. She gasped as he looked into her eyes. "You've pushed me too far already, Lisette. Don't try and play with me anymore."

Avery was shocked by what she saw. She'd waited across the street from the hotel for Carter to drive up. She had known he would get valet parking and run right in, so she'd had to hurry before she lost him. Entering the lobby, she'd caught him just as he turned in to the dark blue corner. She'd half expected him to go through the doors, but when he stopped at the table it was too late for her to see who was sitting there waiting for him. When he sat down, he was still blocking the woman's face, but Avery could see her outline. Carter was already looking around. She would be too exposed if she stepped out to get a better view.

When he grabbed the woman's wrist, pulling her closer to him, Avery's hand went to her chest. What kind of passion did this woman evoke in Carter that he would act so aggressively? He was a grabby man, but his whole body seemed to show this gesture, and Avery began to fear the worst. She'd hoped hearing his threatening phone conversation meant he was meeting someone he at least hated enough not to be sleeping with, but there was more to this.

Lisette ripped her hand away. "You remember, Carter, you made this situation."

"We had a deal." His jaw clenched, eyes narrowing.

"I wanted another one," she answered with finality. "That's what you Chases do, right? You change things until they're in your favor."

"I'm never going to hear from you again." Carter opened the

envelope with the negatives to check and make sure. "That is a fact that you will take to that cold lead heart of yours."

"Awww, I was hoping to get a wedding invitation." Lisette held out her hand. "After all, you can thank me for not losing her. Hell, you can thank me for getting her in the first place."

"I don't want you back in the States." Carter folded the envelope and stuffed it into his jacket pocket.

"Give me the money."

Carter slid the envelope to her but did not release his grip as she tried to pull it away. He felt no guilt about what he was doing, and that didn't particularly sit well with him. But the truth was, he'd crossed a moral line when he'd started this, and there was no point in trying to step back over it.

"Tell me you understand what accepting this money means."

"I have no more ammunition, Carter. It doesn't mean anything if I—"

"Let me put it another way." As Carter leaned in, he stared into her eyes until she blinked, understanding that he was beyond serious. This was all beyond serious.

"If you don't get out of this country and never come back," he said, "you'll be sorry in ways you never thought you could be."

Lisette swallowed hard but still had fight in her stubborn expression. "I'm not afraid of you."

"You should be," he answered. "But if you aren't, that's okay, because I think your mother will be. You know, the one in Chelsea? The one who takes care of the son you have but tell everyone is your nephew."

Lisette's smooth brown skin turned a shade or two lighter. "How dare you threaten my—"

"You have the nerve to blackmail and extort me and ask how dare I? You knew who you were messing with. You're a stupid little fool if you thought you could just ride off into the sunset."

"I don't want anything else from you, Carter."

"Good." Carter let go of the envelope with the check. "Because if you do, I'll have to tell everyone who your son's very prominent father is. That would create a royal world of trouble for you. Emphasis on the *royal*."

"You're bluffing," Lisette said, although her hand was shaking.

"No, I'm promising. I'm promising you that if I see or hear from you again, I will go after you with everything I've got and everything I am. To say you'll regret it would be the understatement of the year."

Lisette's unsteady gaze lowered to the envelope. She looked as if she wanted to open it but didn't have the necessary control of her hands to do so without giving away her fear. She quickly placed the envelope in her purse.

Carter leaned back with confidence as he watched Lisette slowly stand. Finding the news about the paternity of Lisette's "nephew" was what had caused the delay in paying her off. Carter had needed something better than simple threats. He had to pay a London investigator $100,000 but it was worth it.

"Next time you need money," he said, "go to your kid's father. He's got more than I do."

Lisette was visibly shaken. "That's . . . that's not a . . . an option."

Carter smiled. "You've done well at burning all your bridges, haven't you? What would happen to you if word got out? I'm sure his threats hold much more weight than mine. Maybe I'll—"

"You've got the deal you want, Carter," she said, "but you'll lose in the end, because deep down inside you've got a black heart and you'll pay for it."

"Good thing I'm rich," Carter said nonchalantly. "I can afford to pay for anything. I paid for you, and I'm certain you'll never be a problem for me again."

Avery's knees threatened to give out on her as the woman stood, and a sense of dread swept over Avery. Was she seeing things?

The second she saw Carter sitting across from this woman, Avery thought about Alex and his cheating. She just found it impossible to believe that Carter would betray her like this. But when she saw the same woman who had been in those horrible pictures with Alex, the pictures that had broken her heart, she believed she was hallucinating. She was creating this image in her mind, because it wasn't possible. Was it?

This couldn't be the same woman! Avery closed her eyes, picturing the face in those photos. It had been a little more than eight months ago, but the vision was still very clear, and when she opened her eyes again, just in time to see the woman, clearly off-balance, walk past her, Avery was certain.

She ducked away, not wanting to be seen, even though a part of her wanted to run after the woman, jump on her head and beat her into the ground. Avery was dying to know who she was and what she wanted with her man. It couldn't be a coincidence that she would know both of her fiancés. She fought the helplessness that wanted to tell her some woman she knew nothing about was trying to destroy her life. What was her motive?

Avery's stomach was turning as a sense of foreboding came over her. As Carter stood up, she slid farther away, hiding herself behind a group of about seven businessmen discussing their plans after their conference had ended. It seemed unreal to watch the man she loved only a few feet away from her and be scared to death that he would see her.

Carter didn't have to wait for a valet to drive his car around because it was still in the driveway of the hotel. He grabbed the keys from the doorman, tossed him some money and hopped inside. He was already on his cell phone, waving his hand to match his angry expression. She hated herself for being too spineless to confront him. But she knew she wasn't ready to accept that the man she intended to spend the rest of her life with and be the father of her children was a complete stranger—a stranger being the least of what she feared he might be.

Avery knew whom Carter had been talking to on the phone as he drove away. It was the only person on earth he didn't keep any secrets from: Michael.

A 15,000-square-foot house wasn't too big by L.A. standards, but sometimes Kimberly swore the place was bigger than that. Unable to use the intercom because it would make her too noticeable, she'd spent about half an hour tracking Steven down. She finally found him in the workout room in the back of the house. Spying him on the recumbent bike, she had to rush back

to her room, change into her workout clothes and hope he
would still be there when she got back.

In his usual way, Steven nodded an acknowledgment of her
presence when she entered, but nothing more. In an odd way
Kimberly found his on-and-off affection for her comforting. At
least she knew whom she was dealing with.

"I thought I was alone in this big house," Kimberly said as
she leaned against the elliptical machine. "I could hear my own
echo."

Steven realized she wanted to talk, so he put down his copy
of the *Wall Street Journal*, hoping this wouldn't take too long.
"Where are the boys?"

"At another birthday party in Beverly Hills." Kimberly toyed
with the controls of the elliptical. "It's just amazing, the social
life of six-year-olds. I guess we're alone."

"For a while," Steven said. "I have to run by the country club
and then Janet and I are meeting a business partner for dinner."

"You don't have to keep secrets from me, Steven." Kimberly
flipped her hair back in that way that caught the attention of
every man, including Steven.

Steven took the bait. Kimberly was always pleasant to look
at, and he could find her amusing on occasion. "What secret am
I keeping, dear?"

Kimberly winked. "You're not going to the country club. I
know where you're going. It's the same place you went Tuesday."

Steven knew he'd regret pushing this further, but Kimberly
had a way about her that made him give her a second more than
she deserved. "I was at work all day Tuesday. Then I came
home."

Kimberly gasped just slightly, amused at how easily men,
even men like Steven, were reeled in. "If it wasn't you, then . . .
Oh."

"Kimberly, come out with it." Steven stopped cycling.

"Kelly Lancaster said she saw Janet at the Bel-Air hotel
Tuesday. She was going into one of the elevators to the suites. I
assumed she was meeting you. You two have . . . lunch there
sometimes, don't you?"

The line of Steven's mouth flattened. "Yes, we do. Not that it's anyone's business."

"So it was you." Kimberly sighed, pretending to be relieved. "I was worried."

"No reason to be." Steven hadn't been anywhere near the Bel-Air hotel Tuesday, and Kimberly knew that.

"You're such a confident man." Kimberly waved a dismissive hand in the air. "Paul has just been so enamored with Janet since he showed up. They have sort of a mysterious history, don't you think?"

"Not really," Steven assured her.

"Of course not to you," Kimberly said. "I'm sure she's told you everything. Paul seems so . . . I don't know. He's just reluctant to discuss it."

"You spent a lot of time with him?"

She nodded. "I enjoyed listening to his catwalk tales. I was just kind of surprised when I heard about him coming to the house to see Janet. Seemed a little inappropriate."

"He was saying goodbye." No longer interested in playing this game, Steven turned the machine off.

"That's odd." Kimberly stepped aside as Steven got off the bike. "He called me yesterday to say he's staying a little longer."

Steven didn't break stride as he was sure Kimberly was expecting him to. "Good for him."

"But he must have moved," Kimberly said. "He's paying his own way now, so I'm sure he wasn't at the Bel-Air anymore. It is kind of confusing, though."

"Not really." Steven repeated in a tone of finality. This game was over. He turned to her and smiled. "Don't bother yourself with it, Kimberly."

Steven was a remarkable man. Kimberly admired him for her own reasons, but mostly because of how revered he was by Michael. If Steven didn't want you to see him sweat, you didn't. But she'd come to know him over the years and if there was any giveaway to Steven, it was that he loved his wife to no end and basked in the glory that she felt the same. It was an enviable love, and the idea that Janet could be with another man was impossible, unthinkable. It simply was a thought not worth entertaining.

These were the words Kimberly was certain Steven was telling himself right now.

CHAPTER 15

As she sat at her vanity, Janet could hear Steven in the bathroom. He was slamming things around, making too much noise to ignore. This had all been building since yesterday.

As he stepped out of the bathroom, Steven looked across the expanse of their bedroom to Janet, calmly applying her makeup. He appreciated the care she took with her appearance. She understood that it was important for a man like him to have a beautiful, distinguished and elegant wife, and Janet was all that and more.

He hadn't been a perfect husband. He'd put family aside more times than he was willing to admit in favor of Chase Beauty, but only because he knew that Janet could handle it and he could trust her completely. He knew that what they had and what they stood for meant everything to Janet. She would never betray him.

"Are you just going to stand there and stare at me?" Janet asked, glancing at him from the reflection in the mirror. "I picked out two ties for you. They're in the dressing room."

Steven didn't move. He knew the woman before him was not perfect, but she was everything, absolutely everything to him. "What about breakfast?"

"You know Maya doesn't work on Sundays." Janet twisted

halfway around, facing him with a smile and feeling self-conscious. "Just hold off until after church. We're going to brunch with the Ascotts."

His expression was unchanged and Janet was beginning to wonder if he sensed she was back on the Valium. She would have to take a Welbutrin to help her mood. Dr. Gaines had told her they shouldn't be taken together, but when she did, it was the only time she felt even-kiltered enough to deal with her problems.

"You really do need to get dressed, dear."

"Were you going to tell me that Paul Devereaux is still in town?"

Janet felt a pinch in her belly, but outwardly her panic was undetectable. "Why would—"

"How about meeting him at the Bel-Air hotel?" Steven asked. "Were you gonna tell me about that?"

Janet turned around in her seat, placing her hands on her lap. "Sit down, dear."

"Janet, just—"

"Sit down." Janet pointed to the bed, waiting for Steven to do as she told him. "How long have you known?"

"Does that matter?"

"Did Kimberly tell you?" Janet knew the answer to that was yes.

After everything Paul had told her that day in the hotel suite, she felt certain Kimberly was no longer a threat. He'd promised he was no longer working with her. She didn't know if she believed this, but she would worry about that later.

"You should have told me," Steven said. "Unless you didn't want me to know."

"I didn't," she answered, "but not for the reason you suspect. And frankly, Steven, I'm disgusted with you for even suggesting I would—"

"Don't try to turn this around, Janet! Just tell me the truth."

That wasn't possible, but she could make him feel better. "I did go to his hotel room, and you can be assured he's leaving today."

"I've heard that before." Steven slammed his fist against the edge of the bedpost. "Why did you do that? You knew how I would feel about it. You had to know what it would look like."

"I'm sorry. You know I took precautions, but I wasn't doing anything wrong."

"What could be right about going to the hotel room of a man who is clearly attracted to you?"

"Paul doesn't want me." Janet smiled convincingly. "Paul doesn't favor women."

"You're trying to tell me he's gay?" Steven asked. "He certainly wasn't looking at you and Kimberly as if he were gay."

"Paul looks at women that way because he's a man who appreciates the beauty of women. It's his life and his work. It always has been, but you can be assured he hasn't once made a pass at me. He's not interested."

"Then why did you go there?" Steven asked.

Janet sighed. "I know you'll be angry, but I don't care. If you had considered my feelings in any of this, I wouldn't have had to go there."

"Again trying to blame me." Steven was losing his patience. "The route you're taking, Janet, I'm not inclined to believe anything you tell me."

"Do you know why he is still in L.A. after he said he would leave?"

"Because of you?"

"Paul doesn't care about me," Janet said. "He stayed because Kimberly wanted him to. She was making promises that she has no authority to make. More money. More freedom in his designs. She was telling him he could bypass anything you said."

"Kimberly isn't that stupid," Steven said. "He was lying to you."

"You are so foolish when it comes to her." Janet stood up and walked over to her husband. "You're blinded by her beauty."

"Please, Janet. You're the one being foolish."

She wanted to strangle him. "You've always had a soft spot for her."

"She is my daughter-in-law, the mother of my grandchildren."

"I'm your wife," Janet said.

Steven wasn't going to let what she was suggesting slide. "I have *never* put anyone ahead of you."

"You've never believed me when I told you that woman was a threat to our family, to everything that we've worked for. I couldn't stand by while you handed her more power than she already had."

"I wasn't handing her anything," Steven said. "I was trying to keep Michael happy, keep him here. I was never going to go through with it."

Janet paused, taking in this unexpected news. "Don't just appease me."

"Trust me," Steven said. "The last thing I'm looking to do right now is appease you."

"Why couldn't you tell me that?"

"Tell me why you were there, now!"

"I wanted to stop him," Janet said. "I wanted to make sure no matter what Kimberly was telling him, he knew this deal wasn't going to happen."

Steven slammed the top drawer shut hard enough to make the entire dresser shake. "How many times have I told you not to interfere with Chase Beauty business?"

"How many times have I warned you about Kim—"

"Stop it!" Steven yelled. "Your obsession with that girl is insane. Here, I'm going crazy thinking you're . . . all because you can't accept something that has been a reality for over seven years!"

"The more you carry on this charade, the more power Kimberly thinks she has, and she's trying to use it against me."

"Despite you always professing that Kimberly is no match for you. That you can handle her and I should stay out of it."

"I don't want to handle her anymore! And if you don't stop this, she will become more than I can handle. Is that what you want?"

"Fine," Steven said. "I'll make you a deal. I'll stop dealing with Michael, Carter, Leigh and Haley so I can focus 100 percent on giving you what you want. I'm sure you'll be eternally happy then!"

"Wait, Steven, I—" Janet reached for him, but she wasn't

quick enough. He eluded her grasp and stormed out of the bedroom, slamming the door behind him.

Janet didn't hesitate to go to her purse and search for her pills. She regretted her visit with Paul now, thinking that if she'd only listened to him discuss their summer of regret, it would be the end of it. As painful as it was to remember, Janet empathized with him because she believed he felt genuine anguish over the entire ordeal.

He'd told her how Kimberly had sought him out, how she would pay him to cause trouble in her marriage, but that he couldn't go through with it after seeing her again. She couldn't expose Kimberly without exposing herself, but that would be okay because Paul promised to leave. It was supposed to be over.

So why did Janet believe it was only beginning?

"He did something with them!" Avery yelled into the phone as she slammed the dining room curio cabinet shut. "I know he did."

"Why did you even have them still?" Nikki asked, feeling some kind of disaster coming on.

When Avery had called to tell her about the woman at the hotel, Nikki didn't want to believe it any more than her daughter did. Now Avery was manic, convinced this woman was the same one who had slept with Alex. It just seemed impossible.

"Don't quiz me now, Mom." Avery stood up, looking around the dining room. "The only other place to look is his office."

"Stop," Nikki said. "Don't do that."

"I have to find those pictures," Avery said. "I've been searching for two days. I know I brought them here."

"That was your first mistake." Nikki had never bothered to ask Avery what she'd done with the pictures. "I assumed you burned them. You should have."

"It was her!"

"You don't know that," Nikki said. "It just doesn't make any sense."

"She's after Carter. She's up to something and I—"

"You're losing it again." Nikki spoke in the most calming

voice she could muster, even though there was a part of her that wanted to panic. "Remember what I told you."

"I've given him two days to tell me something." Avery felt like she was going to go insane, letting the suspicion and mistrust build up. "He hasn't done anything but tell me he wants me to quit my job. Like I'm going to become dependent on him while he's meeting whores in downtown hotels."

"Tell him you want to talk about trust," Nikki said. "Let him know it's safe to tell you everything."

"It isn't safe! I'm going to kill him if he's cheating on me."

"But that's not what you suspect."

"The way he touched her." Avery winced just remembering. "Even though it was angry, it was passionate. If he isn't intimate with her now, he has been."

"Maybe she's just another ex."

"Who happened to be the same woman who ruined my first engagement?" Avery wasn't going to buy it even though the weaker part of her wanted to. "The world isn't that small."

"It can be." Nikki sighed, unsure of what to do. "Why don't you come stay with me for a few days? I'll tell Carter I'm sick and I need you."

Avery paced the hallway in front of Carter's office. The door wasn't locked. She could walk right in. "That sounds . . . I think I could do that. I just have to find those pictures."

"Does he know you have them there?"

"I never told him, but he finds out everything," Avery said. "This family . . . it's what they do. They just find out everything."

"What are you doing?" he shouted.

Avery screamed, jumping as she turned to see Carter standing in the hallway behind her. The phone fell out of her hand and onto the floor.

"What's the matter with you?" Carter leaned down to pick up the phone, but Avery rushed to snatch it away.

"You scared me." Avery put the phone to her ear. "Mom, I have to go. I'll call you back."

Carter studied her, keeping in mind her behavior over the

past two days. She was completely on edge. There was nothing he could say that wouldn't start an argument. "You've been crying."

"No, I . . ." Avery wiped the tears from her cheeks. "I was just . . . You know how I get with my mother."

"You don't cry."

"We were good crying." Avery cleared her throat, trying to slow her pulse. "I thought you were going into the office."

"For a few hours." Carter passed her and opened his office door. He looked inside, wondering if she'd been in there and why. "What happened?"

"I don't . . . I haven't been in there."

"Not in here." He turned to her as he put down his briefcase. "Out there. The house is a mess, Avery. What have you been doing?"

"I'm looking for something."

"Are you going to tell me what's wrong?" He took a few steps toward her and was surprised that she stepped back.

"It isn't important."

With phone in hand, she turned and headed back for the living room. She could hear him following and thought about the right path to take.

"Avery, stop." When she turned around, Carter could see pain in her eyes. Those were not tears of joy.

"I know you're upset about me wanting you to quit, but you have to understand. I wouldn't want it if I thought it wasn't necessary. I'm asking you to just take my word."

Avery laughed bitterly. "I don't want to talk about the job."

"Then what is going on? You know I can fix it."

"What does that mean?" Avery asked. "I know you can fix it. How can you fix it, Carter? You don't even know what it is."

"If you tell me, I can fix it."

"Because you're a Chase, right?" Avery went first to the bookcase to start cleaning up.

Carter could see this was going to be another fight. It was all she wanted. "My last name has nothing to do with what I'd do for you. I love you and I'd do anything for you no matter who I was or what I had."

Avery's heart softened because she wanted to believe the sincerity in his voice. "I'll clean this up."

"I don't want you to clean it up." Carter grabbed the book out of her hand and threw it on the floor. "I want you to talk to me!"

Avery couldn't believe what she was hearing. "All I ever do is try to talk to you, but no matter how much we talk, I feel this entire aura of secrecy around you. I don't know what your intentions are."

"I'm not a stranger," he said. "I love you and I want to marry you. I want to build a life with you. What intentions do you need to know besides that?"

"Everything," she pleaded. "Carter, I need to know . . . Why don't you trust me?"

"I trust you with my life," Carter said, feeling his frustration build. "Don't you trust me with yours?"

Avery wanted to say yes, but it would be a lie and she couldn't.

Her hesitation cut into Carter's gut in the way only Avery could. "This is where you say yes, Avery."

"Carter, I . . ." Avery placed her hand flat on his chest as she lowered her head. "I love you, but I . . . I need to know more to trust you with my life."

Carter stepped back, letting Avery's hand fall away. This was what he had been afraid of when he'd known he was falling in love with her—this pain he was feeling now; a pain no woman had reached deep enough to cause him.

"I would die for you, Avery."

The troubled spirits inside Avery were so confused, she didn't know what to feel or think. "I love you so much. I just need you to be naked with me."

Carter couldn't suppress his anger. All of the secrets and weaknesses he'd exposed to her. All of the thoughts and fears he'd shared with her and this was his reward? "You ask that while you won't even tell me what's wrong with you now?"

"You want to know what's wrong?" Avery asked. "I'm looking for the pictures and I want to know what you did with them."

Carter felt like he'd been hit in the chest with a brick. This wasn't happening. "What pictures?"

"Alex and that woman. I know they're here and I can't find them."

He was thinking of the negatives he'd burned in his office garbage minutes after he'd left the hotel, but this wasn't what Avery was talking about. She wanted the actual pictures.

"I ripped them up and threw them away," he said.

"How could you do that? Those were my pictures."

"Which you brought into my home—our home. They shouldn't have been here and you know it!"

She couldn't argue that, but it didn't change anything. "You had no right to do that. They were mine."

"That was almost nine months ago, Avery. Why do you still care? Why can't you let him go?"

Avery ached to tell him what she had seen at the hotel, but she didn't have the guts. What if she was right? Everything would be lost. Everything would be over.

"You should have asked me," she said.

"I was too angry, Avery. At the time, I was so insulted to find them, I just wanted to get rid of them."

"Things don't go away because you rip up paper," Avery said.

"You want to cry over your ex-lover?" Carter asked. "Go ahead, but I don't have to watch."

Avery's mind went blank after he passed by her, headed for the door. She winced when she heard the door slam behind him. She kept herself from breaking down by cleaning up the condo—anything to keep from thinking she might have to break off two engagements in as many years.

Ending her life with Alex was hard enough even though he'd given her no choice. But Carter . . . No, Carter she loved in a way she had never loved Alex.

Although she would never admit it, sometimes Haley wondered what was wrong with her. Here she was having an expensive dinner at a hot restaurant with what her mother would call the perfect man. Robert Wickland was thirty, tall, muscular and could be mistaken for the actor Blair Underwood. He came from an East coast family, which Janet assured her was where the best boys came from—Chase boys notwithstanding. The family had several generations of business owners, a few doctors, and a Congressman or two and was prominent in all the right social groups.

Robert carried degrees from MIT and Yale and ran his own management consulting firm. He had money and connections, was very ambitious and for a man who could have his pick of women, he was more than eager to impress Haley. He ordered the best wine and the most adventurous meal on the menu and could carry on an intelligent conversation without once mentioning the sports and entertainment industries.

So why did she want to put a gun in her mouth? She was bored beyond belief. Why couldn't she want what was good for her? After Chris, she was looking for something a little calmer—just a distraction, not a relationship of any kind—but Robert wasn't going to do it for her. Maybe she had to face reality and accept that no man ever would.

After tipping the valet, Robert slid into the seat of his Audi A8 and put the key in the ignition. He turned to Haley with a confident grin only men with his life could pull off. "So, you want to hit a club or something?"

"Dinner is all I agreed to," she answered coldly. It was nicer than saying, *I want to pass out from boredom.* "Maybe another—"

Haley squinted, lurching forward. Her hands pressed against the dashboard as she motioned for Robert to stop the car.

"Well, what do we have here?" she questioned.

"Who is that?" Robert asked.

"Let me out," she ordered, trying the door. "Unlock the door, now!"

When the door clicked, Haley jumped out, turning back. "Just park and wait. I'll be back."

"Where are you going?"

"Just wait." She slammed the door.

Turning to her target, Haley had to control the glee she felt at this opportunity. It was unlikely that she would ever run into Sean in this part of L.A. lined with expensive shops and cafés, especially not on a date with a pretty girl. This was the cherry on top of the hot fudge sundae. Our dear boy was trying to impress.

"You're not off to a good start," Haley said as she approached from behind. The look on Sean's face when he saw her got her so excited, she couldn't help but smile even though she hadn't intended to.

Sean blinked, not wanting to believe his bad luck. When he turned to his date, he smiled apologetically. He already knew he would never see the girl again after tonight, which was exactly what Haley wanted.

"Because," Haley continued, "everyone who is anyone worth dating doesn't have to wait in line here. You have to know the right people, Sean. That was never your strong point."

"Excuse me?" The girl placed her hand on her hip and rolled her neck, eyeing Haley up and down. "Who are you?"

"If you don't know," Haley said, "then you don't matter."

"That's enough, Haley." Sean turned to his date. "Just give me a second, please."

The girl made a smacking sound with her lips and flipped her hand, turning away. Sean stepped a few feet away, guiding Haley with him.

"You've made your point," he said. "You can leave now."

"I'm trying to help you." Haley reached out to rub his arm, but he pulled away. "I can get you and your 'hood rat a table here in five minutes."

"Just go," Sean asserted. "We'll wait in line like everybody else."

"How common," she said. "You and your sisters are so alike—Taylor especially."

"Goodbye." Sean turned to go.

"Although," she added, "I suspect that will change once Chris Reman is done with her."

Sean turned around, rushing back to her, stopping only inches away. "Watch it, Haley. I'm warning you."

"Warn me all you want." Haley shrugged. "But it really shouldn't bother you. I know you didn't think he was good enough for me, but he's probably a step up for her."

"She is not involved with him," Sean insisted.

"She didn't tell you?" Haley's hands went to her hips as she nodded. "Of course not. That would spoil all the fun."

"You're a liar," Sean said. "There's no reason to believe anything you say."

"I don't have to lie," she answered, "because I don't give a damn if the truth hurts. As a matter of fact, if it hurts, I like it even more."

"Chris is your boyfriend, isn't he?"

"Never was my boyfriend," she corrected. "But I dumped him awhile ago. Taylor was quick to pick up sloppy seconds after he promised her a modeling job."

"A modeling job?" Sean knew his parents couldn't possibly know anything about this.

"Don't worry," Haley assured him. "It was just an empty promise to ingratiate himself into her goodwill. He really wants to sell her to his gambling customers."

Haley laughed as Sean took her by the arms and led her away. "What are you talking about?"

"I thought only uniformed cops abused people." Haley pushed free of him. "I don't think your date will be impressed."

"I'm sure she's wishing I'd do worse. Now stop playing games and tell me what's going on."

"All those women who work at Pearl aren't just for show." Haley's lips eased into a wicked smile. "They're for sale."

"They're hookers?" Sean asked, not remembering anything about prostitution or sex trafficking on Chris's record.

"But don't worry," she said, "he won't give her to just anybody. All of his clients are rich businessmen, athletes and movie stars."

"Do you think this is a joke?" He wanted to strangle her, an all-too-familiar feeling for him.

"Actually, I think it's pretty sick, but it's not my problem, so . . ."

"Where is she?" Sean was dialing his parents' house on his cell as he spoke.

"I don't know." Haley gestured for Robert to pull up. "I just thought I'd share the news."

"If you're messing with me, Haley, I'll—"

"You'll do nothing," Haley said, "just like always. Have a nice evening."

As Haley slid back into the car, she savored the frantic way in

which Sean paced as he yelled into the phone. He had completely forgotten his pretty little date, and Haley congratulated
herself for making something out of this evening.

"You can't leave!" Kimberly held the cell phone in her hand
as she yelled into the Bluetooth earpiece. She was circling her
closet looking for something new to wear, but she couldn't concentrate. "I told you I will pay for your hotel no matter where
you are."

"It is not that," Paul said calmly. "Janet does not want me."

"That doesn't matter," Kimberly argued. "It only has to appear as if she wants you. That can't happen if you leave. Paul, we
had a deal."

"There was no deal," he answered. "I was eager to see what
you were up to and eager to see Janet again. I have done both."

Kimberly tossed the phone onto the dresser and knelt down
for a pair of Jimmy Choos. "Look, you jackass, you are not
messing this up. I know I'm close. You have to try one last
time."

"Kimberly, I—"

"I know what's going on," Kimberly said. "She's paying you
to counter what I'm paying you. You're making out well, aren't
you?"

"Janet is not paying me anything."

"Then I'll pay you more."

"More than what?"

"More than I'm paying you now, idiot!" She discarded a Vera
Wang cocktail dress on the floor. "You just stay and give it one
last chance."

"It is a silly game," he said. "You did not think it out very
well at all."

"Don't you worry about that," she ordered. "Just do what I
say."

"Kimberly, I—"

"Two-fifty," she yelled. After hearing no response, Kimberly
felt certain she had the floor again. "That's a quarter of a million
dollars I can wire to your account."

"Can you get your hands on that kind of money?"

"Do you know who you're talking to?"

Kimberly reached for the Dolce & Gabbana silk strapless dress she'd bought on a trip to the south of France last spring. It wasn't the newest of the line, but red always looked stunning against her skin tone.

"Then?"

"You have to come to the house," she said. "When, exactly, I'll get back to you."

Kimberly reached for the phone as she heard noises in the bedroom. Michael appeared in the doorway to her closet as she said a quick, cold goodbye to Paul.

"Hey, baby. I know the dinner is at seven, but I'm having a hard time finding something to wear."

"Who were you talking to?" Michael asked, taking off his suit jacket.

"Don't do that." Kimberly pointed at him. "Don't get undressed in my closet. You're always leaving your things in here. You have your own—"

"Don't make me repeat myself," Michael ordered. "Who are you telling to come to this house?"

"Since when do I have to clear my invitations with you? I realize I'm a second-class citizen in this damn house, but I do live here."

Kimberly was stunned at first when Michael started for her, but she quickly got wind of his intentions. He was going for the pretty pink RAZR in her hand. She tried to stuff her phone into her jeans pocket before he could get it.

"Stop it." She pushed his hand away. "Stop it, Michael."

"Tell me who you were talking to." He could tell she was talking about money. If Michael knew any language, it was the language of money.

"Michael!" Kimberly slapped him across the face, but he didn't even flinch.

Knocking her hand out of the way, he grabbed the phone and opened it up, checking the last number. "The Peninsula Hotel?"

"You are a bastard!" She grabbed the nearest shoe and slapped it against his back before he grabbed her by the wrist and squeezed hard enough to make the shoe fall out of her hand.

"Am I going to have to dial this number?" he asked.

She broke free of his grip. "What will I find when I check your cell phone? And don't think I won't every day from now on, jackass."

"I told you about keeping secrets from me," he warned.

"There's a difference between privacy and lying." She grabbed for her phone, but Michael held it back. "It's Paul, okay? Paul Devereaux."

Michael frowned as he shoved the phone at her. Paul was supposed to be back in France. "What are you up to?"

"What do you think?" she asked. "I'm trying to keep my dream alive."

"I told you to leave the business to me."

"So you'll continue doing nothing?"

"He's been interviewed," Michael said. "He's seen everything he needs to see, spoken to everyone he needs to speak to."

"I want him to be the designer!"

"It's not going to happen," Michael said. "Dad doesn't like him. And why are you promising him money—my money? And why were you telling him to come over?"

"You heard wrong." Kimberly tried to pass Michael, but he jumped in her way.

"I don't hear wrong," Michael said. "You'd better tell me."

"Or what?" Kimberly asked. "Is this where you insert a threat to rein me in?"

"If I wanted to rein you in, I could. The liberty I give you is not—"

"You think you're doing me a favor with the little freedoms you allow me?" Kimberly laughed sarcastically. "Next you'll tell me the control you exert over me is a gift."

"You feeling controlled?" Michael asked. "What choice do you give me when you're always keeping secrets?"

"If you really had me under control, this conversation wouldn't even be necessary." She sized him up to make a statement. "Yes, Michael, you give me a lot, but you haven't been able to give me the one thing I've really wanted, so I'm doing what I should have done a long time ago. I'm getting it for my-self."

Michael was fuming. Kimberly already had too much power over him. If she was going to trip like this, things would have to change.

"What do you think you're getting for yourself?" he asked. "Everything you have, you have because I gave it to you."

Kimberly stood silently as she folded her arms across her chest. She should have felt fear as the look of realization hit his face, but she didn't. She could only smile as his expression went from confusion to awareness and then dark anger. He started for her, and she braced herself but was surprised that he didn't grab her.

"This is about my mother." Michael could hear himself breathing as his pulse sped up. That smug look on her face was going to make him crazy. "Isn't it?"

"You're the one with two Ivy League degrees," she said calmly. "Figure it out yourself."

This time he did grab her and Kimberly gasped as his fingers dug into her arms. "I knew it that first day in the office. You knew something then and you didn't . . . Tell me!"

"I just want the deal to work." Kimberly never tired of the pleasure her power to make Michael crazy brought her. His eyes dancing toward madness made her feel like the most pow-erful woman in the world. "Do whatever it takes, baby. That's what you taught me."

Michael squeezed harder. "I told you to back off of Mom."

"If you plead her case one more time, I'm going to throw up on that expensive suit you're wearing." Kimberly tried to wres-tle free, but it was useless against his strength. "You have a deci-sion to make."

"What decision?"

"Me or your mother." She waited as he loosened his grip. Her arms were throbbing, but she didn't care. "We've had this conversation before, but you seem to forget."

"I don't forget anything," he said. "But that was when I knew what you were up to."

"It doesn't make any difference." She pushed until there was the distance of a few inches between them. "I'm your wife, Michael. Our family is everything and you know that."

"That doesn't mean I won't punish you for hurting my mother."

"It means you know where your loyalty lies," she retorted without uncertainty. "Now tell me, where is that, Michael? With Mommy or me?"

There was no playing this off, Michael knew, and the fact that Kimberly knew as well only made him angrier. And the victory in her eyes made him excited. He would make her pay for that, too.

He grabbed at the neck of her blouse and ripped it open. "If you hurt my mother, I'll still make you pay."

As they both slid to the ground, Kimberly knew it was a price she could live with.

It wasn't that he didn't want to come home; nothing was further from the truth. Before Avery had moved in with him, Carter hadn't thought twice about working until ten on a good day, later on most. He was still in the starting years of his law firm, gaining credibility and prestige as a young lawyer. But now that she was there, always waiting for him with her tender smile, soft body and warm heart, Carter couldn't wait to get home.

The issue was Avery's recent attitude problem. Nothing made her happy, and their evenings together seemed to always end in an argument. They hadn't had sex in a week, which was a long time for them. He wasn't buying the spiel about her staying with her mother for two days. Nikki wasn't sick at all and Carter had put an end to it by coming over to the house and telling Avery to come home, which she did without much protest. Carter had given her jewelry, flowers and Google stock as a gift, but nothing had made a difference.

Carter was willing to put up with it, knowing how much worse things could be if Lisette was still around. He didn't expect the comforting welcome, but neither did he expect what he did get when he entered the living room. Avery was sitting on the floor between the sofa and the coffee table, hunched over in tears with Kleenex littering the floor around her.

She looked up at him as he dropped his briefcase and rushed to her. The stricken look on his face made her feel even worse. She held out her arms to him, having waited all night for the comfort only his arms could bring.

"What is it?" Like any other guilty man, Carter couldn't help but think the worst. "What happened, baby?"

"I . . ." Avery buried her head into his chest, wishing she could just crawl into him. "I got fired, Carter. Steven fired me."

Carter didn't have words. *He really did it. That bastard really did it!*

She wiped her runny nose, unable to imagine how awful she must look to him now. "Is that why you've been pushing me to quit so much this week? Did you know he was going to do this to me?"

"No," Carter lied, straining under the pressure of her emotions. "He fired you? Not a warning or—"

"He called me into his office and . . . I can't go through it again."

"He can't do this!" Feeling as if he would explode, Carter reached into his jacket for his phone.

"No." Avery grabbed the phone from him. "I don't want any more of this. Don't call him."

"Give me the phone," Carter ordered. "He's not gonna get away with this. You're a part of this family."

"But I'm not," Avery said. "I'm not and even when I marry you, I won't really be. Kimberly told me—"

"You are part of this family and I'm not going to let him do this to you. I swear I'll make him regret this."

"You can't do that." Avery was beginning to calm down in the sight of Carter's growing anger. "You've already risked ruining the progress you've made with him over me. I won't let you destroy it all."

"He destroyed it all when he fired you."

"He's your father, Carter. You need him."

"No." Carter reached out and placed his hand gently on her

cheek. "I need you, Avery. I don't need anyone but you and I won't let him or anyone else hurt you."

Avery felt overwhelmed by emotion. What she saw in his face, heard in his words, told her this man loved her completely, and the comfort of that was strong enough to get them past anything. It had to be. She couldn't be here with him like this and feel like she was home if he wasn't the man she thought he was. Could she be so blinded by her love for him that she was forcing herself to be a fool?

"I love you," Carter whispered as he leaned in to kiss her.

When his lips came down on hers, it was almost painful, it felt so good to Avery.

"I can make this go away," he said. "I can make all the uncertainty and fear you feel about us go away if you give me a chance."

She opened her mouth to protest, but his lips silenced her, and her eyes closed. This time, she kissed him back and everything disappeared except how much she loved him and how much she wanted him. If this was being a fool, Avery was prepared to be one. She could never leave him, never walk away from the way he made her feel.

CHAPTER 16

As she sat at her desk in her home office, Janet was having an incredibly hard time concentrating, and it confused her. Usually when she took both pills, they balanced her out, but she felt too on edge and couldn't focus. There was just so much to do.

"Are we finished?" she asked Jeannie, who was on the other line at the Chase Foundation offices. "I do have to make calls for the cancer drive for the hospital."

"We also have to go over your September events," Jeannie answered, her voice trailing off on the speaker phone. "We have about thirty invitations here. The economic council gala, the Shooting Stars ball and the Alvin Ailey Dance Theater benefit. That's just next month."

The social season was beginning again, starting with the museum ball, which Janet felt she finally had under control. What she wished was that she could crawl into a corner after the ball was over, but that wasn't possible. She was Janet Chase, head of the Chase Foundation, a major contributor to the most significant charitable events across the country.

"After the ball," she answered, unable to think past the moment.

"Well, some of the RSVPs are already overdue," Jeannie said. "People are calling. They want to be able to say the foundation will attend."

Janet smiled, appreciating the deference. "Steven and I need to get away. Respond to the East coast events first. I'll deal with the rest after—"

A knock on the door was unusual. Despite asking her children to knock, they never did. Maya knocked but came right in without waiting for a prompt.

"I'll talk to you later." Janet hung up. "Come in."

When Paul entered, Janet's heart surged into her lungs. This man was like a cockroach! There was no getting rid of him! Leaping from her seat, she marched around her desk to meet him. "You can't be here."

"I had to." Paul's voice held a convincing sense of urgency that threatened to turn into emotion.

"Not again." Janet rushed to close the door behind him, but he blocked her way, holding out his hand to her.

"I have called you twice," he said.

"You weren't supposed to call me at all," she argued. "We agreed that you would leave. What was all that in the hotel room for? You said you were satisfied."

"You were just appeasing me to get me out of your life." With his hand to her elbow, he guided her to the sofa.

Janet removed her arm from his grasp. "You can't come to my house like this. My husband . . ."

"He is at work, no?" Paul pointed to the watch on his wrist.

Janet felt real panic take over. "This is when he comes home. He'll be home any second."

"Then you will talk to me quickly."

"Kimberly let you in, didn't she?"

"I have told you I do not want your money." Paul reached into his jacket pocket and pulled out an envelope. "Check for yourself. It is a plane ticket leaving LAX for Paris in three hours."

"I won't believe you until you're gone," she said.

Paul showed himself to the sofa. "This will be goodbye forever, Janet. You can offer me five minutes."

Janet rushed to the sofa. "You're being so dramatic, Paul."

"You are not being dramatic enough," he said. "After you left the hotel, I was thinking about this whole mess and I have come to a conclusion."

"Be quick about it," she said nervously.

"This was meant to happen." Paul reached out and took Janet's hand in his. "The incompleteness of our summer together, the way it ended, has kept me from moving on. It has kept me from forgiving myself for not trying to fight for you."

Janet had no patience for this. "There was nothing to fight for, Paul. I've told you this several times."

He glanced down at her belly. "What we started became something different—very different when our baby—"

"Stop." Janet pulled her hand away. "We have no baby. Paul, please just leave."

"It changed the rules we set for ourselves at the beginning of our affair. I should have tried to fight for my child's life."

Janet couldn't stand to hear these words but couldn't deny that they touched her. "I feel bad enough about what was done. I'll regret it forever, but you're making it worse."

As Kimberly stood by one of the large windows in the foyer, her stomach was dancing and jumping with excitement. Despite knowing so much could go wrong, what could go right had her on a cloud.

This was it. It had all been leading up to this and would work despite the mistakes she had made in her haste. So she would never go down in history as the ultimate strategist. She had fallen ass-backward into an opportunity and crossed her fingers. If she'd had more time maybe she would have thought things out better, but whatever . . . it was going to work anyway.

She was lucky, or she thought she might be until the car that drove past the gates and up the driveway was her husband's Range Rover and not the chauffeured town car that drove Steven from one place to another.

What was this? Kimberly gave up all pretense and opened the drapes wide as Michael stepped out of the driver's side and Steven stepped out of the passenger's side. Steven slammed the door behind him and Kimberly watched as Michael turned to him with an angry stare. Michael loved that car and had a fit if it wasn't treated well.

Kimberly felt her stomach clench so tight, she had to hold on to the wall as Steven started for the house. He clearly was ticked off, and she wasn't sure if this was in her favor or not.

To her delight, Michael was walking the other way, headed for the twins, who were playing on the lawn with Maya watching over them. They rushed to him as he knelt down, dropped his briefcase and opened his arms to receive them.

What was this now? Just as Steven reached the door, he turned around. Maya was calling him. This was not good news.

"Leave them in my office!" Steven yelled back as he opened one of the front double doors and stepped inside.

"Hi, Steven." Kimberly pasted on her winning smile, but it was lost on Steven.

"Not now, Kimberly." After the day he'd had with Avery, all Steven wanted was the comfort of his wife and a stiff drink.

"What's wrong?" Kimberly asked, disappointed.

He looked around. "Where's Janet?"

Michael stepped inside, keeping his distance from his father. "Don't snap at Kimberly, Dad. She didn't make you fire Avery."

The boys, attached to their father's legs, appeared curious, as was Maya as she reached the door.

"You fired Avery?" Kimberly didn't want to be distracted, but this was news. "You can't do that."

"I can do whatever I want! And it's none of your damn business." Turning back to Michael, he added, "You stay the hell out of it too."

Kimberly looked down at the boys, who were staring up at their grandfather with mouths wide open. "Maya."

Getting the message, Maya quickly ushered the boys out of the foyer.

"Do you know where she is or not?" Steven asked.

"She's in her office." Kimberly pretended to look nervous. "But why don't you wait in the great room. I'll tell her you're here."

"How dare you talk to me like I'm visiting?" Steven asked. "What are you up to?"

"You're already upset," Kimberly said. "You look like you're gonna bust a vein."

"Tell me!" Steven yelled.

"Hey!" Michael yelled back.

"Don't fight," Kimberly said. "If you have to know, Steven . . . Paul is in there. He's been in there for a while and Janet asked not to be disturbed."

As Kimberly watched, Steven's expression morphed into something she couldn't decipher. It wasn't anger or jealousy. There was going to be trouble.

"That son of a . . ." Steven's eyes turned to slits in Kimberly's direction. "You invited him?"

"I don't know what you're talking about. I didn't—"

"You've gone too far," Steven warned. "And you're not getting away with it this time."

As Steven stormed off, Kimberly felt her body tingling in anticipation despite the price she might have to pay. Steven didn't make idle threats. Kimberly only hoped his anger with Janet would divert his attention from herself. After all, she hadn't made Janet do anything.

Michael watched her eyes dance as they trailed his father, and he knew something bad was about to happen. He turned and started after Steven, but Kimberly grabbed him by the arm.

"Don't," she said. When he turned back to her, she vented her anger. "It's bad enough you just let him threaten me and do nothing."

"What do you think you can gain from this?" he asked.

"Don't make me the bad guy," Kimberly said. "Janet is the one who lied to her husband, to all of us."

"Are you accusing her of cheating?" Michael ripped his hand away.

Kimberly backed away, eyeing her husband cautiously. "I'm accusing her of lying and being a damn hypocrite. I'm accusing her of tormenting me for seven years and I'm accusing you of letting her get away with it."

Michael reached out and grabbed her by the arms. "Tell me what you did!"

"Oh, Paul." Janet pushed his hand off her thigh. Her heart was beating so fast, but she felt tired. How could that be? "Don't—"

"I am consumed with anger toward you," Paul said, "even though I have no right to be."

Janet felt like she'd been stung by a scorpion. "I was devastated by the choice I had to make. I . . ."

"So why do I feel alone in my regret?" he asked.

"How many times do I have to tell you I regret it?"

"It does not matter how many times you say the words," he urged. "In your eyes, I can see that if you had the chance to go back, you would do it again. I would not, Janet. I would not have."

"But . . . but Steven." Janet felt the warmth of his hand as it gently came to her cheek.

"I would have fought for my family," Paul said. "I would have fought for you and our baby."

Janet was shocked as his lips came to hers, but she didn't push away. Inside she was screaming for him to stop, but her body warmed at the senselessness of it all. Maybe it wasn't really happening. She thought of that summer and of the baby—their baby—and suddenly she wanted to kiss him back. As she lifted her arms to embrace him, she felt Paul pull back and wondered if she had done something wrong.

The look on his face was . . . not for her.

"You son of a bitch!"

Filled with murderous rage, Steven reached for Paul and pulled him up by his shirt just before knocking him to the ground with a hard punch to the jaw. Paul was holding his hands up while yelling, pleading in French.

"I'll kill you!" Steven yelled.

Janet screamed as she jumped up from the sofa. This couldn't be happening. "Steven! Please, Steven, stop!"

After the third blow, Paul stopped resisting and Steven stood up. Turning to Janet, he saw nothing but a blur that began with the pain of seeing her kissing that man. "How dare you? How dare you betray me like this?"

Janet jumped back as Steven took a step toward her, both of his hands still clenched in fists. She had never seen the contempt and fury in his eyes as he held for her right now. Because of the pills, she was reacting too slowly, unable to think of what to say.

"This isn't what you think. It isn't—"

"I saw you!" He pointed to the sofa. "You've been sleeping with—"

"No!" She held up her hand to halt his advance. "No, that kiss you saw, that was all there was to it. I swear to you, Steven. I love you. I would never betray you."

"You expect me to believe that?" Nothing was nearby but her desk, so Steven proceeded to toss and throw everything on it around the room. "He's nothing. He's nobody!"

"That isn't true!" Paul exclaimed as he stumbled to his feet. "Tell him, Janet. Tell him about us."

Steven turned, rushing back to him. He cocked his arm to hit again, but this time Paul backed away like a scared child.

"Tell him about our summer!" Paul pleaded. "We shared something you would never understand. That is why I am someone to her."

Paul tried to fight this time, but Steven was too quick, and another blow to his gut made Paul double over and back into the bookcase.

"Paul, please." Janet felt like she was dying inside with every word he spoke. "Just leave, Paul. Get out before he kills you."

"There's no place he can go to stop that," Steven said, his voice more of a growl than a tone of any kind.

The second he could stand, Paul didn't hesitate. He rushed out of the room with the speed of a much younger man.

"Steven, you have to calm down."

"What is he talking about?" Steven asked. "What is your *gay* friend whom you barely knew talking about?"

Feeling completely defeated, Janet fell into the closest chair and began to weep. "Oh, Steven. Steven, I—"

"It won't work," Steven said. "You're already a liar and a whore! Tell me about your affair. Explain your—"

"How could you call me that?" Janet looked up at him with her tear-stained face. "I'm your wife!"

Steven reached down and gripped the arms of the chair, shaking it until she screamed. "Answer me! What fucking summer is he talking about?"

"It . . . It was years ago," Janet explained through choked tears. "It doesn't matter now."

"What I saw happened a few minutes ago, so don't give me that. I swear I'll kill him, Janet."

"Kill him," she spat back. "I don't care. I hate him."

She was messing with his head, but Steven's heart was hardened to her. "Don't play me. If you don't tell me . . ."

"It was the summer before we were married," Janet said. "I had an affair with him in Paris."

Steven frowned, confused. He backed away, shaking his head. "But . . . No, you . . . What the hell are you saying?"

Janet took a deep breath, trying to compose herself. She felt dizzy and frightened, but she held her head up as she told her husband the truth—finally.

Steven had to sit down as it he took it all in. He tried to reach past the fog of anger and hurt to even make sense of it, to see if what had happened thirty years ago really mattered. But it did, it all mattered. If he hadn't heard this after catching his wife in the arms of another man, it might have sounded different. But he couldn't get that image out of his mind.

"How could you?" he asked, his voice suddenly hoarse from the strain.

Michael appeared in the doorway, seeing the room a mess, both his parents looking completely destroyed. Kimberly tried to keep him away, but after seeing Paul rush by with blood on his face and shirt, he couldn't.

"What happ—"

"Get out!" Steven yelled. "Get out and take that woman with you!"

Michael had never seen this look on his father's face. He looked weak, vulnerable in a way that Michael wasn't able to deal with, so he did what he was told. He couldn't have gotten away from that scene fast enough.

"Steven," Janet began with a shaky voice, "you have to believe me. Everything I've said is true. You have to know how hard it was for me to tell you all of this."

"God forbid you should be forced to tell the truth." Every word was laced with the disgust he felt. "I remember that summer. I hated that you left. I missed you every day."

"Steven, I—"

"I never doubted you." He looked at her and just the sight of her beautiful face, which looked much as it had thirty years ago, hurt him to his core. "I knew you loved me and would come back to mc."

"I did." Finding the strength to stand up, Janet rushed to him and knelt at his chair. She placed her hands on his thigh, looking up at him. "I do."

"How many other men were there?" he asked, unable to look at her anymore.

Janet recovered quickly from the sting of his words. "There were never any others. Steven, I was scared. I knew I was going to spend the rest of my life—"

He pushed her hands off of him and stood up. "I don't want to hear it."

"It's the truth." She stood up.

"It doesn't matter," he said. "All of that I could forgive. It was decades ago. But the lies you've told me in these past few months . . . what I just saw . . . You can't pass those off as being youthful mistakes."

"I didn't want you to know about that summer. I wanted you to believe that you were the only man—"

"I never needed you to be a virgin, Janet! That was your idea. You lied for yourself, not me." He threw his hands in the air. "It doesn't matter. I know what I saw just now. The lies you told me about barely remembering him, about him being gay."

"Steven!" As he began to leave, Janet grabbed him desperately. "Please stay. We have to talk this through."

"I'm sick of talking to you!" Steven tore away from her

strong grip, wanting to make her feel some of the pain he was feeling now. "I'm sick of looking at you."

Following him out of the room, Janet felt like she was going to die. "It isn't my fault. I haven't been myself. The pills are—"

He swung around. "You're back on those pills? The ones you promised you wouldn't take anymore, right? Yet another lie."

Janet only lowered her head, feeling shame so overwhelming she thought her legs would buckle. "I can't help it. With Leigh and—"

"Good," Steven said. "Blame Leigh. That'll work for you. I knew you were taking them, but I refused to accept that because you promised me you weren't. That was when I believed we told each other the truth. How many more lies are you packing, Janet?"

"None," she said. "I swear, Steven. I just didn't want to worry you with everything going on."

"Now it's my fault?" He slapped away her outstretched hand. "Don't touch me. I have to get out of here."

Kimberly ignored her husband's orders. "I'm not going anywhere. I'm not the one who lied."

"Get upstairs now!" Michael yelled. "You wanted out of this house—well, it looks like you're gonna get that because Dad wants you out now too. He wants *me* out!"

"He's just angry," Kimberly explained. "But he's going to realize it was Janet who has been lying to him for years and I'm the one that brought out the truth."

"These are my parents, Kimberly! It's their marriage, not anyone else's to mess with. You thought it was bad? You've made everything worse."

"Michael, I . . ."

Both of them turned their attention to Steven who was rushing toward the door with a screaming, begging Janet behind him.

"Please stop!" Janet grabbed at his shoulders again, but instead of pushing her away, he turned to her and grabbed her by the wrist.

"Get off of me!"

He pushed her arms away and she stumbled to the wall, crying his name.

Watching this, Kimberly didn't understand her own emotions. She wanted to be happy, but she wasn't. The scene before her was pitiful and somewhat sickening.

She turned to Michael, and the look of horror on his face made Kimberly afraid. She'd expected him to hate her for a while, but would he turn on her for this? It was Janet who had lied. He would forgive her. He had to.

She reached out to him, but he didn't even see her. Michael was going after his father, who was halfway out the door.

"Dad!" Michael didn't want him to leave but knew it probably was not a good idea for him to stay. He had never seen him treat his mother that way, and he wasn't sure what to do.

"Michael," Kimberly called after him. "Michael, come—"

She had only a second to react as Janet lunged at her with a wailing shriek. Kimberly grabbed on to her just as they both tumbled to the floor.

"You bitch!" Janet screamed, slapping her in the face. "You filthy, gutter, ghetto bitch!"

"Get off me!" Kimberly kicked at Janet and elbowed her in the stomach, hearing her groan. "Michael!"

"I'll kill you." Janet grabbed a handful of hair in her hand and pulled until Kimberly screamed in pain.

"Jesus Christ!" Michael rushed over to them. "You're both crazy!"

"You don't know who you're messing with, you old hag!" With her free arm, Kimberly connected with Janet's face. Janet's head fell back and she let go of Kimberly's hair.

"What is wrong with you?" Michael grabbed his mother from behind. He tried to stand his mother up, but she was kicking at Kimberly's leg, shouting words he'd never in his lifetime heard her say. "Stop it!"

"You're going to pay for this!" Janet yelled as Michael swung her around. "Let me go, Michael."

"Stop fighting!"

"Let her go." Kimberly backed up on the floor, grabbing the stair's handrail to lift herself up. "Let her go. I got this bitch."

"Shut up!" he yelled. "Just go upstairs."

"No!" Janet yelled. "You're getting out of this house now, you worthless little whore!"

"That's enough, Mom. I'm warning you."

"You're warning me?" Janet asked. "Do you know what she's done?"

"Yes," Kimberly said. "Blame me for all of it. What did Steven walk in on? Were you—"

"You'll pay for this!" Janet yelled as she broke free of her son. "She caused this, all of it. She's tried to . . ."

Janet knew she was still moving her mouth, but no words were coming. She looked at her son, confused, before everything went black.

As his mother went limp in his arms, Michael yelled out, "Maya!"

"Don't call her," Kimberly says. "She's with the boys. I don't want them to see this."

"Then call Dr. Anderson," Michael ordered. "Do it now!"

"She just fainted, right?" Kimberly asked, seeing a lifeless Janet lying in Michael's arms. All she could think was that he would forgive her. He had to.

"Call him now!"

How dare he? This is what was on Haley's mind as she reached the bottom of the staircase. How dare he do this to her mother? This was a complete mess, and it was all his fault. Her mother had tolerated more than thirty years of Steven's tyrannical reign over this house and he responded to one little mistake by leaving. A mistake he really was responsible for anyway.

Now here she was left to deal with the mess he'd left behind. No one had told her what happened. She came home to find her mother lying in her bed refusing to see the family doctor, who had gone out of his way to make a house call for one of his richer clients. Haley wanted answers. She was able to get some from Carter, who wasn't talking to their father for firing Avery.

Haley hadn't left her mother's side that night and much of the day after. She had called Leigh, but Leigh didn't care. She'd refused to come over, instead choosing to side with their father and comfort him. Michael had come by, and he and Carter had gotten into a big argument about Kimberly before Michael left again. That was yesterday, and he hadn't been back. Haley assumed he was with Kimberly wherever she had gone, because he had taken the twins with him.

Janet's focus was keeping it out of the papers. No one could know about Paul and her past. No one could know that Steven had checked into a suite at the Four Seasons. No one could know that the Chase family was a complete mess. Haley sensed that her mother knew that Kimberly, who had to feel like a cornered cat, still had a powerful weapon.

No matter what her mother had done, and Haley still didn't see what the big deal was, she blamed her father for leaving. That was what she had been taught a good man never did. He never leaves. Now her mother was a mess and Haley had to put her life on hold because Leigh was too much of a bitch to help her. She knew she wasn't going to make the big celebrity birthday party at LAX this weekend.

Life wasn't fair. Damn him!

"What do you want?" Haley asked Maya as she stood in the foyer.

"It's for you." Maya wasn't looking much better than their mother. She was in charge of deflecting the curious callers inquiring about Janet's absence at this meeting or that luncheon.

Yes, Janet was coming down with a wicked cold, but don't worry about the museum ball. She'll be there, and everything is on track. All other events, we regrettably have to decline. The house had received at least two dozen GET WELL SOON bouquets.

"I'm not seeing anyone," Haley said. "I told you."

"He insisted." Maya pointed her finger. "And don't you tell him anything."

"Don't tell me what to do," Haley said. "Who is it?"

"It's the detective," she answered. "He's in the library."

Haley didn't know how to react to this news. What was Sean doing here? Had Avery gone and blabbed to her family?

"Haley," Maya called to her just as she started off.

Haley turned back, more concerned with how she looked than with anything Maya wanted. "What?"

"What did she tell you?" Maya asked, coming closer. "When she asked me to leave, what did she tell you?"

Haley rolled her eyes. "If she wanted you to know, she would have asked you to stay."

"It's about the pills," Maya said. "Otherwise, she tells me everything. Only the pills she keeps from me because she knows I won't abide."

"Since when do you get to abide by anything? You work for her."

"And not for you," Maya warned. "Remember that with your tone."

Haley turned and walked away, angry that Maya was right. Her mother was making her get a refill on some "secret" prescriptions that no one was to know about. It was something Maya should have been doing, or Jeannie, but she was making Haley do it and had made her promise not to tell a soul.

When she entered the library, she saw Sean standing at one of the dark cherry wood bookcases that held her father's collection of first editions behind glass. In a polo shirt and shorts, his muscles were prominent and he looked very appealing. She remembered the time they'd almost made love in this room before getting caught by her mother.

Haley wanted to be nasty but didn't have the energy. She didn't know what to say, so she just stood there until he turned around.

"I didn't know you were here," he said, walking toward her. "I didn't . . . Haley, what's wrong?"

Looking at the vacant stare on her face, Sean wasn't sure what to do. He had seen her look this way—vulnerable—only once before, and that was when she had almost been killed.

"What do you want?" Haley couldn't stand that concerned look on his face. On the flip side, Sean didn't play games, so he must not know.

Sean remembered his guard and brought it back. He had sworn never to let it down again around this man-eater, but the look on her face reminded him of when . . . That was a useless memory.

"You just looked upset," he said. "I thought . . . Never mind. I came by to talk to you."

She looked him up and down. "This is business or personal?"

"Both," he said. "Can we sit down?"

"You're not staying long enough," she answered. She noticed his impatient stare. "Seriously, Sean. I'm very busy."

"I need your help."

"Good luck with that," she said.

"I need to know everything you know about Chris Reman."

"You've already done your research," she said.

"I need to know more."

Haley was seriously not in the mood to discuss that pervert. "He's a freak and a crook. There isn't more to it."

Sean promised himself he would stay calm. "Can you get your head out of shopping and Sidekick conversations to focus on something serious?"

Haley's mouth opened in surprise. "You have no idea what's on my mind. Dammit, Sean, just leave."

"Not until you tell me about Chris. You're right, Haley. Taylor is in danger and she doesn't believe me. I keep telling her Chris is no good. I even showed her his record and the files the cops in Chicago had on him. She doesn't care. She's blinded by all the money and people he's introducing her to."

"Stupid is as stupid does," Haley said. "I've already helped you. You wouldn't even know about the two of them if it hadn't been for me."

"I need more," Sean said. "That didn't . . . didn't really work out."

Haley studied his embarrassed head turn. "What? The casino thing? It's a big-ass room in the back of the—"

"He must have someone inside the LAPD. I had to clear it with them first. He cleared out before they could get the warrant and get in there. It wasn't my fault."

"Arrest some of his hos."

"LAPD doesn't care about that. We don't have any proof.

I've tried to send some . . . customers in there. He's not biting. He's not doing anything now with the warrant screwup."

"So you're ass-out, Sean. That's your own fault."

"Can you not be a bitch for five minutes and help me?" Sean asked.

"No," she spat back. "I can't not be a bitch for five minutes, because it's what I am. I thought you understood that."

Sean noticed the look in her eyes, the look she tried to veil with coldness. Haley cared about protecting one person in this world—herself. That's what she was doing now.

"You're afraid," he said. "You're afraid of him."

Haley felt her anger bubbling to the surface. "You're leaving now, Sean."

"Did he do something to you?" he asked.

"Do you think he'd still be alive if he had?"

Sean knew all too well he probably wouldn't. Not if he had hurt a child of Steven Chase. "Then what are you afraid of?"

Haley sighed, shaking her head. "What do you want from me?"

"I need you to get information from him."

Haley suddenly felt a chill down her spine. "I don't like talking to him. There's something wrong with him, Sean."

"I know that," he said. "That's why I need to catch him before he hurts Taylor."

"Tell your dad. He's freakin' chief of police. He can do something, can't he?"

Sean shook his head. "LAPD doesn't care about View Park. Besides, I'm handling this. He'll just think it's about you."

Haley found it all pretty pitiful. "All you Jacksons are short a nail or two."

Sean ignored her insults. "Okay, so you're a bitch, but you're not an animal. You think you'd be able to live with yourself if something happened to Taylor, but you wouldn't. Even you would feel regret."

"I haven't yet and I've done worse. Besides, I'm not to blame for their relationship."

"Haley! You have to help me. I'll protect you," Sean said. "You know that I have and I will."

He had saved her life more than once, which was why Haley had thought she loved him. No, she would never forget that. "I don't need your protection."

"You'll have it anyway." He waited for her to fight her natural reaction and give in. "You always have it, Haley. I need you now."

"Are you trying to appeal to my emotions?" Haley laughed, but it sounded weaker than she'd intended.

"What emotions?" he asked.

He smiled and when she smiled too, he knew he had gotten through. There was a speck of humanity in the woman, and he knew she was vulnerable right now. Whatever Haley was going through didn't matter. This was for Taylor.

"This is what I need you to do," he said.

As soon as he entered his home, Carter could hear the Ludacris track pounding in the background. She was still here.

He played it cool as he entered the living room. The television was on, an MTV reality series, but no one was there to watch it. She had taken over the television too.

As he made his way to his office, Carter told himself to be patient. He loved Avery, and Avery loved her little sister. That meant he was supposed to love Taylor, too. He could at least try to like her. That didn't mean he wanted her in his home.

Whatever argument she'd had with their mother made Taylor decide she'd rather spend a few nights at the condo with Avery, who took her in without question. Carter sensed it was to avoid being alone with him.

His usual practice these days was to close the door to his office and work into the night, avoiding the awkward silence and the discomfort of feeling left out as Avery and Taylor kept each other company. But this was ridiculous. It had to stop. He needed Avery with everything that was going on.

Tonight, he found Avery in the master bedroom, sitting on the bed reading a book. Once inside, he closed the door behind him and could hear the trickling creek from her sound soother.

"Hi." He approached the bed, finding comfort in even the lukewarm smile on her face. She had a sucker in her mouth, and with her hair in a ponytail and her pajamas on, she looked like a little girl.

"There's leftover seafood pomadoro in the fridge," Avery said.

Carter tossed his jacket and sat on the edge of the bed. "I'm sorry I'm late, but . . ."

"It's okay." Avery looked up from the book, forcing a smile. He wanted to talk, and she wondered if her cold shoulder would force him to tell the truth yet.

Of course it was okay, he thought. It wasn't as if she wanted to spend any more time with him than was absolutely necessary. "I was going to say, but we won our case—you know the lawsuit against Montkemp."

"So they didn't have to settle." she knew her pretended interest was obvious. "Congratulations. Big paycheck."

Carter reached out and placed a hand on her thigh. He wanted her, but they hadn't had sex since the night she'd gotten fired. "Avery, I need you with me right now."

"I'm here." Avery looked away, not wanting him to see the emotion in her face. Just his touch made her want to forget everything but how much she loved him.

"No, you aren't." He slid close to her, taking the book out of her hand and placing it on the bed. "Look at me. Can you understand what I'm going through? Baby, my father is living in a hotel and my mother is falling apart. I need you. You're my strength and you're scaring me to death."

"I can't fix your parents' mistakes," she said. "But if you want to talk about us, I'm here to listen to—"

"Stop it!" Carter pushed away from the bed and went to his closet. "Stop baiting me. If you aren't going to tell me what you want me to say, then stop toying with me."

Avery didn't know what she was doing anymore. She wanted to back off, seeing what was going on with Carter's parents. She wanted to back off because after being fired, her emotional state was so uncertain, she didn't think she could handle it. But now she'd waited too long and felt paralyzed. Her spine had disappeared at the prospect of losing him because of the truth.

"I'm not toying with you," she said, sitting at the edge of the bed. "But your anger tells me I'm right. There is something you need to tell me."

"My anger tells you I'm sick of you punishing me for not being able to read your mind."

"If we're going to get married, we have—" Avery was stopped in the middle of her sentence as Carter swung around in a rage.

"'If'? What the fuck does that mean?"

"I . . ." Avery stood up, unsure of how to respond. She couldn't believe she'd actually said it. "I didn't mean that."

"Was that a threat?" he asked.

"No, I . . ."

"Are you crazy?" he asked, all of his secrets feeding an unreasonable anger. "So now if I don't feed your subconscious fears and illusions, you'll call it off?"

"Keep your voice down," Avery said.

"I won't keep my voice down! I'm not taking any more of this shit! I come home to nothing but ice. No matter what I do, what I offer to do, to give to you, you sulk like a child."

Avery's stomach began to tremble as she begged for whatever was lost inside of her that normally would have fought back.

"Now you're threatening me?" he asked. "It ends now, Avery!"

"What ends?" Avery felt her entire body begin to shake as she felt the intensity of the moment go from zero to 300 in less than a second.

"The head games," he said. "The frigid bed, the threats, all of it. That isn't the way things are going to go from now on. I've had enough."

Avery at least was grateful that his controlling turn was making her anger return. "Who do you think you're talking to?"

"You tell me," Carter said. "I don't know who you are anymore. I want the old Avery back and I want her now. I don't want any more games, stupid questions and suspicious stares. I'm not asking you. I'm telling you!"

"Since when do you lay down rules?" Avery was incensed.

"Since now," he said with a hard-as-stone expression.

"What, do you think you own me?"

"Do you think I don't?" he said plainly.

Carter's breath caught the second Avery's did. He heard the words in delayed time as if it was slow motion. The stunned look on her face, her lips parting in disbelief struck him like a bolt of lightning.

He started for her, his right hand outstretched. "Baby, I'm so—"

When she slapped him, the contact was like a sharp whip and stung like a January wind whipping around a corner. Carter's head went all the way to his right and he stepped back. He blinked, seeing spots float in his eyes.

"You son of a bitch!" Avery said, seething. "Get out."

"Avery. I . . . I don't know what I was saying. I'm upset over my parents, with everything—"

"Get out!" Her arm shot up, her finger pointed decidedly to the door. "You self-centered, lying motherfucker. Get out!"

Carter knew the only thing he could do was leave, so he did. Riding the elevator down ten floors to his sister Leigh's apartment, he felt a dark sense of dread. What in God's name had made him say such a thing?

Carter knew what had made him go over the top. He was guilty and that made him defensive. He was desperate and that made him mean. It was a recipe for disaster, which was exactly what he'd gotten.

CHAPTER 17

"Don't waste your time looking at me like that," Michael said. "This is the bed you've made."

Kimberly knew she wasn't going to garner any sympathy from Michael now, but possibly his pity. Anything to avoid what he was making her do.

As they stood outside his parents' bedroom, the anxiety threatened to drive her crazy. She hadn't been in the house since the *incident* and knew she wasn't welcome.

For the past four days she'd been at the Regent with her twins, second-guessing everything. Michael had tortured her with threats of divorce and destitution before he calmed down. There had been a moment there when Kimberly believed she would lose everything, and she couldn't say that feeling wasn't still there.

She had thrown her pride out the window and begged Michael to understand and forgive, but he wasn't hearing any of it. She had gone down the list of every threat and devious action brought against her by Janet over the past seven years, some of which Michael hadn't known about, all while her husband had stood by and let it all happen for his own selfish, insecure needs.

When Michael decided to spend the second night at the hotel with her, Kimberly knew that she hadn't lost everything, at least not yet. There was still something left she had to do, and in her mind it was the most impossible thing.

"I can't go in there," Kimberly said. "She's going to kill me."

"She has a right to," Michael said. "I've thought of it myself a few times."

"Stop talking like that," she pleaded.

"Look at me," he ordered with a cold, sharp tone. "You've torn this family apart. Whatever you have to go through to fix this is what you'll go through. Get in there."

"Why can't we just go?" she asked. "It's not like we can live there anymore anyway."

"We aren't moving anywhere. With my mother in this condition, which you caused, I can't leave her. She—"

"She has Hal—"

"Shut up." He brought his hand up and she flinched, stepping back. He wouldn't hit her, even though he'd wanted to a few days ago. "Just do it."

Kimberly sighed, throwing her hands in the air. "Baby, all I wanted was some peace, the right to live my life without someone on my ass all the time. I swear."

"I've heard enough of your lies, woman." He was being a hypocrite, of course, because he had lied to her as well. "You don't have a lot of time. Haley or Maya will be here soon."

"She won't believe me," Kimberly said. "She already knows the truth. Paul told her."

Kimberly told Michael that the idea to blame this all on Paul wouldn't work, but he insisted that was the story they would tell everyone: Paul had come to Kimberly with the idea in an attempt to get back into Janet's life. After all the pain and suffering Janet had caused Kimberly, which no one in the family could deny, she went along. There was no way Kimberly could come out innocent in this, but at least with this story, she hadn't come up with the idea.

"That asshole isn't here to defend himself," Michael said, "so you're the only truth."

"Michael." Kimberly reached for him desperately, clinging to the fabric of his shirt. "Let's just take the babies and go."

"Me and the boys are staying here. If you want to leave, you're leaving by yourself."

A chill ran through Kimberly at those words. He would never . . .

He could read the fear on her face and Michael nodded. "Yes, I would."

Kimberly bit her lower lip to stop the tears.

"I'll be with the boys." Without a pause, Michael turned and left.

Using her fear of losing their boys was wrong, but he had no choice. Carter had been right that day on the golf course. Despite loving Kimberly with everything he had, Michael knew his only choice was to completely control her. He had lost sight of that and this was what had happened. It wouldn't happen again.

As she heard the door open, Janet turned from her vanity. Something had told her Steven would come by today and that was what gave her the courage to get up and try to make something of her appearance. Her messages begging him to come home hadn't been returned, but he couldn't ignore her forever.

She knew Steven only needed time. There was no way she would lose him, not after all these years. Anyone would react the way he had, but when the anger subsided, he would realize the thirty years they'd been married meant more than any lie or kiss. It was the waiting that was killing her and the fear that others would find out.

Maybe Steven was realizing that. Maybe he was ready to talk without the rage. Her heart told her he would come around sooner than later. Her years of devotion had earned that and . . .

Janet's breath caught in her throat at the sight of Kimberly walking through the door. She had to grab the edges of her seat to keep from leaping into the air and lunging for Kimberly's neck. Despite how she felt, her expression was staid as she reached for the stereo remote to turn down the sound of Beethoven.

Despite all those years on the mean streets of Detroit, Kimberly had never stared down as threatening a face as the one she was confronted with now. She was scared and tried desperately not to show it.

"Sit down," Janet said. "I don't have a gun or anything."

Kimberly took hold of the bedpost, deciding to stay standing in case she needed to run. No, Michael's plan wouldn't work. She would have to go with her own plan.

"Am I supposed to believe that you don't want to kill me?" She noticed the bruise that was still prominent on Janet's lower left cheek and hoped it hurt like hell.

"I don't know." Janet crossed one leg over the other and placed her hands on her knee. "You've dug quite a hole for yourself, Kimberly. I might just let you stay down there and gently kick the dirt on top of you."

"You seem so certain," Kimberly said. "But you can't trust you know everything as long as you lock yourself in your little tower."

Janet smiled calmly. "I know your plan has backfired."

"You think so?" Kimberly looked around. "So Steven must be in the bathroom, right? That's why I don't see him here."

Janet's smile flattened. "This means nothing. You see, Kimberly . . . Men don't leave women like me. You wouldn't understand that because where you come from, men leave all the time. I mean, why would they stay with women like you?"

Kimberly gripped the post. "Let's not turn this into a 'dig at the poor black folks' session. And let's not pretend this is something other than what it is—completely devastating to you. Not only did you lie about Steven being your first, cheating on him before your marriage and getting pregnant, but—"

"Spare me the list of my sins," Janet said. "You're boring me."

"Okay," Kimberly agreed. "I'll leave out the drugs, the lies about Paul being gay and kissing him and God knows what else. The truth is, we're both in a precarious situation."

Janet laughed. "I love it when you use big words. Leeching on to high society has really done wonders for you. It's such a shame those days are over."

"You need to pay attention, Janet, because your list of sins is adding up and you can either work with me or against me. But know . . . if you work against me, I'll do everything in my power to make sure that Steven never comes back here."

Janet rolled her eyes. "What little influence you had with Steven because of your beauty is gone now that he knows the role you played in this."

"Michael is doing everything he can to convince Steven of my"—Kimberly sighed for effect—"desperate attempt to gain peace for myself and my boys that I deeply regret and had no idea you would take it so far."

Janet's face contorted with anger. "He won't fall for it."

"He's not a drug addict like you, but he's pretty vulnerable right now. I think he's prone to believe a lot. If you add to it all the eligible, much younger society women I will go out of my way to inform of his current availability, I'm sure I can distract him long enough to have the desired effect."

Women had always been after Steven, and Janet couldn't lie that it didn't worry her as she got older. It was well known that their marriage was strong, but what would happen once they heard there was a problem?

"A fight does not a marriage end," Janet said. "You know that, Kimberly. Hell, as many times as I'm sure Michael has cheated on you . . ."

"You don't know anything!" Kimberly caught herself when Janet smiled at making her lose control. "Michael has begged me to come back home and I have."

If she had to kick Michael out to get Kimberly out, Janet would. "I'd sleep light if I were you."

"I don't need to," Kimberly said. "Unlike you, I won't be sleeping alone. Michael will be right next to me."

"For now." Janet turned her back to Kimberly, returning her attention to her mirror. "You'll be out of here soon enough."

"Sooner if you work with me."

Janet was curious but didn't turn back around. She eyed Kimberly from the reflection in the mirror. "You want me to convince Michael to move out for good."

"And I'll convince Steven to come back. I'll convince him it was entirely my fault."

"It *is* entirely your fault."

"No, it isn't." Kimberly paused, making sure she had Janet's attention. "It really isn't, Janet. That's the reason you need to work with me."

Janet reached for the remote and turned up the stereo. Over the melodic sounds of the Fifth Symphony, she said, "Go to hell, Kimberly."

"Janet, I—"

"You're not one of us," Janet said. "That's what it comes down to, dear. You're on your own."

"Avery?" Nina Calloway stuck her head out the door of Hue's back room. "Avery?"

Avery took a second to break from her trance to respond to Hue's receptionist. She was looking at one of her mother's paintings, a painting she remembered watching her create. She allowed herself to get lost in the abstract circles and curves as thoughts of her emptiness over the past few days threatened her.

"Yes, Nina?"

"Phone for you."

"Who is it?" Avery hadn't told anyone she would be at the gallery today.

After kicking Carter out and crying into her pillow for hours, Avery had given Taylor the bad news. They would have to leave. Taylor reluctantly agreed to pack up, and they both moved into their parents' house.

After a few days, Nikki had forced Avery to get off the sofa and out of the house. She made herself barely presentable and joined Nikki at the gallery.

Nina frowned. "It's Sean."

Avery made her way to the back room of the gallery. "Can you help out on the floor, Nina? I think it's getting busy."

"I'm done with lunch anyway." Nina wiped her mouth with her napkin before rushing off. "Tell him I said hi. Haven't seen him in a while."

Avery picked up the phone. "Sean?"

"It isn't Sean," Carter said. "It's me."

Avery felt her chest tighten and her temples throb. "How did you know . . ."

"I've been calling everywhere for you."

"So you lied to Nina."

"If I had told the truth, would you have picked up the phone?"

"If you had told the truth," she answered, "we wouldn't be in this situation. Don't call here again, Car—"

"Please don't hang up, Avery." Carter paused with an anxious sigh. "Please."

Avery couldn't resist the desperation in his voice. This was why she had been avoiding his calls. The rare times he showed his vulnerability, she always gave in.

"Avery?"

"I'm here," she answered quietly.

"I miss you," he said. "I love you so—"

"I don't want to hear this." Avery's hand gripped the phone with all her might. "They're just words."

"I have to see you. I know you're angry and I've tried to give you space, but I can't stand it anymore."

"Am I supposed to be concerned with what you can and can't take right now?"

"I know what I said was wrong." Carter still couldn't believe the words had come from his mouth. "But you know how frustrating things have been between us. With my parents' situation getting worse, I—"

"Worse?"

"Dad sent for his clothes and stuff from his office." Carter's tone became erratic and hurried. "Avery, he's not planning on leaving the hotel anytime soon. I can't talk to him because there's been nothing but bad blood between us since he fired you. Michael and I got into a fight over Kimberly. I don't know what to do. Everything is falling apart."

"Calm down," she pleaded.

"I can't," Carter said lowering his head. "I need you, baby. I can't even think, work, do anything without you in my life."

"Carter, I want to help you," she said. "You know that I do, but . . ."

"I'll tell you the truth," he said, even though he didn't even know what truth to tell her. "We can talk, this time for real. No more secrets or lies. What happened with my parents has taught me a lesson, Avery. Please."

Avery wasn't sure she could believe him, but his plea tugged at her heart to the point where it didn't matter. She had to be with him. "I'll agree to talk, Carter, but nothing more than that."

"Will you come home tonight?"

"I can't. I have to help Mom tonight. Tomorrow."

"I'll make dinner for you. When do—"

"Seven."

Carter felt his entire body sigh. "I'll see you at seven. I love—"

"Don't," Avery said. "Because even though I feel it, I won't say it back."

Carter felt the kick to his chest. "Tomorrow night at seven, then."

Avery hung up without saying goodbye, wondering if she had just made a huge mistake. It would just be another of so many she'd made lately.

"I don't have to ask who that was."

Avery acknowledged her mother's worried expression as she stood in the doorway.

"You didn't even notice when I came in here, so I assumed it was Carter." When she reached her, Nikki wrapped her arms around her baby.

"We're going to talk tomorrow night."

"You ready for that?" Nikki asked.

Avery sat down at the circular pine table. "I don't know. I do want to see him, talk to him."

"What he said was horrible." Nikki joined her at the table. "Even for him."

Avery looked up with a frown. "What does that mean?"

"What I'm trying to say is I'm sure he didn't mean it."

Feeling nauseous, Avery pushed Nina's half-eaten ham and cheese sandwich away from her. She thought of the words Kimberly had told her during their last lunch.

"That's just it, Mom. I'm not so sure."

"You don't believe he loves you?" Nikki asked.

"No, I know he loves me, but I think he does believe he owns me, that I belong to him instead of us belonging to each other. It's the way they all live, the Chases. They claim to own things and people, but they only belong to each other."

Nikki couldn't, wouldn't argue that. "This is my fault. I shouldn't have put my two cents in. I should have let you decide what to do on your own."

"You were just trying to help. I'm the one who played passive-aggressive, knowing that I didn't want to hear the truth."

"That's not like you," Nikki said.

"These past few days I've been wondering how I let things go the way I have." Avery looked down at the gleaming ring on her finger. "I kept telling myself the life that came with being with him was just icing on the cake, but it's become more than that. I saw that I could lose it all, and I was scared."

"Baby, you're only human. Everyone wants to live well."

"Don't excuse it, Mom." Avery ran her hands through her hair and leaned back in her chair. "Maybe if it was a little lie, I could see, but . . . I was willing to let something big go. This woman is—"

"You don't know who she is," Nikki insisted. "You can't know unless he tells the truth."

"I'm afraid I won't ever get it out of him," Avery said.

"No matter what happens tomorrow night," Nikki said, "you know you'll be okay, don't you? Like they say, this too shall pass."

Avery laid her head on her mother's shoulder. That may have been true in the past, but she wasn't so sure this time.

Michael didn't bother to knock on his father's office door before entering, because he expected if he had, he would have been sent away. They had barely spoken since Steven left the house, and when Michael heard his father had met with Carter for two hours that morning, the dormant jealousy flared right back up.

Things were not even. Yes, firing Avery had done a great deal of damage to Carter and Steven's relationship, but what Kimberly had started made Michael's situation much more precarious. He had explained to his father the lie that both he and Kimberly agreed upon, but Steven refused to respond. He hadn't been cold or angry or mean; he just said nothing. That was much worse, in Michael's opinion. What had Kimberly cost him?

"Dad, I . . ." Michael stopped halfway into his father's office when he realized Steven wasn't in his chair. He was sitting on the sofa against the wall.

"What do you want?" Steven asked, feeling too miserable to be reasonable.

"Are you okay?" Michael didn't like seeing his father, a man so strong and imposing in his mind, so tired and run down.

"I'm fine." Steven stood up, heading for his desk. "We don't have a meeting scheduled."

"I've never needed to be on your schedule before. Why now?" Michael turned as he heard the sink running in the bathroom. "What did I interrupt?"

"Nothing." Steven pressed the intercom button. "Vivian, call the car for my daughter. She's coming down."

When Leigh stepped out of the bathroom, she noticed the suspicious expression on Michael's face. "Hi, Michael."

"Well if it isn't the Holy Ghost." Michael wasn't sure what to think of Leigh these days. "Taking time away from the indigent to look after Dad?"

"Someone has to." She grabbed her purse from the chair, turning to her father. "I'll come by the hotel tonight if—"

"That won't be necessary." Steven appreciated his daughter's care but wanted to be alone. "I have a business dinner tonight. The car is waiting for you."

"The car?" Michael smiled. "Leigh won't accept that, Dad. She only takes public transportation. She likes to be with the people."

"Shut up," Leigh said. "You're always so inappropriate."

"Keeps things interesting," he said. "Thanks for not returning my calls at all this week, by the way."

"I've been busy," she answered. "I have to go. Daddy, I'll call you tomorrow."

"Goodbye, sweetheart." Steven forced a half-smile as he sat in his seat. "Michael?"

Michael waited until the door closed before taking a seat. He tossed the file onto his father's desk. "Gabriel says we might have some problems with our South Africa office. The financial market there has been too erratic and it's messing with our price . . ."

"I've handled that."

"When?" Michael said, trying to keep the surprise from his voice.

"This morning. I've hired a private firm to take care of retooling the strategic plan to keep things safe until the market steadies."

Michael shifted in his seat. "As CFO, don't you think I should have been a part of that conversation?"

"It wasn't necessary," Steven said. "We've hired them before. They know what we want."

Michael gritted his teeth. "So this is how it goes now?"

"Michael, I don't have time for your insecurities today. You can leave now."

"Well, hell, Dad. I knew you'd have it in for me, but I thought I'd be treated better than Avery. This is how it started, right? First, leaving her out of meetings and—"

"That's enough," Steven said. "I'm sick of you right now, Michael. I won't appease you."

"I haven't asked you to do anything for me," he insisted sternly.

Steven appreciated Michael's confrontational glare. His boy was strong. "I'm not leaving you out of anything. I don't feel like talking to anyone."

"Except Leigh."

"I couldn't have turned her away if I wanted to," Steven said. "That has nothing to do with us or Carter and me. I won't let your wives and fiancées ruin our relationship."

Michael leaned back in the chair, enjoying a brief moment of relief. "When are you coming home?"

Steven looked away, shaking his head. "This is between me and Janet. I want you kids to stay out of it."

"You haven't given me a choice, leaving the way you did. Mom's a mess."

"What do I look like? King of the world?"

"I wish I could stay out of it," Michael said. "I have my own marriage to deal with."

"I don't want to hear about that," Steven said. "You certainly don't want my opinion."

"No, I don't." Michael stood up and reached for his file. "But at least I'm working at fixing mine."

"That's what we have to do," Steven said. "Carter deals with the mess he's made with Avery, you deal with yours and I'll . . ."

The first thing Steven thought when he saw Janet standing in the doorway was that she was such a beautiful sight. This was why he had stayed away. He needed to think, and after only a few seconds in her presence he was already feeling confused.

As Michael's mother slowly entered the office, she turned her eyes from Steven to him with a tepid smile. Michael could see the glossiness in her eyes, the slow way in which the edges of her lips turned.

"Hello, Mom." The words sounded colder than he intended. He had no choice but to blame his mother for most of this. He couldn't blame Kimberly more than he already did.

"Steven, I need to speak to you."

Steven responded by saying only, "Goodbye, Michael."

Michael was already closing the door behind him. He was hopeful. One was never too old to feel the pain of parents breaking up. Even big kids wanted their parents to be together forever.

"I'm not ready to talk to you, Janet. I've told you that."

Janet wanted to rush to him and appeal to his sensibilities, play on the power of her touch, but she knew that wasn't the right strategy for this particular problem. That way would only remind him of what he imagined she and Paul had done, at what he'd seen.

"We have to talk." She kept her voice calm, but with a hint of emotion. "You can't ignore me. I'm your wife."

"So you remember that now?" Steven asked.

"I never forgot," she replied without anger. "I was weak and manipulated. I'm not enough of a fool to think you've never been the same."

Steven shot up from his chair. "What?"

Janet realized she'd made a big mistake. "I just mean that we can work this—"

"Are you accusing me of cheating on you?" Steven's temperature shot up five hundred degrees in one second. "Is that your excuse for what you've done? Because you'd be a fool to think I haven't done the same?"

"No, Steven." Janet could say yes, because that was the truth, but that didn't matter. It wouldn't change what he saw, and she was smart enough to know the rules were different for women. "And I did not cheat on you."

"You've been lying to me for months," Steven said. "Oh no, let me correct that—more than thirty years you've been lying to me. The affair, the abortion, the drugs . . . I don't want to . . . I can't deal with you, Janet. I have a company to run."

"You've always put the company first," Janet exclaimed. "Please put our family, our *marriage* first this time."

Steven slammed his fist on the desk. "I have given you everything you wanted! Everything! And this is what I come home to?"

"I have been a great wife to you, Steven!" Janet dug her nails into her palms to fight becoming hysterical. "I won't let you tell me I haven't. I made a mistake and I'm paying for it, but that doesn't wipe away all I've done for you and for our family."

"Leave, Janet." Steven wouldn't argue with her; he couldn't. "Just leave."

"You can't ignore me forever," she warned. "The museum ball is only a week away. Our family is expected to . . ."

The way he looked at her made Janet stop in her tracks. She swallowed hard as his eyes, the eyes that had shown her tenderness, love and promised protection for as long as she could remember, were threatening her now.

"You can't blame me for thinking about it," she said in her defense. "It's what I do. It's been my job to think about what makes the Chase family what it is. You used to appreciate that. It's made you millions."

Steven sat down and leaned back in his chair. He didn't look at her, choosing instead to look past her at the wall where a picture of her sitting on a horse from her parents' stable in Westchester hung.

"Please leave."

"I will." Janet took solace in her small victory but wasn't so sure she was putting herself in a better position. She knew this man better than he knew himself. She shouldn't be at this much of a disadvantage.

"I know you're miserable without me," she added. "We aren't two people married to each other, Steven. We've been one for decades. You have to deal with me."

Avery stood at Patricia's desk as she scrolled down her computer screen with a confused frown on her face.

Patricia was shaking her head. "No, Carter isn't in a meeting right now. He doesn't have anything for another hour."

Avery had arrived at Chase Law unannounced after spending the morning working up the nerve to face Carter and change the plans they'd made. She was afraid if Carter knew she was coming he would have time to prepare and discourage her.

"Did he go to the men's room?" Avery asked.

"Could be." Patricia leaned away from the computer with a shrug. "I was on the phone when he stepped out and he didn't tell me. It was only about ten minutes ago. Wherever he is . . . Oh, I can call him. He always has his cell on him. He always says never make Avery wait. You want to sit down?"

Avery smiled at the consideration. "No, but I will wait in his office."

At the door, she grabbed the handle and pushed, but nothing happened. "Is it locked?"

Patricia turned around with a nervous grin. "I guess it . . . If he locks it, that means he doesn't want anyone in there. He must have a lot of confidential information out and didn't want to put it away. That means he's going to be back soon. You can wait right here with—"

"I'll wait in his office," Avery said. "Please open the door."

Patricia just stared at her but didn't move.

"I know you have a key, Patricia." Avery held her ground. "I'll wait in his office or I'll tell him that I left because you made me wait out here."

Avery knew that would do the trick. Patricia had to know there were problems between her and Carter; it was impossible for an assistant not to know these things. She wouldn't want to be blamed for more trouble.

Patricia took a deep breath before nodding and reaching inside a drawer for a key. She unlocked the office and opened the door for Avery.

Avery stepped inside the always immaculate office with its mix of traditional law firm decor and modern accessories and art. She could feel Patricia standing in the doorway behind her.

"You're welcome to wait with me and keep an eye on me if you feel it's necessary."

"Of course not." Patricia laughed nervously. "You just can't read anything, you know."

"I'm not interested in reading the latest in corporate law." Avery took a seat on the mahogany brown leather sofa. "If I become impatient, I'll call Carter myself."

"Let me know if you need anything." With another hesitant scan of the room, Patricia left, closing the door behind her.

Avery waited a few moments before getting up and heading straight for Carter's desk. She didn't know what she was looking for, but she felt as if she had a better chance of finding it here than in Carter's office at home, of which she had already gone through every inch.

Everything on the desk was about business: depositions, partnership agreements and trademark assignments. There were notes everywhere written in Carter's flawless cursive, but none of it meant anything to Avery. Sitting down in his chair, she reached for the top drawer to his desk, which she knew was always locked, but this time it was . . . open.

She reached in, grabbing the black Coach portfolio she had gotten him for Christmas. He was always secretive about what he put in this drawer. Could it be here?

Her stomach tightened as she braced herself to see hotel room receipts or receipts for jewelry and gifts for another woman, but there were none. What she found were a bunch of restaurant receipts, some invoices paid to the company hired to handle the flowers and decorations for their engagement party, a retainer agreement for a private investigation company to research a "subject" in Chelsea, England, and a cashier's check receipt for . . .

"Three million dollars," Avery said out loud as she slid the document out from the bunch. She flipped the folded sheet and read the rest of the information. Sum of three million dollars and zero cents U.S. requested from a trust account of Carter Blake Chase wired to the Coutts Bank account of Ms. Lisette Victoria McDaniel in London, England.

Avery knew that even for Carter, three million wasn't chump change. It was intriguing for more reasons than the amount and the fact that it was in the "secret" drawer. It was written on a cashier's check instead of a company or personal check. It was written to woman who apparently lived, or at least banked, in England. Then there was the date on the top of the check.

It wasn't the date she'd seen Carter angrily hand that envelope to the woman who haunted her. It was the day before. The envelope he'd given her was too flat to be money, but just right for a cashier's check. Avery had no proof, but she knew this meant something.

She slid the chair toward Carter's laptop and clicked on the Internet. She was going to Google Lisette McDaniel. She typed in the name and immediately got eight hundred hits. Google's engine didn't just return Web site hits, it categorized them into Web pages, news reports and images. She went straight to images.

The images that appeared as thumbnails on the page were too small to recognize. Avery clicked on the first one and saw a picture of a group of white college girls at a keg party in Durham, North Carolina, one of whom was named Lisette McDaniel. She went back and clicked on the second picture. What she saw made her gasp and sent a chill down her spine.

It was her.

Avery stared at her beautiful face, unable to do anything else. There was no doubt it was the same woman she'd seen sitting in the dark corner with Carter. She looked glamorous in an ivory white designer gown that draped to the floor as she smiled for the camera. Her arm was entwined with that of a handsome, distinguished-looking older white man in a tuxedo.

The picture was one of several taken at a New York society event. The caption read only LISETTE MCDANIEL, BEN CALDWELL.

Avery needed more, but before she could begin looking, the office door swung open and Carter rushed in. From the look on his face he expected to see her and was excited, but he quickly adjusted to the look on Avery's face, which she assumed was scary if it was at all as frantic as she felt.

"What's wrong?" Carter paused, assessing the situation. The drawer was open. "What are you doing?"

Avery opened her mouth, but it took a few tries before words actually came out. "Lisette McDaniel."

Carter flinched, too upset to act nonchalant about her discovery. He could see the pleading and anger in her eyes, ready to erupt. He had a choice and quickly made it.

"What about her?" He approached the desk, seeing the document in her hand. He couldn't spend a second thinking of all the times he'd planned to put that somewhere no one could find it. Too many times. "Why are you going through my drawers? I told you that stuff is—"

"For clients?" Avery asked, standing up. "Not this drawer, Carter. Remember, this one is for non-business, personal papers. So you need to tell—"

"It's still private," he said, holding out his hand. "Give it to me."

"You can't lie to me anymore." Avery heard the weak tone of her voice and cleared her throat, hoping that would help. She had to call on her pride to give her strength. "I know who she is."

"What are you talking about?" he asked, fighting the desire to shut off. It would only make things worse. He had to play this right. "Lisette McDaniel is a client, and that is a confidential docu—"

"Stop it!" Avery turned the laptop to face him. "It's her! I saw you with her at the Westin. I followed you."

"You followed me?" Carter wasn't sure he knew exactly what he was dealing with and he didn't like the disadvantage. Looking at the laptop, he wondered if there were any pictures of him with Lisette. "Where do you get off—"

"Where do I get off?" Avery was angry enough to strangle him now. "I'm not explaining shit to you. Your games are over, Carter. I saw you with her, handing her an envelope. It was the cashier's check, right? The three million?"

"It was a business transaction and I want to know why you were following me."

"Because I don't trust you," she answered with a hand on her hip. "And I was right not to. Meeting in dark hotel corners with a beautiful woman who ruined my life."

Carter clenched his fist in anger at her words. Did she still think losing Alex had ruined her life? "You don't know her."

Avery pointed to the computer. "She's the woman in the photos with Alex. I know it's her. I won't ever forget that face. What does she want with you? Why are you doing this . . . ?"

"Don't you see what you're doing?" Carter asked. "You're projecting everything onto me. You found out Alex was cheating on you when you were engaged. You think I'm hiding something from you, so you expect it to happen all over again. You see me with a woman and you convince yourself it's the same one who was with Alex."

"I'm not projecting anything," Avery said. "And I don't believe in coincidences."

"It isn't a coincidence." Carter came around the desk, slamming shut his laptop. "Ms. McDaniel has been a client of mine for a long time. I'll admit what I'm doing for her might be a little unethical, but she needed to move money that didn't hit her company."

"What company?"

"I've already told you too much."

"You haven't told me nearly enough," she answered. "I want to know her company. What you were doing for her. How you know her. Why is the money coming from your trust fund account?"

"That's easily expl—"

"Why," she pleaded, "were you so angry when you gave her that envelope?"

When she said things like that, Carter felt naked. She really saw him. "I saw those pictures, Avery. That woman may resemble Lisette, but it isn't her. She told you her name in that letter. What was—"

"Oh yes, that letter that you got rid of along with the pictures."

"What difference does it make that I threw them away?" he asked. "It hasn't stopped you from crying over him, a man who never really loved you."

Avery gasped. "Alex did . . . he loved me, but he . . ."

"He didn't love you," Carter said. "You admitted that yourself, but you still can't let him go."

"This is not about Alex," Avery said. "I don't love him anymore. This is about her; that woman. She wants something from me. Why are you paying her three million dollars?"

"You're making yourself crazy," Carter said. "I can't answer your questions, Avery, because they're not real questions. It's not her. Now give that to me!"

"I want to meet her." Avery tossed the paper to the floor. "Call her now."

"I won't do that," Carter said. "She's a client and if she knows I'm exposing what we've done with her money, she'll—"

"She'll what . . . call the bar? Or the cops? I don't think so. Whatever you say you did for her would get her in trouble too."

"Not as much trouble as it would get me into." Carter took a step closer, but she backed up. He had never seen this darkness in her eyes. If he had the time for it, he would be frightened by what it meant.

"You never get in trouble, Carter." Avery smirked. "You Chases get away with everything."

He studied her, completely unaware of what to do. He

couldn't plead, because he had already made his bed with this lie. "I can't risk my practice just because of your paranoia."

Avery turned away from him to hide her doubt. She wasn't crazy. She wasn't being paranoid. "It's her."

Carter came behind her and placed his hands gently on her trembling shoulders. "Listen to me, baby. I know you're scared and it's all my fault. But I promise I will make things better. I will fix all of this. Let's just wipe it clean from this moment on. Let go of Alex, let go of—"

"You can tell me." Avery turned around to face him, her hands moving to his cheeks. She held them gently, looking up at him with tears in her eyes.

Carter blinked with a short gasp. He leaned back, the depth of emotion he felt from her look, her touch, frightening him. This was killing her. He was killing her.

"You can," she pleaded. "Whatever she's doing to you, tell me. If she's blackmailing you or if—"

"Stop it." Carter pushed her hands away and backed up. "Avery, you're gonna kill us if you keep this up. I'm not having an affair. That woman is not who you think she is."

Avery knew he was lying. Her arms fell to her sides as she asked, "Do you want to marry me, Carter?"

He stared into her eyes and knew she wasn't going to break for him. He had pushed her too far. "I love you more than—"

"Then I want to meet her," Avery interrupted. "And if you want to marry me, you'd better make it happen now."

CHAPTER 18

"Well, she has to be somewhere," Haley said as Sean paced the interrogation room. "Call her cell again."

"I've called her a million times," Sean answered in an irritated tone. "So has my mom and my dad."

Sean was panicked after Haley had told him everything she knew about Chris. He was certain Chris was planning to pimp Taylor out with the promise of a modeling career. He had found out from Avery that Taylor probably knew the Chase fashion line wasn't going to happen and Haley expected that this made Taylor more vulnerable to Chris's promises.

When he'd confronted Taylor about it, she'd refused to listen and ran off. According to his parents, she hadn't come home for two nights, saying she was staying with friends in L.A., which turned out to be a lie. No one had heard from her. He had to tell them; knowing what he knew, there was no other choice. He couldn't be worried that his father thought this was about his obsession with Haley.

"I thought she was staying at Carter's." Haley leaned away from the female officer, who was trying to apply a wire to the spot between her breasts.

"Avery isn't with Carter anymore," Sean said. "She's been staying at my parents' for the past week."

Haley's lips formed a quick smile. "That's good news."

"Hey, are you taking this seriously?"

"I'm the one being poked and prodded here."

The female cop turned to Sean. "You aren't supposed to be here, you know."

"He's seen it all, sister," Haley said, "and then some."

"Let me do it." Sean waved the cop away. "Just go. I can do it."

After rolling her eyes, the officer walked out of the interrogation room.

"You have to get him to tell you where she is," Sean urged. "You have to do it right away. There isn't time for small talk."

"I know what I'm doing." She really didn't, but she had come this far. "What about the room at the Beverly Hills Hotel?"

"We have it staked it out, but there's nothing going on there."

"Haul him in and beat him up until he talks." Haley felt her skin prickle just a little at his touch. This really wasn't the time, she knew, but she felt it nonetheless. "On second thought, forget that. He'd enjoy it."

"We don't have anything to haul him in on," Sean said. "That's what this is for. We have to keep this low profile so whoever in the department is tipping him off doesn't know about it. What do you mean he'd enjoy it?"

"Pain is what he likes," she answered. "You know, biting, slapping, pulling, whipping and—"

"That's enough." Sean didn't have the time to be frustrated about Haley's sex life. "That just makes him more dangerous."

"Not really." She liked the fact that this was bothering him. "He's kind of a pussy after you—"

"I don't want to hear any more," Sean said. "We have to go. He's at the club now."

"You could be a little more appreciative." Haley slid off the table and reached for her purse. "I am helping you out. You know, if my parents found out about this, they would stop it."

"I'm not afraid of your family," Sean said. "Not when my family is in danger."

"All I'm getting out of this is the good news that Carter and

Avery broke up." She tilted her head to the side, smiling wickedly. "The best news I've gotten since we broke up."

"Is that how you remember it?" Sean asked. "I recall you taking it differently."

Haley huffed. "You deserved everything you got."

"I didn't," he said, "but that's beside the point."

Haley wasn't going to stand for that. "It isn't beside the point, Sean. You lied and you used—"

"I didn't use you!" Sean didn't want any emotion about the past to mess with him now. All he wanted was to find Taylor. "Look, Haley, let's not get into it. I appreciate what you're doing. Let's just—"

"Don't think things have changed," Haley warned. "I don't even know why I'm doing this, but it doesn't mean—"

"I think there is some good in you," Sean said, "despite you fighting it every chance you get."

Haley laughed. "Don't lie, Sean. You don't do it well."

"That's where you're wrong," he answered, taking a step closer to her. "I lied well enough to fool you. I loved you, Haley. I really did."

Haley sighed. "Enough, Sean. I said I'll do this. You don't have to—"

"I know I don't." He pushed his arm against the wall to keep her from passing. "When I ended things between us, I didn't want to."

"Stop it," Haley warned. "You're going to make me change my mind."

"Your mother was right," Sean said. "You would have been miserable with me. We were too different and we were both uncompromising."

Haley refused to let herself get emotional about this. "My mother told you that?"

"She said you loved me and because you hadn't loved anyone before that, you would try to please me. But you can't change and I can't either."

"What are you saying?"

"I'm saying I'm sorry. I listened to your mother, so I blamed her. But it was my choice, so I'm sorry."

Haley just stared at him, not knowing what to think. She wanted to have a snappy comeback to show she didn't care either way.

"We have to get going," Sean said, stepping out of her way.

"I don't understand." Haley didn't move. "You didn't want to break up with me even though it was the right thing to do?"

"I loved you, Haley. But we don't belong together. You know that, don't you?"

Haley nodded, looking away. Damn, how did she let him get to her? "So you didn't lie. You ended it because that's what you wanted. So why are you apologizing?"

"Because I hurt you," he said softly. "And I didn't want to do that. Haley, I—"

He reached for her, but she slapped his hand away. "It's too late, so why bother?"

As she walked away from him, Sean felt like such a fool. Why had he believed this would end on a good note? There was no ending anything on a good note with Haley Chase.

Everything looked glorious, and Janet savored the chance to feel good about something. She had a right to be proud. The museum ball wasn't only the kickoff event of the social season; it was now the best event since she'd been in charge. Heading the occasion, which this year would donate all proceeds to the American Cancer Institute, was such a competitive event, Janet had to call in her markers.

It was the day before the big event and being busy beyond human capacity was just perfect for Janet. She had thought of Steven only a few hundred times that day. And yes, the pills were helping as well.

Looking around, Janet was so proud of her attention to every little detail in the decorations. What she'd put together would be touted as the greatest work of art in the entire museum tomorrow night. The pictures, the publicity and the prestige would reach the elite families on the East coast, the ones who always said that L.A. can have only so much class. Steven would be proud. He would see how much she'd done for their family and their community.

"You don't have much time," Jeannie looked exasperated; her arms overloaded with packages and papers. "*Town and Country* wants to interview you at three. You also have to provide a pre-event quote for *Savoy*, *Angeleno* and *L.A.* magazines."

"You wrote something up, didn't you?" Janet hoped there wouldn't be any photos today; there was no reason for them. "Just give that to them. I have too much to do without . . ."

She stopped as she noticed the extremely inquisitive look on Jeannie's face as her eyes were focused on Janet's shaking hands.

"Are y-you . . ." Jeannie stuttered. "Are you o-okay? Your hands are . . ."

Janet quickly swung her arms behind her. "I'm just nervous. I want things to go well."

"How could they not?" Jeannie looked around. "The attention to . . ."

Janet followed Jeannie's gaze and felt her stomach turn at the sight of Chloe Johnson, social maven in training, walking their way.

Chloe Johnson was a thirty-five-year-old Janet Chase. She had grown up in one of the best black families in Philadelphia; a descendant of investment bankers and physicians dating into the middle 1800s. The best of breeding and education had helped to mold a wonderful high society role model.

One problem: She didn't know her place. After moving to L.A. a year after her husband had died in a tragic car accident while in the Caymans with his mistress, she expected to have the same status here as she'd enjoyed in Philadelphia. Not only was she new, but she was without a husband and, unfortunately, that limited her.

She wanted to be in Janet's social circle and had been jockeying for that position nonstop. She was a pain but had been able to procure enough status that Janet had to acknowledge her.

"Isn't the museum closed today?" Jeannie asked. "I'm going to call security."

"It's all right," Janet said. "I'll handle her. Go work on that statement."

As Jeannie walked away, Janet took a deep breath with one hand firmly on her hip and the other gripping her purse so neither would shake. The pills were wearing off and Janet knew from the look on Chloe's face that she would have to pull from her reserves.

"Janet, dear." Chloe approached with the quintessential fake grin and blew her air kisses. "I'm so glad I found you. I thought you'd be here since tomorrow is . . . Well, isn't this lovely?"

"Thank you, Chloe." Janet smiled wide enough to be just a little too polite. "I'm actually very busy so . . ."

"I was going to offer help," Chloe said as if she hadn't even heard Janet speak, "but I don't think you need it. How brave of you."

"Brave?" Janet asked. "I've managed this ball for a few years now. When you know what you're doing, it's quite easy."

"Of course," Chloe said, "but you've never done it under this pressure. I mean, your marriage falling apart has got to be a distraction. I wasn't sure things would be—"

"I don't know what you're talking about," Janet said, gripping her purse tighter. "But I am very busy, so—"

"No need to cover up." Chloe pouted with pitying lips. "Unfortunately, word has gotten out and . . . well, I just feel so bad that he's left you."

"Steven hasn't left me." Janet remembered Kimberly's threat to spread word that Steven was on the block. "Those are just silly rumors."

Chloe tilted her head to the side as if to say, *Bitch, please*. "Janet, darling, you don't have to kid with me. Actually, I'm quite impressed with your ability to keep things up as you have."

"I'm sure you're enjoying yourself," Janet snapped, "but you're boring me. You don't know what you're talking about, so why don't you mind your manners?"

Chloe, always quick to anger, straightened up. Her plastered-on smile faded as both hands went to her trim hips. "I apologize. I have to remember to be more considerate of my elders."

Janet's lips formed a thin smile. "So quick to use the age card, Chloe. You have to be smarter than that."

"I don't have to be smarter," Chloe said. "I'm younger. And I know Steven is staying at the Four Seasons. For whatever reason he's left you, being without your powerful husband hurts your place. You know that. And now that Steven is available, you'll find—"

"Steven is not available." Janet took a step closer to Chloe with a threatening stare. She could have destroyed her long ago but had taken pity on her because of the humiliation her husband had caused.

"But he is," Chloe corrected her. "And there are women at the top who know that snagging him would put them right where you are now."

"Women like you," Janet said.

Chloe shrugged. "He's an incredibly handsome man. And I'm sure it's been a while since he's touched young skin."

Janet came back with, "Or in your case, youngish."

As Chloe smiled sarcastically before turning and walking away, Janet heard herself exhale. She wouldn't let this get to her. It wasn't as if Chloe was the first woman to openly tell her she wanted to take Steven away. Women had always been jealous of her. They thought their youth, beauty or sometimes being white gave them an advantage over her, but they were all wrong. They underestimated her and Steven.

But now word was out that there was trouble, and the women would pounce. Women like Chloe salivated at the chance to grab a man like Steven and everything that came with him. Even being his mistress would be profitable; but being his wife would be a gold mine in more ways than money.

Janet had to get her man back home—and quick.

Avery hung up the phone, bringing her hand to her chest. A breaking heart was more physically painful than she could have imagined. This was much worse than Alex. Just speaking to Carter on the phone made her burst into tears and run to the kitchen for whatever ice cream she could find.

Not bothering to wipe her tears, Avery tossed every thought from her mind except getting that pint of Häagen-Dazs in her stomach. Only she faced an obstacle standing in front of the refrigerator.

"You're going to get fat," Nikki said. "You've got enough to deal with."

Avery sighed, not wanting to fight. "Fine."

She turned and headed upstairs for the bathroom. It had been an entire two days since she last bawled out while sitting on the toilet. It was time again. Avery thought she was alone, but when the door wouldn't close behind her, she knew she wasn't.

"Mom, please," she said. "Can I be alone for five minutes?"

"I'll leave you alone for ten if you tell me what's going on." Nikki stood in the doorway. She was worried sick about both her girls. How she wished for the days when they were little and she could control where they went, what they did and who they saw.

"You've got enough to worry about with Taylor." Avery felt the weight of worrying about her baby sister's disappearance. "I can take care of myself."

"That's the wonderful thing about family." Nikki came behind her daughter, caressing her hair with her hands. "Even if you can take care of yourself, you don't have to."

"I'm gonna to be fine." Avery leaned over the sink, calming at her mother's touch. "We're meeting at the condo tomorrow night."

"For what?" Nikki asked. "Another set of lies?"

"Not this time," Avery said. Carter had promised that Lisette would be there.

She had been tempted to find out more about the mystery woman since the argument in Carter's office, but he'd called her while she was driving away. He pleaded unlike ever before, in a way Avery couldn't imagine a man like Carter would. Love was love. Being a fool until the end meant giving him chances until you couldn't excuse giving him any more. Carter had one last chance, and he'd promised he would not need another one. So she denied herself and gave him a chance.

"Do you have to go to the condo?" Nikki asked. "You'll end up sleeping together."

Avery thought back to the last time they had made love, the night Steven had fired her. "Maybe you're right."

"Maybe?" Nikki smiled, letting Avery's hair go. She searched for a brush on the countertop. "Where's your . . ."

Avery pointed to the right-side drawer. "Things are bad between us, Mom. Sex is the last thing on my mind. And with Taylor—"

"That's when it happens." Nikki grabbed the brush. She was just about to close the drawer when something caught her attention. "When your emotions are all . . ."

"All what?" Avery rubbed her red, swollen eyes. Sex did seem to be best between them when there was conflict.

"What's this about?" Nikki held out the object in question to her daughter.

Avery glanced at it quickly and smiled. "Those are birth control pills, Mom. What did you think we used, the rhythm method?"

"The dates are wrong." Nikki shoved the pill box at her daughter.

Avery frowned, trying to remember if she'd taken the pill this morning. "I think I forgot this morning's."

"But this says you've forgotten the last six morn—"

Avery snatched the box in a panic. She was looking at it but wanted to believe she wasn't really seeing it. "No, I . . . I took it yesterday. I remember because I'd just thrown up and—"

"You've been throwing up?" Nikki felt her heart beating fast.

"It's . . . stress. I've been under . . ." Avery was feeling dizzy now. She remembered her nausea and lack of appetite followed by being ravenous. "It's because of everything, Mom. It . . . It can't be . . ."

"Oh my God."

"No!" Avery threw the box in the sink as if it was on fire. "I threw up because I was upset over Carter and Taylor and . . . No, I'm not."

"He uses a condom, right?"

Avery shook her head, afraid to open her mouth for what might come out.

"You thought he might be cheating on you and you didn't use a . . ." Nikki threw her hands in the air. These children of hers! "I'm going to the store."

"Mom!" Avery's voice shrieked in panic. "Wait, don't do that. I'm not . . . I can't."

"Don't tell your father," Nikki said. "Whatever you do, don't let him know. I'll be right back."

Avery's knees went weak as she leaned against the sink to stay upright. Looking at herself in the mirror, she saw that her face was already two shades lighter. What had she done?

Haley kicked open the door to Chris's office just as she was grabbed by Lincoln, Chris's wannabe-someone bodyguard.

"Let me go!" She struggled to free herself.

Chris was leaning back, talking into the Bluetooth headset in his ear with his feet on the desk. If she'd surprised him, he didn't show it. He looked more annoyed than anything as he quickly ended his call.

"What are you . . ." He sighed, frustrated. "Let her go, man."

"Fine." The second Lincoln let her go, Haley turned and kicked him in the shin.

"Do you know who I am?" she yelled. "Don't you ever touch me, you piece of shit!"

She didn't flinch as he turned toward her. She knew he wanted to do something but wouldn't. She grabbed the door and slammed it in his face.

"Hey!" Chris yelled. "What's your problem?"

Haley swung around and tossed her purse at him. He grabbed it before it could hit him in the face. "You stupid jackass! I'm going to make you so sorry, you—"

"You need to slow your roll, girl." He stood up as she reached the desk, seeming to brace himself for whatever was to come.

"You made a big fucking mistake trying to get me in trouble." She was showing her most serious psycho-bitch face. "You forgot who I am."

"I don't know what you're talking about, and you best stop getting in my face."

"You think I'm in your face now?" She laughed. "You wait until my daddy gets in your face. You've done it now."

"I didn't do anything." He shoved the purse at her, pushing against her chest. "I'm busy, so—"

"It's too late. You think you can get the cops to pick me up, question me, threaten me with arrest and you just walk away smiling?"

"What?"

With a clenched fist, Haley swung at him, but he backed out of the way just in time. "Was this supposed to be a joke? Your little idea of getting back at me?"

"What in the hell are you talking about?"

Haley was breathing hard as she blinked, trying to appear confused. "You can play dumb all you want, Chris. My daddy is coming after you."

"Either tell me what you're talking about," he said, "or get out of my club."

With a sly side smile, she turned and started out.

"Wait," he said after a moment's hesitation.

How could she have ever doubted her skills? This was going to be so easy. She swung around with a look of fury on her face. She was very impressed when she saw Chris's expression. He was nervous.

"Tell your daddy I didn't talk to the police about you or anyone else," Chris said.

Haley feigned debating whether to explain herself, but she knew there wasn't a lot of time. Sean was listening and he wanted to get in there.

"The police picked me up," she said. "They came to our house and picked me up!"

"To ask about me?"

"They said they'd been tipped that I was running drugs for you. You know I have a record. They threatened me."

"Did you tell them anything about me?"

"Fuck you!" Haley slammed her hands flat on his desk and shoved a stack of papers onto the floor. "I'm the one they're looking at now, and you're the criminal."

"You're the one with the rich daddy who can get you out of anything like he has been doing for the past twenty-three years." Chris started pacing behind his desk. "Did you say something about me or not?"

"I don't talk to cops," Haley said. "I kept quiet until my

daddy's lawyer came and got me out of there. But I do talk to my daddy, and you'd better watch your back."

"It wasn't me," he argued vehemently. "Tell your dad it wasn't me. I don't need him on my ass either."

"It's you or me, Chris." Haley stared at him intently. "If my dad thinks I'm involved, he's going to send me back to Europe and I'm . . ."

As Haley's incredulous expression took over, Chris's curiosity got the best of him.

"What?" he asked.

Haley nodded with an angry grin. "That bitch. It was her. He got her to do it."

"Clue me in, Haley. This isn't just about you."

"The cop said 'she,'" Haley said. "He said, 'she told us . . . she said.'"

"A woman called them." Chris was already appearing relieved.

"When I got back, Sean said I should've stayed in Europe and Taylor said she wished I'd go back."

Chris was taken off guard as Haley was around the desk in a flash. She grabbed his silk shirt and pulled him to her. "Where is she? Where is that bitch?"

"Let me go." He pushed away. "That's between you two. Just keep me out of it."

"Too late for that." She slammed a fist on his desk. "Either you give her up or I give you up."

"What do you mean give her up?" he asked. "I'm not her keeper."

"You're pimping her, aren't you?"

"I thought you didn't care about that."

"I don't, you stupid idiot. I want to find her and kick her ass."

"Wait till she's done." Chris went back to his desk.

Haley's stomach tightened. "Done? What do you mean? She's . . . working right now?"

"I got her at a party." Chris sat down looking extremely proud of himself. "You know the Japanese boys like the sisters."

"You're pimping her out to Japanese businessmen?"

"Hell, yeah. They love it all, gamblin', blow and hos." He

glanced down at his watch. "At fuckin' 2:30 in the afternoon, no less. That's how I—"

"So she's at the Beverly Hills?" Haley turned to head out, but Chris grabbed her by the wrist, turning her back to him.

"No," he said with a pompous smile. "That joint is hot. Besides, it isn't good enough for the yen boys. I went Steven Chase kind of style on this one."

Haley thought for a second. What had she told Chris about her father entertaining business associates? It was hard to remember. She had been high and . . . "The Peninsula Hotel. You've got her at the California Suite?"

"The party will be over in a few hours." Sitting down, he tugged at her, bringing her closer to him. "You've got some time to waste before you beat her down. Why don't—"

"I have to go." Haley pulled away, but Chris tightened his grip. "Chris, I have—"

"There's no rush." He reached around and grabbed her by the waist. "All this attitude has turned me on."

"Not a chance, loser."

Haley slapped at his hand, but he only pulled her closer.

"Stop it." She fell onto his lap, hurting her ankle from the resistance. "That hurts."

"That's the idea, baby." He shoved his face into her neck, starting with a sharp bite.

"Don't bite me, you diseased freak!" Haley slapped at him, pushing away. He was only getting more excited. "Let me go."

"For old time's sake, baby." Standing up, he grabbed her with force and lifted her body in the air.

Haley let out a pained moan when he slammed her flat on his desk.

"I like that," he said. "Sing some more."

"Stop!" Haley was in panic mode now as images of their past encounters threatened her. The last thing she wanted was to be degraded by him again. "You can't."

"I can!" He reached out and grabbed her shirt.

"No!" Haley was scared now because no matter how hard she tried to push his hands aside she couldn't stop him from ripping her shirt open and seeing the wire. She was going to die.

"What the . . . ?" At the sight of the wire taped in her cleavage, Chris jumped back. "You bitch!"

Before she could think, Chris grabbed her by the legs and pulled her back toward him. Her butt slid on the desk and she fell on her back.

"I'm gonna kill you!"

Haley felt her entire body being lifted as he grabbed her sides. She couldn't even scream as she felt herself suspended in the air one second before hitting the ground.

She was seeing lights and then black and then lights again. It wasn't clear, but she looked up in time to see Chris reach into the top drawer. She knew what was in there and she knew if she didn't do something, she was going to die.

He had turned his back to her at an angle as he reached into the drawer. Thank God for Manolo Blahniks.

The end of her ultra-thin four-inch heel went straight into the back of his knee, and she knew from his howl she had pierced skin. He bent inward and fell to his knees with the gun in his hand.

Turning sideways, he raised his arm to aim at her.

Was this when her life was supposed to flash in front of her eyes? Haley wasn't sure. All she knew is that in one-tenth of a second, she saw a vision of her fabulous, privileged existence being ripped from her. She didn't want to die. Her heaven was being a rich, spoiled, beautiful bitch on Earth, and she wasn't about to give that up.

There was no superhuman strength she mustered to lift up her body. She just did it and in enough time to move out of the way of the bullet. Before he could aim again, Haley lurched forward and both of her fists made contact with his face, making him fall back with her on top of him.

With his right hand, he slapped her away and she fell beside him. Her head hit the floor and Haley knew she was about to pass out, but she wouldn't give up. As she shouted obscenities, she kicked again, this time connecting with his right thigh.

He yelled out again, but it didn't stop him. He aimed the gun at her. Haley heard a shot and nothing else.

* * *

Avery knew something was wrong the second she opened the door to the condo. Carter was standing in the hallway, looking perfect as usual, but as she took a step closer, there was a look on his face that she had never seen—fear.

"Hi, baby." Carter had learned at a very young age to conquer his fear. Some things took more work than others, but there wasn't anything he couldn't fix in his favor.

Avery smiled only because that was what her heart always wanted to do the second she saw him. It had nothing to do with how she really felt. "Is she here?"

Carter held out his hand, and Avery didn't want to take it, but she did. She wanted to touch him, connect to him. She hoped it would make some of the fear go away—fear about the future. There was no turning back from the news she had found out yesterday. Three tests had changed her life.

Carter squeezed her hand tight as he led her down the hallway and into the living room. "Let's sit down."

Avery looked around the room and saw no one. She pulled her hand away. "Where is she?"

"Avery." Carter reached for the glasses of wine on the coffee table and offered her one.

"No." Avery stepped back. "Where is Lisette?"

Carter put Avery's glass down but kept his own, taking a long drink. "She isn't coming, Avery."

Avery couldn't believe it. *It's all over* was repeating in her mind. Everything was all over. This man was a complete liar and it was all over. "I'm leaving."

"Wait," Carter gestured for her to halt. "I have to tell you why she isn't coming."

"I only came here to see her," Avery said as she turned to leave, "nothing else."

"Lisette is who you think she is." Carter knew she would stop and she did. When she turned around, he opened his hand to the sofa. "Sit down."

Avery sat down only because if she hadn't she would have fallen. "Where is—"

"My whole world has always revolved around me." Carter sat next to her, trying to stay focused despite the completely injured look on her face. "Even after I met you and fell in love with you, I only wanted what I wanted. It's all I've ever known."

"I don't want to hear this," Avery said. "Who is she?"

"Being with you changed everything," Carter said. "For the first time, I care about someone else's happiness more than my own."

Unable to bear it any longer, Avery grabbed his shirt and yelled, "Tell me!"

"Listen to me." Carter took her hands in his and looked into her eyes. "The past doesn't matter, baby. Our future is limitless. You have to think of that. Our life is going to be incredible. I will give you everything and—"

"I only want the truth," Avery said. "That's all I've ever wanted."

"Don't think I haven't wanted to tell you the truth. Since the night we first slept together, I've wanted to tell you the truth, but it was too late."

Avery remembered the night they'd made love. Despite being half drunk and angry at the world, she would never forget. She had been reeling from the discovery of Alex's cheating . . .

It hit her like a streak of lightning and just as fast. Avery's mouth fell open as a tortured gasp escaped. "No, Carter. Please."

"I wanted you." He squeezed her hands tighter. "You wanted me, but your feelings of loyalty and obligation kept us apart."

Avery felt like the room was spinning around her. "He said he was set up. He blamed you."

"I wanted him out of the way so we could be together," Carter said. "That's where Lisette came in."

Avery felt her chest constricting. She could barely breathe. "She was his lover and she said . . ."

"She was my lover," Carter said, "a few years ago, and she needed money. I needed you."

Avery shook her head. "It can't be that easy. You can't have just done something like that."

"It wasn't easy, Avery. It was hard and it haunted me, but all I cared about was you."

"No!" Avery ripped her hands away and stood up.

"I regretted it the moment it came true, but then you—"

"You knew I'd come to you," she said, looking down at him. "You knew I'd leave him. I'd be vulnerable."

The look of disgust on her face made him falter. "I . . . I knew you . . . you would be with me and that's all that mattered."

"You can actually try to justify shattering me into pieces."

"I make no excuses," Carter said, "but I didn't force him. Neither did she."

"You paid her to seduce him!"

"She picked him up at a bar." Carter stood up. "It took less than an hour before he came back to the hotel with her."

"Shut up!" Her hand went to her mouth to stifle a whimper. "It was my fault. I pushed him away because of you."

"You didn't love him the way you love me," Carter said. "You told me, and you don't lie."

"But you do." Avery felt an eerie sense of calm. "It's all you do."

"She came back for more money. I didn't have any choice, but I couldn't let you know. I couldn't hurt you."

"You mean you couldn't hurt me anymore," Avery said. "Right? Because you had no problem hurting me before. You had no problem ripping me apart as long as Alex got all the blame for it."

"Back then, I only saw—"

"What about now?" she asked. "You wanted me to think I was crazy. You lied and you were perfectly fine making me think I was imagining things."

Avery's hands went to her head, feeling it beginning to split apart.

"I was scared," Carter said. "I know you hate me now, but you have to know that I was scared because I love you so much. When you wade through all of this, that's what it comes down to, Avery. And I know you love me."

"Why?" she asked sarcastically. "Because how could I not? That's what your master plan was tonight, right? Tell me how you destroyed my life, lied to me and made me a fool. It's okay, because no matter what, I've still gotta be grateful to have a rich man that wants to marry me."

"Avery, that's not—"

"Good thing you're not poor," she said, "because you'd be in deep shit now."

She was laughing now and Carter sensed her hysteria. "Please understand."

"You would have kept that lie forever if Lisette had let you get away with it."

Carter wasn't about to lie again, so he didn't answer as Avery's mixture of laughter and tears dug into his gut. "I didn't tell you because I wanted to protect you . . ."

Avery opened her arms wide. "Well, you certainly did a bang-up job of that."

Carter nodded in agreement, too ashamed to try to defend himself.

Avery felt like she was going to throw up. Looking at him standing in front of her, she knew the truth. It was too big and loud to hide behind his handsome face or the appeal of his last name and his money. He was the man she'd thought was the answer to all her dreams, but had turned out to be just another liar. And she still loved him. She still wanted him. That was what made her sick to her stomach.

"I have to go," she said. Half in a daze, she was looking around, unaware of which way to turn.

"We have to talk about this," Carter said. "What we have is worth saving. It's worth more than my stupid mistakes. We can work through this. I will do anything."

"Yes," she said, nodding. "But I have to go now. I can't talk now. I have to think."

"Avery." Carter heard the strain he felt in his voice. "I can't let you leave. I want you—"

"I don't give a fuck what you want!" The venom in her tone jolted him. "You selfish bastard!"

"I deserve that, I know, but—"

"You deserve a lot more," Avery said. "What you don't deserve is anything you want right now. So I'm going to leave because if I don't, I'll probably say—no . . . *do* something I'll regret."

Carter believed her. He had never seen her this angry. "No matter what we have to go through, we will work through this."

"I have to go home." Avery slowly turned and stumbled a few steps.

"This is your home," Carter said. "This is where you belong."

She looked back at him, seeing the fierce resolve in his eyes. She remembered what Kimberly had said and she read between his lines. He was telling her she belonged to him.

CHAPTER 19

Everything was wonderful. Just wonderful enough to make Janet not want to fall to the ground and come completely apart. Everyone who made up the fabric of L.A. society was there: politicians, business leaders, philanthropists and a few celebrities who were known to be charitably inclined. They were all beautiful and their wallets were full. In the past hour, the governor of California, the mayor of Los Angeles and the senior senator of California had arrived with the press flashing wildly outside.

Janet had received nothing but compliments and knew she looked just as stunning as everyone said she did, despite being two seconds away from completely losing her mind.

Arriving early was a small diversion from the fact that she was alone. Only a few people asked about Steven and the children, and she smoothly evaded having to answer. No one would have the nerve to ask about her marriage, but some of them had to be whispering. Word was getting around. Janet had spent so much of her life cleaning up the messes her children made, but this mess was her own making and there was no telling what damage could be caused before she fixed it.

"Janet, dear." Phoebe Stahl stepped into Janet's line of sight as she approached.

She was a seventy-year-old pasty-white vision of big hair, broad shoulders and fat jewelry. Phoebe was a throwback from the '80s, when every society woman looked like Joan Collins from *Dynasty*, and she'd never given it up. Excess was her daily mantra. Janet found it a little tacky, but she found Portis Stahl's shoe magnate money too appealing to not invite them to every fund-raiser.

"You look lovely," Phoebe said as the two blew air kisses at each other.

"Thank you." Janet pasted on her perfect smile, fighting the urge to take more pills. She couldn't remember when she'd taken her last dose. "So do you, dear. I hear Portis is up and running again."

Phoebe beamed. "My husband isn't going to let a little thing like a heart attack keep him down."

"He looks well."

"He's not as dashing as Steven is tonight, but he has his color back."

"I'm sorry." Janet was shaken. "What did you just say?"

"Just that Steven looks particularly . . ." Phoebe's eyes danced as someone across the room caught her interest. "Oh! Alexandra is here. I have to hear about her new yacht."

"Phoebe." Janet reached for her. "Did you say . . ."

"Lovely party, dear." Phoebe blew her a kiss before rushing off.

Janet's pulse raced as she searched the enormous room. There were too many people. She tried to keep from looking desperate but couldn't help herself. Was it possible? If he was here, it meant he cared, as she knew he did.

Janet stopped, her breath catching when she saw him. Standing next to a column near the end of the room, Steven held court looking like a king among men.

He had come for her.

"Excuse me, gentlemen." Janet smiled politely as she stood outside the circle of men surrounding Steven. "Might I borrow my husband for a few minutes?"

The men parted quickly and when he saw her, Steven allowed the emotion to pull him toward her. How he had managed to go this long without going nuts amazed him. Even when he went on long business trips or the family spent the week at the Vineyard while he stayed in Los Angeles until Friday, he would talk to her on the phone at least once a day.

"I'm so glad you came." Janet pressed against him, placing her hand on his chest. "I knew you would."

Steven wished he had the strength to step away from her, but he found too much comfort in her touch. "Janet, understand something. I'm not here for you."

"Of course you are," Janet said. "You hate these things. You came because you knew I needed you here."

"I'm here because Michael said no one else from the family was coming," he said. "And I don't intend to stay long. It would be best if we kept our distance to avoid any problems."

Janet's hand fell to her side as her heart sank. "How long do you intend to punish me?"

"This is what I mean," he said coldly. "I won't start this here."

"But—"

"I didn't want tonight to be about our conspicuously absent family." He looked away from her hurt eyes.

She wanted to grab him as he turned to walk away, but she couldn't. What if someone was watching? So despite feeling her soul being crushed, she smiled and followed him with endearing eyes. Just in case gossipy lips wanted to say they saw anything other than a kind exchange between spouses.

That was until she saw Chloe Johnson make a beeline for Steven, cutting him off. She looked incredible in a strapless lavender satin gown, and her young, eager, wide eyes had Steven's attention. Feeling the air being sucked out of the room, Janet watched as Chloe briefly touched Steven's upper arm and laughed. Steven laughed too and that was all Janet could take.

"Mom."

Janet turned to see Haley standing behind her. She was all dressed up for the occasion, but with a noticeable bruise on her left cheek. By instinct, Janet rushed to her and raised her hand to the bruise.

"Baby, what—"

"Don't." Haley moved her face away. "I tried to cover it up with makeup, but it keeps getting darker."

"What happened?"

"Not that it would matter to you, since I haven't seen you at all, but I was almost killed yesterday."

Janet wasn't sure if she was kidding or not, but she looked too angry to be fooling with her. "You'll have to be more specific."

"I tried to help Sean get information on Chris."

"I thought you were through with him," she said, "with both of them."

"It's a long story."

"I want to hear it." Janet took hold of Haley's arm and led her aside.

She glanced back in Steven's direction and fumed at the sight of him still with Chloe. She seemed closer to him now and they were both still laughing.

As they reached a quiet corner of the room, Haley pulled her arm away. "Chris was about to pimp Taylor out to some Japanese businessmen and Sean needed to know when, so he wired me and—"

"Are you insane?" Janet didn't understand much of that but knew it wasn't good. "What did he do to you?"

"He tried to kill me." Haley rolled her eyes. "Do I need to repeat it again?"

"Let me get your father."

"No! I don't want him. I want to talk to you."

"Has he been taken into custody?" Janet asked.

Haley nodded. "And Sean got to save Taylor before anything happened to her, but not before he saved me. Again."

Janet saw a flicker of emotion in Haley's eyes. She hoped it didn't mean she was falling for the detective again.

"Chris was about to shoot me point-blank," Haley said, "but Sean busted in the room right before and shot him. Sound familiar?"

"All too." Janet shuddered. "How could you do something like this without telling me?"

"Sean could hear everything from the wire I had on," Haley

said. "He knew where his sister was and that she was in danger of being raped. He could have bolted and let the other cops save me, but he didn't. He made sure I was safe before he went after her."

Janet took a deep breath. Why did she have to be so reckless? "You could have been killed. Why would you put yourself in that—"

"Because Sean loved me," Haley said. "He still cares about me, but that's all ruined because of you."

Janet knew immediately what she was talking about. "Haley, that's the past. It doesn't mean anything now. All that matters is that you're okay."

"You made him dump me."

Janet looked around before taking a closer step. In a low voice, she said, "I didn't make him do anything. I told him what he should do and he made the choice to do it. I didn't threaten him or bribe him."

"You knew I loved him and you wanted him to hurt me." Haley lips pressed together in anger as the whites of her eyes got smaller and smaller. "I will never forgive you for that."

"You thought you loved him," Janet said. "Remember, daughter, I know you better than you know yourself."

"I did love him."

"I think you could have," Janet answered, "but you love being Haley Chase more. You would've had to give that up to be with him and I'm not just talking about the lifestyle, although that would have been enough to make you miserable."

"Then I would have ended it. That should have been my choice. Do you know how hurt and humiliated I was?"

"I think all of Los Angeles remembers," Janet said.

"You had no right."

"I had every right," Janet said. "I'm your mother. No one loves you more than I do and no one knows what is better for you than me. If you had stayed, it would have caused you pain. He would have made you try to be something you aren't and that would have been worse. Trust me."

"Trust you?" Haley laughed. "Never again."

"Haley!" Janet surprised herself with the volume with which she called after her daughter, who stormed off. She garnered a few looks, but that didn't matter.

Haley was all she had left.

When she turned back to Steven, he was gone. So was Chloe. Ignoring anyone who called her name, Janet searched the vast room for her husband, trying to fight the images in her head. Steven was a good man, but he was a man and Chloe was a beautiful young woman with a plan. She had to find him.

Her mind floated to Haley, and the effect on her psyche only got worse. She was beginning to feel confused and was frightened to death that people were noticing. Suddenly it seemed like everyone was staring at her, laughing at her.

What kind of woman was she? They all had to be asking how she could manage to lose both daughters and a husband in the span of one year. How her oldest son seemed to barely know she existed and her youngest son had turned on her in favor of trash. How could everything so quickly fall apart when all she wanted was to make things right?

"Janet?"

Janet felt someone grabbing her arm. She turned and snapped, "What do you want?"

Phoebe snatched her hand away, letting out a quick gasp of surprise. Janet never lost her cool in public this way, but she was barely holding on.

"I have to go, Phoebe."

"I just wanted to know if you were all right," Phoebe said. "You're almost as pale as me."

Janet tried to smile but couldn't. "I'm fine. Enjoy yourself. I'll be back in a moment."

She searched the room but couldn't find either Steven or Chloe. As her head began to pound, Janet was feeling frantic. The images of her husband, the man she couldn't live without, hidden somewhere in the crevices of the museum with that woman's hands on him, made her want to go crazy.

Janet knew what she had to do. She had to get out of the spotlight, stop the staring and laughing. It was too humiliating.

They all knew that Steven was with Chloe and she was the old hag who had been tossed aside. She couldn't take their glares anymore.

Finding her way to the back room, behind the stage where the band was performing, Janet pushed inside. She was grateful no one was there because she wasn't sure she could hold up a pretense anymore. She rushed to the drawer under the vanity, where she had left her purse. Ripping it open, she reached for her pills and grabbed the bottle of wine sent to her as a gift from the museum. If she could just take them together, they would balance her out and she would be fine. She just needed a little more than before. In a few minutes, she would calm down and be Janet Chase again. Then she would find her husband and make things right.

Carter knew it wasn't a good sign that Avery rang the door-bell to their condo instead of using her key to come in. It meant she didn't think this was her home anymore. But it was and he was going to make her remember that. He would have to change everything, but he was willing to do that. No matter how long it took, he would win her forgiveness. It would be on her terms; giving her the power so she wouldn't be afraid. His desperation told him to push, but he knew that wasn't going to work. He had to give her space, give her time.

He smiled but didn't say anything as he opened the door. Looking into her eyes, he could see how far into the hole he was. Those eyes that had always held warmth and need for him offered nothing now. It was worse than anger.

Avery felt queasy as she walked down the hallway into the living room. She wasn't sure if it was the pregnancy or the situation. She had made up her mind and cried her eyes out over it, but that was it. There was no turning back now.

"I don't want to sit down," she said as he gestured toward the sofa. "I have something to say."

"I know." Carter felt his chest tightening. He looked down, noticing the ring was not on her finger anymore. As much as it hurt him, he held his chin up. He was prepared for that.

"I've been doing a lot of praying," she said, "and I think you know that I can't marry you."

You expected this, Carter told himself. *Stay calm.* "I know a wedding isn't in the cards for us right now. We have a lot to work through and I know what that means for me. I have to change the way I do every—"

"You don't understand." Avery felt certain there was nothing he could say or do to make her change her mind, but she still loved him too much to be sure, so she had to halt him. "We're over, Carter. I've canceled the wedding and I—"

"No." Carter saw her reach into her purse and knew what she was about to do. "The ring is yours. You'll wear it again, Avery. I know you don't think you will. I know you don't think you want to, but you will. I'm going to fix this."

"You can't fix this." Avery offered him the ring, but he stepped back. She bit her lip to keep from crying. "Take it, Carter."

Carter shook his head. "You want me to accept that we're over. I love you too much."

"I don't think you understand what that means," she said.

"I didn't," Carter said. "I admit that. But I do now and I will earn your forgiveness."

"You don't have to," she said. "I'll forgive you one day, Carter, but I'll never trust you again. And I don't believe I'll ever respect you again."

That was a blow to the gut and Carter faltered a bit. "I . . . I made a mistake. It was a horrible one, but it doesn't make me a horrible person."

"I know that." Avery prayed to keep some control over her emotions. "I never said you were horrible. I just can't be with you."

"But you want to," he said, "because you love me."

She had expected manipulation. "I don't want to see or hear from you again. Is that clear enough?"

"No," Carter said flatly. "If you want space, I can give you that, but don't ask me to give up on us. I can't do that. I love you too much."

"How can you . . ." *No, girl, get hold of yourself. Don't let him take you there. He's too good.*

"I know what I did was awful," he pleaded. "But, Avery, I loved you and I wanted you more than I've ever wanted . . ."

"Stop it." Her anger at his audacity made her stronger. "Don't say that. This wasn't about love. It was about winning. It was about you thinking your blessed genetics allowed you the right to manipulate people's lives to get what you want. You didn't care who you hurt, including me. I wasn't even the prize. That self-satisfying desire you have for victory was the prize."

Carter ignored her truth; it was too unsettling. "There was something between us, Avery. It wasn't just a game. You wanted me."

"I wanted Alex!" When she saw him wince, Avery felt pain too.

"You wanted me!" Carter felt himself losing control. "I was the one who made it happen."

"Because I was too chicken to turn my back on the promises I'd made. Let's not do this, Carter. Please, this is hard enough." She leaned over and placed the ring on the table. "God, this is so hard. Please, let—"

"It started as a game," Carter admitted, "but you know I cared for you. And when we were finally together, I knew I was in love with you."

"Then why did you keep doing it?" she asked. "Why did you keep lying? Why did you steal those photos from me? Why did you keep trying to trick me? Why did you try to make me think I was asking for too much when I just wanted the truth? You don't do that to someone you love."

"I was trying to save us."

"No." Avery shook her head. "You were trying to save your win."

Haley wasn't sure what was wrong with her. She was just off her game. She had been since she'd gotten back from Europe. All these emotions were clouding her thoughts. She didn't do regret well, but couldn't seem to avoid feeling it. She had every right to be mad at her mother, didn't she? She hadn't been looking for forever with Sean, but it was the first time she'd felt something real; the first time she hadn't spent most of her time with a guy trying to figure out when she would have to dump him. She'd had better sex before, but it was still great and . . . maybe he did love her. Maybe Sean was the guy who could have loved her despite herself. Her mother never gave him the chance to . . .

Who was she fooling? Haley knew she couldn't stay mad at Janet. Her mother was the only person she really cared about— except the twins, of course. She was certainly the only person Haley knew she could trust. She couldn't justify letting a man, who would be temporary at best, come between them.

"Haley?"

Haley turned from the terrace railing as her father approached. *Oh, this one*, she thought. "What are you doing here?"

"Hello, little one," he said. "Nice to see you too. You know I've left messages on your cell. I want you to come visit me at the hotel."

Haley laughed. "And you know you weren't serious, so I didn't bother."

"I was serious." Steven usually brushed Haley's insincerity aside, but it hurt this time. God help him, he missed the little hell-raiser.

Steven set his glass of wine on the tray of a passing waiter and came closer to his daughter. "I know this hasn't been easy on you. You're the baby and you're so close to your mother."

"Someone has to be." There were those damn emotions again. Haley was furious with him and his trying to play the loving father was making her angrier. "Why did you come here? To taunt her? To hurt her more?"

"I came for our family and I still . . ." Steven was hit with alarm as Haley, who had only turned halfway, finally faced him and he saw the bruise on her face. "What is this? What happened?"

"Nothing." Haley covered her cheek with her hand. "I fell."

"What happened, Haley?" Steven's tone was insistent.

"I said nothing, and since you aren't talking to Mom, she can't tell you. So I guess you're ass out of luck."

"Watch your mouth."

From his tone and the look on his face, Haley knew she had reached her limit. "Leave me alone, Daddy."

"I love your mother," Steven said. "That's not what this is about."

"If you loved her, you wouldn't hurt her like this. She's a mess and you're enjoying it."

"I am not." Steven wouldn't bother explaining things to this unreasonable girl. "This is between me and Janet. Not you. Now tell me what happened. Did you get into a fight? Did you—"

"Sorry," Haley said. "You don't get to play Daddy anymore. If you leave, you're out."

"I'll always be your father."

She turned away from his stern look. This was craziness. What was wrong with her? Maybe it was the near-death experience with Chris. Yes, that had to be it. What else could make her this sensitive?

"You want me to believe you care about me?" she asked. "Well, I don't, because if you cared about me and what was best for me, you wouldn't have left my mother."

"I haven't left Janet. She and I aren't getting divorced. We have a problem."

"And ignoring her is fixing it?" Haley threw her hands in the air. "I don't care. I'm not a kid anymore. I don't need you around. She'll find somebody else. She's a beautiful, wonderful person and she'll find someone to replace you."

"Haley." Steven took hold of her arm as she was about to walk away. "Wait. I want to tell you—"

"Don't talk to me," Haley said. "If you care, talk to her."

"Where are you going?" He refused to let go even though she pulled away.

"I'm going to do what you don't love her enough to do," Haley said. "I'm going to apologize for thinking she would want to hurt me, for doubting that she really loved me."

"If you explain yourself, I'll let you go."

"You'll let me go because I'll make a scene if you don't. And you know I'm better at that than anyone."

She was, but Steven didn't care this time. Usually he'd leave her to Janet when she acted like this, but the bruise was upsetting him too much. "I'll make you a deal. You tell me what happened and we'll both go talk to Janet."

Haley paused and stopped pulling away. "You can't go nuts, 'cause I'm fine now."

Steven saw Jeannie poking her head out, and he waved her over.

"Where is Janet?" he asked.

Jeannie's brows furrowed. "I think I saw her go in the back room, behind the stage. Do you want me to get her?"

"No," Steven said. "I'll get her. Thanks."

He turned to Haley, finding it surprising that she was the one who'd made him come to his senses. "Let's go."

Steven reached for the cell phone he had clipped to the inside of his tuxedo jacket. "I don't understand you, Haley. It's like you're insane or . . . I just don't know."

"What are you about to do?" Haley put her hand on the back room door, blocking him from going inside.

"I'm making sure this asshole doesn't get out on bail."

"He tried to kill me," Haley said. "It's on tape. Besides, he got shot in the arm, so he isn't going anywhere anytime soon."

"Get in there," Steven ordered. "This isn't over yet."

With him right behind her, Haley opened the door, and what she saw made her heart leap out of her chest. "Mommy!"

It looked like a scene of overacting in a tragic play. Janet's body was laid out on the sofa, one arm swinging to the ground, the other reaching over the back. She looked regal in her pearly white gown, everything perfect except that she appeared to be dead.

Both of them rushed to her side, hysteria and panic sweeping through them at the sight. Steven felt more frightened than he ever had in his life.

"Janet!" He pulled her to him, but she seemed lifeless. "My God, Janet! Haley, call 911."

"What's happening?" Haley was pulling at her hair, feeling her body shivering. "What happened to her?"

Steven put his fingers to her neck and felt a pulse. He slapped Janet's face, but she didn't respond. "Please, baby. Wake up."

"Someone shot her?" Haley asked, tears flowing down her cheeks.

"Call 911!" He felt all over Janet's body. "She isn't shot. It's something else."

Haley stumbled for her cell phone. She dialed 9 before it fell out of her shaking hands. When she went to pick it up, she saw the bottle. No, she saw both bottles.

"Daddy!" She picked up the bottles, offering them to her father.

Steven snatched them from her. "Call them, Haley."

As Haley cried over the phone with the emergency operator, Steven cradled his wife in his arms, caressing her face gently. He said her name over and over again, feeling himself dying inside. This was his fault. If she didn't make it, Steven knew he wouldn't either.

"You can't fix it," Avery responded to Carter's pleas. Expecting to get weaker as he continued to beg her understanding, she was finding herself only getting stronger, more resolved. "You can't fix it because it's not all your fault. It was my fault too."

Carter angrily picked up the phone, which had been ringing nonstop for the past ten minutes and slammed it back on the receiver. He returned to her, unwavering in his case.

"I knew something was wrong," she confessed. "I knew in my gut, but I put up with it because I loved our life. I loved being with you. You were so incredible to me, and that you wanted me was so compelling. The lifestyle I had with you only made loving you so much more rewarding. I tried to believe none of it mattered, but it did. It was all so seductive, and I can't blame anyone but myself for wanting it so much I could ignore the truth."

"But you can have both now," Carter promised, "the life and the truth for us and our children . . ."

"No." Avery was thinking of the life inside her, knowing what she had to do. "I don't want any of it anymore. I don't want to be so drunk with material things that I'm willing to give up my self-respect."

"You won't have to," Carter said. "I'm going to change, Avery. You'll never have to give up anything ever again."

She looked him in the eyes, knowing that she loved him but wondering if she'd ever really known him. He was waiting for her to give him hope, give him something. But all she could do was tell him, in a soft, broken voice, "I don't believe you."

Carter felt like someone had grabbed his insides and was wringing them like a wet rag, tighter and tighter. "Avery, our future is worth more than our past. It's—"

"It's over."

Keeping his eyes set on hers, Carter took a deep breath and stood up straight. With a voice that showed not even a hint of uncertainty, he said, "I won't let you go."

Avery believed him, which was why she wouldn't, couldn't tell him about the baby. "You don't have a choice."

That didn't matter to Carter, but before he could tell her that, there was a pounding on the door followed by the doorbell ringing.

"You just need time," he said, distracted by the pounding.

"Just get it," Avery said. "I'm leaving anyway."

She rushed down the hallway, knowing he was right behind her. When she opened the door, they were both surprised to see a frantic Leigh standing on the other side.

"What is wrong with you?" she asked. "I've been trying to reach you for ten minutes!"

"We were talking," Carter said impatiently. "This isn't a good time, Leigh."

"It's Mom," Leigh said. "Daddy just called. Something bad has happened."

Carter gripped the door. "What?"

"Is she all right?" Avery asked.

"Daddy said she was unconscious and they were in the ambulance on the way to Cedars-Sinai. They were at the museum ball."

"Let's go." Carter rushed back to grab his keys off the console. "I'll drive."

"No." Avery stepped back.

"Avery, please," Carter said.

Leigh looked between them, unaware until now that there was a space of about a million miles there. "What's going on? Carter, this is an emergency."

"I'm coming," Avery said. "But I'll drive myself. I'll come behind you."

"I need you there," Carter pleaded.

Avery nodded. "I'll be there. Go ahead of me, please."

"Come on." Leigh grabbed her brother and dragged him to the elevator. "Carter, come on."

Carter kept his eyes on Avery until the elevator door closed between them. The entire time, she kept her eyes to the floor.

Leigh, Michael, Haley and Carter all stopped their pacing as Steven came out of the hospital room. The way they looked at him reminded Steven of when they were all small children with eyes wide in search of his wisdom and reassurance. They were all his; this was his family and it would have all been destroyed without Janet.

"She's going to be okay," he said.

Leigh rushed to him, wrapping her arms around his waist and burying her head in his chest.

"You've said that," Michael said. "Why can't we see her?"

"She hasn't woken up yet." He held Leigh tight. "When she does, I'll go in and when it's okay, I'll call you in."

"They pumped her stomach?" Carter asked.

"That wasn't necessary," he answered. "She didn't OD. She had a bad reaction to the combination of medications. The alcohol put her over the edge."

"This is your fault!" Haley blurted out. "You drove her to this."

"Don't," Carter warned. "Haley, not now."

"It's the truth." Haley wiped the tears from her cheeks with the back of her hand. "She took the pills because she was afraid to tell you the truth about Paul. She knew you would turn on her. When you left, you pushed her over the edge. You almost killed her!"

"Haley." Leigh let go of her father and went to Haley. "Calm down. Come and walk with me."

"No." Haley pulled away from her grip. "I'm just speaking the truth. We almost lost everything because of your male pride."

"Haley!" Carter yelled.

"It's okay," Steven said. "She's right. This was my fault. Your mother deserved more from me. Haley, no matter what has happened up to this moment, I know that this family is all that matters. Your mother is going to be fine."

He reached his hand out to her, but she didn't accept it. Turning away from him, she saw Kimberly in the distance.

"Who invited that bitch?" Haley asked.

Everyone turned to see Kimberly looking on cautiously.

Michael turned back to them. "I'll take care of it."

Before she could get a word out, Michael grabbed Kimberly by the arm and pulled her around the corner.

"I told you not to come," he said menacingly.

"I want to be here for you." Kimberly reached for him, placing her hands on his cheeks. She was grateful beyond words that he didn't push them away. Instead, he closed his eyes and leaned into her.

"She's going to be okay," he said. When her lips came to his, he kissed her, finding the comfort he needed. "She could have died, Kimberly."

"You can't believe that's what I wanted," she pleaded. "Baby, I love you and I love our children. I wouldn't want them to lose their grandmother. No matter how I feel about Janet, she loves the boys and they love her."

"I know." He opened his eyes, looking into hers. She was afraid and she should be. He was angrier at her more than ever, but he also needed her now more than ever. "But you can't be here."

"The press is outside," she said. "Cameras, everything."

Michael cursed under his breath. "You don't say anything."

"I never would," she promised. "I just need to know that everything between us is going to be okay."

He didn't say anything. He couldn't tell her what she wanted to hear, because he wasn't so sure. Michael stepped away from her, his hands falling to his sides. "Go home, Kimberly. We'll talk later."

As she stood at the corner, watching him return to his family, Kimberly knew she was in trouble. They all hated her now. She was more of an outsider than ever before. She couldn't live without Michael.

"Kimberly."

As soon as she saw Avery, Kimberly fell into her and broke down in tears.

Avery wrapped her arms around her. "What . . . Oh, my God. Is she?"

"No." Kimberly tried to pull herself together. "She's gonna be fine."

"That's good news, right?" Avery asked.

Kimberly was shivering, suddenly feeling like ice all over. She stumbled to a bench along the wall with only Avery to hold her up. When they sat down, Kimberly took Avery's offered hand and squeezed tight.

"Kimberly, you're scaring me."

"Michael hates me now."

"No." Avery rubbed the back of Kimberly's hand comfortingly. "Michael loves you and the boys more than anything. You're in a bad patch, but you'll recover."

"Not this time," Kimberly said. "He couldn't tell me we'll be all right."

"He's only thinking of his mother right now."

Kimberly looked at her, wishing she could be as naïve. "My boys are all I have."

"Stop talking like that," Avery said. "You're putting the cart before the horse. You'll fix your marriage."

"What if I don't?" Kimberly asked. "What if he wants me out? I'll lose the boys."

"They're your kids," Avery said. "Children belong with their mothers."

Kimberly laughed. "Avery, I know you've only been around us for a year, but you can't be that stupid. Haven't you listened to anything I've told you?"

Avery couldn't begin to tell her how much her words had been on her mind these past few weeks. "Yes, but the twins are—"

"They're Chases, Avery. That's who they are. I'm not. If that family is against me I have no chance with my kids."

Avery didn't want to hear this. "Yes, they have money and they have power, but those boys came from your belly."

"When that family bands together," Kimberly said, "they always get whatever they want. Blood is thicker than water, but their blood is thicker than blood. You haven't seen what I've seen. When you cross them, you don't have a chance."

Avery took her words to heart, unable to appreciate the irony. Kimberly's imagined problems were more than real to her. She was turning on Carter and pregnant with his child. He'd already made it clear he wasn't going to let her go. What would he do when she gave him no choice?

"Avery." Kimberly winced. "Avery, please."

"What?" Avery broke from her trance.

"You're hurting me." Kimberly looked down at their hands.

Avery realized she was squeezing Kimberly's hand with both of hers and let go. "I'm sorry. I'm . . . I have to go, Kimberly. I can't be here."

"I'm here, baby." Janet's eyes came into focus as Steven looked down at her.

"Steven," came as a hoarse whisper from her lips. "What . . . ?"

"Shh." Steven brought his finger to her lips before trailing her cheek gently. "You're weak now, sweetheart. Let me do all the talking."

He told her everything that had transpired from the moment he and Haley found her. Janet couldn't believe she'd let her baby see her looking like a half-dead drug addict and put the family's name in such jeopardy.

"Steven, I swear I thought . . ."

"You don't have to explain now," Steven said. "I thought I'd lost you. I thought I'd lost the love of my life."

"I'm so sorry."

"You just get well and when we get home, we'll work it out."

"Home?" she asked.

"Home." Steven smiled. "But first, I have a surprise for you."

Janet's eyes lit up as Leigh came from around the curtain with a warm, loving smile on her face. Tears were coming down her cheeks as she approached the bed.

"Hi, Mom." Leigh took her father's place as he got up to leave the room.

"I'm so sorry, baby." Janet lifted her arm and Leigh reached out to take her hand. "This isn't how I wanted . . ."

"I'm the one who's sorry," Leigh said. "We're family, and you never turn your back on family. I forgot that."

"I made it easy for you," Janet said. "I hope you can forgive me."

"Mom!" Haley rushed around the bed and threw herself on top of her mother.

Janet smiled, running her hand over Haley's hair. "I'm okay, baby. Don't worry about me."

"Take it easy, Haley," Steven instructed.

Carter and Michael stood at the end of the bed and she blew them both a kiss. With her family around her, Janet forgot about the mess she'd caused, the trouble she'd made and the pain she'd endured. Everything was going to be okay.

She knew she had her family back. All that was left was to make Kimberly pay.

EPILOGUE

Janet watched as Maya placed the plate of fresh strawberries, pineapples, cherries and mango on the table in the middle of the Florida room.

"I told you I was fine with coffee," Janet said.

Maya looked at Steven, who was sitting across from Janet reading that morning's issue of the *Wall Street Journal*. He shrugged and buried his head in the paper.

"Blame him," Maya said. "He said you have to eat."

Janet eyed Steven, who glanced up from the paper and winked at her. "I'll try to put a dent in it."

"Thank you," Maya said before walking off.

It had been three days since the incident and this was her first morning at home. It was a beautiful early September morning—not as hot as usual and the view from the room this time of morning was perfect.

"I talked to Dr. Gaines yesterday." She picked up a fork and retrieved a chunk of pineapple.

"She's safe, isn't she?" Steven asked.

Janet nodded. "She's a doctor with the best reputation. Trust me, she won't leak anything to the press. She recommended the doctor in South Africa."

"Someone you can talk to?"

"Hopefully someone *we* can talk to." She ended her statement as more of a question.

Steven smiled. "Of course."

"She thinks, and I agree, that my anxiety really stems from the abortion. Even though my Valium abuse started before Paul showed up, it was still my biggest regret and I never faced it."

Over the past few days, Steven had learned everything about Paris, the affair, the abortion and Paul's attempt at seduction. All he cared about was Janet getting better and the two of them getting back on track.

"Leigh has agreed to move back home." He relished the smile on Janet's face. "I thought that would make you happy."

"I can't wait." Janet ate a bite of mango. "Although it seems like a shame since we'll be leaving tomorrow."

"She'll be here when we get back. Plus, maybe she'll come visit us while we're gone."

Janet put her fork down and sighed. "Steven, where—"

"Michael is living at the Regent with his family for a while. They're moving into Leigh's place while they look for a house."

Janet nodded, looking out the glass doors. She had hoped to see the twins before they left. "You're not happy about this."

Steven reached across the table and placed his hand over Janet's. "Michael should have left a long time ago. I was reluctant to let go of him, but he doesn't belong here anymore."

"It still hurts you."

"We're all doing the best we can," Steven said. "Michael and I are going to be okay."

Although she was disappointed Michael was still with Kimberly, Janet knew it wouldn't be long before they would have Michael and the twins back and Kimberly would be out of their lives for good. She would make sure of it.

Haley made her way to the table with an annoyed grin on her face, focused on her mother. "I hope you're happy."

"What is it now?" Steven asked.

Haley ignored him, offering the sheet of paper in her hand to her mother.

Janet smiled as she read the paper. Today was turning out to be a wonderful day. "Classes have started? You're already behind."

Haley nodded, rolling her eyes. "I got no time to prepare."

"Well you have nothing to do, so there's plenty of time to catch up."

Haley snatched the paper back. "I was going to go to Venice to visit some friends I made there."

Janet leaned forward, offering her cheek. "Venice can wait. I'm very proud of you."

Haley leaned down and kissed her. "Whatever."

Janet's eyes softened as she looked up at the biggest challenge God had ever given her. "You aren't still angry with me?"

Haley shrugged, unsure of how she really felt. "No, I . . . I guess I just wish I'd had a chance with Sean. You know, just to see."

"To see what?" Janet asked. "Things fall apart?"

"To see what it would have been like," Haley said. "I mean, it could have been nice for a while. You know, because he was . . . he was normal."

Janet sighed, touched by her daughter's attempt at honesty. "Yes, he was. Sean was very normal, but you aren't. You aren't normal, Haley. You're exceptional; quite something else. The right man for you won't be normal either. He'll be exceptional too."

"Mom."

"No," Janet protested. "Listen to me. He won't try to change you or ask you to change anything about yourself, because the right man will be able to handle you just the way you are."

Haley smiled, knowing this was the truth. "I'd like to see him try."

"Good morning, Haley." Steven thought he would give it a try, considering the tone of the moment.

Haley glanced at him and mumbled something before turning and walking away. As she stuffed the UCLA class schedule in the back pocket of her jeans, she already knew that once her mom was back in the swing of things, UCLA was going to have one less student to worry about.

Steven looked at his wife, who managed a smile. "You're amused?"

"At least she said hello."

"That was hello?"

"It was something," Janet said. "Accept it and be happy."

Janet opened the newest issue of *L.A. Weekly*, confident that she wouldn't find anything about herself that would be embarrassing. The media had taken the bait. Her trip to the hospital was a result of exhaustion. Janet's unlimited desire to raise money for good causes drove her to collapse as she pulled out all the stops for the social event of the season.

With the myriad flowers arriving at the house on the hour, Janet's image as selfless society heroine was set in stone. Word around the country club circles was that she and Steven were going on a well-deserved and much-needed European cruise for the next month. In reality they were going to stay at a hotel in South Africa that had a recovery spa.

"Do you really think you can do this?" Janet asked. "Be away from Chase Beauty for a month?"

Steven was already feeling anxiety about it. It had been more than a decade since he'd spent that much time away from the office. "I'll be calling in every day. Michael is in charge of things and Carter has promised to help out."

"You have Carter working at Chase Beauty?" Janet could barely believe that.

"It's all about you," Steven said. "Carter's love for you is stronger than whatever allergic reaction to working at Chase Beauty he seems to have."

"But you must be happy," Janet said.

Steven smiled. The idea of both his boys running Chase Beauty was his dream. It was a shame he had to leave to make it happen. "I'm only thinking about you."

"Where is Carter?" Janet asked. She hadn't seen him since he'd visited the hospital the first night.

"He has his own problems," Steven said. "I'm worried about him. He's getting manic over this thing with Avery."

"Can you hire her back?"

"That's the least of it," he said. "You don't know everything that's been going on, and you don't need to."

"She called me yesterday to see how I was doing," Janet said. "I asked her what was going on and she just cried."

"I don't think it's going to work out." From what he had been able to get from both Michael and Carter, a web of lies and deceit had come full circle with a bang. "With any other woman, maybe, but Avery . . . I think she's gone."

"I don't think I can stand it," Nikki said as she vigorously wiped down the living room coffee table. "I just don't think I can."

"Then why did you agree to it?" Charlie asked.

He stood in the doorway to the living room watching as his wife wiped down every inch for the second time. Cleaning helped her deal with stress, but the tears on her face told him it wasn't helping this time.

"There was no other choice." Nikki rearranged the items on the table in perfect place. "You understand that."

"I disagree." Charlie was angry about the whole thing and mad that he hadn't really been given much choice. "I can protect her. I'm her father and chief of police, for Pete's sake."

"She doesn't need your type of protection," Nikki said. "Our family needs to stay out of it. We have enough to deal with with Taylor now."

After the difficult summer, it was agreed that Taylor needed to delay her return to Spelman and spend more time at home.

"Taylor is out of danger," Charlie said. "Avery is the one who—"

"Why is Taylor out of danger now?" Nikki asked as she stood up and approached her husband. "Because of something Steven Chase did."

"We don't know that."

"You know that Steven had a meeting with the district attorney, who quickly announced that Chris was confessing and going straight to jail. He admitted to things Sean hadn't even known about, things that weren't in his file."

"So what are you saying?"

"I'm saying that this type of influence is what Avery is up against. That's why she made the choice she did."

"He can't force her to be with him if she doesn't want to."

Nikki sighed in frustration. "That isn't the problem. Weren't you listening?"

Charlie wanted to punch a hole in the wall. "I can't be trusted to protect my own daughter."

"Stop thinking this is about you," Nikki pleaded. "I hate it more than anyone. I don't know how I'm not going to cry myself to sleep every night, but we have to trust her. She knows what's she's doing. She needs to fight him, and right now, she can't focus on that. She has to focus on more important things."

"What if she needs us?"

"You said your contact at the FBI is going to make that possible in a way that the Chase family won't be able to take advantage of." Nikki wrapped her arms around her husband and laid her head on his chest. "As soon as that happens, we'll contact her. After a while, maybe Carter will give up and we'll contact her."

"She still has time," Charlie said. "She doesn't have to have it."

"Don't even say that." Nikki looked up at him, surprised he would even suggest it. "That was her choice and she made it."

"I'm sorry." Charlie turned as the doorbell rang. He saw the Mercedes in the driveway and felt rage build inside him. "I want to bash his head in."

"But you can't," Nikki said. "If you were anyone else other than the chief of police, maybe you could. But you aren't, so you can't. If he were anyone other than a Chase with extensive knowledge of the law, maybe you could. But he isn't, so you can't. There's no way to win here. We know what we have to do."

"What do you want?" Charlie asked as soon as he opened the door.

Carter eyed the man directly—the one who'd hung up on him the last three times he'd called the house. "Where is Avery? I need to speak to her."

"She isn't here." Nikki emerged from behind Charlie.

Carter knew something was wrong, not just from Nikki's tear-stained face, but from the way that Charlie tried to block her from coming forward. "Where is she?"

"None of your damn business," Charlie asserted. "You come by this house one more time, I'm gonna knock the crap out of you."

Carter didn't give a damn what this little man thought he could do. "This is between Avery and me, Charlie."

"That's Chief Jackson to you," Charlie said. "Do you understand that? Chief Jackson. So I suggest you go on about your business."

"Where is she?" Carter turned to Nikki.

"She needed some time off," Nikki said, squeezing Charlie's hand tight. "She needed a couple of weeks."

"Where did she go?" Carter asked. He was trying to keep his cool because he knew he wasn't helping himself by pushing her parents around. "I just want to know where—"

"She just wants to be alone for a couple of weeks," Nikki said. She was disturbed by the look on Carter's face. He was desperate. Rich and desperate was a dangerous mix. "Can't you just give her some space?"

"I just want to talk to her," Carter said. He wasn't asking for the world. Just the sound of her voice would hold him for a few days.

"I don't give a—"

"She doesn't even want us to call her," Nikki said, interrupting her husband. "Carter, it's just a couple of weeks. You owe her that much."

Carter grunted off the truth of her comments. "When is she coming back?"

"When she gets back," Charlie said.

It was very difficult for her, but Nikki reached out and placed her hand gently on Carter's arm. Looking into his eyes, she told herself that her daughter was relying on the appearance of sincerity. "I'll let you know when she's back."

Carter wasn't buying it for a second and when Charlie slammed the door in his face, he knew something was up.

"Why did you do that?" Charlie asked after the door was shut.

"That was the plan," Nikki said. "You're the one who veered off course."

"So now he thinks she'll be back in two weeks."

"Yes. It buys her two weeks to do what she has to do without his interference."

"So are you going to say two more weeks when he comes back?"

"Maybe," Nikki said. "Maybe I'll have something different then."

"He's not buying it," Charlie said, nodding toward the window.

Nikki looked outside and saw Carter on his cell phone. "It won't matter. She's safe from him and that's all I care about."

"Matt Tustin here."

"Tustin, it's Carter Chase." Carter opened the door to his Mercedes and stepped inside. "I need you to find Avery."

"You mean . . . your girlfriend? She's missing?"

"She's my fiancée," Carter corrected. "She's not missing. She's just gone. I need to know where she is and I need it yesterday."

"Do you have—"

"I have everything," Carter said. "Her social security number, credit cards—everything."

"Then I'll have it for you in a second. Hold on while I get a pen."

Carter leaned back in his seat, feeling relief just around the corner. He was going to find her and get her back. Nothing was more important, and no one was going to stop him.

NEVER ENOUGH

Angela Winters

The following questions are intended
to enhance your group's discussion of
this book.

Discussion Questions

1. Should Avery have listened to that voice in the back of her head that day Carter proposed or not? Why did she fight her instincts for so long? Do you know any women who would do that? Would you?

2. Why do you think Sean and Haley still decided not to try again even after Haley found out the real reason Sean broke it off and he saved her life . . . again?

3. Did Steven overreact to Janet's behavior? What was worse? What she did thirty years ago or today?

4. Understanding how important trust is to Avery, do you think she was right to end the relationship or should she have forgiven Carter? Should she have told him about the pregnancy before leaving?

5. Do you feel sorry for Kimberly or did she get what she deserved for trying to destroy Janet's marriage?

6. Knowing how difficult it has been for his wife, is Michael a bad husband to have stayed at the Chase mansion for so long? Should he take some of the blame for what Kimberly did?

7. What did you think about Haley's reaction to Chris's disregard for her? She seemed to like it at first. When did it change and why?

8. Is it possible for Carter to really love Avery and try so hard to deceive her at the same time? Was he really sorry for what he'd done or was he just sorry that he got caught?

9. What did you notice in the Chase children regarding their reaction to their father leaving the home? They are all adult children, but they were still affected. What did you think about their reactions?

10. In the end, Janet was the victor. Do you think she deserved to get Steven and Leigh back just because she has a drug problem? What do you think she has in store for Kimberly now?

The following is a teaser from the
third installment of
Angela Winters's exciting View Park trilogy.
ENJOY!

"What is this, Daddy?" Six-year-old Daniel Chase was standing in the hallway of his uncle's luxury penthouse condo in downtown L.A.

"What is what?" Thirty-year-old Michael Chase waited for Evan, Daniel's twin brother, to get inside before closing the front door behind him.

"It's a bra!" Daniel held the lacy pink lingerie up for his father to see, his little brown hand waving it in the air.

Michael sighed, realizing it was a mistake to bring his boys over to his brother's place. He should have known something this like would happen. He'd been warned last month when he walked in on Carter and a Brazilian model having loud and what seemed like dangerous sex halfway off the dining room table.

"Put that down," Michael ordered. "Just drop it."

"These are panties!" Evan was reaching for the matching bottoms just a few feet away, lying on top of a silk cocktail dress.

"Don't touch that." Michael took his son's arm.

"Mommy has these." Evan struggled to get away from his father. "Is Mommy here?"

"All mommies have these, silly." Daniel rolled his eyes.

"Uncle Carter needs to do laundry." Michael cautiously led his boys down the hallway, praying that he wouldn't have to explain the birds and bees to them today.

"Where is he?" Daniel asked impatiently as soon as they were at the steps to the living room of the 3,500 square foot, three-bedroom home.

"He's probably working in his office," Michael answered. "Working hard."

He led his boys to the living room sofa and reached for the remote. "You boys stay here. Do you understand?"

Evan was already looking antsy, as if eager to get out of his church clothes. The boys were used to being able to run wild whenever they were at their Uncle Carter's house.

Michael found a suitable station on the big-screen television. "Just watch this and don't move."

"Why not?" Evan asked.

"Look at me," Michael ordered and waited until both of them did so. Keeping stern eye contact, he said, "Because I said so. Do you understand?"

Daniel nodded, but Evan just shrugged; always the difficult one.

As he made his way to the master bedroom, passing scattered pieces of clothing along the way, Michael wasn't looking forward to the reason he was sent to Carter's house by their mother. He had to remind Carter to show up tonight at their parents' house, the largest in all of View Park, to celebrate in his honor. Carter hadn't been answering his phone for three days now, so Janet sent Michael to track him down.

This wasn't the first time in the last six months Carter had 'disappeared.' Ever since his fiancée, Avery, left him, Carter would leave for long periods of time. Avery not only left Carter, but left L.A. and didn't want to be found. Carter had gone ballistic when he realized she had no intention of coming back. He had become a Jekyll and Hyde, moving between two states of being.

One was an obsessed psycho desperate to find Avery, who he swore on the Bible was the only love of his life, using the considerable means at his disposal whether legal or not. The other was a reckless drunk who didn't care about Avery, who he swore he was better off without her and went on to prove it by nailing every woman he could get his hands on.

Michael figured these past few days had been the latter, as the bra and panties in the hallway suggested. This was the Carter that their parents were concerned about; the one who could get the family in trouble.

Finally, Michael stood in the doorway to Carter's bedroom, observing the mess in front of him. He could only smile because Carter was such a neat freak—almost to the point of obsession—and here he was, living like a frat boy complete with a naked woman sprawled face down on the bed beside him.